HOW THE EARL ENTICES

ANNA HARRINGTON

COPYRIGHT

This book is licensed to you for your personal enjoyment only.

This is a work of fiction. Names, characters, places, and incidents are either products of the writer's imagination or are used fictitiously and are not to be construed as real. Any resemblance to actual events, locales, organizations, or persons, living or dead, is entirely coincidental.

Dedicated to the real Gracie
Love always, Mom

Special thanks to
Sarah Younger for insisting that I write about the Carlisle men,
the NYLA interns for their feedback,
and Natanya Wheeler for creating such a beautiful cover

PROLOGUE

On the English Channel
April, 1823

"Where are the documents?"

Ross Carlisle, Earl of Spalding, spat out a mouthful of blood onto the midnight-black deck of the pitching ship as the storm intensified around it. "Go to hell!"

A fist slammed into his stomach. He doubled over in gasping pain, coughing and struggling for breath, yet thankful for the pouring rain that cooled the bruises the men had already put on his ribs and face.

The two Frenchmen holding his arms jerked him up straight.

Their leader grabbed him by the hair and yanked back his head. "You are a murderer and a traitor. No one will care what happens to you."

Ross gritted his teeth against the pain.

"So I will ask you one more time before I cut off your kneecaps," the thug threatened in street French, having to yell even at such close range to be heard over the wind and driving rain. In his free hand he brandished a knife. "Where are the documents?"

Ross glared at him, refusing to answer.

So it all came to this...a decade serving the crown as a soldier and diplomat, an unblemished reputation without a hint of scandal, more recently a dangerous pursuit in which recognition would never have been possible—only to end ingloriously on a fishing boat being tossed about on the Channel.

He'd been running for the past week, fleeing for his life from Paris to the coast with hired henchmen on his heels. First on horseback, then on foot, changing identities as easily as other men changed clothes. But he'd been unable to throw them off his trail, and always they'd been less than a day behind. Then a handful of hours. By the time he'd reached Calais and found a captain brave enough to take him across the Channel in this storm, they'd caught him. In a matter of minutes he'd be dead.

And damn the world that the last person he thought about was Christopher! Not one of his French mistresses, not one of his first loves as a boy, not even his mother—but his brother. How the last thing Ross did in life was prove Kit right, that eventually he'd be discovered and that even his post at the Court of St James's wouldn't be able to save him.

The Frenchman released his hair and stepped back, struggling to keep his footing on the wet, rolling deck. With a menacing gleam in his eyes, he lowered the knife toward Ross's legs. "Where are the papers?"

The knife tip sliced across his left thigh and through the rough work trousers he'd donned in his last attempt to hide, biting into the flesh beneath. Ross sucked in a pain-filled gasp through clenched teeth and bit back an ironic laugh—his *left* thigh.

The boat rose on the swell of a wave, then dropped with enough force that the men holding his arms wobbled to keep their balance. His interrogator stumbled backward—

Now.

Ross lunged toward the closest railing, tearing his arm free of the man on his right and catching the one on his left off-balance. He lowered his shoulder and rammed it into the man's chest to push past. All went dark as he tumbled over the railing and into the black sea below.

CHAPTER 1

Sea Haven Village on Winchelsea Bay
East Sussex, England

Grace Alden lay in her bed, staring at the dark ceiling and listening to the storm raging around her. The wind and rain roared so loudly that she couldn't hear her own heartbeat. But she knew it was racing because it jumped into her throat each time she heard something bang against the cottage. The wind howled like a banshee over the cliff tops, screaming through the eaves and bringing with it a torrent of black rain that fell with the force of a hurricane.

"Please God, let the roof hold."

Around her, the old limestone and timber cottage groaned beneath the fierce battering of the storm.

"And the walls, too," she whispered in afterthought, "if not too much trouble."

After ten more minutes of staring at the ceiling, she slid out from beneath the covers. Sleep was proving impossible tonight.

The cottage was dark as pitch as she made her way slowly across the main room to the hearth, where a bed of coals hissed and snapped angrily against the few drops of rain that found their way down the chimney from the force of the wind. She stirred the ash bed with the iron poker to raise a flame, tossing in a few more chunks of coal to feed the fire enough to last until morning. Normally, she never would have burned a fire through the night, but tonight, she sought its comfort.

Taking a brass candleholder from the mantel, she bent over to light the wick in the flames and let out a soft sigh when it caught hold. After nearly ten years of fearing things that bumped in the night, would she ever grow comfortable in the darkness? But the most frightening things weren't the unseen. She'd learned the hard way that the worst were the ones a person knew well.

She lifted the candle to read the storm glass fixed to the wall. The water in the spout had been rising during the past two days, and now it stood higher than she'd ever seen it. She bit her bottom lip. It could be hours before the water level dropped and the temperature fell, before the clouds rained themselves dry.

Before she could bring Ethan home.

Her chest tightened with aching worry. Sending her son into the village to spend the night with Alice Walters at the apothecary shop had been the right decision. She knew that. But oh, how much it hurt to be separated from him! For the first time in his life, too. But the sailors who had come ashore all day predicted that tonight's storm would be the worst in memory. Ethan was safer within the shop's thick stone walls, while she had to be here to rescue their belongings in case the roof caved in. Holding everything she owned in the world, this cottage had been her own safe port over the past stormy decade, where she and Ethan had been safe since he was born.

But he wasn't a babe anymore. He was nine years-old now, and growing so fast that it pained her to think of it.

He'd soon reach an age when he should be going off to school. Instead, he'd have to stay here. Guilt gnawed at her. He deserved better, was *born* for better—fine schools, hundreds of books, private tutors, trips across England and the continent to see in person all the wonderful things that the world had to offer. Instead, they had to make do with the few books she could scrape together enough money to purchase and the tutoring sessions with the local vicar she'd negotiated in trade for cooking and cleaning the vicarage.

But he could never have that other life. As far as Ethan knew, his father was a sailor who died at sea, and she fully intended to keep it that way. Because if Ethan ever discovered the truth, if he ever got the foolish notion into his head when he was older to pursue what was due to him...She shuddered.

At least now, he would have a life. She would never regret what she had to do to keep her son safe.

A loud banging shot through the noise of the storm. She jumped with a small scream, her hand going to her throat.

The pounding came again. This time she recognized it—a shutter had broken loose and was banging wildly against the side of the cottage in the howling wind. Her chest sagged. She had to fix it. If she didn't, not only would it continue to bang all night, but it might also smash through the window it was supposed to be protecting.

Setting the candle onto the table, she moved toward the door, where she pulled on a pair of fisherman's boots and an oilskin coat. The last thing she wanted to do tonight—oh, the *very* last thing!—was go out into the weather and be soaked, chilled to the bone, and battered about. But she had no choice, because she couldn't afford to replace the window if it broke. At least she could brew up some hot tea when she returned. Taking comfort in that, she threw back the bolt and opened the door, only to have her breath ripped away by a burst of icy cold wind and rain that slammed into her.

Pulling the old coat tighter around herself, she shouldered her way into the wind and along the front of the cottage. It took only a moment to close the shutter and fasten the hook that had somehow come undone.

She turned to scurry inside—

A strong arm went around her waist and swung her back against the side of the cottage. She screamed, but the sound was lost beneath the noise of the raging storm. A forearm pushed against her upper chest, pinning her against the wall.

Another scream ripped from her throat. She kicked and punched with all her might at the man who'd grabbed her, who now held her a helpless prisoner as he leaned into her, his muscular legs forcing hers to still. With one large hand, he grabbed both her arms and pinned them over her head, while the other pressed the barrel of a pistol beneath her chin.

"Who else is inside?" he demanded.

She couldn't see his face as the rain pelted down upon both of them, so fiercely that she couldn't blink the water away fast enough. The black night covered his features, but nothing could hide the strength of him as he held her against the wall.

He pressed the pistol harder against her. "A husband, brother —who?"

"My husband!" she lied, so frightened that she nearly crumpled to the muddy ground. "He's certain to have heard me scream, so you'd better leave!"

He laughed, a terrible sound that scratched and screeched nearly as much as the wind howling over the bluffs. "No husband, then. Anyone else?"

She was terrified and freezing, but she refused to submit to this man. Not to *any* man ever again. She'd rather die than surrender. "Go to hell!"

His eyes gleamed in the darkness. "I'm already there."

Keeping the pistol pressed against her throat, he grabbed her arm and tugged her toward the door, which had blown open in the hurricane gale. He pulled her inside and kicked the door closed. Twisting from his grasp, she yanked her arm away. He let her go, only to reach behind him and throw the bolt to lock them inside.

Grace ran toward the fireplace, snatched up the iron poker, and brandished it like a weapon. All of her shook so violently from cold and fear that she didn't know how she managed to hold onto it. But he'd have to rip it from her hands before she released it. And if he took a single step toward her—

But he didn't. Instead he watched her silently from the shadows near the door, not making a move to force himself on her.

"You need to leave. *Now.*" She prayed her voice didn't sound as terrified to his ears as it did to hers. "I will use this if you come any closer."

"If I come any closer, I certainly hope you'd try," he drawled dryly, amused at the idea. "But I have a gun. I don't need to come closer."

Oh God. Fresh fear shuddered through her.

"But I don't plan to use it. Nor do I plan on hurting you."

A bitter laugh tore from her. "You shoved me against the cottage!" She kept the poker raised, holding it in front of her like a sword. "Then forced me inside, to—to—" The horrible words choked her...*To rape me.*

"To be out of the storm," he finished pointedly, as if reading her thoughts. "You never would have opened the door if I'd knocked."

"You unlatched the shutter." The realization soaked into her as coldly as the rain. "It was *you.*"

"Yes."

She whispered, too frightened to find her voice, "What do you want?"

"A place to spend the night. That's all."

"There's an inn in the village." She waved the poker in the general direction of the harbor. "You can spend the night there."

He tilted his head, as if listening to the storm. The silence that stretched between them only accentuated the howl of the hurricane gale that swept in from the Atlantic like a banshee from hell. Then he shook his head.

"As soon as the weather breaks, I'll leave."

Her hands gripped harder around the poker, so tightly that her knuckles turned white. "You need to leave *now*."

His deep voice matched the intensity of the rain lashing against the cottage. "I have no intention of going back into that storm."

He stepped away from the dark shadows by the door and came slowly forward toward the firelight, as if no more troubled by a woman brandishing an iron poker than he would have been by a gnat. He set his pistol down on the wooden settle yet kept it within easy reach as he peeled off his fisherman's peacoat, which was sopped with water, and laid it over the back of the settle. Then he sat down and began to remove his boots.

Her heart lurched into her throat. God help her, he was removing his clothing!

"What are you doing?" she demanded, slashing the poker back and forth in front of her.

"Taking off my boots." He pulled the left one off his foot.

Her eyes narrowed with suspicion. "Why?"

In answer, he stoically held up the boot, then tipped it over and poured out the water onto the floor in a puddle.

Her mouth fell open.

He tugged off the other one and poured out just as much water, then looked at her solemnly. "Only Jesus should walk on water."

She snapped her mouth shut. Oh, his audacity! She jabbed the poker at him, pointing first at the boots, then at his feet. "Put them back on this instant! And leave. *Now.* You are not welcome here!"

He reached beside him to rest his hand meaningfully on the pistol. Icy fingers of fear curled around her spine.

For one long moment, they held each other's gaze through the thick shadows of the dark cottage, lit only by the weak flames in the fireplace beside her and the flickering candle on the table. Darkness hid his face, but his eyes were bright as he silently studied her. Then he stripped off his neckcloth, tossing it across the back of the settle beside his jacket. Around him, the puddle on the floor grew larger, evidence of how exposed he'd been in the storm and how drenched through to his skin.

But that didn't give him the right to force his way into her home at gunpoint. And it certainly didn't give him license to remove his clothing...which he was still doing, now unbuttoning his waistcoat.

"Stop that! Put your clothes back on."

"I'm cold, and I'm not going to sit here freezing for the rest of the night." He pushed himself to his feet and nodded toward her. "I advise you to do the same."

With her free hand, she clutched at her coat's lapels, to keep it closed so that the villain couldn't see her night rail beneath. He said he didn't want to hurt her, but how could she trust him?

He shrugged and peeled off his waistcoat, then tossed it onto the settle with the rest of his clothes. His wet shirt clung to his broad shoulders and narrow waist like a second skin.

He held out his arms, inviting her to look. "No hidden weapons."

But Grace knew well that a man didn't need weapons to harm a woman. She wore the proof of that in the scar on her cheek. Brute strength and anger could be enough to destroy. Although this stranger wasn't in a rage, the muscles on his broad frame seemed more than powerful enough to harm.

Not threatened at all by the iron poker she still held ready to strike, he walked slowly toward her—rather, toward the warmth of the fire beside her. As he approached, the dim light of the fire chased away the shadows and finally revealed his face. A light growth of beard covered his cheeks, cuts bled at his brow.

A distant memory triggered in the far back of her mind, but it swirled away before she could latch onto it. That face. So familiar...

Or perhaps she was simply so frightened that she'd gone daft. To think she'd know a stranger who'd forced his way into her home, who even now could lunge for the gun still resting on the settle before she could strike with the poker—madness! His large presence in her small cottage was enough to make her tremble, if she wasn't already freezing from the icy rain.

He unfastened the half dozen buttons at his neck. "You can put that poker down now."

"I'll keep it right where it is, thank you very much," she shot back, gripping it more tightly. *Why* was he so familiar?

In coarse and ill-fitting clothing, he was dressed like one of the sailors who filled the boats that sailed from the harbor to ports all along the western coast of England. But in the ten years she'd lived in Sea Haven, she'd never seen a sailor like him. He wasn't one of the men who worked on the docks, either. Oh, he had the muscles for that, certainly, but his bearing was too commanding, too proud. He wasn't one who took orders. She could read that in every inch of him.

No, *this* man was used to giving them and having them followed without question. Even now, from the way his mouth pulled down, he was irritated that she continued to defy him, with the poker still raised to strike.

"I'd prefer that you put that down." He nodded toward the poker and said wryly with a quirk of his brow, "Wouldn't want it to go off accidentally and hurt someone."

"Yes, that would be a great shame," she muttered, not lowering it even though her arm had begun to ache, "if *someone* got hurt because he didn't leave when he was asked."

"You didn't ask."

A tendril of irrational hope rose amid her fear. "Would you please leave?"

"No."

She bit back a cry of frustration. Oh, the infuriating devil! Her fear was quickly being replaced by anger, and by that nagging feeling that wouldn't go away that she *knew* him.

Untucking his shirt, he stripped the wet material up his body, over his head and off, baring himself from the waist up. Her gaze darted to the bare chest he'd so scandalously revealed—

She swallowed. Hard.

No, definitely not anyone she knew.

Instead of tossing the shirt over the settle with the rest of his clothes, he carefully draped it over the iron arm where she hung her kettle and swung it closer to the fire to dry. The firelight played over his smooth muscles and the faint tracing of hair on his chest that narrowed across his ridged abdomen before disappearing beneath the waistband that hung low around his slender hips. He wore only his trousers now. She couldn't help but bite her bottom lip as she wondered if he planned on removing even those.

Then she *would* have to hit him with the poker.

He turned around to heat his backside. With that too familiar face once more plunged into the shadows and the firelight behind him outlining his broad shoulders, he resembled a devil escaped from hell.

He nodded at her. "You need to take off that coat now and warm yourself up."

Dangling the poker at her side in one hand, she grabbed at the front of the coat with the other to keep herself covered. "No."

He shrugged. "Then freeze. Makes no difference to me."

Her lips fell open at his callous comment. Why that *arrogant*—

She bit back a laugh. It *did* make a difference to him, or he wouldn't be asking her, repeatedly, to remove it. The same strategy she used against Ethan—tell him to do what she didn't want, in hopes that he'd do the opposite. Well, years of mothering had taught her that the strategy failed more often than it worked, and she wasn't some nine-year-old boy refusing to do his chores. If he thought—

She sneezed.

The stranger arched a brow.

Her shoulders sagged. Oh blast the devil!

"I cannot take off this coat," she explained with a haughty sniff to cover the flushing in her cheeks, "because I'm in my night rail."

"Then go dress." He turned back toward the fire. "Because we're going to be up all night."

Her stomach plummeted to the floor. She wanted him gone. *Now.* "You need to leave," she pleaded in a desperate whisper. "Just go. I won't tell anyone you were here."

He said nothing.

"I don't have any money. Search through the cottage if you'd like, you'll see." When he continued to remain deaf to her pleas, her frustration changed to panic. "Take whatever you'd like. Just take it! And leave. Please." A tear fell down her cheek. "Please just *go!*"

He stiffened at the sight of her tears, yet he made no move to dress and leave. "I cannot."

"Please!" Each plea sliced into her. She'd sworn to herself long ago that she'd never again beg any man for mercy. But that old helplessness was surging to the surface, and she hated herself for it. Hated *him* for stealing away the strength that had taken her years to find.

"I need shelter from the storm." His voice remained calm and quiet even as hers rose toward hysteria. "This was the first cottage I came across." His gaze pinned her with a gravity that made her shiver. "If I go back out into the night, I'm dead. And several other good men with me."

When he faced her, she reflexively took a step back, once more raising the poker.

"So you can stand there all night holding that damnable poker if you desire," he continued in the same quiet, controlled voice, "and I'll sit there on the settle with my pistol pointed at you to make certain you don't get some fool idea about hitting me over the head with it." His eyes flickered with steely resolve. "But I am *not* leaving until it's safe for me to travel. So go dress if you'd like, or stay in that coat and freeze. As I said, it makes no difference to me."

He reached toward her—

She swung. The poker arced through the air toward his head.

Startling her with how fast he moved, he grabbed the poker in mid-swing with one hand while the other seized her arm. He twisted the poker from her grasp and held it away so she couldn't reach it.

Grace stared up at him, her heart pounding so hard with fear that each beat knotted her belly impossibly tighter. Dear God, what would he do to her now? Oh dear God!

He tossed the poker away, and it clanged against the stone floor. He lowered his face until his eyes were level with hers, his mouth so close that his warm breath shivered across her lips. Anger simmered inside him. "I told you that I wouldn't hurt you."

"You were reaching for me," she choked out, all of her shaking violently as old memories came crashing back, ones she'd thought she'd buried long ago. Now they returned with the same fierce intensity as the storm raging outside.

"Because I hate to see a woman cry." He slowly raised his hand to her cheek and finished the gesture he'd started moments before —to wipe away the tear with his thumb, as gently as his other hand held her like an iron manacle. "But if you try something like that again, I *will* tie you up. Understand?"

Blinking hard to keep another tear from falling and giving him cause to touch her again, she gave a jerking nod.

"Good." He released her.

As Grace shoved away from him, she saw the gaping gash in his right bicep and the trickle of blood seeping down his arm. But she hadn't hit him!

Her eyes narrowed on him, now that she was standing close enough to notice not only the bleeding cut on his arm but all the wounds that the black shadows inside the dark cottage had hidden before, that she hadn't noticed in her fear of him. Bruises dotted his arms and chest, and a hideous purplish black-and-blue spot on his right side marked a bruised rib, if he were lucky. More than likely a broken one. Heavens, the pain he must have been in...

She knew now that she didn't need the poker to defend herself. Even if he tried to attack her, she could drop him to his knees in agony with a poke of a single finger into the bruise on his side. How he'd found the strength to hold her immobile only moments before she had no idea, or how he managed to keep standing upright on his feet even now.

"You're wounded," she whispered, surprised out of her fury and fear. "Your arm..."

He glanced down curiously, as if he'd forgotten it was there. Then he turned back to the fire without comment.

Her lips parted; she was stunned. A cut that deep, the bruises and damaged ribs—the storm hadn't done that. Good God, what had he been through tonight? And who were those other men he said would lose their lives if he headed back into the storm?

Who on earth *was* this man?

"Go dress," he said quietly into the fire. "I need your help, and you can't help me if you catch fever."

"I won't help you anyway." Defiance lifted her chin. "I might be stuck here with you, but I won't—"

He turned his head and pinned her beneath a look so black that she gasped. Her hand went to her throat.

"Go." His low voice slithered down her spine.

Her hand rose to her cheek to reflexively cover the pink scar with her trembling fingers. Nodding, she backed away. Desperation seeped from him and grew the fear that roiled in her stomach, making him more dangerous than she'd first realized.

"I'll trust you enough to remain here," he called after her as she retreated toward her bedroom, not turning her back on him. "But keep the door open."

She froze in her steps. "You expect me to change in front of you? I'll do no such thing!"

"The door stays open." He glanced past her into the bedroom. "It's dark enough in there to keep you covered by the shadows." Then his lips twisted grimly. "And I won't risk that you keep another poker hidden beneath the mattress."

"You are not a gentleman." Her words were so soft that they were nearly lost beneath the rain pounding against the roof. "You are despicable."

She stood her ground, waiting for him to unleash his fury on her. It was what Vincent would have done. Just like her brother-in-law, would this stranger have enjoyed hurting her?

But instead of a harsh warning—or making good on his threat to tie her up—he turned back to mutter into the fire, "So much more than you know."

He was quickly lost in his own thoughts, but Grace knew he was still aware of her and every move she made. If she attempted to run, he would pounce before she reached the door.

She walked into her bedroom. Part of her contemplated defying him and closing the door anyway. Would serve him right! But something in her gut told her not to press him. So far he'd kept true to his word and not attempted to hurt her, and the last thing she should do was provoke his anger. The night was half over now; by dawn the storm would be weakening, and he'd leave. She only had to wait him out.

Even knowing that, she still couldn't stop the shaking as she shrugged out of the wet coat, then reached for her dress and undergarments in her dresser. The room was dark, and the shadows hid her from view, yet she took repeated glances over her shoulder to make certain he kept his distance, still standing at the fireplace with his eyes focused on the flames.

After she'd changed into her dress and wrapped a shawl securely around her shoulders, she blew out a deep sigh of relief, both at finally being properly dressed and that the stranger hadn't moved from where she'd left him.

Her hands fumbled with putting up her damp hair as she emerged from the bedroom, with two hairpins between her lips. Grudgingly, she mumbled around them, "Thank you for not—"

He glanced up from the fire as she stepped from the shadows, his face fully visible in the firelight.

She halted in mid-step at the intensity of his gaze as it trailed slowly over her in an assessing manner, a look filled with such deliberate aloofness that she couldn't help but see the arrogant reserve beneath, the cool detachment. That look crystallized a long-forgotten memory at the back of her mind, so distant as to be almost a dream...

Ross Carlisle, Viscount Mooreland, heir to the Earl of Spalding.

Dear God—so much worse than a stranger!

CHAPTER 2

*F*rowning both at her reappearance and at the relentless pounding in his head, Ross turned his gaze back to the fire as the woman slowly approached. She'd changed, and more than just her dress. The difference was palpable.

"Better?" He carefully kept the suspicion from his voice, along with his surprise at seeing her looking so pretty in that plain dress and wool shawl, all soft and warm.

Yet at the same time, he sensed an inexplicable hardening in her. Oh, she was still afraid, certainly. Even now she moved stiltedly as she approached, each step uncertain and cautious, reminding him of a skittish doe. But she no longer exuded the fury and terror of before. Thank God.

She stopped beside the fireplace, close but cleverly just beyond his reach. Her gaze dropped to the iron poker that he'd returned to the rack of tools beside the hearth while she'd been changing. Her mouth twisted, but she didn't deign to answer his question. Instead, she lifted her chin and defiantly narrowed her eyes.

Stubborn woman.

Not that it mattered. Once the storm broke, he would be on his way. If he somehow managed to wrangle himself out of the mess he was in, then he would make certain she was well compensated for any trouble he'd caused her.

But tonight, he needed her help.

"I need a bandage for my arm." When she didn't reply, he added with grim humor, "Unless you'd rather I keep bleeding all over your floor."

"*I'd* rather you leave." She fumed that he'd expected her to help him, yet she turned to the hutch and lifted up on tiptoes to reach for the workbox sitting high on the top shelf.

His eyes darted over her lithesome figure, noting her thin waist and round hips, her slender shoulders…She'd pinned up her hair. Damnable shame, that. He would have liked to have seen what it looked like when it dried, whether it would have hung down her back in chestnut waves or dried to light brown curls. After all, tonight was going to be hellishly long and quite possibly his last as a free man. He might as well enjoy himself a bit.

She took down the box and sat at the table. "There's a lamp on the peg near the door. Light it and bring it here." A hostile brow arched high. "Unless *you'd* rather I sew you up in the dark."

Well. *That* was certainly a change in attitude, all right.

He suspected as he fetched the tin lantern and lit it on the fire that he'd have little rest tonight, if any, with her here with him. Dear God, he desperately needed rest! The weakness in his limbs from swimming for his life in the Channel, coupled with a growing headache, proved that. Yet as tired as he was, he couldn't let his guard slip or his journey might end right here. Wherever here was.

He sat at the table and extended his arm toward her. With an irritated scowl, she reached for his bicep, which she inspected by jabbing at it with her fingertip. Gritting his teeth, he held perfectly still, even when she gave him a hard poke right in the bruised muscle. Pain shot all the way up his arm to his pounding temples. *Christ!*

Given all he'd been through during the past sennight, she'd have to try a hell of a lot harder than that to wound him.

With a disappointed sniff—perhaps unhappy to find his arm still attached—she leaned back and reached into her workbox to retrieve a large square of cloth, most likely one she'd been saving for her embroidery. Then she pulled out a needle and thread.

He grabbed her wrist, stopping her. "Is that necessary?"

"A big strong man like you, frightened of a bitty needle and thread?" she taunted. "Then you shouldn't have gotten into a fight in the first place."

He released her wrist and let her jerk herself away. "It wasn't a fight." *Not exactly.* "And I didn't have a choice."

She eyed him warily. "Then what was it?"

He gestured at his arm, silently ordering her to continue. He wasn't willing to share that piece of his story.

With an irritated huff, she rose from her seat and returned to the hutch, where she angrily poured water from a pitcher into a bowl and snatched up a hand towel. In afterthought, she bent over to retrieve a small brown jug from the lower cabinet. She carried it all back to the table. The jug came down with a thud, the bowl of water with a splash.

He bit his cheek to keep from laughing.

If he weren't in such danger and utterly exhausted, he'd find her hostility amusing. In his normal life, society women didn't dare show him such irritation, even when they wanted to slap him. No, they kept false smiles plastered firmly on their faces, no matter how much he irritated them, because they all hoped they might become his countess, not knowing that they didn't have a chance. He couldn't stand the preening lot of them.

He watched her closely as she returned to her chair and soaked the towel in the bowl. "What's your name?"

"Apparently, it's Captive," she answered flippantly, wringing out the excess water. When she leaned toward him to dab at the wound to clean it, he grabbed her wrist again, silently pressing for her name. She shook her head. "You first. You're the stranger here, not me."

"Thomas." He released her arm to let her continue to nurse him. "Christopher Thomas."

His brother's Christian name rolled easily off his tongue and without a prick of guilt at lying to her. Self-preservation. By now, there must have been a reward out for him, with notices plastered in all the posting inns and every constable and soldier in south-eastern England on watch, just in case he made it out of France. He expected no less from King George and the Court of St James's, who would certainly hang him for a traitor if they caught him.

The woman's eyes flickered. "Christopher Thomas, is it?"

"My friends call me Kit. And you are?"

"Grace Alden." Her eyes lowered to the wound on his arm as she began to clean it.

"Grace," he murmured. A beautiful name and, from watching her closely as she'd moved about the cottage earlier, an apt one. Even when she'd been wielding a poker she'd revealed an innate elegance he never would have associated with a woman living in a fishing village.

She arched a brow. "And *my* friends call me Mrs. Alden."

Cheeky chit. But there was no husband here. A quick glance revealed a pair of boy's boots, a small jacket, and school books. A child lived here, but there was nothing that signified a man's presence.

"Where's your husband, Mrs. Alden?" When she began to answer, he interrupted, "And don't tell me that he's due home at any moment, because you and I both know that's a damn lie."

She froze with the towel against his arm in a heartbeat's pause, during which that sharp mind of hers calculated her options and weighed the best. "My husband is dead," she answered softly. From the pained timbre in her voice, she was telling the truth.

"I'm sorry."

"Thank you." The swipes of the towel against the cut gentled beneath his sympathy.

She was much friendlier when she spoke of her husband, so he pressed his advantage. "Was he a sailor?"

Another pause, as if gauging how much she should reveal. "Yes."

The hair at his nape prickled. She'd just lied to him. He could read it in the way she kept her face lowered, her eyes averted. In the way her fingers trembled when she rinsed out the cloth. But why would she lie about that?

"How did he die?" A gentleman would never have asked such a thing, but tonight he was no gentleman. And there was more to the woman in front of him than a simple fisherman's widow. He sensed it the way old sailors felt changes in the weather. In his bones.

"He was lost at sea." She shoved the jug across the table toward him. "You'll want this."

He uncorked it and sniffed. Whiskey. Judging from the sharp odor that bit his nose, not expensive single malt. He handed it back. "No, thank you."

"Suit yourself." She snatched up the bottle and poured it into his wound.

"Christ!" The pain splintered his insides. Through clenched teeth, he panted down the burn, if not the fierce pounding in his head like an iron hammer, until the sickening nausea in his stomach subsided and the sharp pain mellowed into a dull ache. But the throbbing at his temples remained strong and relentless. "Warn me next time before you do that."

She set the jug down and shot him a look of pure vengeance. "Will you warn the next woman you attack?"

He gritted his teeth against his headache. "You were less trouble when you were armed with the poker."

"And *you* were less trouble when you were outside in the storm." Her chin rose icily with all the haughtiness of an old governess. "Would you care to leave? And we can end this madness right now."

Madness. His situation was certainly that. "I cannot."

"Then tell me why you were out in that storm tonight." Not a request but a demand for information. "Why are you hiding here?"

Oh no. He had no intention of answering *that.*

He shoved away from the table and snatched up the square of white cloth. Taking it between his teeth, he ripped off a two-inch wide strip. Her eyes widened when he tore off a second piece, then dropped the rest to the floor. He wrapped the first strip around his bicep, covering the wound.

"It doesn't need stitches," he told her when she continued to gape at him. And thanks to her, there was enough whiskey inside the cut to prevent any infection from taking hold. For the rest of his life.

He'd gotten enough wounds over the years, first at Eton and later during a two-year stint in the army, to know the difference between those which threatened a man's life and those which simply hurt like hell. However, the sharp pain that came from the cut on his left thigh might just prove him wrong. Even now he limped as he stepped back, tying off the second strip of bandage with his teeth.

But he was still alive, that's what the pain meant. And he was damned lucky to be.

"I'm here to be out of the storm." He placed a hand on the fireplace mantel to steady himself against the swaying that his exhaustion started in him. "That's all you need to know."

"How were you hurt? Can you at least tell me that?"

He rubbed his forehead and the pounding headache. Damnation! Wouldn't the woman give him peace? "No."

"This is my house. You've barged in here like a criminal." Her voice rose in anger, nearly as loud as the storm raging around them. "I deserve answers."

The headache was blinding now, and he gritted his teeth. "I cannot tell you."

"Why not? I deserve to—"

"Because they'll kill you!" His patience snapped, and he wheeled on her, fisting his hands at his sides. "If they find me here, if they suspect you've helped me—you're as good as dead. And I will *not* have another death on my head."

She froze, her eyes wide at his outburst. Even in the flickering shadows of the firelight, he saw the blood drain from her face.

Guilt assaulted him for frightening her. He raked his fingers through his damp hair and dragged in a breath. For God's sake, was this really what his life had come to? Forcing his way into a woman's house and yelling at her simply because she wanted answers?

In stealing those documents from the British ambassador, he'd lost himself. He didn't know if he'd ever be able to find his way back.

"I'm sorry." He turned toward the fire. "But the less you know, the better."

His heart pounded frantically now, the rush of blood through his body searing like liquid flames. He squeezed his eyes closed and focused on calming his breathing, which only increased his swaying. Sheer exhaustion ached in every muscle, burned at his throat which was raw from hours spent gulping salt water as he fought the waves to stay alive, throbbed in the bruises from being slammed against the rocks when he finally reached shore.

But he couldn't stop now, not when he was so close to destroying the inner circle of the Court of St James's, those Englishmen working in France who had pledged their loyalty to the British ambassador. Not when he could still feel the blood on his hands from the murder of Sir Henry Jacobs.

That was what had kept him ceaselessly plotting during the past year. What had driven him to steal the documents and sent him on the run, hiding from both the French and the British.

What had kept him alive for hours in the Channel, tossed and battered by the storm, before he crawled up from the beach and found this cottage, with the dim light of its fire shining through the cracks of the shutters and promising rest and warmth.

Five years ago, if anyone had asked him what he wanted most, he wouldn't have hesitated to say an ambassadorship. It was what he'd *always* wanted. But that was before his parents died, before he'd discovered his brother Kit's role with the Home Office. Before he was responsible for Sir Henry's body lying in a pool of blood, his throat slit from ear to ear. Before he'd committed treason.

Now he wanted nothing more than to rain vengeance down upon the heads of the men responsible for destroying everything he'd believed in.

But first, he had to get to London.

He glanced at the woman, still sitting at the table, gaping at him.

Get to London? He bit back a laugh. First, he had to survive the night!

"So you didn't come here to seek shelter from the storm." Her voice was barely loud enough for him to hear over the driving rain. "You're here because you're hiding."

"I'm hiding from the storm." Not entirely a lie. Although at that moment, the immorality of lying was the least of his worries.

"You're being hunted."

His head snapped up. He narrowed his gaze on her.

"That's why you were out in the storm." She tilted her head as she studied him. "A man like you, I bet you have plenty of money at hand to afford a room at an inn while you wait out the weather."

He repeated in an amused drawl, "A man like me?" He shrugged a shoulder, but he was so exhausted and weak that even that small movement set him swaying and unleashed fresh pounding in his head. "I'm no one important."

"Important enough that whoever is after you might just kill me because of something you've done."

"I won't let that happen." The cottage began to roll and pitch around him, and he grabbed once more for the mantelpiece to keep his balance. "You can trust that."

She rose slowly to her feet. Her soft voice joined the spinning in his head. "What did you do?"

He smiled grimly. "Defended my country."

She carefully stepped toward him, taking slow but deliberate steps. "Are you a criminal?"

"That depends on who you ask." He shook his head but couldn't clear away the light-headedness. But at least the wound in his arm and leg were turning numb. Thank God for that.

She drew closer, but her voice reached him as if through a tunnel. "Did you break the law?"

In two countries. In both, hanging offenses. "Yes," he murmured. That single word took such concentration to utter that he couldn't be bothered with finding his full voice. The room grew dark around him, the shadows closing in upon him. Even the howling of the raging storm grew muted. Distant. He felt himself swaying widely now.

"What did you do?" Through his fogged mind he saw her approach, like a ghost through the shadows. Or an angel bringing light to the darkness. "Did you hurt someone?"

Her beautiful face danced before his darkening vision. "Yes..." *Murder.*

Both hands gripped at the mantelpiece now. Swaying, spinning...shadows closing in, his body turning numb...He fought to remain conscious.

"Who's after you?"

"Everyone." Then the darkness claimed him.

CHAPTER 3

*N*o! Grace lunged to catch him as he sank toward the floor.

But he was tall and broad, solid muscle, and heavy. Oh so *very* heavy! She gasped as his full weight fell against her and struggled to keep him from collapsing. If he fell, she'd never have enough strength to lift him.

Staggering as she slipped his arm around her shoulders, she half-dragged him across the cottage to her bedroom and brought him to the side of her bed. With a loud groan of exertion, she shoved him forward. He collapsed over the mattress, his face buried in the counterpane and his body lying lifeless, half off the small bed.

She pressed her fingers against his neck, offering a silent prayer of mercy. It was bad enough that a peer had forced his way into her cottage tonight. But God help her if he died here.

His pulse beat strong against her fingertips.

Thank God. She heaved out a sigh of relief and pressed the back of her hand to her forehead.

Her eyes trailed over him. Dear lord, what was she supposed to do? He couldn't be a gentleman and leave when she'd asked. Or even when she'd demanded it. *Oh no.* Now the troublesome man was lying all akimbo in bed. In *her* bed. And not a very big one at that, which now looked impossibly smaller beneath his large body.

She wrung her hands. He was hiding from someone who wanted him dead. But he was the son of a *peer*, for God's sake! Peers didn't have people wanting them dead, apart from their own family sometimes. Peers had people envying them for their lands and fortunes, hating them because they'd won or lost too much money at White's, loathing them because they had the better horse or hound. Because they were pompous, arrogant, lazy, paunchy, self-entitled—

But they didn't hunt them through hurricanes in order to kill them.

Yet from the looks of him, someone had already tried. And very nearly succeeded.

Carefully, she straightened his body on the mattress, rolling him over onto his back and stretching out his arms and legs to make him more comfortable. She stepped back and bit her lip. What was she going to do with him now? Tie him up, that was a certainty. But then what? The last thing she could do was go to the authorities. He was the son of an earl, and claiming that he'd attacked her would draw far too much attention. Her description would run in all the papers, and she might have to testify before a magistrate. Vincent would surely hear of it and recognize her, would realize what she'd done all those years ago—

"Damn you, Ross Carlisle." Her eyes burned with hot tears of anger and exasperation. "Damn you to hell for coming here."

She couldn't even run away. Even if she hid until he left, there was no guarantee he wouldn't be found by the authorities, give up her name, and implicate her in his mess, if only as an innocent victim. The *very* last thing she needed was to have any attention at all brought down upon her.

He had no idea that he possessed the power to end her. And her son.

She would *never* let that happen.

With resolve, she left the bedroom. "I'll be right back." Then she tossed wryly over her shoulder at his unconscious form, "Don't go anywhere!"

When she returned a few minutes later, she carried everything needed to patch him up—cloth for bandages, hot water, scissors, needle and thread. Because it wasn't enough to let him remain until the storm broke. In the condition he was in, he wouldn't make it very far down the road before he collapsed again, and she had to make certain that he could get as far away as possible.

The cut on his arm needed stitches, no doubt of that. But the wound on his leg worried her more. A long deep slash, most likely from a sharp knife. Had he gotten into a bar fight? Had he cheated at cards or attempted to trick a group of local sailors—was that what he'd meant when he'd said he'd committed a crime?

No. Gentlemen didn't gamble with sailors, and they certainly didn't appear out of the dark of night in Sea Haven. It wasn't a bar fight; neither was it an attack by a footpad. He wouldn't be hiding from either of those, or have so many harsh cuts and bruises.

A chill spiraled down her spine. Something worse had brought him here.

"Got yourself into a mess, did you?" She sat on the edge of the bed and eyed him grimly. "Now you've left it to me to clean up."

Her eyes darted to sneak a glance at his chest. But she certainly didn't need a reminder of how broad and muscular it was, how the dusting of hair trailed over the hard ridges of his abdomen and disappeared beneath his waistband. Or that she couldn't very well sew up his leg with his trousers in the way.

"Well, you're already *half* naked." As she looked once more at his left leg, she gathered her nerve and reached for the fall of his trousers. "And you've nothing I haven't seen before."

Despite that reassurance to herself, her hands shook as she

unbuttoned his trousers, then wiggled them down, careful not to jostle his leg and make it bleed more. She averted her eyes as she stripped off the wet material. Down over his hips, along his hard thighs, over muscular calves, and off, to drop them onto the floor.

Thunk.

She glanced at the pile of wet material and saw a small bulge sewn into the left cuff. Tiny, not much bigger than her thumb, yet definitely not part of any tailor's handiwork she'd ever seen. Frowning with curiosity, she reached—

An unconscious groan came from him.

Straightening, she glanced at him and gasped, unprepared for the sight of him, lying sprawled across her bed. Completely naked.

She rolled her eyes and blew out a mouthful of air. Just her luck. Of all the men she should finally have naked in her bed after nearly a decade of chaste widowhood, it would have to be *him*. A Carlisle. Not just any Carlisle, either, but the one who'd claimed her first-ever society waltz, only to have it stolen away by the man who very shortly afterward became her husband.

Ross hadn't remembered her, but then, why would he? The ball had been a masquerade and only her second society outing, and at sixteen, she was unknown to the rest of the *ton*, even without her mask. They'd not spoken more than a handful of words when he requested the waltz, then none ever again after David took her into his arms and whirled her around the floor, stealing both the waltz and her future.

Moreover, she certainly wasn't the same person now as before. During the past decade, she'd gone from being London's Incomparable to a widowed mother in a fishing village. Whatever aspects of her previous life that her new identity, time, and age hadn't managed to hide, the scar on her cheek successfully concealed.

She repeated in an unconvincing mutter as her gaze traveled over him, "Nothing I haven't seen before."

Her face heated when her gaze strayed beneath his waist. Well, she might have seen *something* like that before…but apparently there were things the cold rain didn't shrink.

As she let herself take a good long look, the heat in her cheeks changed from embarrassment to something intense, something unexpected that tickled at the backs of her knees and stirred in her core. Hot and achy. Oddly urgent. She couldn't help but stare.

He was beautiful. The strangeness of that realization struck her, that a man could be beautiful. But he was. She'd seen naked men before, had been married for nearly two years. Yet she'd never seen one like him. The sculpted panes of his chest that gave way to the chiseled muscles of his abdomen, the long and graceful stretch of muscles in his thighs…He reminded her of a Greek sculpture, one of those gods from Lord Elgin's marbles, except fashioned in warm flesh and blood that had her longing to run her hands over him, to touch him and prove he was real. To simply *feel* him.

Her hand reached toward him of its own volition—

No. She snatched it back. What on God's earth was she thinking, losing her control like that? And losing of her mind, too, apparently. She simply couldn't touch him beyond tending to his wounds. Could *not!* A whole new ocean of trouble would drown her if she did.

So she focused her attention on the gash that sliced across his thigh and set to cleaning and sewing it. "A knife did this to you."

The cut was too smooth, too clean to be anything else. She'd tended to the wounds of enough sailors over the years when she'd helped Alice at the apothecary shop to recognize the slash of a blade when she saw one. Her hands trembled, not from each unconscious flinch he gave when the needle popped sickeningly through the skin and the thread pulled through after, but in fearful worry. Why had someone done this to him? They'd meant to hurt. Possibly even to kill.

Dear God, what had he gotten himself into?

She finished her gruesome sewing and sat back with a ragged sigh of relief that it was over. Then her gaze dropped to the cast off trousers on the floor.

Well, there was no way to put those back on. Not as wet as they were, not over damp skin. And certainly not as large and unwieldy as his muscular body was. So she picked up the throw from the back of her rocking chair and spread it over him. Faint disappointment panged inside her that his beautiful body was now covered.

"The worst is over." She sat on the side of the bed and frowned guiltily at the beads of sweat that had blossomed across his forehead at her handiwork. "Should I distract you from the pain the same way I distract Ethan whenever he skins a knee, with a spoonful of sugar?"

She wiped gently at his forehead with the towel, careful to avoid the small cuts and bruises at his brow and cheek. *Those* marks had been made by fists, as had the bruises on his chest and ribs. "Perhaps you'd prefer to change your mind and accept that jug of whiskey after all?"

After several ragged breaths that moved his bare chest up and down in small spasms, she saw his brow relax as the pain eased from him. His heavy body seemed to soften into the mattress, and his breathing grew deep and steady. Finally calm.

Asleep like this, quiet and still, he seemed almost harmless. She reached to touch his face, to delicately trace her fingertips along the soft curve of each brow, carefully skirting the cut at the edge of the left one.

Good God, what had he been through? To be this badly beaten, so exhausted and weak that he'd collapsed…*Why?*

"Ah, but you *are* a Carlisle. Bare-knuckled fights are your family's forte, from what I understand."

So were their handsome looks. This one, even battered and bruised, owned that trait in spades.

With a faint smile, she traced her fingertip along his jaw. She couldn't stop touching him. No matter how slight the connection, he was still a link to her old life and to the woman she'd once been. A young woman who'd once had so much promise, shining like a diamond—

A lie. That wasn't why she couldn't tear her hands away from his body or her eyes away from his sandy blond curls and sculpted face.

She couldn't stop because she simply enjoyed it too much.

Twelve years since she last saw him...Ross had just entered the army after finishing at Oxford. He'd been so dashing in his red uniform, with sparkling blue eyes and a commanding presence that claimed the attention of every room he entered. Now, age had mellowed his brashness, but he was still handsome. The years had been good to him, maturing him into a man in his prime, and not one bit of the lanky young man she remembered remained beneath the strength he exuded, even while asleep.

Her hand trailed down to his chest. Dear God, it had been so long since she'd touched a man! Even so innocently as this. How could she have forgotten the warmth of male skin, the steely firmness of muscles beneath soft flesh? Or the delicious solidity of him, a feeling so tantalizing that even now she ached from remembering the pleasures of joined bodies, of welcoming a man's hardness inside her softness—

She squeezed her eyes shut against the stinging that suddenly sprung up in them. She'd forgotten because the loneliness had consumed her.

At first, she'd mourned David's memory. Then her full attention had been on Ethan, a tiny babe who needed her undivided devotion. There had been no time to consider her own selfish needs as a woman. The years stretched on after that, filled with busy days and long nights. Of course, there had been offers of intimacy from the sailors at the docks and the men in the village. A few had even been bold enough to propose marriage. But she knew better than to let any of them into her life, and certainly not into her heart. The risk was simply too great.

"You're the first man who's been in my bed since my husband died. Just my luck that you would be a Carlisle." She was unable to keep her lips from twisting in amused irony. "And unconscious."

He slept on, replying with a faint snore.

CHAPTER 4

*R*oss opened his eyes.

A blinding pain gripped his forehead and temples so hard that he winced and squeezed his eyes shut. He sucked in a deep breath and waited for the throbbing to subside before attempting to slowly open them again as he struggled to sort through the fog dulling his mind and to remember where he was. And how he'd gotten here.

He lifted his arm to scour a hand over his face—

His arm jerked to a stop. Ropes tightened at his wrists, keeping his hands fastened to the side rail of the bed frame. He couldn't move them. Or his legs, with his ankles tied to the footboard. *Christ.* With gritted teeth, he yanked his arms to break through the thin rope.

"There's no point in struggling," a soft voice assured him. "You've been tied up."

"Obviously." His eyes narrowed on the expertly knotted ropes, before turning to the woman sitting in the rocking chair in the corner, who'd most likely done the tying. The same woman whose cottage he'd forced his way into last night, seeking shelter. He remembered that much, if not clearly. "Is this really necessary?"

"I think so." She didn't move to stand, her feet remaining tucked beneath her as if she'd spent the entire night right there, keeping guard. "I used sailors' knots, too, so the more you struggle, the tighter the ropes become."

"Of course you did," he muttered as he stole another glance at the knots, then lay still. Although, if truth be told, he wasn't feeling up to struggling, despite the sleep he'd finally gotten after days on the run. And apparently, he'd been asleep long enough that a glance at the window told him it was morning and that the storm had spent itself. Despite still being shuttered, gray light shined dimly around the window's edges, and rain now fell over the cottage in a steady drizzle instead of the driving hurricane gale of last night.

"I also took the liberty of sewing up your wounds and applying salve to the cuts." She mentioned that as casually as if she were a hostess chatting over tea instead of the woman who had turned the tables on him and gone from captive to captor. Complete with slipknots that would have made Horatio Nelson proud.

"Why bother, if you're going to send for the authorities to have me arrested?" To think he'd survived flinging himself into the ice-cold Channel to escape the French, only to end up caught by a widow—his brother Kit would have a grand laugh over this, if his situation weren't so deadly. After all, if a wisp of a woman could capture him, how little would it take for one of the Frenchmen to slit his throat if they found him?

"I'm not turning you over. I'm holding you to your word that you'll leave without harming me." Her eyes flickered as she added, "The word of a gentleman must be worth something."

"No gentleman I've ever known," he muttered, only half facetiously. "So untie me, and I'll be on my way."

"Oh, I don't think so. Not yet anyway." She nodded toward the window. "You arrived under the cover of darkness. That's the same way you'll leave."

Interesting…if not for the fierce pounding in his head that had him desperate to close his eyes again and fall back into sleep's sweet oblivion. She wanted to keep him from being seen. Good. At least they agreed on that. "So we're to wait until sundown before you release me?"

"Before I place a pocket knife in your hand," she explained calmly, as if discussing nothing more distressing than the weather. "Then I'll leave and let you cut yourself free. The rope is loose enough for you to maneuver the blade beneath and fairly thin. You should have yourself out in no more than twenty minutes, and by then I'll be safely away."

So that he couldn't change his mind and do her harm after all. "Very clever."

She shrugged a slender shoulder. "A widow lives on her wits."

She was no more a fisherman's widow than he was the king. Her plan for him proved that. Only a woman who had been harmed by a man would think to go to such extremes to ensure she couldn't be hurt again. Was that how she'd gotten that scar? A permanent reminder to always be cautious?

"So you plan on spending the day together like this? Making pleasant conversation, with me lying here." He glanced at the pile of his clothes folded neatly on top of the dresser and grimaced. "Naked."

"I had to undress you. I couldn't sew up your wounds through your clothes. Besides, you've nothing I haven't seen before." But she glanced away, a faint pink staining her cheeks. "And yes, I plan on you lying there all day."

"And if I have to relieve myself?" he challenged impudently.

She snatched an empty pitcher from the washstand and set it on the bed next to his hip. "Don't miss."

He narrowed his eyes on her. *Damnable woman.*

She returned to her chair. "So you'll stay right there, tied up. Unless you tell me the truth about who you are and how you ended up here."

"You first," he dared. "You're no fisherman's widow."

To her credit, her expression never changed, although he saw a darkness cloud her eyes. The Home Office was recruiting its operatives in the wrong places. They should have been looking in fishing villages.

He continued, "We can end by you telling me why you don't want me to be seen leaving. Or why you've not already sounded the alarm for the villagers to raise their pitchforks against me."

"I would never ask the villagers to raise pitchforks." With faint indignation, she reached casually for a cup of tea resting on a small tray on the dresser. "We're a fishing village. They would raise oars."

Not moving her gaze from his over the rim of her cup, she lifted it to her lips and took a small sip. His stomach rumbled. He couldn't remember the last time he'd eaten, and watching her partake of something even as unsubstantial as tea made him ravenous.

She asked softly, "What's your real reason for being here?"

He closed his eyes and tried to relax, to make the best of a brutally bad situation. If he hadn't been so desperate to leave France, he would have been able to take better care of himself, and he wouldn't have let his guard slip to the point that she'd been able to tie him up. "First, you'll have to tell me where *here* is."

"Sea Haven Village on Winchelsea Bay." Her bewilderment rang out loudly in her pause. "How could you disembark at the dock and not know where you are?"

"Because I didn't disembark." His lips curled in foolish pride at his own perilous behavior. At least this part of the story Kit would love. "I jumped overboard."

"In that storm? I don't believe you."

"Good. It makes it easier for a man to hide his secrets when a woman won't believe the truth."

He heard the soft rustle of her skirts as she stood. "Why on earth would you do something like that? It was tantamount to suicide." Her voice grew closer as she stepped toward the bed. "Was the boat sinking?"

"Perfectly good boat. I simply preferred to be off it." To die by drowning rather than torture. With his kneecaps intact.

He felt the bed sink beneath her light weight as she sat beside him, and he opened his eyes to see her reach forward to set the little tray on the bedside table. In the faint gray morning light that filtered in around the edges of the shutters, she was just as pretty as he remembered from last night. Beautiful, in fact, with a delicately pretty face and hair a shade he would have called toffee. An apt description, as it so perfectly complimented the chocolate brown of her eyes.

It wasn't only her physical appearance that struck him, but also the way she moved so gracefully, even just to reach for a teacup. She had blue blood coursing through her veins. He would have bet his fortune on it.

"So you jumped overboard." She carefully brought the teacup to his lips and helped him take a sip. He closed his eyes at the exquisite sensation. The grassy-sweet liquid soothed his parched throat, made raw by swallowing what seemed like half the Atlantic Ocean as he'd struggled in the waves. "And came ashore here at the bay."

She offered another sip of tea.

Not tea, he now understood, but a reward for confiding in her. He had no choice. He was too famished to deny himself sustenance because of something as malleable as the truth. "Yes."

She reached for the tray and what looked deliciously like a cinnamon biscuit, then poised it at his lips, just out of bite-reach. "Why were you on a boat in the middle of that storm?"

"Lives were at risk. Mine especially." He opened his mouth, and she placed the small biscuit on his tongue. He mumbled through his starved chewing, "And now yours, if anyone finds out that you're helping me."

He watched her closely, expecting her to pale at that. Instead she remained calm, as if not surprised in the least. He would have found that to be another intriguing facet to her, if she hadn't tied him up.

"Then they shan't find out." She picked up a second biscuit and held it to his lips. "So you were being chased from France."

He jerked his head back, his eyes narrowing. "I never said that."

"You implied last night that you were being chased." She gave him the biscuit, then reached into her skirt pocket to pull out a small sheath of papers.

He froze in mid-chew, his heart stopping.

"And I found these in a little water-tight vial sewn into the leg of your trousers." She placed the documents on the side table. "They're in French."

He choked down the biscuit, no longer hungry.

"They're nothing," he lied as she raised the teacup to his lips again. "Just papers I needed for travel."

Her gaze hardened on him, and she lowered the cup away. "I'm fluent in French." She reached for a small sandwich on the plate and broke off a corner with her fingers. "Leftover roast beef from yesterday's dinner. Very tender." She showed him the bite of food in blatant bribery. "Want to try that again?"

Damnable woman. Despite himself, his eyes fixed on the beef, and his stomach growled. He was starving, and the small biscuit had only whetted his hunger. "You read them. What do you think they are?"

"A letter requesting payment and three lists of names. One list is all in the same handwriting, but the other two…" She eyed him warily. "Something tells me none of those pages are what they seem."

"Because they're not."

"What are they, then?"

He looked at the bite of beef and arched a brow, opening his mouth and refusing to say more. Two could play this bribery game.

She placed the piece of food between his lips. He chewed it slowly, savoring the flavor. Never had beef tasted better in his entire life.

He swallowed. "You cooked that?"

"Yes. But with yesterday being the cook's day off and the butler and housekeeper both ill, what choice did I have?"

Cheeky wench. "I meant that it's very good."

The quiet compliment struck its mark, and she gave him a second piece without preamble. "Thank you." And another biscuit. "I had to learn to cook when I first came to Sea Haven. It wasn't pretty." A self-deprecating smile lit her face, one that warmed him through. When she wasn't threatening him with an iron poker, she could be quite alluring. "I'm surprised we all didn't die of food poisoning."

"Your mother didn't teach you?"

She stiffened at his question. Her reaction was barely perceptible, but he noticed. "My mother died when I was a baby."

"I'm sorry."

Not meeting his gaze as she tore off another bite of beef, she shrugged a shoulder. "I have no memories of her, but Papa assured me that she was always kind and loving, intelligent, and beautiful."

"Like her daughter," he murmured.

She laughed, the sound soft beneath the faint drone of falling rain. "Flattery won't make me untie you any sooner." Yet she smiled faintly as she gave him the bite of food, placing it between his lips. "What were you doing in France?"

He chewed slowly, taking the time to consider what he should tell her. She knew too much as it was, but resisting her gentle interrogation would only result in his starvation. "I was working."

"At what?" She cut him off with a pointed glance. "Before you attempt to lie and tell me that you're a fisherman, you should know that I won't believe you. I live among sailors here, and you're most definitely not a man who makes his living on the sea."

"I'm not a sailor." In reward, he accepted the biscuit she raised to his lips. "I work for King George in the Court of St James's."

Her fingers froze as they reached to brush a crumb from his chin. When a slight frown creased her brow, he suspected that he'd just surprised her for the first time since they'd begun talking. "The diplomatic corps?"

"Yes. In Paris." When her thumb caressed gently over his lip, his gut tightened reflexively. He was used to having women's hands on him, but certainly not like this. Her innocent caress was…nice.

"What kind of diplomat dons workmen's clothes?" Her question was a disbelieving challenge, yet her voice held a knowing edge to it. As if she knew more about him than she was letting on. *Impossible.* She might have figured out on her own that he'd been in disguise when he boarded that ship to England, but she certainly didn't know who he was. And better that she didn't.

"The crown's budget has fallen since the wars," he drawled wryly. When that earned him a scolding glare from her, he answered truthfully, "I had to leave France unexpectedly."

"Flee, you mean?"

"Chased."

"Caught," she corrected, her hand reaching up to trace featherlight caresses over the cut at his brow. Soft, soothing…He ached to take her into his arms like a child with a treasured toy and fall back to sleep. "We don't have a doctor in the village, so I've helped patch up a lot of sailors over the years. The only times I've seen wounds like these were when they'd been in drunken fights." Her fingers trailed down his temple to the bruise on his cheek, then along his jaw. "You didn't receive these wounds from washing ashore in the bay, even in storm-tossed seas."

"No." His breath hitched when her hand trailed down his neck to his bare chest. "I didn't."

She lightly touched the stitches in the cut on his arm, each flutter of her fingertips easing away the heat of the wound. But she also sent his heartbeat racing when she swept her hand slowly across his shoulder and down the plane of his chest. "Someone wanted to hurt you."

"No." Warm tingles spread out from beneath her fingertips. He could no longer call her touch soothing. It was so much better than that. "They wanted to kill me."

Her hand stilled on his chest. "Why?"

He shook his head. Damn those knots, that he couldn't slip his arms around her and pull her down on top of him. After all, a condemned man deserved a last request, and kissing her senseless would be a damnably fine one. "It isn't safe for you to know."

"Protecting me, are you?" A sardonic smile curled her lips, and her hand moved again. This time, her fingers played lightly over his abdomen, following along the dusting of hair on his chest that disappeared beneath the edge of the blanket draped across his hips. Her hand slipped beneath—

His cock jumped. Only for the immediate ache to turn ice-cold when her hand slid over to feel along his bruised ribs to check for wounds.

He bit back a curse at himself. He was a damned fool.

"You're not proving to be much of a protector," she chided, her brown eyes gleaming with dark amusement. "Perhaps you shouldn't have let yourself be caught." Although she said that while examining the bruises on his side, he knew she didn't mean by the Frenchmen. The aggravating woman meant *her*. Which only proved how exhausted he'd been last night that she was able to best him.

"Then untie me," he cajoled in a husky murmur.

"I'm afraid not."

"I told you—I won't hurt you."

Her somber eyes held his for a long moment. "Oh, but you could," she whispered, so softly that he barely heard her. "More than you possibly realize." She slowly pulled her hand away from him, as if reluctant to stop touching him—*he* certainly wouldn't have minded if she continued. She forced a wry smile. "You picked the wrong cottage last night, and the wrong woman to hold captive. I'm not one to fall for flattery and manly assurances, no matter how charming."

Oh, he certainly realized *that*. "Then I'll be blunt. I need to travel to London. Immediately. Before the men who are after me get there first."

"Why are they after you, exactly?"

"I can't tell you."

"Because you're protecting me?" She didn't bother trying to hide her skepticism.

"And myself. But if you keep me here until dark, I'll lose an entire day." God only knew how much damage could be done in that time. How much of a traitor he would be revealed to be. Or a murderer.

"I don't have a choice. I can't risk that anyone might see you, especially if you've broken the law."

"Why does it matter who sees me?" he dodged, avoiding her attempt to pry deeper into his criminality. "No one here knows me."

She hesitated, as if she'd started to answer but changed her mind. "Because I have a reputation." Another hesitation. Then quietly, but in a voice filled with resolve, "And I have a son. I cannot take any risks that might put him in danger. Not from you, not from *anyone*."

"I won't put you in danger."

"You already have just by being here." She suspiciously eyed the documents. "It's those papers, isn't it? Why you're being chased. What are they?"

"A letter and three lists of names." The last thing he needed was for her to learn the truth about those. "Nothing more than that."

She waited for him to offer more. *The hell he would.* The stubborn woman had already placed both their lives in danger. Any more, and they'd swing together at Newgate before this was over.

When he remained silent, she slowly set the tea tray aside, then wiped her hands on her skirt and collected the pages. Standing to walk away, she slipped them into her pocket.

Panic spiked in his gut. "Don't!" He thrashed against the ropes but only worked the knots tighter and increased the pain in his ribs. "Don't take them! You don't know what they are."

"A letter and three lists," she pointedly repeated his words with a shrug of her shoulders. "Nothing more."

When he didn't contradict her, she took a step toward the door.

"They will kill you if they find them on you!"

She froze. "Who?"

"The men I'm running from—men who want me dead. If they discover that you've read them, they'll kill you, too, just to keep you silent."

"What did you do?" Her face paled.

He bit down a soft curse. "I trusted the wrong man."

She gazed at him, as if deciding whether to accept this fractured half-explanation. Then she shook her head. "I can't believe that—"

"And I don't believe for one moment that you're a fisherman's widow protecting her son," he shot back, putting her on the defensive as he attacked. He prayed that he might anger her enough to make her leave those pages behind. "What did *you* do that you don't want to be noticed?"

Her gaze didn't stray from his. The silence stretched between them for so long that the sound of the drizzling rain striking the roof filled up the little cottage.

Finally, she answered, "I refused to die."

Well aware of his gaze on her, she carried the papers to the dresser and hid them inside his clothing.

Relief eased away his alarm. Not that having the papers nearby did him any good. The ropes at his wrists were tighter than ever, and he had no hope of retrieving them until the blasted woman allowed it. But at least she wasn't carrying them on her person.

"I have to go into the village." She stepped into the main room to fetch the oil slicker and slipped it on. "And no, I won't tell anyone about you or those papers."

"Thank you."

"I'll be back in about an hour." She tossed dryly over her shoulder as she left the cottage and closed the door after herself, "Don't go anywhere!"

With a frustrated curse, Ross lay back on the bed and seethed. Never in his life had he met a woman like her.

If he weren't careful, he wouldn't live long enough to meet another.

CHAPTER 5

"For heaven's sake!" Alice Walters called out in surprise from behind the counter as Grace rushed inside the apothecary shop to escape the rain. "What on earth are you doing out in this weather?"

"Swimming," Grace answered, deadpan. She stopped just inside the door to peel off her hat and slicker and shake out the water before it pooled on the stone floor. And also to gather herself before she faced her old friend. Thank God she could blame her shaking on the cold.

Alice ignored her quip, allowing only a concerned huff as Grace hung up her coat and then stuck her head into the adjoining room in search of her son.

"Ethan?" she called out, hearing the panic in her voice but helpless to prevent it. "Ethan! Where are you?"

"He's upstairs cleaning out the storage room." Alice circled around from behind the counter and took Grace's hands in hers, squeezing them reassuringly. "Calm down. Everything's all right. He's perfectly fine. Slept through the storm like a log."

A harsh sigh of relief tore from her. "I can't help it. I—"

The words choked in her tightening throat.

Now that she was here in the shop, knowing for certain that Ethan was safe, the fear and distress that had kept her on edge since the moment Ross forced his way into her cottage eased from her. It left her body trembling, her stomach roiling, and oddly enough, somehow even more panicked now than when she'd been held prisoner.

She blinked back tears and admitted painfully, "I was worried about him."

With a motherly smile, Alice tucked a wet curl behind Grace's ear. The affectionate gesture wasn't enough to soothe away her agitation at Ross's unexpected return into her life, but thank God she could blame all that on being apart from Ethan.

"Come warm yourself." Alice slipped her arm around Grace's waist and gently led her to the small stove in the corner. "You shouldn't have come out yet, not with the rain still falling like it is."

But she definitely couldn't stay home. "I needed to see Ethan and make certain he was safe."

That was the God's honest truth. She'd always put Ethan's well being before her own, and today was no different, especially with the man-sized threat of Ross Carlisle bearing down upon her.

Alice reached for a mug, then filled it with tea from the kettle sitting on the stovetop. "You know I'll protect him like he was my own. You didn't have to risk your neck."

"I wasn't risking my neck." Although she certainly now craned it toward the stairs, still searching for her son. She wouldn't calm down until she saw him with her own eyes. "The storm's nearly over. Just a bit of rain. Nothing worth fretting about it." *A lie.* She was nearly soaked through by the half-mile walk into the village, although the winds had howled themselves out. "And I—I have to ask you a favor." She bit her bottom lip. "Can you keep him here with you for the rest of the day?"

Alice frowned. "Don't you want him home with you?"

What she wanted was for Ethan not to discover a large—and currently naked—man tied to his mother's bed. There was no good explanation for that, and no way to be rid of Ross until nightfall. She simply couldn't risk that he'd be seen leaving. "I need him to stay here."

Alice stiffened. She was the only other person in the world who knew the truth of Grace's past. "Is something wrong?"

More than I can say. Yet she dissembled, "Just a problem that blew in during the storm."

"Do you need me to fetch Mr. Dawson to help you?"

"Not at all." She feigned a smile of embarrassment and swallowed down the guilt of lying to her closest friend. "One of the shutters came unfastened last night, and there was some damage to the window. I don't want Ethan there underfoot while I'm trying to fix it." When that lie didn't seem to mollify Alice, Grace added, "I also didn't sleep a wink last night. I don't think I'm in the proper condition to take care of Ethan today." That was the God's honest truth.

"All right." But the way Alice said that made Grace suspect that she didn't think she'd be catching up on her sleep this afternoon.

"By evening, everything will be back to normal." If she could take Ross at his word as a gentleman that he would leave, that is, taking those peculiar pages right along with him. With a flicker of worry over the new mess fate had flung her into, she paused to listen for her son. Hearing nothing, she called out, "Ethan, now!"

A head peered over the top of the stairs. "Yes, Mother?"

Thank God. "Come down so I can see you." And pull him into her arms. Even now she ached at having been so long apart from him, from worrying about him every minute since she'd left him here yesterday afternoon—twice as much since she recognized Ross and realized the threat he unwittingly posed. She shuddered, the fear so strong that it pained her.

"All right," Ethan heaved out in aggravation. When she saw him grimace, her heart tore.

He dutifully thumped his way down the narrow stairs, taking his sweet time. Every second of delay agonized her. When he finally got close enough, she flung her arms around him and pulled him to her, not caring that she was crushing him.

She closed her eyes, choking back the soft sob of relief that he was safely back in her arms where he belonged.

With a scowl, he pushed her away and stepped back. His face darkened with that same defiant expression he always wore lately, which ripped her heart even more.

"Were you all right last night?" She brushed her fingers through his hair the way she'd done since he was still in leading strings. "Did you listen to Mrs. Walters and do as she asked?"

"Yes." He ducked his head away, just out of her reach.

Her hand fell to her side. She forced a smile, pretending that it didn't pain her that her son was no longer a baby. But he needed her protection now more than ever. "What did you two do to pass the time?"

He shrugged a shoulder.

"We played games and sang songs," Alice answered for him. "And roasted apples over the fire."

Her smile widened with relief that his night away had been so ordinary. "That sounds wonderful."

"Guess so," he grumbled.

At that moment, Grace had a terrible glimpse of how sullen and dour he would be as a young man. He was already becoming a handful and challenging her more and more every day. However would she handle him?

"What did you do last night, Mother?"

Her stomach somersaulted. He was watching her closely, waiting for an answer—Heavens, she could never tell him the truth! "I went to bed early." Not entirely a lie. She *had* gone to bed early, only to be taken prisoner a few hours later. "Then spent the entire night missing you terribly."

At that, Ethan scowled. Only a few months ago, he would have flung his arms around her neck and hugged her, happy to see her and eager to return her affections. But not now. Her little boy was disappearing before her eyes.

"I'm helping Mrs. Walters sort through some old boxes." He glanced longingly toward the stairs, and toward escape from his mother. "Can I go back up?"

Forcing her smile not to waver, Grace pressed her lips tightly together to hold back a sob of emotion and nodded jerkily.

If Ethan saw her eyes glistening, he didn't pay it any mind as he hurried upstairs, his shoes thumping just as loudly as when he'd come down. Except now much faster in his rush to be away.

"He's a boy who wants to be a man," Alice explained quietly in an attempt to assuage the pain of his rejection. "You remind him that he was a babe not so long ago."

Grace knew that. Yet that bittersweet knowledge didn't lessen the sting.

Alice handed her a mug of tea, then fixed her with a hard look. "He needs a man's influence in his life. It was fine before, when he was a babe and you took care of everything for him. But he's growing now, and he needs a man to show him how to behave."

"He has men in Sea Haven who can teach him that." She bristled at the implication that Ethan lacked anything so essential. She'd given him everything. Including her life.

Alice scoffed. "The men down at the docks and in the public house?"

"His schoolmaster," she countered, listing every man whose orbit brought him into her son's life, "Vicar Brennan, Mr. Dawson at the mercantile…" Even as she said their names, the list of men seemed pathetically weak. "I'll teach him what they can't."

"You're going to teach him to shave, are you?" she pressed. "The difference between when a man needs to answer with his fists and when he's better off walking away? What he needs to know about being with a woman and how babes are got?"

"Yes, I will," she said as resolutely as possible, despite the doubt pinching in her belly.

The dubious look Alice sent her was piercing. "He needs a man in his life." She gave a curt nod. "And so do you."

Grace nearly choked on the tea. Oh, the very last thing she needed in her life was a man!

"You should have a man to take care of you, one who spoils you the way you deserve and protects you." Alice's face softened. "One to put another babe in your belly. You know you want that."

Her chest tightened at that temptation. How many nights since David died had she lain awake, staring into the darkness and wanting exactly that...for a man to put his strong arms around her and make her feel safe? To make her feel desired and beautiful again? To give her another child that she could love as much as she loved Ethan?

But all that died with David and was buried deep beneath his brother Vincent's threats.

The tea turned to acid on her tongue. "I can never have that, you know it."

"What I *know* is that you've been keeping secrets for so long that you don't recognize the truth. It's time you stopped now. For your sake *and* Ethan's."

Alice's quiet words stabbed her with a spike of fresh guilt. *Secrets.* So many secrets! How could she even begin to sort through them all? At that very moment, in fact, she was keeping one very large, hard bodied, and handsome secret from the world.

She swallowed down the urge to confide in her friend, knowing the risk was simply too great. Later, when Ross was gone and no longer a threat, they could both have a good laugh at the desperate measures she'd once again been forced to take. Until then, he had to remain her secret.

"The boy has to be told the truth about his father."

Her shoulders sagged with exasperation. That Alice would bring this up, now of all times, nearly ten years to the day when she'd fled the only life she'd ever known—she was overstepping.

But Grace would never have survived without her. When she'd first arrived in Sea Haven, with her large belly nearly bursting, she had no money, no family, and nowhere to go for sanctuary. By sheer luck Alice had stumbled across her, quite literally, when she'd collapsed outside the apothecary shop. The woman took her in, at first only to nurse her through the birth and help with the newborn whom Grace knew nothing about how to care for. But then the two became best friends, and Grace stayed in Sea Haven long after she should have moved on, settling into the old cottage on the bluff with Ethan, helping Alice in the shop, and taking whatever work she could find to support them.

She'd struggled to make a safe life for herself and Ethan here, and she hoped to continue to live unnoticed, in peace and security, dead to the rest of the world. Given her past, she didn't dare ask for more. She wanted only for Ethan to grow into a good man, one who was successful but not so accomplished as to ever move to London, where someone might see his resemblance to David, might put the pieces together and realize—

Worse, that Ethan might meet his Uncle Vincent.

"Ethan has to be kept safe." Even if that meant never sharing his true past with him.

Alice's face grew grim. "What would your husband have wanted for his son?"

That simple question cut Grace to the quick. She'd wondered exactly that nearly every time she looked at Ethan.

"He would have wanted his son to live," she answered in a whisper, unable to put voice to that half-lie.

David would have wanted Ethan to have the life of privilege and status he deserved. That was why she'd gathered whatever evidence she could about Ethan's conception and birth. Her diary and household records that showed she and David had been together when her baby was conceived, a statement from the midwife who helped Alice deliver Ethan that proved the date and time of his birth, the record of his christening in the parish church in Sea Haven...everything she could to prove that Ethan was David's son. But the timing had never been right to attempt to reclaim his inheritance. The threat to Ethan had always been too great.

Not that it mattered. Even if she wanted to pursue justice, what good would it do? She'd spent too many sleepless nights trying to think of any way to claim what they were due, only to come up with nothing. She had no one to help her present a petition, and no way to pay for attorneys even if she did.

No. Her safest strategy was simply to wait.

Grimly, Alice picked up a newspaper. "This arrived two days ago. I finally read it this morning." Her voice was grim. "You need to see this."

Her belly knotted as Alice opened the broadsheet and laid it on the counter. Grace scanned it—

The gossip page?

She rolled her eyes. That page was home to all kinds of salacious news about the *ton's* happenings during the London season. She knew Alice eagerly followed such nonsense, but Grace had lived it once and had no desire whatsoever to relive it, even in newsprint from half a country away.

Alice tapped her finger on a small bit of news tucked in between all the wedding announcements. Biting back an annoyed sigh, Grace read:

LOCKWOOD STRUTS THROUGH MAYFAIR LIKE A PEACOCK THESE DAYS, *now that his American heiress wife is finally* enceinte *and sharing her good news with her friends—and more importantly, with her dressmaker. Could this be the long-awaited Lockwood heir?*

· · ·

THE EARTH PITCHED SICKENINGLY BENEATH HER. SHE GRABBED FOR the counter to keep from collapsing.

"Like I said," Alice whispered, the soft sound reverberating inside Grace's chest. "You've run out of time."

CHAPTER 6

"*You.*"

Ross opened his eyes. Grace had returned.

And something was wrong.

She stood in the narrow bedroom doorway, her fingers clasping the doorjamb on either side of her so tightly that even from the bed he could see her fingertips turning white. The oil slicker was open, and rain had soaked her through, leaving her dress wet and her hair lying plastered against her head. Raindrops clung to her cheeks and eyelashes—rather he hoped they were raindrops. From her stricken expression, they might have been tears.

"Me," he returned dryly. "You said not to go anywhere, so I made myself at home."

For once, his taunting didn't draw an irritated reaction from her. Which worried him. She continued to stand there, wild-eyed and struggling for breath. *Good Lord.* Had she run back from the village?

She panted out, "I know who you are."

He kept the surprise from his face. She couldn't possibly know his true identity. "Because I told you. Christopher Thomas."

"You're Ross Carlisle, Viscount Mooreland." The certainty with which she said that belied the violent shaking in her limbs. "Christopher is your brother."

He froze. *That* bit of information wouldn't be on a bill for his arrest. How the devil did she find out?

She came forward and pulled a pocketknife from her oil slicker. The blade sliced through the rope tying his right wrist. Then she slumped down in the chair, still trying to catch her breath. Her slender shoulders slumped as the rainwater puddled on the floor around her boots, but she kept the knife clasped tightly in her trembling hand.

Her gaze locked with his. "You and I are going to have a little talk."

Despite himself, the corner of his mouth twisted into a wry smile. His situation had suddenly taken an interesting turn.

However she'd learned of his identity, it wasn't from news of what he'd done in France. That information couldn't possibly have reached all the way here so soon, to a tiny fishing village in East Sussex. Not when boats had been safely docked against the storm. No news in or out. He'd counted on that to secure a jump in the race to London that he'd been thrust into.

Not saying a word, with only the sound of falling rain and her ragged breathing breaking the silence, he reached over and untied his other wrist. He paused to rub the red marks where the slip-knots had tightened against his skin, then sat up and untied both feet.

He swung his legs over the side of the bed to stand up and warned, "Better look away so I can dress."

"Not on your life." Her hand clenched tighter around the knife.

With a roguish arch of his eyebrow, he pushed himself off the bed. The throw fell away, leaving him standing there naked, daring her to look. But she kept her gaze firmly fixed on his face, despite the soft hitch of her breath.

He would have laughed if he didn't suspect that she might very well use that knife on him for it.

Turning his back to her, he reached for the stack of clothes on the dresser. "Why do you think I'm a peer?" He smiled to himself as he tugged on his trousers. The aggravating woman had mended them for him during the night. "Is it my fashionable attire?"

"I *know* you're a peer, those clothes notwithstanding. It's clear in every inch of you."

Just as he knew that she was no sailor's widow. Stowing the papers carefully beneath his waistband at the small of his back, he turned to face her, then gestured at the knife. "You can put that down. I won't hurt you."

"So you say." She kept it pointed at him. "Why did you lie about who you are?"

"How did you find out?" He snatched up the beef sandwich still sitting on the tea tray that she'd left beside the bed, most likely to torture him while he'd been tied up and unable to reach it. He hungrily sank his teeth into the sandwich and nearly groaned with pleasure. After so many days without food, the taste of it...*ambrosia.*

"We met once, a long time ago."

He paused in mid-chew, his eyes narrowing on her. *Impossible.* He would have remembered a woman like her. "Where?"

"Mayfair. At a masquerade ball."

He swallowed down the bite and laughed. "*Masks?* You'll have to do better than that if you want me to believe that we—"

"You had just joined the army," she interjected calmly, "so you didn't deign to wear a mask, not for that ball. You wanted everyone to see you in your brand new uniform and shiny black boots. Your father, the Earl of Spalding, was incredibly proud of you for taking a commission, although most peers would have suffered apoplexy if their heirs put themselves in front of Boney the way you'd planned to do"

A prickle of unease snaked up his spine. No point in denying his identity. But who the hell was she that she'd been at a masquerade? "Lots of balls in Mayfair. You'll have to be more specific."

She shook her head, unwilling to divulge more. "You are Ross Carlisle," she declared firmly, as if daring him to contradict her. "Everyone in Mayfair knows the Carlisles. For heaven's sake, it isn't as if any of you try to fade into the background."

True, although more so his cousins than he and his brother. The Trent side of the family had certainly rained havoc upon England, while the Spalding side had fought to serve her. And look where it had gotten him. An accused traitor, hiding in some godforsaken fishing village with a lying widow. At knifepoint.

"While I don't know what you've done to end up here or why anyone would chase you—nor do I care—I do know that if those wounds of yours are any indication of your last run-in with them, they will not hesitate to kill you if they catch you." Her eyes glowed with a soft intensity in the dim light. "You need my help."

Ross reached for the leftover cold tea and raised it slowly to his lips, assessing her over the rim of the cup. Why would she help him? "I told you that I was a criminal. How do you know that I won't kill you to keep you quiet, now that you've untied me?"

Not at all afraid of him, she replied, "Because the man I knew wasn't a murderer."

More than you know. "Men change."

"Not that much. Besides, if you wanted to harm me, you would have done so last night when you forced your way inside." She folded up the knife and tossed it onto the bed beside him. "You're not that kind of man. But you *are* wealthy and powerful with influential connections in Parliament. Most likely at court, too."

Not anymore. "If I'm all that, why would I need your help?"

"Because you're famished, covered in wounds, and two hundred miles from London without a farthing on you. Believe me, I know, because I've seen all of you."

He grimaced at the reminder that she'd stripped him bare. And sadly, while he wasn't awake to enjoy it.

"You have no way to hire coach nor horse, and if you felt desperate enough to force your way into my cottage last night in order to hide from whoever is chasing you, then simply walking on the roads puts you in danger of being recognized. Or arrested for vagrancy, once you're seen wearing those filthy clothes." She squared her slender shoulders with the resolve of a man walking to the gallows—one with nothing to lose. "If *I* could recognize you, despite ten years and all that beard, then the men who want you dead would certainly have no trouble."

Damn her, she was right. "How could you help me with any of that? Feeling charitable enough to purchase me a seat on the mail coach, are you?"

She shook her head. "They'll be watching the stage routes. Go as you are, and you'll be spotted before you reach the first inn." She said that with a well-practiced assurance, as if she'd known when she'd burst through the cottage door what she would propose. "You need money from me to hire a post-chaise, and you need me to come with you in order to disguise you. They won't be looking for a couple traveling together."

He laughed at that, nearly choking on the last bite of the beef.

But she wasn't laughing, and her eyes lacked that teasing glint he'd come to appreciate. *Good God—*

"You're serious." His laughter died when she didn't contradict him. "And utterly mad."

She ignored that. "Once we're in London, you'll repay me in kind."

A knowing smile tugged at his lips. "Extortion, is it?"

"Extortion, blackmail...call it whatever you'd like." She shrugged, her gaze never leaving his. "But you'll agree to it, or I will let you rot right here, trapped in Sea Haven until those men who attacked you arrive to finish the job."

Well. She certainly had spine. He would have admired her for it, if her offer to help him weren't so ludicrous.

Or tempting.

He took another sip of tea. "So you want money."

"Yes."

A pang of disappointment pierced him that she should prove so predictable.

"But not yours."

He froze, the cup halfway to his lips. Not so predictable after all. "Whose?"

"My late husband's."

"An inheritance?"

"The birthright that my son was denied."

He narrowed his eyes on her. "*Whose?*"

"You don't need to know that. Not until we reach London. Then, once you're safely back in Spalding House or Albany or wherever you're living these days and back into your own clothes," she muttered, her eyes trailing critically over him, "you'll help me hire whatever solicitors I need to file suit in the courts and put up your word to vouch for my good character."

"Of the woman who tied me up and blackmailed me," he drawled, deadpan. "Of course."

She ignored that but hesitated before adding, "My husband was a gentleman. The inheritance is quite substantial. You'll be compensated for your trouble."

Good God. A gentleman? That explained her presence at a Mayfair ball. But it didn't begin to explain everything. "So you're really...?"

"Mrs. Grace Alden." She stood and folded her arms across her chest, refusing to reveal her true identity. Frustratingly, he still couldn't place her in his memory. "I'll tell you more when we're safely in London and you're in a position to help."

He might never be in that position. Certainly if he didn't arrive at St James's Palace soon. Yet the only way to safely travel was exactly what she'd offered—moving quickly under disguise.

He set the empty teacup down and scoured his hand over his face, feeling the prickly bristle of three days' worth of beard. "You're putting your life in danger. It's a long way to London, and if we're caught together—"

"I'm willing to risk it. Are you?"

Did he have any other choice? The only thing now standing between him and the gallows was a woman with the audacity of Napoleon. One who possessed deep secrets of her own and apparently had nothing to lose. His life now rested in her delicate hands.

"I cannot promise you any kind of success," he warned. "I'm not in a very authoritative position these days to make requests of the courts." Or of anyone, for that matter.

"I'll take that chance."

He drawled, "You're making a deal with the devil."

Her face hardened with a world-weariness that startled him. "When the angels turn their backs on you, the devil is all that's left."

But she didn't know the devil he'd become. How could she, when he barely recognized himself?

He took a slow step toward her. She stood her ground, her only reaction a slight lifting of her chin as he approached in order to keep eye contact with him. She had courage, but his army days had taught him that there was a fine line between bravery and foolhardiness.

He stopped in front of her, his hands falling to his sides as he towered over her, to emphasize their difference in physical size. "Aren't you afraid of me?"

"No." She reached out and jabbed a single finger into his bruised side.

Excruciating pain shot through him. He doubled over in agony and pressed his hand against his ribs.

"Point taken," he forced out as he reached for the dresser to steady himself and panted down the pain. *Christ.* If the French didn't kill him, this woman just might.

"Remember that," she cautioned. "I'm not some helpless society lady."

Certainly not. He muttered as he straightened, "But you're a natural at blackmail."

With a wry smile, she stepped past him to collect the tray from the bedside table. "Then you shouldn't have picked my cottage to force—"

Without warning, he grabbed her around the waist and tossed her onto the bed. He knocked away the little knife, then covered her with his heavy body to hold her trapped beneath him.

He pinned her arms over her head and smiled. "And you shouldn't have untied me."

CHAPTER 7

"*L*et go of me!" Grace couldn't pull her arms and legs free, able to do little more than wiggle. Last night she'd wondered what it would feel like to lie beneath him, his weight pressing down upon her— Oh, fate was surely laughing at her! "I agreed to help you!"

"You blackmailed me." His face hovered so close to hers as he leaned over her that his breath tickled her lips. "Why?"

"I told you." She stilled beneath him. There was no point in struggling. She wouldn't be released until he was ready, blast him!

"You've told me practically nothing. And most of that was lies."

"Because I cannot tell you the truth." Not yet. She couldn't risk that Ross might discover who she was and refuse to help. Or worse, somehow alert Vincent to Ethan's existence. "And *you* certainly haven't told *me* the truth."

He smiled, his sensuous lips pulling into a dark grin. "This isn't about me. I've got the upper hand now." His eyes stared into hers so deeply that she could see flecks of indigo in their sapphire depths. "Unless you want me to tie *you* up, you'd best start giving explanations, Mrs. Alden. Starting with the real name of your husband."

"He was a gentleman," she repeated. "He died, and I was forced out of my home and our son out of his inheritance by my brother-in-law. That's all you need to know for now."

He laughed. The deep sound rumbled from his hard chest into hers, tingling through her from head to toes. "Not even close."

Ironic. She couldn't be any closer if she tried. Not with his bare chest pressing down against her breasts beneath her damp dress, his heavy leg tossed over both of hers.

"Tell me his name."

"No." She'd go to her grave keeping that secret if she had to, because revealing it might very well mean putting Ethan into his.

His eyes flickered, as if he knew it was useless to press. "How did he die?"

"Unexpectedly." Her eyes stung at the memory. She'd long ago stopped mourning David's death, but she would always grieve for how his life was cut short. "From fever."

She turned her head away and closed her eyes, unwilling to let him see any tell-tale tears. Guilt still ate at her that she hadn't been at his side when he'd passed away. She'd been ill and in her own bed, with Vincent standing watch at his sickbed. At the time, she'd believed that she'd come down with the same sickness, only to realize later that her illness had portended a miracle. She'd been with child.

"I'm sorry."

She opened her eyes and saw genuine concern in his. "Thank you."

His expression softened, so did his voice as he asked quietly, "You were cheated out of your inheritance?"

"Yes." All she'd been able to keep were a few jewels she'd taken with her when she'd fled. The same jewels she'd been forced to sell one by one over the years in order to keep a roof over their heads and food on the table. "But my inheritance doesn't matter. I don't care if I never receive a penny of that. What matters is that my son gains what is rightfully his and the life he deserves."

He frowned. "As a gentleman, your husband should have had a will in place, and you should have had a dower. How could anyone have stolen your inheritance?"

"When a powerful man wants to steal from a young widow with no other male relatives," she said quietly, "who would dare stop him?"

He grimaced at the brutal truth of that. "And your son's?"

"Ethan wasn't born yet. No one knew I was with child."

"You can't keep a thing like that hidden."

She held his gaze as she whispered, "You can if you flee."

His dark blue eyes narrowed. "Why would you do that?"

"Why are *you* fleeing?"

"Because I'll be killed if I don't."

When she answered that with a silent arch of her brow, grim understanding hardened his face. For a long while, he said nothing, and she knew from his silence that he understood why she was so desperate for help.

"How long ago?" he pressed gently.

"A lifetime." Literally. Because the only way to protect her unborn baby had been to let Susan Montague die and Grace Alden rise from the ashes. "Ten years."

Disbelief flashed across his face. "You've waited that long? Why try to claim it now, after all these years?"

"Because my hand has been forced." And because she'd been too afraid to pursue it before. Always before, she'd claimed she was simply waiting for the right moment, using her lack of money and power as an excuse. But now, with the possibility of Vincent siring a legitimate heir and all her evidence of proving Ethan's paternity circumstantial at best, she had no choice but to swallow her fear and act. "It has to be now."

He slowly shook his head. At least he had the decency not to laugh at her. "After that long, with a babe no one knew existed, no one will believe you."

"They will if you make them. There's precedent, if someone like you holds them accountable."

He searched her face and puzzled in a low murmur, "But I don't even know who you are." A mystified expression softened his features. "Sweet Lucifer, how could I not remember a woman like you, even from behind a mask?"

"Because I wasn't the same woman then." Her chest knotted with the irony of that. And from something hotter, a dim yet thrilling awareness of her femininity that she hadn't experienced in a decade, that had her asserting breathlessly, "And because you weren't looking."

He admitted in a husky rasp that melted all the muscles in her belly, "I'm certainly looking now."

He couldn't have meant that the way it sounded, not a rake like him for a disfigured widow like her. Yet an undeniable longing to be kissed twined heatedly through her. Confused by the attraction sparking between them, she asked, "Why?"

He curled an amused smile at her question. "Because you're beautiful."

As if to confirm that, his gaze languidly drifted over her face, taking in her chin and jaw, moving over each brow in turn before returning to her mouth...before sweeping sideways to her cheek. And the jagged scar that marred her there.

From a self-consciousness built over a decade of stares and pitying looks, Grace turned her face away, to press her cheek into the mattress and close her eyes. To see the same look of pity from Ross—she couldn't have borne it!

He affectionately nuzzled her face with his, his beard scratching softly against her cheek and sending a soft warmth down into her breasts. "Don't," his lips murmured against her cheek as he gently nudged her face back toward his. "Don't hide from me."

"I can't help it," she whispered.

"Neither can I." He slid his mouth along her jaw and caressed her lips beneath his.

She gave a trembling gasp at the contact, which was surprisingly tender, almost delicate, and so very assuring. As if he were afraid of frightening her, yet couldn't deny himself this taste of her. His concern tugged at her heart, and she relaxed with a sigh, her body softening beneath his.

He brushed his mouth back and forth over hers. His sensuous lips teased hers with a skilled gentleness that shook her to her core, yet one that declared a single purpose—to take as much pleasure as he gave.

When the tip of his tongue dared to sweep over her lips, she sighed at the bittersweet ache of it. So long without enjoying a man's kiss, so long without the wonderful pressure of strong arms holding her close...She didn't stop to let herself think of the danger she might be putting herself into, how little she could trust him—all she could do at that moment was let long-dead sensations inside her blossom back to life, and drink him in.

"Ross," she murmured and opened her mouth, inviting him inside.

Her senses filled to overflowing when his tongue slipped between her lips, to sweep along her smooth inner lip, carrying with it the earthy flavor of tea and the heady taste of man. So long, so unbearably long...When his tongue swirled around hers, teasing it out so he could close his lips around it and gently suck, the pull wound through her like a silk ribbon slowly unspooling, to pile between her legs with a shiver of need.

It *was* need. That was the only explanation for why she let him kiss her like this, why she encouraged it with tiny nibbles of her own against his lips and soft mewlings that told how much she enjoyed it. Right then, with her breath coming in shallow little pants and her body arching beneath his, she needed him to kiss her. So much that she whimpered for it.

He loosened his hold on her wrists to slide his hands up, bringing palms against palms and lacing his fingers through hers. Then he began to thrust his tongue repeatedly between her lips in a possessive and relentless kiss, as if trying to discover her secrets by turning her traitorous body against her, until she was willing to bare all.

God help her, he was doing just that. He sent her spinning, and her soft mewlings turned into a moan of desire.

When she finally tore her mouth away to gasp for air, he gave her no quarter. He released her left hand only to cup her face against his large palm, to hold her still while he placed soft kisses along her rough scar.

"Don't," she pleaded, her hand going to his shoulder. But instead of shoving him away, she clung to him. Her fingers curled into his bare flesh, and the warmth of smooth, soft skin covering hard muscle tingled under her fingertips. "Don't kiss me...there," she panted out, trembling, as she tried to make him stop. To make him leave that hideous mark alone—

"But you're beautiful." He nuzzled his lips against her cheek. "Even here."

When he kissed her lips again, tears stung her eyes. She wanted to believe him but couldn't. He didn't remember what she'd been like before, when she'd been so full of beauty and life that men had complimented her by calling her flawless. A flawless diamond shining so brightly...But *she* knew. Every morning when she looked into the mirror, she was reminded of all that had been stolen from her, leaving nothing but ugliness in its place.

"I'm not beautiful." She twisted her mouth away from his. "Don't lie to me."

"I would never lie to a woman about that."

"Just other things?" she countered peevishly.

But she couldn't stop a hot shiver when he grinned at her in reply. Such a tantalizingly rakish smile that her heartbeat leapt into a frenzied tattoo so fierce she was certain he could feel it, especially when he strummed his thumb over her bottom lip.

Certainly when he caressed his hand down her neck, to that spot where her pulse pounded wildly in the little hollow at the base of her throat. And undoubtedly when he trailed lower still, his fingertips fluttering lightly over the swells of her breasts.

She wore layers upon layers, including the still damp slicker, all of which clung to her skin and grew a damp heat between their two bodies. But she might as well have been utterly bare for the way the intensity of his light touch electrified her.

"You *are* beautiful. You might be keeping secrets, but you can't hide that, no matter how hard you try." He traced his fingers along her neckline. "I'd be very happy to prove it to you."

A strangled sound of desire tore from the back of her throat when his hand slipped beneath her bodice and stays, cupping her fullness against his palm. Warm flesh heated her bare skin, cold from the rain. His fingers teased at her nipple, and the already aching bud tightened even more as he rolled it between his fingers.

He leaned over to claim her mouth again beneath his. Soft sucks at her bottom lip, featherlight caresses over her nipple, the weight of his body pressing deliciously down onto hers— She spun weightless beneath his hard body, ready to float away.

Crash! The sound of splintering wood broke through the silent cottage, followed by the groan of twisting metal.

Ross's hand covered her mouth. "Shh," he whispered. "Someone's breaking in."

With an arch of his brow for her to keep silent, he rolled away and snatched up the little knife.

"Stay here. If they come after you," he warned, placing the blade into her shaking hand, "you'll have to use this. Understand?"

The bottom dropped out of her stomach as she realized that he intended to confront the intruder, and without a weapon.

She grabbed for his hand. "Your pistol! When you were asleep, I hid it in the dresser, beneath my undergarments."

He crooked a half grin, but his eyes remained serious. "Lucky pistol."

Then he shook off her hand and headed toward the doorway without it.

"Let me come with you!" The fear flaring inside her pushed her to fight. But more glass shattered, and she flinched, biting back a soft cry.

"Stay here, and do *not* come out until I tell you."

He cautiously slipped into the main room. Grace held her breath as shouts of anger and surprise rang out, followed by more crashes and dull thuds—

She couldn't bear it a second longer and raced to the dresser, yanked open the drawer and shoved her hand down into a stack of chemises to find the pistol. She ran out into the main room, with the knife gripped tightly in one hand and the pistol in the other, its hammer cocked and ready to fire.

Then she stopped, stunned.

Ross held a young man of no more than fifteen pinned against the wall by his throat. His jaw was set hard and his teeth bared as he leaned threateningly over the lad.

"Do not *ever* come around here again, do you understand me?" Ross growled menacingly.

The young man nodded, his hands clawing at Ross's forearm as he dangled against the wall, the toes of his shoes barely touching the floorboards. A gurgling sound came from his throat.

Ross glanced over his shoulder and saw Grace and the weapons she wielded as boldly as last night's poker. For a fleeting beat, admiration flickered in his eyes.

"She has a pistol," Ross warned the lad. "And she's a good shot."

Grace pointed the gun at the young man and echoed, "A damnably good shot."

Despite the twitch of Ross's lips in stifled amusement, the young man's face paled. Ross yanked him away from the wall and shoved him toward the door.

"Leave," he ordered as the scrawny lad staggered back and tripped, then scrambled across the floor to flee from the cottage.

Ross slammed the door closed after him.

Grace sank against the bedroom doorframe, her arm falling to her side and the pistol dropping to the floor with a quiet clatter. All of her shook violently with equal parts fear and relief.

He crossed to her and cupped her face between his hands, his eyes narrowing as they swept over her. "Are you all right?"

She gave a jerking nod. "Fine."

He grimaced, recognizing that for the lie it was, yet softly stroked her cheek. That did more to reassure her than all the fists and weapons of moments earlier.

Until she saw the blood on his arm.

"You've torn your stitches," she whispered, reaching a shaking hand toward him.

"It's nothing," he dismissed quietly, shifting his arm just out of her reach. He gently chastised, "I told you to stay put."

"But you didn't take your pistol with you."

"Because that pistol went into the Channel with me. The charge is useless." He bent down and picked it up, then frowned as he cautiously eased down the still-cocked hammer. "But let's not take any chances."

Her mouth fell open. If that pistol didn't work, then last night when he'd forced his way into her cottage by gunpoint—

She snapped her mouth shut and scowled furiously. "Why you lying, conniving devil of a—a *Carlisle!*"

"You can yell at me later." He pointed at the shards of broken window on the floor and the shutter hanging half-twisted from the casement where the young man had pried it open to break in. "We need to leave."

A chill slithered down her spine. "But he's so young! He can't be one of the men who are after you."

"He's not. Just opportunistic. Most likely he was walking by, thought the cottage was empty because of the storm, and decided to commit a quick robbery." His expression turned grim. "But he saw my face."

"Why should that matter, if he's not chasing you?"

"It matters." His eyes narrowed on her, once more sizing her up. At that look, the prickling suspicion at her knees grew into full-out apprehension. "If you're serious about helping me, we have to leave. Now."

"I'm very serious." Once again she felt a ribbon of connection winding between them, pulling her toward him.

"Then pack your things." He nodded toward her bedroom. "We're late for London."

CHAPTER 8

*K*eeping his face down and his collar high, Ross placed his hand on the small of Grace's back as he followed her into the apothecary shop on the village's High Street. If the British ambassador had already gotten word to London and England had declared him a traitor, then notices for his arrest would soon be plastered all along the coast. But the storm surely bought him a few days' reprieve in the manhunt, and he prayed it would be enough to travel to London before word of what he'd done saturated the countryside. Before anyone else recognized him.

The bell on the door jingled softly as Grace shut it behind them.

"Alice?" She set down the little travel bag, the one she'd refused to pack until he'd agreed to let her bandage his arm. Tugging off her gloves and slipping them into the pocket of her coat, she moved past him to glance up the stairwell and called out, "Where are you?"

He gently took her elbow. "Is this necessary? The fewer people who see me, the better." *For everyone.*

"Alice can be trusted." She gazed grimly at him. "Besides, we need her."

"Grace?" A woman entered from the backroom, wiping her hands on her apron as she circled the counter. "I didn't expect you —" She saw Ross and froze, then forced a smile. "And with company."

"Alice Walters, this is Christopher Thomas." She didn't stumble at all over his false name as she made quick introductions. "An old acquaintance from my London days."

The woman's smile vanished. She didn't even bother at a pretense of welcome as her eyes narrowed. With her gaze fixed on him as if she didn't trust him not to turn into a viper right then, she muttered to Grace, "Do I need to fetch my gun?"

Grace laughed, a genuine and soft sound that lilted through the room. Musical. And lovely. A man could certainly grow used to that sound.

"No." She smiled at Ross as she placed a reassuring hand on her friend's arm. "But perhaps you should keep a butcher knife at the ready, just in case." Her eyes shined as she finished the introductions. "And this is Mrs. Walters, our local apothecary and the dearest woman in the world." She gave her a brief hug. "Where's Ethan?"

"Upstairs." Alice eyed Ross warily. "Do you think it's wise to have him here with the boy?"

"It's all right." Although the look she cast him was just as uncertain as her friend's. "He's going to help us."

Alice didn't bother trying to hide her disbelief as she raked a deliberate glance over him. "Where did he come from, poppin' up out of the blue here?"

"It was a miracle," Grace replied with teasing mockery. "You know, the kind of angel Vicar Brennan is always preaching about on Sundays." As she stepped past him toward the stairs, she slide him a sideways glance and murmured, "Or perhaps one of the devils."

Ross saw the amused glint in her eyes. She was sharp, all right. Perhaps too much for her own good.

"Ethan, come down please," she called up the stairs. She turned back to Alice and clasped both of her hands. "I'm traveling to London with Mr. Thomas. Will you look after Ethan for me until I return?"

That surprised her friend. "London?"

"It suddenly came up." Offering no other explanation, she pressed, "Will you watch him?"

"Of course." From the way Alice Walters continued to glare at Ross distrustfully, she most likely expected him to murder Grace right in front of her. "You trust this man?"

"Not at all," she answered quickly, and far too earnestly for his comfort. "But if he gives me any trouble, I'll simply tie him up." She cast a sly glance in Ross's direction that told him she meant just that. "He also needs a change of clothes." She added in a private jab, "Something that doesn't make him look as if he fell into the English Channel."

"And a shave," Alice muttered.

He rubbed a hand against his jaw and flashed the older woman his best rakish smile. Her cheeks flushed, and she glanced away.

Grace narrowed her eyes and mouthed, *Stop that!*

He winked at her. Which caused *her* cheeks to flush. He was beginning to find a new appreciation for women in fishing villages.

"Do you think you have an old set of your late husband's clothes that might fit him?" Grace asked.

The older woman mumbled, "Might have."

"You're the one who keeps telling me that it's time I claim Ethan's inheritance for him," Grace reminded her in a soft voice that Ross suspected he wasn't meant to overhear. "This might be my only chance." Her frown softened. "It *will* work out, I know it."

Alice nodded, although reluctantly, and pulled her hands away from Grace. Sending a suspicious glance at Ross, she walked into the backroom.

Ross folded his arms across his chest. "She doesn't seem happy about this."

"We've surprised her, that's all."

He suspected they'd done a lot more than that. "She knows about your past?"

"The only one who knows, except for you." Lowering her voice and glancing toward the stairwell, she rested her hand entreatingly on his upper arm. "Ethan can *never* know, understand? Not unless I'm successful in retrieving his inheritance. I can't risk that he might tell someone, or attempt something foolish when he's older."

He placed his hand over hers, pinning it there. "You think his uncle would harm him?"

"I know so." Her scar showed bright pink as her face paled beneath it. She slipped her hand away and turned back toward the stairs. "Ethan!" she called out again. When silence greeted her, she slumped her shoulders with a frustrated sigh and grumbled, "How is it possible that he can hear whispers about birthday and Christmas gifts from two rooms away but can never hear me when I call for him?" Losing her patience, she shouted, "Ethan, *now!*"

Stomping steps reverberated overhead, then slowly down the stairs. A boy who couldn't have been more than eight or nine, slight of build and with a shock of unruly hair, grudgingly emerged from the stairwell and went to his mother.

She dropped to her knees and pulled him into her arms, to hug him tightly to her. But the boy scowled and stepped back, darting an embarrassed look at Ross.

"Mother, I'm not a baby," he protested wearily.

Ross suspected that Grace had heard that same admonishment countless times before, yet that didn't stop a pained expression from flitting across her face.

She plastered on a smile as she rose to her feet and took the boy's shoulders in her hands, to turn him to face Ross. "Mr. Thomas, this is my son Ethan. Ethan, this is Mr. Christopher Thomas."

Ross noted that she didn't add any further explanation of who he was or how he knew her, although *that* was still just as much a mystery to him. He inclined his head and held out his hand. "A pleasure to meet you, Master Ethan."

"Sir." The boy shook his hand.

Ross smiled. "How old are you?"

"Nine and a half, sir."

"And a half, hmm?" Well, Grace certainly had her hands full with this one. "So you're in year five at school, then. When I was in year five, I loved geography and despised math."

The boy's eyes gleamed. "I like math. It's Latin I don't like."

"Don't worry." He couldn't resist tousling the child's hair, drawing a duck of his head and a soft laugh from the boy. "You'll never use Latin outside the schoolroom."

"Mr. Thomas," Grace warned quietly.

Both males promptly ignored that—Ross because he wanted to be on the boy's good side, and Ethan because he seemed determined to ignore all of his mother's warnings. As any nine year-old boy would. "Unless you become a vicar," Ross added. "Do you want to be a vicar? My brother claims he does."

He proudly stuck out his chest. "I want to be a ship's captain!"

Behind him, Grace blanched, her hands tightening on the boy's shoulders. "Honey, we've talked about this." She brushed her hand through his hair, combing it back into place. "Being a sailor is dangerous."

"But it's what I want to do." When he scowled and shoved her hand away, an injured expression flashed over Grace's face. "Why can't I? I want to be on a ship, sailing around the world." He grumbled, "Away from here."

That peevish dig hurt Grace, and badly enough that she didn't answer right away.

So Ross intervened before the boy could realize that he'd wounded her. "When I was younger, I was an officer in the army. Traveled all over the world—France, Spain...once all the way to northern Africa."

Ethan's face lit up with excitement. "Truly?"

"The God's truth." He smiled at the boy as he flicked a gaze up to his mother, who bit her lip in worry over what future distress he might be causing for her with such tales. "I hated every moment of it."

Ethan's excitement waned. "You did?"

"I missed my home and my family, all my chums back in England." Realizing that he wasn't persuading him as much as he wanted, he changed tactics. "And the food was terrible."

The boy stilled for a moment at that revelation. Then he jutted up his chin defiantly. "But I won't be in the army. I'll be on a ship!"

"Even worse. Homesick *and* seasick. Three years away from England with only salt pork and hardtack to eat." Knowing more of the lesson would sink in if the lad were eavesdropping rather than receiving a lecture, he glanced up at Grace, changing his tone from addressing a child to one of conversing with an adult, and talked past the boy. "My brother served in the navy and swears that hardtack's not that bad." He chuckled then, as if sharing a joke between adults. "He said that mealy worms are the only fresh meat sailors get when they've been out on the water for six months straight."

He didn't dare lower his gaze to the boy without giving himself away. Nor did he want to when he saw Grace's unease melt into amusement.

"So your brother was at sea." Her bright eyes shined knowingly as she joined in. "Of course, we have mostly whole sailors here in Sea Haven, those who still have both arms and legs. But I've heard stories about how many men in London and further along the coast are missing parts. Did he lose a leg?"

"Both," he answered, deadpan.

From the bottom of his gaze, he saw the boy's eyes widen, and he bit his cheek to keep from laughing. Grace beamed with conspiratorial glee at Ross over her son's head.

"How do you know my mother?"

The unexpected question froze the smile on her face. He could almost see the wheels turning in her head as she raced to come up with an answer.

"We're old friends," Ross answered for her. "From long before you were born."

That answer seemed to satisfy him. Until... "Why are you in Sea Haven?"

"The storm forced me to come ashore." Not technically a lie. "And I unexpectedly came across your mother." Also not a lie. "We spent all night becoming reacquainted." Unable to help himself, he added, "I couldn't bring myself to leave. It was as if I were tied in place."

A strangled sound came from her throat. Her eyes narrowed murderously on him for just a beat, then she forced a smile and turned the boy to face her. She lowered herself to her knees as she reached up to brush at his hair. Ethan rolled his eyes.

"But Mr. Thomas is needed in London." She paused. "And I'm going to travel with him."

"You are?" Ethan asked warily, sliding a distrustful glance at Ross. "Why?"

"Because I have business in London, and it isn't safe for women to travel alone."

"Then I'll come with you." Another look at Ross, this one purely territorial.

The boy was a handful and chafed beneath his mother's care, but he clearly loved her. Which was more than could be said of most sons of the aristocracy, who were raised by nannies and tutors and whose only interactions with their parents before the age of thirteen was to be paraded out nightly for a cursory review before being promptly returned to the nursery. Thank God he and Kit had been given a better childhood than that.

"You can't, honey. You've got school, and I could be away for several weeks. You'll stay here with Mrs. Walters and have a grand time." Her forced smile faltered. "You won't give me a second thought while I'm gone. So be a good boy for Alice, and kiss me goodbye."

When she leaned in to kiss his cheek, Ethan scowled angrily and pushed her away. "I told you—I'm not a baby!"

Grace rocked back onto her heels and gaped at him, this time unable to hide the hurt from her face. Her lips parted delicately, stunned.

"Ethan," Ross called out sharply.

The boy's head jerked up in surprise.

He pinned the child with a hard look. "If you want to be a man, then you'll respect your mother. In every way. Good men *always* treat their mothers well."

He held Ross's gaze for a long moment beneath that chastisement, as if contemplating how far he could push back.

"Apologize to your mother," Ross ordered. "Then be a man and kiss her goodbye."

A sheepish look clouded the boy's face, and he turned apologetically toward Grace. "I'm sorry, Mother." Dutifully, he placed a contrite kiss to her cheek. "And I'll be good for Mrs. Walters."

"Thank you," she whispered, blinking rapidly. "Now go on back upstairs. I'll send letters as soon as I can."

The boy nodded, then turned to Ross. "Goodbye, sir."

"Goodbye, Ethan."

The boy hurried off, whether to escape his mother's coddling or further scolding, Ross couldn't have said.

"And thank *you*," Grace repeated, solemnly meeting his gaze.

"It was nothing." He took her elbow and helped her to her feet.

"But you don't need to worry too much. I was a rough and tumble boy once, too." He grinned at her. "I'd like to think I turned out all right."

She squeezed his hand. "You turned out just fine."

He wished he could believe her.

Then her face darkened as she confided, "He deserves better than to die at sea. Your help in obtaining his inheritance will prevent that."

Yet after so many years, the odds of it happening—Ross wouldn't have placed that bet into the book at White's.

But he also wouldn't have bet on his odds of surviving his own flight from Paris, or the fate awaiting him in London.

"Here." Alice Walters returned with several pieces of clothing in her arms. She set them on the counter, then picked up one of the shirts and held it up to his shoulders. She frowned, and for a moment, he wondered if she'd demand he strip to his breeches so she could measure him. "This one will work." She tossed it over his shoulder and snatched up a jacket, quickly measuring it across the breadth of his shoulders. "This one might be a bit tight, but it'll do." Then she reached for a pair of trousers—

Ross grabbed them from her before she could measure other parts of him that she had no business being that close to in the first place. "These will all do nicely, thank you."

She arched a brow. "Is there a reason you don't have your own clothes?"

"I had to leave home quickly. There wasn't time to gather my things." He'd been prepared to leave everything behind. Once he stole the last of the documents, he knew that his life would never be the same again. "I hadn't planned on getting caught in the storm."

He hadn't planned on getting caught at all.

"Hmm." She raked her gaze over him once more, folding her arms across her chest as if she found him lacking. "A friend from Grace's London days, huh?"

Suspicion panged in his chest at the way she said that, almost as if leveling a challenge.

"Alice," Grace warned softly. "That doesn't matter—"

"Not really," he confessed, deciding that the blunt truth was best. "But she needs to go to London, and so do I. We might as well travel together."

Grace interjected before Mrs. Walters could protest. "He might be able to help me once we're there."

Or get her arrested as an accomplice in treason. He didn't dare put voice to that, or Mrs. Walters might just fetch her gun after all.

Alice narrowed her eyes on him. "If you hurt her, Mr. Thomas, I swear that I will hunt you down and make you pay for it."

"Alice!" Grace exclaimed, shocked. But her friend didn't lower her resolute gaze.

Neither did Ross. "I won't let any harm come to her." He meant it.

At that, Alice snorted in distrust and walked away. "That's not the only way for a man to hurt a woman, is it, Grace?"

But Grace kept her gaze straight ahead and her face turned away, to hide as much of her scar as possible, and said nothing.

CHAPTER 9

*I*n the dim light from the inn's lamps, the post-chaise swayed to a stop, and the postilion gratefully slid off the horse's back. Ross opened the door and swung stiffly to the ground, then reached a hand back to help Grace.

"Watch your step," he warned, reaching a second hand up to take her arm as she descended.

She gave him a tired smile. After six hours in the hired carriage, stopping only to change out horses and postilions, her legs prickled with pins and needles, and all of her ached. But they'd made good time over the roads, which couldn't decide whether to jar their bones with rocks and bumps or mire them in mud.

He picked up her travel bag in his left hand and took her elbow in his right to guide her to the wooden planks that had been laid across the yard as a temporary footpath so passengers wouldn't sink up to their ankles in mud and manure. Even though Ross hadn't complained, he must have been even more tired and travel-sore than she was, given how he limped slightly on his wounded leg. Around them, the inn bustled with activity, despite the early evening darkness, as hostlers and drivers busied in the dim lamplight to care for the teams and carriages. Raucous laughter and music drifted from the inn's common room, the light spilling out of the windows and open doors into the night.

"We'll buy some food here and rest a bit," he told her, "then see about securing seats on a stage coach heading out yet tonight."

A sharp ache pinched her back at the thought of traveling on. But it was an inexplicable pang in her chest that snared her attention, a disappointment that they'd be crammed into a mail coach with other passengers when she'd had him to herself since they'd left Sea Haven. She'd enjoyed that time alone with him, far more than she wanted to admit.

It had been only the two of them in the post-chaise all afternoon and past sunset. They'd passed the time telling stories, with Ross avoiding sharing any more details of his flight from France and those odd papers he'd carried tucked beneath his waistcoat, just as Grace foiled all his attempts to wheedle out of her when they'd originally met and her husband's identity. It had become a game, each knowing exactly what the other was attempting. Their own version of a traveling chess match, played to a stalemate as the miles slipped past.

"We can travel faster if we hire another post-chaise," she countered. And continue the game they'd started, one she'd found herself liking a great deal.

"Not tonight." He glanced up at the pitch-black sky overhead, not one star or a sliver of moon to be seen. But the chilly air held the promise of more rain to add to the mud and standing water from the storm. "There's safety in numbers on a night like this." He grimaced. "I wouldn't want Alice Walters to chase me down with that gun of hers for letting you be robbed by a highwayman."

"Don't be silly. She wouldn't really come after you with a gun." She gave him a smile as they entered the crowded inn. "She'd use a knife."

He laughed as he led her up to the innkeeper. He rapped his

knuckles on the counter to get the man's attention. "My wife and I need two seats on the next coach to London."

Wife...the word skittered through her. Of course, they were traveling under the pretense of being married. But this was the first time she'd heard it said aloud, and she wasn't prepared for the pulse of shooting electricity it brought. Or the faint niggling of guilt that she was betraying her late husband.

The innkeeper shook his head. "None goin' out t'night. Roads 're too bad. None o' the drivers wants to fight the mud i' th' darkness, 'specially when passengers have to get out an' push."

Ross looked down at Grace, his expression held carefully inscrutable. But she'd come to know him well enough during the past few days to sense his simmering frustration.

"A wagonload o' chickens is headin' out in 'bout an hour," the man offered. "Ye might be able t' ride i' the back with 'em, if'n yer in a hurry t' get on. Can't say ye won't end up helpin' t' push that one through the mud neither though."

Ross's gaze never strayed from Grace's, but she saw a flicker of amusement light his blue eyes. "What do you say, Mrs. Thomas? Ride with the chickens or take a room?"

"Whatever you think best, dear husband." When he looked back at the innkeeper, she muttered, "Either way, I have a feeling that I'm going to be plucked."

He froze, except for a twitching of his lips. The only visible sign that he'd heard her.

Recovering himself, he reached into his jacket pocket for the money. She'd given it to him before they left Sea Haven because he would need to pay for everything as long as they pretended to be married. Yet it wasn't until that moment that she realized what he'd done with it, how he'd kept it separated from the French papers. If they were robbed or pickpocketed, whoever took the money from that one pocket would never think to search him further and find the papers. Clever.

"We'll need dinner and a private room," Ross said as he set a coin onto the counter. "And my wife will want hot water."

Her chest tightened at his thoughtfulness. How heavenly a warm dinner, hot water, and a soft bed sounded! When she'd been on the run from Vincent, she'd only been able to afford a shared bed, sometimes sleeping with four other people, and there had *never* been hot water for washing. There had barely been day-old bread and whatever burnt stew was left at the bottom of the pot.

"Not t'night." The man reached for the small lockbox beneath the counter. "We're full up. Best I can do is a room we normally keep fer the postilions an' drivers. Nothin' fancy, but it has a bed an' door that locks." He held up the last of the room keys. "Ye want it?"

It was either that or the chickens, so Ross gave a solemn nod and reached for the quill to sign the guest registry. Grace sneaked a glance, and her chest warmed inexplicably...*Mr. Christopher Thomas and Wife.*

The innkeeper slid the key and a candle stub across the counter toward Ross, then nodded at a buxomly woman carrying six tankards of ale in both hands as she weaved her way through the crowded room. "Ye can see ol' Bess o'er there 'bout gettin' dinner an' hot water."

From the dozens of calls and shouts that went up across the room for the woman's attention, Grace knew it could be hours before they had their turn getting dinner, if anything was left by then. And no chance at all of hot water.

"It's all right." She rested her hand on Ross's arm. "I'm exhausted. Let's just turn in."

The innkeeper jerked a thumb toward the stairs. "Second floor, all the way t' the end."

"Thank you." Ross handed the candle stub to Grace, picked up the bag, and took her arm.

As they moved toward the stairs, drunken revelers broke into an Irish drinking song, followed by hoots and jeers. Hot water and dinner might be in short supply, but ale and whiskey were apparently still well stocked. The din of noise followed them as Grace lit the candle stub on a lantern hanging at the base of the rickety steps and led the way upstairs.

She threw a backward glance downstairs as they rounded the first floor landing and continued upward. "They're not going to be fit to travel in the morning."

"Better for us, then. We'll have a good night's rest and be on the road early, taking their places on the coach." He gave her a faint smile of reassurance. "We should be in London in two days."

Two days. She inhaled a steadying breath. This confrontation with Vincent had been ten years in the making, yet now that it was approaching, the enormity of it made her tremble.

He glanced down at her with concern. "Are you having second thoughts?"

"It's either share a room or sleep with the chickens," she reminded him, purposefully misunderstanding his question.

He stopped her with a gentle tug at her elbow. They were alone on the stairs, with the noise from below keeping their conversation from being overhead. "I meant about helping me."

"No, not at all." Not *quite* all anyway. But the way he gazed at her in the flickering candlelight made her admit, "It's just that...I don't want to put my son into danger."

His face softened at the first true revelation she'd given him since they'd left Sea Haven, despite hours of attempting to wrangle information from her. "Don't worry." He reached to tuck a stray curl behind her ear. "I won't let you do that."

She wanted to take comfort in his quiet offer of protection, yet he had no idea of the storm she was heading into.

Trembling as that old feeling of helplessness returned, she reached a hand to his arm, to let him be her anchor as thoughts of what lay ahead stirred up fresh dread. "I need you, Ross," she whispered, "and I haven't needed anyone's help in a very long time." *A lifetime ago...*

This time when he lifted his hand, it wasn't to touch her hair but to stroke his knuckles across her cheek, in a gesture filled with such tenderness that she sucked in a pained mouthful of air.

His gaze dropped to her mouth, and she stilled, waiting for him to lower his lips to hers—

A mud-covered postilion bounded up the steps and squeezed past them on the landing, breaking their cocoon of privacy. The noise and business of the inn descended once more over them, and she shifted away, feeling like a fool for sharing even this much with him when he'd told her practically nothing about his own situation.

They might have needed each other, but they also needed to keep their own secrets.

Sensing the change in each other, they moved on up the stairs and down the hall to their room. Ross unlocked the door and shoved it open. Grace walked inside, holding the candle stub high.

"I've changed my mind," she announced. "I'd rather be with the chickens."

He looked over her shoulder, and from the way he tensed she knew the moment he saw the bed. Just as narrow and small as the room around it, which couldn't have been originally planned for anything more than a closet sandwiched beneath the back stairs. So sandwiched, in fact, that the backstairs angled upward across the ceiling from the floor and turned the whole room into a tiny triangle. So tiny that Ross had to duck his head to keep from hitting it on the sloping ceiling when he stepped past her.

"The innkeeper didn't lie," he drawled, placing the key onto the narrow washstand beside the bed, which was the only other piece of furniture in the room and the only other thing that could fit. "It has a lock and a bed."

Her eyes didn't move from the narrow mattress where a single driver or postilion could catch a few hours of sleep. But where two would *not* fit. "Of a sort."

"I'll sleep downstairs on one of the benches. You'll be fine here for the night."

Grace eyed the rusty lock. She wasn't so certain. "The benches will all be taken." If not with travelers who weren't lucky enough to snag beds, then certainly by men too drunk to stagger upstairs to their own rooms. As if fate had read her mind, a raucous cheer went up from downstairs. Besides, with his wounds still healing, he wouldn't be fit to travel in the morning if he slept on a hard bench or the floor. "We can share this room."

Somehow. Good Lord, it was tiny, so very tiny. And Ross was big. She swallowed hard and didn't dare let her gaze drift to him. So *very* big.

"Are you certain?"

When she jerked a nod, Ross pulled the door closed and flipped the lock.

Doing her best to calm her racing heartbeat, Grace watched Ross sit on the bed and yank off his boots. As he placed the second boot under the bed, he glanced up. "Aren't you going to undress?"

"Of course," she murmured, thankful that in the dim light from the candle he couldn't see the flush that rose into her cheeks as she reached for her travel bag and realized that in order to put on her night rail she'd have to remove her clothes. *All* of them. With him sitting on the bed less than four feet away. *That* she simply would not do.

But she couldn't ask him to step out into the hallway, not when they were supposed to be married.

She was being silly. She was a widow with a child, for heaven's sake! She certainly wasn't an innocent who needed to protect her virtue. Both of them were adults, after all, with nothing the other hadn't seen before. In his case, most likely hundreds of times with dozens of women. And it wasn't as if he cared what she looked like beneath her clothes.

But *she* cared, even if that made her a goose to be nervous. It had been ten years since a man had seen her undress, since before she'd given birth—

"Would you like me to turn around?"

Oh please God yes! She forced a casual shrug of her shoulder. "If you'd like."

The scoundrel arched a knowing brow but wisely said nothing. He pushed himself off the bed and turned his back.

She let out a deep but silent sigh and grabbed up her night rail. Keeping an eye on him to make certain he didn't turn around, she quickly kicked off her shoes and stripped off the kerchief at her neck, before reaching to remove her dress. "This must be difficult for you."

"It's a pleasant change."

That wasn't the answer she expected. "Oh?"

"Usually I'm the one undressing the woman who's sharing my bed for the night."

She froze, her dress half off. "That's not what I meant."

"I know." Amused laughter colored his deep voice. "But my interpretation is far more entertaining."

Blast the devil! She snatched up her travel cape and threw it at him, hitting him over the head with it. Chuckling, he hung it on a nail jutting out from the wall.

"I *meant* the lodgings." She untied her petticoat and let it fall away from around her waist. "You're a viscount. You must be used to private suites, feather beds, brocade curtains—"

"Earl."

She paused as she reached for the front lace of her stays. "Pardon?"

"I inherited four years ago," he said quietly. "I'm Earl of Spalding now."

Her stomach roiled. She'd tied *an earl* to her bed and then blackmailed him into helping her? Oh good Lord.

He turned his head slightly to ask over his shoulder, "You didn't know?"

Heavens no! "We don't receive a lot of society news in Sea Haven."

"Does it make a difference?"

She shrugged off her stays and set them onto the growing stack of clothes on the floor at her feet, with no other place in the tiny room to put them. "Will you try any less hard to help me once we're in London, simply because you're an earl?"

"Of course not."

She reached beneath her chemise to untie her stockings. "Then it makes no difference to me who you are."

A lie. She knew how powerful the Spalding title had become, how protective his family was of it. What would stop him from changing his mind and deciding that helping her posed too great a risk to his reputation? Being a notorious rake with wild ways was one thing; helping a dead woman was something completely different. Even now the thought of it made her tremble as she lifted her chemise over her head and off, leaving her momentarily naked. And less than four feet behind him.

She said as she snatched up her night rail, "King George or a chimney sweep...as long as you keep your word."

"I'm a gentleman," he reminded her, a touch of pique in his voice.

"Like I said," she repeated pointedly, having had first-hand experience with his sort, "as long as you keep your word."

He chuckled.

"I'm sorry to hear about your father." She pulled on her night rail and tugged it into place. "The earl was a good man."

He stiffened. "You knew my father?"

His surprise caught her off-guard. She continued, careful not to let slip too much information, "I met him a few times in London, at various events. He was always kind to me." She hesitated before adding, "And always very proud of you, Ross."

"Was he?"

The tone of his drawl pricked at her. She'd meant her

comment to reassure, yet he seemed anything but that. "Very much so. He was always bragging about you, about how brave you were in fighting the French."

"Then thank God he didn't live to see me now," he murmured, half to himself.

The way he said that sparked her sympathy for him. He might be a rake and some kind of petty criminal, but his father's opinion of him had always meant a great deal to him. She shuddered to think what low opinion he now held of himself to say such a thing.

In order to lighten the suddenly serious conversation, she pressed teasingly, "You mean because he'd wonder why you didn't ride off with the chickens when you had the chance? After all, in for a penny, in for a peck."

He gave a grim laugh at the absurdity of that. "Actually, he'd wonder why I'd turned my back while a beautiful woman was removing her clothes."

She twisted her mouth in aggravation at that wholly exaggerated compliment and looked down at her night rail. The formless, frumpy white thing covered her from neck to wrists to toes like a billowing tent. *Perfect.* There was nothing beautiful about her in this, and no worry about what he'd think of her body, because as long as she was wearing this there was no chance of him seeing any of it.

"All right." She drew in a deep breath. "I'm dressed now."

He turned around, and Grace busied herself with gathering up her clothes, pretending not to notice the way he raked his gaze over her. Yet that look made her tremble. He'd gazed at her the same way once before, that night twelve years ago at the masquerade when she'd descended the stairs into the ballroom. As if he couldn't quite fathom that someone like her existed. Even after all these years, she remembered the intensity of him that night. It had frightened her then, yet excited her, too, in a way she would never admit.

That same feeling now began to creep up from her toes.

He removed his jacket and hung it over her cape on the same nail, then began to unbutton his waistcoat.

"Stop!" She put up a hand. "What are you doing?"

"Undressing." He shrugged out of the waistcoat and tossed it over the end of the bed. With that, the old feeling he stirred inside her turned into a low tingle. "You don't expect me to sleep fully clothed."

"Of course not."

Actually, she'd expected exactly that, and the thought of him removing his clothes made the tingle grow stronger. She'd seen him without them before, and he'd been breathtaking, even lying unconscious on her bed. God only knew the damage that magnificent body could do with both of them fully conscious.

She nervously gestured at the growing pile of clothes as he unwrapped his neckcloth. "Would you like me to turn around?"

"Absolutely not." His eyes pinned hers as he untucked his shirt and let it hang loose around his waist, as if daring her to keep looking.

Her belly heated at his brazen audacity. The devil deserved to have her turn her back on him. But she didn't. Nor did she look away, continuing to watch shamelessly as he stripped off his shirt and bared himself from the waist up. From the gleam in his eyes, he was enjoying it.

"After all," he taunted, his hands going to the fall of his breeches, "what kind of marriage would ours be if my wife couldn't stand to watch me undress?"

"A typical society marriage," she answered, a bit too breathlessly.

He laughed, undermined in his attempt to goad her, and he dropped his hands to his sides, leaving on that last piece of clothing. Given that the borrowed breeches were a bit too small, though, not much was left to her imagination. Even now her fingers itched to touch him as they remembered what it felt like to run over the smooth, hard planes of his chest, once again bare to her eyes.

God help her. He stood far too close. Her eyes darted to the bed, and she nearly groaned. He was about to come even closer.

As if reading her mind, he murmured thoughtfully, "It could be worse."

She pointed at the bed. "It's the size of an army cot. How could this possibly be worse?"

"I usually sleep nude."

For a beat, she froze. Then she slid him a murderous glare, her hands going indignantly to her hips.

The rascal had the nerve to chuckle at her and reached to pull back the covers. "Come to bed, Mrs. Thomas."

"I believe our marriage just became estranged," she muttered.

With a laugh, he blew out the candle.

In near total darkness, she slipped beneath the covers. She lay on the edge of the mattress, but even that barely gave them enough room on the narrow bed. So narrow that Ross lay on his side with his back pressed against the wall, yet she could still feel the heat of his tall body radiating all along hers.

His arm slipped around her waist.

She tensed. "What are you doing?"

"Dancing a quadrille," he answered wryly, then shifted until his chest rested against her back, his legs nestling against the backs of hers. "I'm making more room in the bed." His warm breath tickled against her nape, and the tingle settled low in her belly. "You don't mind, do you? Surely, a beautiful woman like you is used to having a man's arms around her."

She rolled her eyes at his blatant attempt at flattery. "Yes, because this night rail is so bewitching that they simply can't resist."

A deep chuckle rumbled into her back. Oh, that did *not* help! "I like that nightgown."

"Good, then *you* can wear it tomorrow night."

Ignoring that, he languidly brushed his fingers up her arm, from her wrist to her shoulder. Goose bumps sprang up beneath her sleeve everywhere he touched. "All soft cotton, lace, ribbon..."

Oh, how she wished he would stop touching her like that! "And yards of billowing material hanging like draperies." But her awakening body wished he would touch her even more.

"Which only makes it more alluring."

She knew she shouldn't ask, shouldn't rise to the bait..."How could that possibly make it more alluring?"

"Because it makes a man wonder what's hiding beneath."

The tingle in her belly shifted lower between her thighs and turned into a soft ache. Yet she found the resolve to force out a laugh. "Best to keep wondering, then, because I'd hate to disappoint you."

"Something tells me," he murmured against the back of her neck, his hand trailing down her body to her hip, "that you wouldn't disappoint."

That sent the aching tingle shooting through her on a wave of deep longing, followed swiftly on its heels by a cold slap of reality.

For the past ten years, she'd focused only on keeping her son safe, sacrificing her life for his. That meant suffering through long nights alone and denying any urges she had as a woman, never allowing herself to contemplate the possibility of having a man in her life again. It had nothing to do with her husband. Oh, she'd cared for David certainly, but theirs hadn't been a love match. Not on her part, anyway.

No. She'd not allowed herself the comfort of a man because she didn't dare risk bringing harm to Ethan. Now that she was so close to gaining back what she'd been forced to surrender all those years ago, so close that she could almost touch it, the very last thing she would do was risk it all for one night of intimacy.

No matter how wonderful it would be.

"I've already agreed to help you travel to London." She

removed his hand from her hip. "So you needn't attempt to seduce me."

He stiffened against her back. "That wasn't what I was doing."

She sniffed in disbelief. "Then seduction has become such second nature to you, Spalding, that you don't even realize when you're doing it."

"*Spalding*, is it?" He hadn't shifted away, but she felt a chasm slowly widening between them. *Good.* Because as large and hard as his body was as he pressed against her, the masculine scent of him filling her senses, it was becoming harder and harder to deny herself the pleasures she knew he was capable of giving.

She'd touched a nerve and was glad for it, if it kept him on his side of this poor excuse for a bed. "That is your title now."

"It is," he said guardedly, "but only women who want something from me use it when they're in bed with me."

"And only a man who wants something from *me* would pretend that this night rail is anything but frumpy."

He laughed and nuzzled his cheek against her shoulder, mumbling with amusement, "*Touché.*"

"Good. Then we both know that we each shamelessly want something from the other."

"And aren't above blackmail to get it," he added, a teasing edge to his voice.

"Or seduction," she shot back.

Another laugh rumbled into her back. Despite the tightening of his arms around her, she gave a silent sigh of relief. The battle was over. For now.

His laughter died away, and silence filled the darkness. Around them, the inn was still wide-awake, the travelers and hostlers continuing to drink and carry on downstairs. But cocooned inside the tiny room with Ross, she felt warm and protected. *Safe.* For the first time in a decade.

"It's a long way to London," he said quietly. "If something should happen to me along the way, if I'm caught by the men chasing me, you need to claim that I forced you to help me. Understand?"

It was her turn to laugh. "Anyone seeing us together like this would never believe that."

"I'm serious, Grace." So was the grim tone of his voice. "The closer we travel to London, the more dangerous it becomes."

Her heartbeat faltered. "But I thought...I thought whoever was chasing you would be looking for you along the coast."

"It's not them we worry about now."

She stared into the darkness, her belly pinching with dread. "You have more than one group of men chasing after you?"

Not answering that, he tightened his arms around her. "You have to claim that I forced you to help me. Promise me that." When she didn't answer, he pressed, "If not for me, then for my father's memory."

With a soft sigh, she reluctantly nodded against the pillow.

"And no matter what happens, those papers I'm carrying have to be given to my brother in London. You can reach him through any of the clubs on St James's Street."

Another nod. Then a hesitation—"What are they?"

"Christopher will know what to do with them," he dodged. "He *has* to get them, understand?"

"Yes." Christopher. He was using his brother's name as an alias. Clever. And yet..."You should have picked a different name. Something random."

"Is that how you picked your alias? A random name?" he prompted gently. "Or was there a real Grace?"

She hesitated. They'd been pressing each other all day for details, yet never giving ground..."Grace was my mother's middle name." She tamped down the faint uneasiness at revealing this secret, when she'd never told anyone else. Not even Alice. "Alden was my nanny's name."

He nuzzled her neck in silent gratitude for trusting him this little bit. Yet it didn't stop him from pressing for more. "What's your true name?"

Not daring to answer, she closed her eyes and whispered, "Good night, Ross."

"Good night," he murmured against her nape, "whoever you are."

CHAPTER 10

"Ross?" a soft voice called to him. A hand pushed at his shoulder—"Ross, wake up!"

The fog of sleep ensconced him, made even deeper by the first chance in days to sleep well. In a warm bed, no less. Next to a soft woman.

With a heavy sigh, not opening his eyes, he tightened his arms around her and rolled onto his back, to nestle her into the hollow between his arm and chest and fall back to sleep.

A hand slapped his cheek.

That woke him.

His eyes flew open and blinked to bring into focus a beautiful face peering down at him through the blue light of pre-dawn. *Grace.* He was in her bed. And this time he wasn't tied down.

He reached to stroke her cheek. "What are you—"

"Shh!" Her hand covered his mouth. "Listen."

A commotion resonated through the inn. Loud knocking and shouts, heavy footsteps on the hallways and stairs—

"They're searching the rooms," she whispered. Panic flashed in her eyes.

He came instantly alert and reached up to remove her hand

from his mouth. "It's all right," he assured her in a soft murmur, placing a kiss to her trembling fingers.

He cocked his head and listened. Down the hall, someone banged a fist against one of the doors and demanded to search the room. Angry shouts answered, followed by the opening of doors, hard steps, then the slamming shut of the door. A brief pause, only for the noise to be repeated at the next door. Two men were moving down the hall room by room, coming closer.

The alarm in her eyes shined brighter as the pounding of fists on doors and shouts to open grew louder. "What do we do?"

"Let them in." And be arrested. He prayed she'd keep her promise and claim he'd kidnapped her.

A fist banged on their door, and she jumped with a soft gasp. The door shook on its hinges beneath the fierce pounding. "Open up!"

Ross moved to ease her aside and slip out of bed to open the door.

Without warning, she grabbed onto his shoulders and slid over on top of him, straddling him to hold him in place beneath her slight weight. Well, *that* certainly captured his attention…in all kinds of delicious ways.

She called out before he could stop her, "What is it? Who's there?"

She didn't have to fake the surprise in her startled voice. Or the determination in her eyes when she touched a finger to his lips in a plea to keep silent.

Ross narrowed his eyes. What the devil was she was doing?

"Constable's men," a man shouted back.

"It's the middle of the night, for heaven's sake!" She turned her head to yell at the door but kept her eyes locked with Ross's. Bewildered anger rose in her voice. "I was sound asleep. What do you want?"

"We're searching the rooms. Open your door."

"I will do no such thing!" Indignant outrage now overtook any lingering panic or surprise.

His chest tightened with trepidation. She certainly had spine. But she'd get both of them hanged if she wasn't careful.

"Sir, I am a lady!" she shouted, loud enough for the drunken hostlers all the way down in the yard to hear. "You expect me to open my door to a stranger when I'm *dishabille?*"

He mockingly mouthed, *Dishabille?* Then arched an eyebrow as he raked his gaze over her, taking in the tent of a night rail and how her hair hung in a riot of toffee-colored curls across her slender shoulders. Oh, he could think of lots of adjectives to describe the way she looked at that moment, all right, deliciously sleep-rumpled and warm, with her thighs straddling his waist, but *dishabille* wasn't one of them.

Her shout took the men in the hall by surprise, as well, based upon their momentary silence. Then one of them called out, "We're searching the entire inn. There's a dangerous criminal on the loose."

She stiffened instantly. Wariness flashed in her eyes.

He knew exactly what she was thinking, how she was doubting everything he'd told her. She practically pulsed with distrust. *Damnation!* He couldn't even plead his innocence to her, with those men within earshot at the door. All he could do was hope she didn't give him up.

Not moving her suspicious gaze from his, she asked, "What did he do?"

"Broke out of the gaol at Chilworth last night."

Her shoulders eased in a silent sigh of relief, yet her fleeting doubt of him pricked more than he wanted to admit.

When she began to slide off him to open the door to let the men search the room, he stopped her with a hand to her hip and a warning shake of his head. Those men might not be actively looking for him, but that didn't mean they wouldn't recognize him. So far, she'd managed to keep them outside in the hall. He prayed that's where they stayed.

"Well, he's not in here with me!" she shouted back, once more seizing upon anger as a way to fight against opening the door. "The only man I'm concerned with is my worthless husband who's spending the night downstairs in his cups." She couldn't stop the smile playing at her lips as she looked down at him and added, "And most likely between the thighs of whatever pox-ridden wench will have him. Woe to her for her pains. Believe me, *I* know!"

That stunned the men into silence.

Ross studied her closely. Sweet Lucifer, she was good at deception. *Too good.* What on earth had she been through to make spinning pretense like this second nature?

"That damnable nodcock hasn't been in any jail, although if you feel so inclined, do me a favor and take him away," she ordered with all the imperial haughtiness of a gentleman's wife in a long-suffering marriage. "And leave me to my sleep! The coach leaves in a few hours, and if my eyes are puffy because of this—oh, the magistrates will certainly hear of how you've treated a lady! Forcing yourselves into her room in the middle of the night!" She paused, then added in a calculating voice, "You men report to the Justice of the Peace in Chilworth, do you not?"

At her subtle threat, muffled conversation rose in hushed tones behind the door. Then one of the men called out, "Apologies, ma'am."

They moved on, heavy footsteps pounding up the backstairs and across the slanted ceiling of the tiny room.

She let out a heavy sigh, and the tension drained out of her. A relieved smile pulled at her lips, and she moved her hand down to the middle of his bare chest to give him a gentle pat.

"Quite a performance." He didn't know whether to admire her talents or be terrified.

She laughed softly. "It worked, didn't it?"

When she moved to slide away, he slipped his hand behind her neck and tugged her down across his chest.

She tensed with a sharp inhalation as she landed on top of him. Both of them were suddenly aware of the way she was straddling him in the narrow bed, how her full breasts pressed against his chest through the thin cotton of her gown and her thighs hugged his hips. He could see the fierce pounding of her pulse in the hollow at the base of her neck as he placed his mouth close to her ear.

"That was an unnecessary risk," he murmured, slipping his hand up to shove his fingers into her silky hair. Despite the pinch in his side from his sore ribs, his discomfort already heightened by the way she straddled him, the siren song of her was simply too tempting to resist.

She closed her eyes against the brush of his hand through her curls and whispered, "There was nothing to lose…everything to be gained."

When he massaged his thumb in hard, slow circles against the base of her skull, she shivered. He drank in deeply the spicy-sweet jasmine scent of her, reveling in her softness and warmth as she still sat perched over him.

"You shouldn't have done that." The harshness of his chastisement was lost as he brushed his mouth over her cheek.

"Had to protect you." She lifted her chin, just enough to keep his lips frustratingly away from hers, yet her fingers curled into the hard muscle of his chest. She wanted him to kiss her; he could tell from her quickening breaths and racing pulse. But the damnable woman was too stubborn to let herself claim the pleasures he eagerly wanted to give. "You're no good to me in gaol."

He grinned at that blatant lie and slid his hands over her, from her shoulders down to the small of her back. Her thighs clenched against his hips and jolted a throbbing pain both into his ribs and down the length of his hardening cock.

He smiled at her obstinacy. So determined to deny herself,

even as her body ached for his. And he certainly wanted her. If she simply writhed her hips against him, she'd discover for herself exactly how much.

Unable to resist, he rose up to kiss her.

But she shifted away and sat up, keeping her mouth just out of his reach. So he took what little taste of her he could with an open-mouth kiss to her throat, eliciting a soft whimper of longing from her. He smiled against her neck. That kiss almost had her surrendering in his arms. How many more could she withstand before she surrendered?

"You make it damnably difficult for a man to properly thank you," he drawled, frustration audible in his voice. His hands on her hips slid lower—

Cold water splashed over him.

He let out a curse of surprise as she poured the water from the basin pitcher over his head, instantly cooling his ardor and ending all thoughts of thanking her further.

He narrowed his eyes. The damned woman still sat perched on top of him, holding the pitcher between them like a trophy. Or a weapon.

She gave him a wide, saccharine smile. "You're welcome."

Then she slid off him and returned the pitcher to the washbasin beside the bed.

"I think we should dress and see what kind of transportation we can hire this morning, don't you?" she asked casually as she reached for her clothes, as if dousing a man in her bed was a common occurrence. For this hellion, it might very well have been. "It's still a long way to London."

Flicking the water off his face and chest, he blew out a hard sigh and bit back a second, far less complimentary curse. *Damnable woman.* With a hand pressing against his ribcage—which wasn't the only part of his body that now irritated him—he stood and turned toward her to fling a cutting reply.

At that moment, the first bright rays of sunlight fell through the tiny window high in the wall. Bright enough to stream through the thin cotton of her night rail and silhouette the curves beneath. Every tantalizing inch of her was revealed, from the dusky rose of her nipples to the soft patch of feminine curls between her thighs.

Dear God, she was beautiful. And that, along with her sharp mind and the challenge she posed every time they sparred—

He fought down a groan of longing and turned away.

The road to London had just become insufferably long.

CHAPTER 11

"*A*ndover Pike!" The driver slapped his hand on the roof of the mail coach as he stopped the team.

While the men on top of the coach tossed down the mail to the post boy waiting at the crossroads, the eight passengers inside the compartment shuffled positions on the bench seats as two of them disembarked. The compartment was still cramped, but Grace was no longer squeezed against the wall. Not the most comfortable travel arrangements, but at least they were moving.

"Where are you two headed?" the vicar traveling with them asked with a friendly smile.

"Basingstoke." Ross threw a glance at Grace as he settled onto the seat facing hers. His long legs brushed against hers as he stretched them across the small compartment, sparking a prickle at the backs of her knees. He knew it, too, based on the knowing curl to his lips.

With a peeved sniff, she tucked her legs back against the bench beneath her so that she wouldn't accidentally touch him.

Accidentally touch him? Good heavens, she'd straddled the man that morning! Starting innocently enough, just to keep him quiet while the men were at the door, the encounter had grown into so much more. And quickly. So quickly, in fact, that she almost couldn't find the will to stop it.

She'd wanted him to kiss her. God help her, she'd wanted him to do so much more to her than that.

It simply could *not* happen again.

Ross sent her a private smile, as if the aggravating devil knew what she was thinking. Or worse, as if he were remembering that pre-dawn encounter and what it was like to have his hands on her. And wanted to do it again.

With a flush heating her cheeks, she turned toward the rain-drizzled window. If he didn't stop looking at her like that, she'd have no choice but to kick him.

"Ah, lovely town! Should be there in less than two hours," the vicar informed them. As if in challenge, the coach lurched as one of its wheels stuck momentarily in the mud before breaking free. He amended grimly, "Perhaps."

Tonight, they'd have separate rooms. Sharing a bed again was unthinkable. She couldn't risk that Ross might attempt to kiss her again, or the even greater risk that she'd let him.

"Where are you traveling from?" the vicar pressed politely.

"Weymouth," Ross answered, the lie coming easily.

"Traveling on business or pleasure?"

"Business of a sort. I have a bit of land in this area." Ross fell into easy conversation. "Rocky sheep pasture mostly, with an old hovel I've been meaning to tear down."

She arched a brow at that whopper of a lie, only to earn a conspiratorial wink from him. The Spalding fortune was one of the largest in England, and the bit of land was most likely thousands of acres, the hovel a grand manor. But the vicar believed him, and their ongoing conversation made the otherwise mind-numbing travel bearable.

The coach groaned around them as its large wheels dipped into a deep hole on the muddy road, and she offered up a quick prayer, hoping they wouldn't have to step out and push. Again. No post-chaises had been available that morning, so they'd gotten the last two seats inside the fully loaded mail coach. They weren't making nearly as good of time as they'd done yesterday, thanks to rutted roads, frequent stops, and mud puddles so big they threatened to swallow the entire team. But each mile still brought them closer to London.

An hour later, the coach stopped again. This time, all four of the other passengers disembarked, with the vicar wishing them well on the rest of their journey. When two women climbed onboard, Ross changed seats to sit beside Grace.

The coach rolled on, but now there was none of the friendly banter that had made the past hour tolerable. Instead, the two women huddled closely together and whispered frantically to each other. *So peculiar.* They clutched at each other's hands, their eyes glued to Ross as if they expected him to pounce like a wolf.

"Is something the matter, ladies?" he asked with a concerned frown, exchanging a glance with Grace, who was as bewildered about their odd behavior as he. "Should I signal to the driver to stop the coach?"

They both froze, like deer startled by a hunter.

Then one of them swallowed nervously and replied, so softly that her quavering voice was barely audible above the rumble of the wheels, "You look like that man."

The other woman nodded. "The one who's wanted by the authorities."

Ross didn't move, yet Grace felt him stiffen.

"Oh yes!" She laughed to alleviate the sudden tension. "The dangerous fugitive from Chilworth gaol. We were caught up in the search for him last night, weren't we, Mr. Thomas?"

"No, not him," the first woman countered.

"The man on the bill," the second one clarified. "There's a sketch…"

When her voice trailed off, the other woman added, "We saw one at the inn where we bought our ticket. You resemble him." A long, tense pause filled the compartment before she whispered, "The Earl of Spalding."

Grace froze as a chill spiraled down her spine.

Ross laughed, almost too quickly. "This is the first time anyone's accused me of being quality!" He playfully nudged her leg with his, as if sharing a joke. "Isn't it, dear?"

With no other choice unless she wanted to cause a commotion that would stop the coach, Grace awkwardly smiled as her stunned surprise turned into bitter betrayal.

"Can you believe that, Mrs. Thomas?" Another nudge... another secret communication for her to play along. "Someone confusing me with an earl."

"I wish I'd married an earl," she forced out, stiltedly joining in with the pretense despite the frantic pounding of her heart.

He said he'd broken the law, but a manhunt by the authorities, with bills posted across the countryside—oh God, what had he done? She fought to keep the smile on her face as she realized how close they'd come that morning to being discovered by the men in the inn. Her stomach sickened.

She had to make it through this conversation. There would be time later to hear his explanation. Or more lies. But now she had to protect him, in order to protect herself.

She nudged him back. Hard. "Maybe then I could buy those new curtains for the parlor that you've been promising me."

His smile tightened. "I told you, love. Profits are down. Blunt doesn't grow on trees."

"Yet you harvest enough of it to spend nearly every night with your chums." As she'd done that morning—and ten years ago when she fled to protect her baby—she let the anger rise to the surface, to use it to her advantage and feign a fight. "Always enough money for drink and cards." She slid him a sideways glance and sneered, "And women."

That took him by surprise for a beat, his eyes widening. Then his gaze narrowed sharply. "Now is not the time nor place to—"

"I am so *very* tired of your lies!" The raw honesty in that soft comment was brutal. She certainly hadn't needed to pretend *that*. Ignoring Ross as he sat beside her, so close that the side of his body brushed hers as the coach rocked down the road, she pinned the women beneath her gaze. "Tell me. What is it that my *dear* husband has supposedly done? Then I can turn him in, collect the reward money, and buy the curtains on my own."

The two women exchanged a nervous glance. Although they were still just as uneasy as before, now their faces darkened sheepishly for inadvertently causing a fight between a married couple.

The one with spectacles perched on her up-turned nose rasped out a forced laugh. "You could certainly buy a lot more than just curtains with that reward!"

"Oh?" Grace whispered. *Good God, what had he done?*

The other woman nodded with an apologetic glance at Ross. "A thousand pound reward."

Icy dread numbed her limbs. She rasped out, "For what?"

"Treason."

Her gaze snapped to Ross. Her chest squeezed so hard that she winced, despite the rest of her having gone completely numb.

With all eyes on her, she laughed awkwardly. "My husband would never commit treason. He's a staunch monarchist. Isn't that so, Mr. Thomas?" She should place an affectionate hand on his knee or shoulder—*anywhere* to physically demonstrate that Ross was her husband and not a traitor. But she couldn't bear the thought of touching him. Instead, she shifted away and forced out, "I'll have to try harder to get you out of my hair."

The woman with spectacles gave a grim shake of her head. "Not just treason—"

"Murder."

Grace's gaze flew to the other woman. Her heart stopped, and when it started again, each beat came like canon fire, so hard and jarring that her hand went to her chest.

She couldn't joke her way out of this, and too much fear blossomed inside her to feel anything else. Not anger. Not even betrayal.

"Then you ladies are safe," Ross drawled, flashing them his most charming smile. "The only things I murder are bottles of port and overpriced cigars."

Grace couldn't find enough trust in him to muster even a smile at that. *Breathe*...She stared out the rain-speckled window as the sun began to set and saw nothing. Her concentration—*all* of it—focused solely on not screaming. *Just breathe*...The conversation died, and they traveled on in silence, with Grace unable to look at him. Whenever the coach lurched over a rut and he brushed up against her, she inhaled sharply.

"Drummond's Crossroads!" the driver called out with a pound of his fist on the roof.

The coach stopped, and the two women departed.

Grace jumped to the other seat to move as far away from Ross as possible. Her gaze bore into him as she fisted her hands in her lap.

"Basingstoke in five miles!"

No new passengers were taken on, and the coach started again with a swaying jerk. Leaving Grace alone with Ross.

"You bastard," she hissed quietly, aware of the proximity of the coachmen and afraid they might overhear despite the loud rumbling of the wheels. All of her so brimmed with anger and fear that she shook. "You lied to me!"

His gaze pinned hers as he replied calmly, "I told you that I broke the law."

"I thought you'd cheated at cards, perhaps gotten involved with smugglers or taken bribes— You didn't tell me that you were wanted for treason!" *And murder.* She forced herself to breathe past the dread gripping her chest. "Did you do it?"

He paused for a long moment, as if debating how to answer.

Or how to most effectively lie. "That would depend on who you asked."

A strangled laugh fell from her lips. Heaven help her! She'd tied her future hopes to a man wanted for treason and murder, and he possessed the nerve to prevaricate with her. "Let's say the British, shall we?"

"Then yes. The British would consider it petty treason and espionage."

Oh, this was not getting any better! "And the French?"

"They would consider it an act of war."

The blood drained from her face. He wasn't teasing. *Dear God.* "What did you do?"

He reached beneath his waistcoat and pulled out the papers.

"I stole these." He held them up. "And now people on both sides want me dead."

He placed them on the seat beside her.

She tore her gaze away from him to glance down at the sheets, not daring to touch them. They were like a snake, coiled and ready to bite her. "What are they?"

"Documents that prove the existence of a spy ring within the Court of St James's." When she gaped at him, he nodded toward the papers. "Go on. Look at them."

"I've already read them."

"Then look at them again."

Knowing he wouldn't tell her more, she reached for them. Her fingers trembled as she unfolded each sheet.

He leaned toward her across the compartment. "They fit together, each a piece in a puzzle." He touched the top page. "A list of workers at a textile factory in Le Havre, from which the British ambassador planned on ordering bolts of fabric to redecorate his Parisian townhouse."

He removed the first sheet from her hand and gestured at the next one.

"A March letter from the ambassador to André Delacroix,

thanking him for meeting with him in Le Havre and reminding him that payment needed to be made for the bolts of cloth before he could send on the list of factory workers. On the surface, a typical request regarding a personal matter of no consequence. The embassy sends out dozens of correspondence like this each week, all approved by the ambassador. See there?" He tapped the bottom of the page. "The ambassador's signature."

Grace's gaze darted to the signature, then back to his. A list of workers, a letter from a creditor—how could these possibly be state secrets? Or was he merely lying to her again?

He took the third sheet by the corner and held it up. "The page from the embassy's register for December 8th, 1821." He gestured at a signature toward the bottom. "The ambassador's signature, verifying that he'd checked in to work that day. Odd thing, though—it doesn't match the one on the letter. Or any of the letters or documents he's ever signed. But this one does, only it's on the register for the same date at an inn called Le Chat Noir." He held up the last page, one from a hotel register. "In Le Havre."

"I don't understand." What was he trying to prove with all of this? Her confusion warred with distrust, and fear had her fingers trembling so hard that she couldn't refold the papers. "What does this have to do with treason?"

"Because nothing is as it appears." He took the pages from her. His eyes never left her face as he watched to gauge her reaction and held up the first list of names. "This list of factory workers contains a hidden list. The first name, second, fourth, eighth…the pattern continues until the last name, each a man working as a secret agent for England inside France."

Her blood turned to ice, her hands now shaking so hard that she had to twist her fingers in her skirt to hold them still.

"*This* is why England thinks I'm a traitor, because I stole this list of names from the ambassador's office in the Paris embassy, and then I ran." He added gravely, "For Le Havre."

She shuddered and pulled back against the squabs. Good God, he was admitting to treason. She didn't want any part of this!

"As far as England knows, I stole this list to sell to the French. I'm certain that's what the British ambassador has told the Court of St James's, and that's why they've put out a reward for me. If I'm caught in possession of that list, I'll swing." He paused, the silence grim. "I knew that when I took it."

"Then why did you?" she whispered. Fear was winning against her confusion. "You're an earl, for God's sake! You don't need the money."

"I didn't do it for money. I did it to save the lives of every man on that list." Then he added quietly, "And to avenge the death of a friend."

"So you're a noble traitor?" She gave a short laugh of disbelief at the story he was spinning. As far as she knew, every word was a lie.

He didn't answer that. Instead, he held up the papers. "On December 8th, 1821, a man named André Delacroix, a mid-ranking official in the court of King Louis, took a room in Le Chat Noir in Le Havre." He traced his finger over the guest registry, circling the date at the top and then drawing a line down the page to the name. *André Delacroix.* "So did Charles Wentworth." His finger moved lower, to a name at the bottom of the list, written in a distinctive, scrolling handwriting. "British Ambassador to France. The two men were in the same inn on the same date."

"So two government officials had a meeting." She shook her head, unable to fathom the importance of that. "They have meetings all the time. What does any of this have to do with your innocence?" *Or your guilt?* The question hung on the air as clearly as if she'd uttered it.

He held up the page torn from the embassy guest register and tapped his finger on the name...*Charles Wentworth.* "How can the same man be in two different places at once?"

"I don't know." At that moment, she didn't care. All she knew was that she'd put Ethan's life at risk by trusting in Ross.

"This name is a forgery. It doesn't match the ambassador's signature. He had a crony sign the register to make it appear as if he were in Paris that day, when he was actually two hundred miles away in Le Havre, negotiating the sale of that list of agents to the French." He held up the letter. "By March, the French still hadn't provided the money they'd agreed upon. So the ambassador sent this reminder. Wentworth kept the list of agents in his office, with all the other personal documents related to his housing and general living expenses so that it wouldn't draw suspicion, waiting for payment so he could send it off to the French."

"That's why you were in Le Havre," she mumbled as the pieces began to fit together. "To steal the inn's guest register."

"Yes. I already had the letter he was planning on sending to Delacroix. So I stole the list from the ambassador's office and tore the page out of the embassy visitor log on my way out the door. His signature in the hotel register matches his official signature. He was there in Le Havre and arrogant enough to use his real name."

"So you didn't..." Her voice trailed off, almost too afraid to utter the words. "You didn't do as they're claiming?"

"I did exactly as they claim." He tapped the list of names. "This one by itself makes me a traitor." He refolded all the pages and slipped them beneath his waistcoat. "But all of them together shows treason by the ambassador."

He eased back against the seat, stretched out his legs as far as possible in the cramped space, and fell silent. He watched her closely, waiting for her reaction.

Good God. Her mind spun with all he'd just revealed, with everything he'd told her since the moment he'd forced his way into her cottage. All of it seemed plausible.

Except... "Then why are you still running? You're on English soil now, safe from the French. You could go to the authorities and show them the evidence. The ambassador would be arrested for treason, not you."

"Because I don't yet have everything I need. It's all circumstantial at best, with no inarguable way to put Wentworth in Le Havre except for that signature in the guest registry."

"What else do you need?" The question emerged as a breathless whisper. God help her, she was afraid of the answer.

"Wentworth's personal diary. It will put him in Le Havre by his own admission and also reveal the other men who are working for him, because he isn't doing this alone. That list of names had to have come from someone attached to the War Office. If I go to the authorities now, I catch only Wentworth, and only if I'm lucky. But I want to bring down every single one of them and make the bastards pay for what they've done."

The venomous resolve in his voice played down her spine like icy fingers, eliciting a shudder. "How do you acquire the diary?"

"From the ambassador. Which is why it's good to know that I'm wanted for treason."

"That's *good*?" The man was mad!

He sent her a lazy smile. "That means Wentworth has made it to London before me and convinced the Court that I've turned, which proves that he's worried about me and the evidence I have against him. He'll be in London, his diary with him, and preparing for a fight."

"Which is why you're going there." She pressed her hand against her chest, as if she could physically push down the frantic pounding of her heart. "For a fight."

He turned toward the window. "There are names of over a dozen men on that list, all of them deep operatives hidden in France. They would have been murdered, their throats slit one by one, if that letter to Delacroix hadn't been intercepted. I'm fighting for them."

She wanted to believe him. *Desperately* so. But…"You're also wanted for murder. Do you have papers that prove that away, too?"

His lips curled grimly, his attention still focused beyond the glass. "Do *you* think me a murderer, Grace?"

She simply didn't know what to think. "Are you?"

He murmured, "As surely as if I put the knife to his throat myself."

Her body flashed numb. *Dear God,* what had she gotten herself into?

"I was the one who found that letter," he continued quietly. "By utter accident. The seal was broken after Wentworth posted it and before it could leave the embassy, so the clerk who caught it brought it to me." He reached up to draw an idle fingertip along the window's edge. "The clerk thought it was an accounting matter, and part of my duties was to serve as the embassy's quartermaster, responsible for all accounts in and out. But something about that letter struck me as odd. Why should a buyer of expensive fabric care about the names of factory workers? So I took it to Sir Henry Jacobs, my mentor and the man who'd helped me gain my post." His hand dropped away. "At the time, I had no idea what I'd found. But Henry knew. He confronted the ambassador, who killed him for it. I found his body draped over his desk in a pool of blood, his throat slit from ear to ear."

When he looked back at her, she gasped at the grief that darkened his face.

"I promised his widow that I would catch the men responsible, and I won't stop until I've found them. Wentworth is only the start of the work I have to do." So much determination rang in his voice that it dripped with resolve. "Now you know what I've done to be accused of treason and murder, why I was out on the Channel during that storm, why I forced myself into your cottage…why I'm innocent."

But she wasn't at all certain of that. "It only proves that you stole those documents. For all I know that letter and hotel register have nothing to do with your story, that you were the one who forged the ambassador's name on the embassy log to place blame on him, while you planned to give that list of names to the French yourself."

His eyes narrowed on her for a beat, studying her closely. Then he shrugged a shoulder, a forced gesture of nonchalance that contrasted sharply with how his jaw tightened beneath his week's growth of beard. "Then turn me in. Call out to the driver and make him stop, reveal who I am, and claim your reward."

"You know I can't," she shot back, keeping her voice low even as her frustration rose.

He shook his head, dismissing that. "You don't trust me because I'm not the only one keeping secrets."

"Because I am keeping my son safe!" she ground out, her alarm and unease almost too much to bear. Revealing Ross's identity would rain all kinds of unwanted attention down upon her.

"The woman who captures England's greatest enemy since Napoleon would surely be awarded her son's inheritance." His midnight blue eyes gleamed like the devil's own as he tossed out that temptation. Fitting. Since he was offering up her dearest wish in exchange for her soul. "But the ambassador also goes free to sell more secrets, to reveal more of our agents to the enemy. Can you live with their deaths?"

She fisted her hands in her lap. The impossible choice he was presenting to her was far more complicated than it seemed on the surface. This wasn't about choosing between revealing his identity or not. It was about deciding to trust him. The blasted devil knew it, too.

"Better make up your mind soon. We're almost to the inn. If you wait until then to send up the alarm, you'll have your reward ripped away from you by every driver and hostler in the yard." He leaned forward, his elbows resting on his knees and his hands clasped together between them. His eyes were piercing. "What's it going to be, Grace? Does it all end here, or do you trust me enough to help me the rest of the way to London?"

Damn you. Her eyes burned, blurring with hot tears. After ten years, to come so close to giving her son the life he deserved, the one he was meant to have— All her hopes for Ethan's future were slipping through her fingers as easily as the miles beneath the coach's wheels. *Damn you to hell.*

Not answering, she slumped back in the corner of the seat and turned her head to stare out the window. But she saw nothing, her tear-filled vision blurring until the landscape became nothing more than a mass of dark reds and golden yellows of a smeared sunset, edged by the oncoming darkness of night.

Over the final mile of the stage, her fear gave way to frustration, which turned into silent fury that she should discover now the odds that they were up against. He'd warned her before they left Sea Haven that he might not be able to help her, but she'd gambled on him anyway. What other choice did she have? But now, unless she continued to help him, they would never reach London, and whatever small chance she had at successfully pleading her case would crumble to dust. So she sat there, doing nothing to signal to the driver to stop.

The coach slowed before passing through a narrow archway into the inn yard. She'd opened the door and had her feet on the ground before it came to a complete stop, to stay as far away from him as possible.

But his hand closed around her elbow from behind, halting her.

"You said you needed me," he murmured, his mouth lowering to her ear to keep from being overhead by the hostlers around them. "Now I need you, Grace. I can't do this without you."

Her chest tightened, and not because she needed him in kind, to help her with Ethan's inheritance, but because it had been a very long time since she'd been needed by a man.

That it was him, of all men, made her heart bleed.

"All right," she whispered grudgingly, blinking the stinging anger from her eyes.

"Thank you for trusting me." He affectionately squeezed her arm.

"I'm not keeping silent because I trust you," she flung back just as quietly. "I did it because keeping you from being arrested is in my own best interests."

Wordlessly, he lifted her hand and placed a kiss to her fingers. His eyes gleamed at that wholly blatant lie.

She snatched her hand away and grabbed up her bag that a hostler had unloaded from the rear luggage rack and dropped to the ground, then stomped away toward the inn door. Not caring if he followed her or not.

A flash of red—

She halted. Half a dozen soldiers gathered on the far side of the inn yard, their red uniforms torn and dirty, all of them travel weary. But it was the soldiers' arms and legs that caught her attention. Because they were missing.

She stared, gripped immobile by the harrowing scene. None were whole men anymore. Two had wooden spindles fashioned where their legs should have been. Three others were missing hands, and one had lost an entire arm. Another was missing half of his face, with no chin or jaw beneath the wide bandage tied around his head. They were waiting for transportation to take them onward, finally going home to families and loved ones.

"Now you know why I risked my own life to save the lives of every agent on that list," Ross said quietly over her shoulder, following her stunned gaze to the soldiers. "How do I tell men like these that I couldn't find it within me to sacrifice my life to save others who are fighting for England, when they've given so much?"

Harsh remorse assaulted her. When his hand closed around her elbow again, she grudgingly let it stay.

"We're both exhausted. Let's take a room and settle in for the night." He placed her hand on his arm and led her toward the inn. "We can argue more about my treason over breakfast."

"But there are guards here." Her fingers tightened on his arm. Three soldiers with rifles slung over their shoulders stood on the opposite side of the inn yard, keeping their distance from the others. As if being wounded in service was contagious. Their bright red uniforms stood out boldly in the darkness of the foggy, rain-drizzled night.

"I see that." Playing the part of the doting husband, he slipped his arm around her waist as he lowered his lips to her ear with a casual smile. "They're taking the coach home, that's all. They'll be gone in a few hours and won't bother us."

Her fingers trembled against his sleeve, but she fought to make every inch of herself appear calm and composed. She forced a smile in case anyone was watching. "Are you certain?"

"Yes." That was clearly a lie. But when she parted her lips to challenge him, he took her bag from her hand and nodded toward the wet ground to distract her. "Watch your step."

As he led her toward the inn's entrance, she lowered her head and pulled the hood of her cape further down over her face. She'd grown more self-conscious about hiding her scar the closer they drew to London. She didn't dare tell Ross, knowing he would demand more information from her, but that afternoon, when they'd stopped at an inn to stretch their legs and buy food, she'd thought she'd seen Vincent among the crowd of other travelers. A mistake, of course, one that left her momentarily gripped by terror, then feeling like a fool for seeing ghosts when she realized that the man wasn't her brother-in-law. But it was also a warning not to take any chances that she might be recognized.

A commotion rose behind them. The strike of horseshoes across cobblestones, shouts, the creak of wood and ping of metal—

A team of horses broke loose and scattered the grooms who were changing them out. The coach lurched forward out of control. The rattle and movement frightened the horses more as they scrambled to find footing on the slippery stones. The team charged forward, right toward a little boy who had toddled away from his mother.

Ross dropped the bag and sprinted into the path of the uncontrolled horses.

Grace's scream pierced the clattering noise of onrushing hooves. But Ross didn't hesitate as his arms went around the child, tackling him to the ground and rolling away, just inches from the horses' hooves and crushing wheels.

They lay together on the wet ground for a long moment. Grace gaped at them, terrified they'd been hurt. Or worse. All of her flashed numb with fear.

Then Ross slowly sat up and drew the boy onto his lap. "It's all right," he assured the child as he quickly checked him over to make certain he hadn't been hurt. "You're fine."

But the toddler looked at Ross with frightened horror, then let out a wail at the top of his little lungs. His face contorted with terrified cries, and he punched at Ross to move away from him, blaming this big stranger for frightening him by hurling him to the ground.

"John!" His mother ran to them. She fell to her knees on the wet cobblestones to grab the crying child to her bosom and poured out an endless stream of relieved tears and gratitude to Ross as he climbed to his feet.

With a grimace, he reached down for his hat that had fallen off when he'd tackled the boy. New fear stuck Grace— His face had been revealed for all to see, including all the drivers and hostlers in the courtyard, and now all the people in the inn who poured outside to see what the commotion was about.

Including the soldiers.

Knocking his hat against his leg to shake off the mud, he returned to Grace's side. The faint smile of reassurance he gave her wasn't enough to vanquish her worry.

"You saved his life," she whispered. And in doing so, jeopardized his own.

As if reading her thoughts, his gaze darted past her to the soldiers, who were now staring openly at him and talking with one of the drivers, who gestured from Ross to the mail coach.

"Let's go," he said calmly, collecting her bag and taking her arm to lead her inside.

"But they—"

"Won't bother us."

Grace ignored that and glanced at the three soldiers, who were now walking straight toward them.

With a panicked gasp, she halted in mid-step and threw her arms around Ross's neck. She leaned against him as she rose up onto tiptoes and brought her lips against his.

Ross froze, startled by the unexpected kiss. He took her arm to steady her as she slowly pulled back, forcing a brilliant smile onto her face that belied her increasing panic.

"Isn't my husband just the most wonderful man in the world?" she called out over his shoulder as the soldiers approached, her beaming smile and the affectionate expression meant to throw off their suspicions. But it didn't hide the true terror she'd felt when she saw him run in front of the horses, which still had her shaking. "He's a store clerk, so he thinks he isn't important," she continued. "But he risked his own life to save that boy."

She directed her proud smile at Ross and ran her fingers lovingly through the hair at his nape. Fingers which trembled harder as the soldiers drew nearer, their boots scuffling softly over the wet cobblestones. *Dear God, please let them believe me!*

With a trace of legitimate pride in her voice, she asked as the soldiers stopped just behind Ross, "Did you gentlemen see that?"

"Aye, ma'am, we did," one of the men answered.

Ross forced his own smile and shook his head. "My wife is exaggerating. It was nothing."

The soldier stepped up to his side, and a small smile tugged at his mustached lips. "'Fraid I have to agree wi' yer wife, sir." A touch of a northern accent colored his voice. "Ye hit the ground a bit hard. We wanted t' make certain ye were all right." His eyes glinted as they slid over Grace. "An' yer wife."

"Thank you." Grace blew out a tired sigh and gave a relieved sag of her shoulders as she placed her hand over her abdomen and arched her back in exaggeration to jut out her belly. "Especially a woman in my condition." She lowered her voice as she clarified in a whisper. "*Enceinte*."

She saw a flash of amused surprise glint in Ross's eyes, but his well-trained expression never changed.

"Aye, ma'am. The scare must've startled ye."

"Terrified me, more like." Her eyes never left Ross's as she touched his cheek. "Don't ever do anything like that again, Christopher, you understand?"

Then, because she couldn't help herself, she rose up on tiptoes and kissed him again.

As she pulled away, her eyes locked with his. She only half pretended when she murmured, "What would we do if we lost you?"

His lips twisted with amusement, not catching her deeper meaning. "Yes, Mrs. Thomas. Next time I'll let the boy be trampled, shall I?"

"Impertinent," she scolded, falling back into her role of irritated wife.

"And on that," he muttered, giving the long-suffering sigh of a beleaguered husband as he took her arm and led her forward, "we'll depart. Gentlemen, I wish you a good night's rest away from your wives." He cast a roll of his eyes at them and muttered, "Lucky devils."

The three soldiers laughed. Grace's cheeks grew redder with peevishness that she'd been the butt of his joke, which only added to their disguise of a bickering married couple.

They crossed the courtyard to the inn, and Ross held the door open for her.

"Do you really think those soldiers only wanted to find out if we were all right?" she whispered as she started past him.

"No." He reached for her arm, stopping her close to him in the small doorway. "Did you really kiss me just to throw them off?"

She didn't dare answer. The truth would undo her.

His eyes fixed on her mouth for a long moment, as if he were contemplating kissing her again, right there in the doorway. And not a peck like she'd given him, but one that would have left her begging to be ravished.

Hearing his explanation of the papers and why he'd done what he had, and then seeing him risk his life to save that child, she couldn't remain furious at him. He was proving himself to be the selfless, courageous hero she'd suspected him to be.

Although trusting him again would take more time.

As if recognizing the conflict he spun inside her, he mercifully looked away from her mouth and dropped his gaze to her belly. "*Enceinte?*"

"It seemed a good disguise at the time."

He drawled dryly, "Is it mine?"

She flashed him the most mischievous smile she could summon. "I'll never tell."

Then she stepped past him into the inn.

CHAPTER 12

*T*he soldiers were moving again.

Ross stood beside the window in their dark room and watched the activity in the yard below. Not because he worried that the men would realize that he and Grace had lied to them, but because he couldn't sleep.

He raked frustrated fingers through his hair. It was official now. England had declared him a traitor, when all he'd ever done was fight to protect his country. Even now he was risking his life for it. Yet everyone who saw those bills posted across the countryside or read the reports in the London papers would believe he'd turned his back on England, when that was the very last thing he'd ever do. But if he couldn't convince the Court of the truth, he'd go to his grave marked as a traitor.

To think that he'd once wanted nothing more than to be an ambassador, that he'd admired Wentworth and considered him a mentor—*lies.* Nothing but lies now, leaving the taste of ashes in his mouth.

And Grace...*Christ!* He'd wanted to punch his fist through the coach wall that afternoon. Not because those two gossipy old women had identified him, but because of the terrified look Grace had given him.

As if he were some kind of monster.

He bit back a curse. He shouldn't have revealed the truth about the pages and how they fit together. Telling her put her life at risk. Yet he needed her to trust him, and he couldn't bear the cold accusation he'd seen in her eyes, the fear and doubt. He'd wanted her to trust him—

No, he'd wanted her to *believe* in him.

At that moment, caught up together in the coach, with the full ramifications of what he was doing staring him in the face, he'd needed to know that what he'd done mattered. That someone like Grace, a good and caring woman, could believe in the importance of his mission and support him in his actions.

Leaning his shoulder against the casement, he glanced at her as she lay in bed, drawn up beneath the covers as she slept, once more in that frumpy tent of a night rail. She might not believe in him, but at least she hadn't given him up when she'd had the opportunity. He'd claim his victories wherever he could. Especially with Grace, because every minute with her was like being immersed in a game of chess in which she constantly challenged him to keep up.

Who the devil *was* she?

She said she'd been part of his Mayfair world, but how was that possible? How could he not remember someone like her? A woman with that much fearlessness moving among those spoiled society ladies who fainted at the first sign of distress. A woman who was filled from head to toe with determination, whose sharp mind could have run circles around most of the men in Parliament. A woman who had the spine to tie him up, then blackmail him into helping her.

He should have been furious at her for that. Should have left her behind in Sea Haven when he had the chance, tied up to her own bed in revenge. But she also intrigued him, flaming all kinds of wicked thoughts, until revenge was the last thing he wanted from tying her up.

She stirred as she awoke, taking a moment to clear the sleepy confusion from her mind as she sat up and glanced at the dark room around her. Then she looked down at the trundle bed that he'd claimed for the night instead of pushing his luck and trying for a repeat of last night's sleeping arrangements. Better that he hadn't, given the way she looked, all deliciously sleep-rumpled, with her hair lying in a riot of thick toffee-colored curls down her back and the loose neck of her gown sliding down to reveal a smooth, bare shoulder.

He'd lied to her last night when he'd denied attempting to seduce her. God knew he'd been doing just that. Given half a chance, he'd unrepentantly do it again.

"Ross?" A hint of panic rose in her voice at not finding him near.

"I'm here," he called to her through the darkness.

With a soft sigh that she wasn't alone, she brushed a hand through her hair to push the unruly curls away from her forehead. "What are you doing?"

"Watching." He turned back toward the window, his gaze once more falling to the soldiers below who paced the corner of the yard to keep their blood circulating against the chill of the damp night.

Behind him, he heard the soft rustle of the covers as she slipped from bed. "The soldiers?"

He nodded, his eyes following them in the halo of light from the stable lamp. "They're waiting for the night coach." He felt her come up behind him, his body instantly alert with the nearness of her. When she remained behind him, lingering fearfully in the shadows, he assured her, "They don't suspect us."

"How can you be certain?"

"Because they would have arrested us by now."

That blunt truth didn't put her at ease. Instead, she came

forward just long enough to peer down at the soldiers, to see for herself that they weren't a threat, then stepped aside.

He expected her to flee back to bed, especially since she'd spoken less than half a dozen words to him since they settled into the room. Instead, she remained just behind him at his shoulder. Close enough that he could catch the faint scent of jasmine that surrounded her like a cloud and sense the warm softness of her body. Close but not touching, and driving him mad with frustration.

"I forgot that you used to be a soldier," she said quietly.

"In a different lifetime." More truth lingered behind that than he wanted to admit.

"This must be so very difficult for you."

Not difficult. *Hell.* He was in hell. He rasped out the quiet confession, "My world has ended."

He heard the quiet catch of her breath at that soft revelation and felt her hesitate, so attuned had he become to her. He thought that comment would drive her back to bed for certain, to maintain the distance between them that had formed that afternoon in the carriage. Instead, she slowly placed her hand on his bare shoulder.

Her soft touch was absolution. The sensation spooled through him like a ribbon, tying the two of them together in the darkness and giving him solace.

"Everything I believed in has turned out to be a lie. The men I admired, the ones whose careers I wanted to emulate—" He shook his head, still watching the yard below, even though the soldiers had boarded the night coach and were now waiting to leave. "Wentworth welcomed me with open arms the day I arrived at the embassy in Paris, did you know that? To bring me into the fold and guide me on the right diplomatic path so that I could serve England to the best of my abilities." Bitterness burned on his tongue. "His patriotism was only a charade."

She said nothing, but in that silence he felt her sympathy. Her fingers tightened against his shoulder, then slid down his arm in a reassuring caress that soothed the simmering anger he'd carried with him since the moment he'd discovered Wentworth's treachery.

"I've wanted nothing more in my life than to serve England. That's why I became a soldier, why I took a diplomatic position when the wars ended." He wanted to make her understand— No, he wanted to share this part of his life with her because he knew she *would* understand. The only woman who could, now knowing what depths that service had taken him to. "I wanted to serve my country beyond the wars and into the peace." Then he shared with her the secret that he'd kept from everyone, including his brother. "To know that I've earned the right to serve in Parliament, rather than being there only due to fortune of birth."

"You have." She squeezed his arm. "In so many ways."

If only he could believe that himself. With a sigh, he lifted her hand to his lips, to place a kiss on her palm, then lowered it to his chest. "My country thinks I'm a traitor."

Instead of pulling away, she laced her fingers through his. "Only until you show them those pages."

"But I *did* commit treason. I stole those names and carried them out of France—"

"To save the life of every man on that list." Her voice was as quiet as the sleeping inn around them. "That wasn't treason. That was heroism."

He squeezed his eyes closed against the doubts that whispered inside his head, putting voice to his worst fears. "And if I prove no better than Wentworth in the end?"

"You're already better." Her fingers curled into the hard muscle of his chest, as if she could hold his heart in her hand and keep it safe. "So much more than you realize."

A shudder tore from him, and in its place came comforting warmth. Her touch proved to be a benediction. It was the belief in him that he'd been seeking since that afternoon, when he'd revealed everything. The forgiveness and blessing he needed to keep going, to survive.

They stood together like that for a long moment, with his heart beating strong beneath her fingertips, and the closeness of her made him ache. Unable to resist, he turned toward her and cupped her face in his palm, then lowered his head to kiss her—

She moved her mouth away only a hairsbreadth before his lips touched hers. Stepping back, she slipped away from him.

"That's not..." She swallowed hard and twisted her hands in that tent of a night rail she insisted on wearing, as if distrusting herself not to reach for him. "That's not a good idea."

"Seems like a fine idea to me," he murmured, wanting very much to find solace in her arms tonight. "One we'd both enjoy a great deal."

Her lips parted delicately from the temptation he presented. She was a widow and knew the pleasures a man could give her, and a longing for exactly that showed in every inch of her. She wanted him as much as he wanted her.

But the stubborn woman shook her head and took another step backward, increasing the distance between them. Instinctively he knew not to follow, no matter how much he wanted to.

"You're wrong," she countered.

"I'm not." He arched a brow to punctuate his point. "You kissed me twice in front of the soldiers."

"I had to convince them we were married."

"One kiss would have done that. There was no need for a second, unless you simply wanted it." He pinned her with a look so blatant in its declaration of desire that she shivered. "If you wanted something as small from me as a kiss, just think of what other pleasures I could give you if you allowed yourself to accept them."

Accept them...as if he were giving her a gift. He nearly laughed at the irony. The truth was that the gift would be his, to show him that she trusted him enough to make herself vulnerable to him in the most exposed way. To prove that she glimpsed the good still inside him.

"None of that matters," she whispered, yet he noted with a tightening of his gut that she didn't deny it. Even now her voice dripped with so much need that it trembled. "What matters is Ethan."

That snapped him up straight. What the blazes did her son have to do with this? "I told you. You'll have my help with his inheritance. Nothing will change that."

"Not if we...if we..." She gestured her hand toward the bed, unable to say the words. After all, speak of the devil...although at that moment, Ross would have sold his soul for one night with her and the absolution he knew he'd find in her arms. "It will only cause problems between us."

"That won't happen."

She challenged, "So you've walked away as good friends with every woman you've ever bedded? You've never had a bad parting afterward?"

Christ. He couldn't answer that, not without lying. Her sharp mind was one of the things he liked best about her. Until right now.

"Then you'd better stay on your side of the room," he warned, deadly serious. "Because if you touch me again, I won't be able to resist stripping off that frumpy gown of yours." He paused to emphasize exactly how serious he was. "With my teeth."

Her eyes widened like moons at that declaration, one he wholly meant to keep if she dared come closer. Understanding how completely earnest he was, she took another step away. *Smart woman.*

His frustration burned hot. To tamp down his rising desire—and other shamelessly rising things—he moved to the other side of the window, putting further distance between them. He forced his thoughts away from Grace and back to London and what awaited them there. It was as good as a dunk in cold water.

"If I'm to have any chance of being exonerated," he said quietly, "then I have to get to St James's Palace to see the king."

"They'll arrest you as soon as you arrive."

He slid a sideways glance at her through the shadows. "Then I have to get there very carefully." When she didn't find his dry attempt at humor amusing, he turned back toward the window and the now deserted inn yard below. "I'll need help."

"*We'll* need help," she corrected, unaware of how that single word, uttered with such resolve, pierced him with pleasure. "You're thinking of your brother, aren't you?"

Not taking his eyes away from the window, he smiled. She'd begun to understand how he thought. "Yes."

"The authorities will be watching. How will you send a message to him?"

How, indeed? He couldn't send a message directly to Christopher, she was right about that. Nor would Kit accept it unless he was certain no one had seen it being delivered. Yet it wouldn't arrive at all without the help of someone the authorities would never suspect, someone removed from his social circle yet close enough to the periphery to make contacting Kit appear wholly innocuous. Someone who knew the risk yet would be willing to help anyway, simply out of love for England, for duty and honor—

Or for the sheer excitement of it.

"Evelyn," he murmured as the solution struck him.

"Who?"

He stifled a laugh. She would be *perfect*! "Evelyn Winslow."

"Who is Mrs. Winslow?"

"*Miss* Winslow." A young woman with more daring than prudence. One who loved adventure and excitement to the point of distraction. And the very last person whom the authorities would suspect knew anything about his whereabouts.

"Is she someone special to you?"

Right then, Evelyn Winslow might just be—"My salvation."

"I see."

He looked up at the odd tone of her voice. He didn't dare let himself consider the delicious possibility that Grace was jealous. Or how a less scrupulous man might use that to his advantage to fill the long night ahead. "She's my cousin Robert's sister-in-law."

But that admission didn't relax her. She remained as uneasy as before as she folded her arms over her chest. "Someone you trust, then?"

"I trust *you*, Grace." Although he had every reason not to, given that she was keeping secrets of her own. But when she'd had the opportunity to betray him, she'd kept his confidences. For that, she'd earned his loyalty. "Our situation would be much easier if you'd trust me."

He turned and sat down on the windowsill, kicking his long legs out in front of him to physically keep her away. *Sweet Lucifer*, even now all of him ached to be buried between her thighs, to feel her writhe beneath him until she broke with pleasure. If she kept up this tension between them, then God help him.

"But I do trust you." She purposefully misunderstood his meaning by adding, "I wouldn't be sleeping in the same room with you if I didn't."

"Perhaps you shouldn't be," he drawled in a wicked murmur, unable to help himself from trailing a shamelessly lascivious gaze over her. "I am a Carlisle, after all."

Her sensuous lips twisted into a wry smile at that reminder, drawing his eyes to her mouth...to that delectably kissable, wholly eager mouth of hers. And if she kept that up—

God help *her*.

"And who are you?" he asked. Despite her claim to the contrary, she didn't trust him enough to reveal her true identity.

"I can't tell you, you know that."

"Not until you know whether I'll be able to help you or be set swinging at Newgate, you mean," he drawled with a touch of resentment. This new turn of conversation was doing wonders to tamp down his lust.

"Not until I'm certain that Ethan cannot be harmed."

"He won't be." Then, just because he was in a self-punishing mood tonight, he added, "As long as you stop putting him in danger yourself."

Her eyes blazed in the darkness. "I have dedicated my life to keeping him safe. I would *never* put my son—"

"Then stop taking unnecessary risks. Your acting ability is quite impressive, and I nearly applauded this afternoon in the carriage. But then, with the soldiers—" He gestured in aggravation toward the inn yard below. "You need to stop doing that because sooner or later you're going to come up against someone who sees through your act."

"Like you?"

He ignored that bait. "I don't want you to be hurt because of me."

Grace stared at him, as if sensing the raw honesty behind that. "What do you care about me? I'm nothing to you but a means of getting to London."

She was becoming so much more. Heaven help him when she realized it.

He pushed away from the windowsill and pulled himself up to his full height as he slowly stalked toward her. Standing her ground, she let her eyes roam over him, taking him all in. Bare chest and bare feet, with only his trousers doing a poor job of keeping any part of him covered, given how the sight of her in the shadows, all bed-ready and warm had him nearly hard.

"I mean it, Grace. Don't take any more risks for me."

"I'm not doing it for you." But there was no conviction in her voice.

"Then you can stop doing it completely. I'll keep my word to help you once we reach London. If not me, then Kit and my cousins. Ethan will have everything he deserves, I promise you."

He reached out and tucked a curl behind her ear. Then he opportunistically sifted his fingers through her silky tresses as he drew his hand away. "But I won't allow you to be hurt. Understand?"

She stared at him defiantly for a moment. Then she grudgingly nodded.

"Now go back to bed and sleep. You'll need rest for tomorrow's travels."

Knowing to take his victories wherever he could, he returned to the window, to keep watch a little longer into the night. And to keep away from her before he took more than a caress of her hair. Behind him, he heard her footsteps as she returned to bed and the soft rustle of fabric as she nestled down beneath the warm blankets.

It took all his strength not to follow her.

CHAPTER 13

London
Two Evenings Later

C hristopher Carlisle lifted a glass of Madeira from the
tray of a passing footman. He leaned a shoulder against
the Grecian column at the edge of the Marquess of Totteridge's
ballroom and cast a bored glance around the crowded room.

No one dared approach him. Word had flowed through the *ton*
faster than the Thames through London that Ross was wanted for
treason, and the news had made him a social pariah by proximity.

Not that Kit had ever cared what polite society thought of him.
He had his work with the Home Office to give his life purpose.
And now, he had a new mission—redeem his brother's
good name.

Which was the *only* reason why he was here tonight, why he'd
attended a musicale this afternoon, and why he would drop by as
many of the clubs tonight as he could tolerate once he'd left this
ball. And at each place he went, letting himself be cut. He needed
to be visible to show the world that he considered the news about
Ross to be ridiculous, and to remind them that the Earl of

Spalding occupied a respected place in society and would again as soon as the charges were revoked.

Hiding would only fuel the gossip.

Yet how much longer could he continue the show? In the four days since Ross had been declared a traitor, the invitations had already stopped coming and his name stricken from the guest list at White's. In truth, he was only allowed into the ball tonight because the soiree came so quickly on the heels of the treason declaration that the invitation was already in the post and so Lady Totteridge had been unable to rescind it. But sweet Lucifer was it entertaining! He smiled with private amusement at the way the merry widows tripped all over themselves to catch a good look at him, how the innocent young misses gave him wide berth, how the men simply ignored him.

Not all. A few longtime friends had greeted him when he arrived, to tell him that they hoped the charges would be dismissed and to offer their support. He was certain their loyalty was helped along in no small part by his cousins' devotion. The Duke of Trent and his brothers refused to believe that Ross was a traitor. Sebastian Carlisle wielded a great deal of power these days, and no one wanted to cross him. Neither did they want to be at odds with Robert and Quinton, both of whom were now successful in their own right and highly influential in all quarters.

But most were happy to cut him, and Kit was happy to keep a list of their names for when this whole mess ended and they once again wanted the favor of the Earl of Spalding.

If it ended.

He hadn't heard a single word from Ross since his brother fled Paris, and dread sat like a lead ball in his chest as he feared the worst. From what little information he was able to gather from his contacts within the War Office and the Court of St James's, Ross was most likely dead. The last time anyone could pinpoint him he'd boarded a fishing boat in Le Havre to cross the Channel right as the storm hit. There was no record of him disembarking on English soil.

So now Christopher was here, drinking watered-down Madeira and pretending to watch the dancing, because he hadn't yet given up hope. If Ross were somehow still alive, then he would need Kit's perseverance in protecting his name. But if he were dead...well, it was only a matter of time before the family was stripped of the title and all of its possessions. The standard punishment for traitors. Already the Home Office had taken Kit's assignments away from him. The crown was simply waiting to lower the axe.

Since the moment Kit learned what Ross had been doing in Paris and the risks he was subjecting himself to, he'd publicly threatened his older brother with the prospect of becoming a vicar, in order to make a point about the uselessness of martyrdom. But if Ross couldn't miraculously resurrect himself, then Kit might very well have to become a vicar after all just to survive. Ross would laugh from his grave at the irony of *that*.

"Good evening, Mr. Carlisle," a soft voice said from behind him. "I'm so glad to find you here."

He tensed, the glass stopping halfway to his lips. God help him, he *knew* that voice. Because the woman attached to it frightened the daylights out of him.

"Miss Winslow." Lowering the Madeira, he sketched a polite bow as she approached him. "A pleasure to see you again."

Her eyes gleamed at that, as if she knew it was a lie. But she was too polite to dispute his untruth—or more likely, the unpredictable chit simply saw it as a challenge. Instead, she sank into a curtsy.

Evelyn Winslow. A more intimidating creature the good Lord had never made, except perhaps for her sister Mariah, who was now married to his cousin Robert.

At first glance, Evelyn seemed as ordinary as any other unmarried young lady, from the rosebuds in her hair to the bow-capped toes of her pastel satin slippers, complete with an intoxicating smile.

What lay beneath, however, was a different matter entirely.

Her unassuming façade hid a woman so confident and sure of herself that she made grown men quake. One who possessed an endless supply of energy and an intense love of life, coupled with a tendency to leap without looking that was seemingly always putting her into one kind of scrape or another, including some undisclosed predicament during Robert and Mariah's elopement to Scotland that mandated that she be on her best behavior ever since. No more racing horses through Piccadilly or shooting off guns in the park. No more swimming in the Serpentine. No more parading down St James's Street beneath her parasol as if she were on the Promenade instead of strolling past rows of gentlemen's clubs.

For once, Evelyn Winslow had been on an extended stretch of proper ladylike behavior. Which frightened Kit even more.

"I hope you're enjoying the ball," he commented, because it was expected.

Her face lit up with a barely controlled excitement. "It's the most thrilling night of my life!"

That stunned him, certain that no one had ever before called Totteridge's annual ball thrilling.

Before he could think of a reply, she added, "I've come to ask that you request a dance from me."

She'd come to ask…He blinked. "Pardon?"

"And it *has* to be a waltz. The very first waltz of the evening, in fact."

She smiled and flitted her fan at that, as if requesting a dance from a gentleman—and from him, no less—was her birthright. As if he wouldn't dare dream of denying her.

"Haven't you heard?" He gestured at the crush around them, which was now leaning in to eavesdrop on their conversation. "I'm a social outcast these days."

"Well, isn't that convenient? Because so am I." She smiled, undaunted. "What better way to thumb our collective noses at society than by waltzing together? Besides," she murmured as she leaned in closer so she wouldn't be overheard, "it's not as if you have anyone else requesting a dance from you tonight."

So she *did* know what the gossips were saying about him yet wasn't at all wary of it. "Perhaps you shouldn't either," he warned gently. "I would hate for you to be cut simply because you danced with me."

With a mysterious smile, she tapped her folded fan against his shoulder. "The waltz, Mr. Carlisle." Then she ordered outright, "Come for me when it starts."

Without a backward glance, she retreated through the crowd.

Kit stared after her. What the devil was she up to, asking him to dance? No, not asking. *Demanding.* She'd sidled right up to him and demanded a dance. A waltz, no less.

And not just him, apparently. She was circling the room, stopping to converse with every unmarried gentleman—and some attached—who had the misfortune to stray into her path. A flirtatious smile from her, a nod from the man, another dance most likely secured...At this rate, she'd have every dance for the evening spoken for.

He couldn't remember Evelyn Winslow dancing that much at any society ball before.

Come to think of it, he couldn't remember seeing Evelyn at *any* society event except those she'd been forced to attend with her sister, who was nowhere in sight tonight.

His eyes narrowed. What did the trouble-making gel have up her satin sleeve?

He continued to hold up the column through the next dance, in which Evelyn reeled with Hugh Whitby, Baron Whitby's youngest son, then through the next one with a man Christopher didn't recognize. She didn't glance his way, presumably filling up the rest of her dances between sets.

The Master of Ceremonies called out the first waltz of the evening, and the orchestra sent up the opening flourish of notes. Around him, the partygoers pulsed with excitement as they began to pair off and find their way to the dance floor.

Kit tossed back the last of his Madeira. With a determined squaring of his shoulders, he moved through the crush to claim his waltz, feeling every bit like a condemned man marching toward the scaffold. When he reached Evelyn, he wryly arched a brow and held out his hand.

She slipped her trembling fingers into his. He almost stopped this fiasco right there. *Should* have stopped it. The chit didn't have any idea what she was getting herself into by asking him for this dance. But when she felt him hesitate, she grabbed his arm and pulled him onto the dance floor.

He took her into position and twirled her into the waltz.

"Your brother's alive," Evelyn announced without preamble. Then ordered, "Don't look shocked!"

"I won't." Just damned confused, he was certain. Then he did his best to keep down a look of grief as he squeezed her fingers. Although the way she'd gone about expressing her support was unusual—*everything* about Evelyn Winslow was unusual—he was grateful for her optimism and her attempt to keep up his spirits. "Thank you. I appreciate your kind words."

"They're not kind. They're factual." She lowered her voice until he barely heard her over the orchestra. "Spalding sent me a letter."

Only years of training as a Home Office operative kept him from stumbling in surprise. He held his face carefully stoic as he studied her. "My brother contacted you, of all people? When?"

"Today." Then she gave a peeved sniff, clearly offended. "Why *not* me?"

"Why not, indeed?" He supposed it made sense, in a way that was completely brilliant. Or utterly mad. All their family members and close employees were being watched, the houses all under guard, in case Ross attempted to contact any of them.

Which was also why Kit persisted in making the social rounds, and especially to the clubs. If Ross wanted to send a message to him, he would have to do so through alternative means.

But through Evelyn Winslow? Kit never would have thought of her. Yet she was a woman who so craved adventure and excitement that she'd eagerly participate in espionage if given a chance, and one to whom the authorities wouldn't give a second thought. "What did he say?"

"'Tell Kit to contact the man we once raced against on donkeys in dresses,'" she recited with exacting precision. "'Tell no one else, not even Mariah. My life depends upon it.'"

He waited a beat for her to continue. When it became clear that she was finished, he pressed, "That's all?"

She smiled proudly. "Every last word."

His chest tightened with suspicion. "He signed it?"

"No."

"Then how do you know it was from Ross?"

She looked at him as if he'd escaped from Bedlam. "How many other people do you have in your life who would be passing secret messages to you?"

Dozens, actually. But the gel had a point. "So Spalding sent you that message, and you didn't think to take it to the authorities, or at least show it to your father?"

"Of course not!" The suggestion appalled her. "And let them ruin all the fun?"

Oh, what a stroke of genius Ross had in sending his message through Evelyn! A more perfect conspirator Kit couldn't have imagined.

"So all this means that your brother is still alive? That he hasn't committed treason?"

"That's exactly what it means." His chest soared with the news.

She frowned as they reached the end of the room and turned to circle back along its length. "But there's one thing I don't understand."

"What's that?" he asked, distracted. Already his mind was spinning with plans for how to meet Ross without being followed or alerting the authorities to Evelyn's involvement.

"Who wore the dresses—you or the donkeys?"

"The donkeys," he answered, deadpan. Then he squeezed her hand, interrupting before she could interject, "What did you do with the letter?"

"I memorized it and then burned it, of course."

"Of course." He grinned at her, the widest beaming smile of his life. "Miss Winslow, I could kiss you!"

She leaned scandalously closer. "By all means," she purred, "don't let me stop you."

He laughed and shifted back to put more distance between them as they continued to twirl around the dance floor. He realized then why she'd gone through the room, reserving every dance she could. So her waltz with him wouldn't stand out from any of the others.

Frighten him?

No. The chit downright terrified the daylights out of him.

"In fact," she continued, "I think this proves that I would make a good spy, don't you?"

He didn't let his expression change. She didn't know about his work with the Home Office. No one outside the department did, except for Ross. But that didn't stop the tightening of his gut at her question.

"You're far too beautiful." He distracted her with a tight, fast twirl. "In all the novels, the best spies are people who blend into a crowd." He twirled her again, out of step with the rest of the crush and not giving a damn that they were as long as he could take her mind off spies and Carlisles. "And you, Miss Winslow, definitely do not blend."

She laughed brightly at the compliment, drawing the scowling attention of the couples surrounding them. Kit didn't give a damn about them, either.

"Are the rumors true? Do you really want to become a vicar?" Her eyes sparkled, as if *this* were the big secret of the evening and not Ross's return from the grave.

They came to a stop as the dance ended. "Don't tell a soul." He lowered his mouth to her ear. "It was only an empty threat to irritate my brother."

She dropped into a deep curtsy, extending her hand to him with all the polished grace of a princess. "Then I hope you can continue to irritate him," she said in low voice, "for a very long time to come."

He bowed over her hand and mumbled earnestly, "Me, too."

CHAPTER 14

*G*race heard the midnight bell from All Saints peel through the rain-dampened streets along the Chelsea Embankment as the hackney stopped at the alley behind Cheyne Walk. Ross opened the door and swung to the ground, then reached a hand back into the dark compartment for her. She stepped down carefully, then glanced uneasily at the terrace houses fronting the Thames, most of which were already shuttered and locked up tight for the night.

Ross tossed a coin to the driver and sent the man off. He waited for the carriage to disappear from sight before taking her arm and leading her down the alley.

"Where are we going?" she asked quietly.

"Someplace safe."

She heaved out an irritated sigh. That was the same answer he'd been giving her since they arrived in Richmond that afternoon by post-chaise. He'd refused to be more forthcoming even when he'd sent off a message just before evening, not telling her whom he was contacting except that the man was an old friend. Then they'd settled into a room at an inn and waited, with Grace filling the time by writing and posting a long letter to Ethan to tell him that she was in London and safe.

Then, two hours ago, under the cover of darkness, they'd hired a hackney to take them into the city. He hadn't told her the exact location of where they were headed then, either. Or after they'd switched carriages two times so that the same driver who delivered them to their final destination wouldn't be able to trace them back to the inn.

Well, she knew where they *weren't* going—not to Spalding House nor the residences of any of his relatives. Those would all be watched. Just as they couldn't risk renting a room now that they were in London, where an opportunistic landlady or innkeeper might recognize him and call for the watch. But an alley in Chelsea...She hadn't expected *this*.

"We've arrived." He stopped outside one of the carriage houses.

She looked up at the two-story façade, with its massive double-doors and large fanlight and saw nothing to identify the place. "Where?"

"Domenico Vincenzo's studio," a deep voice answered.

Grace grabbed at Ross's arm in surprise as a black form emerged from the shadows.

But Ross recognized the man, who was nearly as tall and broad-shouldered as he was, and extended his hand in greeting. "Ellsworth."

"Spalding," he returned tightly and shook his hand.

The man was clearly not happy to be called into service, certainly not at such a late hour. And not dressed as he was, in evening finery that proclaimed he'd been interrupted from a night at a society event, right down to the silver and gray striped satin waistcoat and diamond cravat pin.

He gestured a white-gloved hand down the alley. "You weren't followed?"

"No."

The man swung his gaze to Grace and raked an assessing look

over her. Then he turned his head slightly to ask Ross, his eyes not leaving her, "Can she keep secrets?"

"You'd be surprised how well," Ross drawled with a touch of private amusement.

She glared daggers at him.

But the stranger was satisfied. He walked up to the wicket gate set into the carriage doors and reached into his breast pocket for the key to the padlock. He unlocked it, and the door opened with a creak. He disappeared inside.

Grace clutched Ross's hand to stop him as he began to follow. "Who is he?"

"Dominick Mercer, Marquess of Ellsworth. An old friend from university."

Unease trailed down her spine. Another peer, another man who might recognize her. "Can he be trusted?"

He leaned over to whisper, "You're not the only one keeping a secret identity, Mrs. Alden. Ellsworth will do whatever it takes to keep his hidden from the world."

Her eyes widened. "You *blackmailed* him?"

He grinned. "I learned from the best."

She scowled at him. But as he shifted away, he brushed his lips opportunistically over her cheek, eliciting a tremor from her. Then he took her elbow and led her inside, closing the wicket after them.

A spark flared as a flint struck on the far side of the room, and an oil lamp hissed to life. Ellsworth hung the lamp from a peg on the central post. As he turned up the wick, the dim halo of light grew in brightness to reveal a large room that had once been a carriage house but now served as—

"An artist's studio?" she murmured in surprise as she looked around, taking in the dozens of canvases of all sizes leaning against the walls, the worktables covered with bladders and jars of paints and pigments. Bookshelves lined one of the walls, filled with large folios of prints. In the middle sat a half-finished painting on a large easel draped with a sheet. Over it all lingered the stench of linseed oil and charcoal.

"It belongs to Domenico Vincenzo." Ellsworth's lips twisted as if at a private joke. "The most brilliant Italian artist since Titian."

"The most notorious anyway," Ross clarified.

Ignoring that, Ellsworth nodded toward the stairs. "There are living quarters above that you can use." Then he fixed a knowing look at Ross. "Don't touch anything down here. You might move something, and I'll never find it again."

Ross nudged her shoulder with his as he confided, "Dom's still angry about the time we helped him move into a new set of rooms when we were at Oxford."

"You didn't *help*, and I wasn't moving rooms." Ellsworth leaned a shoulder casually against the post, his arms folding over his chest and drawing the jacket tight across his broad back. "I returned from a meeting with my don to find all my belongings and furniture gone."

"We put everything back exactly as you had it," Ross defended himself.

"Two days later and two halls to the south." His gaze swung to Grace. "If he offers to help you, refuse."

He pushed himself away from the post and stalked slowly toward her, completely unaware of how that innocuous comment sliced into her.

He stopped in front of her and held out his hand. "Dominick Mercer."

"Grace Alden."

"My pleasure."

He smiled flirtatiously as he lifted her hand to place a kiss to the backs of her fingers with a slight bow, as if she were a society lady. A fearful tremor slid through her. Had he recognized her, even with—

"How did such a beautiful woman end up entangled with a

rascal like Spalding?" Instead of releasing her hand, he covered it with both of his.

As relief flooded over her that he didn't know who she was, she gave him a friendly smile. "I always take in strays who come sniffing around my door."

Ellsworth laughed as she slipped her hand away.

"She's not kidding." Ross wrapped her arm around his. The move was more than just a protective gesture; it was a jealous one. Before she could fully consider the significance of that, his handsome face turned serious. "Thank you, Ellsworth, for your help."

"When I heard the charges that had been brought against you, I knew they were nonsense." His expression was just as grim as Ross's. "You've done a lot of questionable things in your life, but you'd never betray England."

"Thank you." He squeezed her arm, drawing her attention to the marquess's comment. A recommendation for his character, in case any doubts still lingered in her regarding his innocence.

But she could have reassured him about that. Her unease now had nothing to do with treason.

Ellsworth handed him the key. "The place is yours. I've hired workers to reface the brick and make repairs to the façade, so no one else is currently using the building. I've halted work for the sennight while you're here. But I won't guarantee your safety." The marquess paused meaningfully, leaving no room for misunderstanding. "If you're discovered, I won't come to your defense."

"I wouldn't let you."

The two men silently held each other's gaze for a long moment, both faces dark and unsmiling.

Then Ross pressed gravely, "And the other item I requested?"

Ellsworth retrieved a wooden case from the bookshelf and set it down on the worktable. He opened it and pulled out a short-barreled pistol. "Caplock."

Ross let go of Grace's arm and stepped up to the table.

"Powder, caps, balls, wad—everything you need."

"Thank you." Ross picked up the pistol and examined it, then expertly set about loading it.

"If you have to use it," Ellsworth drawled, "try not to splatter blood on the canvases, will you?"

Ross smiled wryly at that. When he looked up at Grace, his smile faded. "Do you know how to use a pistol?"

She nodded, not at all liking this turn of conversation.

"We'll keep it loaded at all times while we're here." He tucked it into the middle drawer of the worktable, his eyes not leaving hers. "You'll have to use it if anyone comes after you. Can you do that?"

A chill bit at the base of her spine. "Is that really necessary?"

The two men exchanged grim looks. Then Ross said quietly, "It might very well be, if Wentworth discovers we're here before the British do."

"Before we go to the palace, you mean," she corrected, her faith in him undeterred.

His eyes softened at that, and warmth filled her chest. "It's only a precaution." He lowered his voice, and the husky timbre tightened all the tiny muscles in her belly. "I won't let anything happen to you, Grace. I promise you that."

She nodded, unable to speak past the knot in her throat. It had been years since she'd had a man's protection. For once, the night ahead didn't feel quite so lonely or frightening.

"You're set, then. I'll leave you to your plans." With a parting incline of his head toward Grace, Ellsworth sauntered toward the door. "By the way, the neighbors are used to all kinds of characters coming and going from here, although it would ease their suspicions if you'd speak in Italian."

Then he slipped through the wicket and out into the dark alley. Ross locked it after him.

Grace blinked. "What on earth did he mean by that?"

"When it comes to Ellsworth," he cautioned as he took the papers out of their hiding spot at the small of his back, then knelt down to feel at the floorboards beside the center post, "best not to ask too many questions."

He found a loose board and lifted it, hiding the papers beneath. Then he took the lamp down from its nail and held out his hand to her.

She took it and followed behind as he led her up the stairs. "And the same with you? Don't ask too many questions?"

He paused in mid-step to look down at her, his midnight blue eyes nearly black as he searched her face in the dim lamplight. "You can ask me whatever you'd like."

Perhaps. But she also knew that there was no guarantee he'd answer.

CHAPTER 15

"Good God," Ross muttered to himself. "I look terrible."

Grace caught her breath as she emerged from her bedroom and found Ross peering at himself in the mirror above the men's dressing stand in his room, bare from the waist up in the morning sunlight. While he might have grown comfortable enough around her to think nothing of wearing only a pair of breeches, she doubted she would ever grow used to seeing him like this. Despite all his wounds, with his broad back, muscular shoulders, and hard ridges of his abdomen so casually on display, *terrible* wasn't the word she'd used to describe the view.

When he caught her staring, she quirked up her brow and prayed her face didn't flush, revealing her true thoughts. "Ghastly."

"And you look…" He slid an appraising gaze over her reflection, taking in the night rail she still wore. "Tempting."

His deep voice vibrated down her spine, making her breasts feel suddenly heavy and sparking a faint throbbing between her thighs. She'd felt a wave of relief last night to discover that they had separate rooms and that she wouldn't have to fend off any nighttime flirtations, not realizing how much more seductive this devil could be in daylight. Or how much weaker her own resolve had become.

"You are mistaken," she countered in enough of an icy rebuke to keep him at a distance.

But not enough, apparently, to keep a wicked, knowing grin from his face. Or a blush from hers.

Yet he gave her a reprieve by looking back at his own reflection. He turned his head left and right to examine his face, especially the faded bruises and cut to his brow that had now healed almost completely. Then he scrubbed a hand over the growth of beard. "They won't recognize me at the palace looking like this."

She stiffened at that stark reminder of his situation. In quieter moments, when he was smiling at her or they were sharing parts of their lives, she forgot the danger hanging over them, only for it to come crashing back without warning. "When do you plan to go there?"

"Have to talk to Christopher first." He poured a splash of water into the shaving mug and began to whip up the soap with the brush. Tossing a hand towel over his shoulder, he lathered up his cheeks until most of his face was hidden beneath the foam, then mumbled at his reflection, "Well, that's a decided improvement."

Grace couldn't help but smile. Or keep from shamelessly watching him, mesmerized by the sight of a man performing his morning ablutions. It had been so very long since she'd experienced this private moment, and her chest warmed at its quiet intimacy. She knew the ache of long, lonely nights and had been surprised at how easily she'd grown used to having Ross with her in the darkness, how much she'd grown to depend upon his protection, even last night when they'd been in separate rooms. But she'd forgotten how sweet mornings with a man could be. Her chest ached with an unbidden longing to have more than only this morning's brief glimpse into his private life.

And not just as a lover. If it were only physical intimacy she craved, that could easily be satisfied. With the way he'd looked at her this morning, like a starving man who wanted to devour her, all it would take would be a whisper of permission, and she'd be in his arms, ending a decade of longing and loneliness.

But God help her, that wouldn't be enough. She wanted more.

Somewhere along the road from Sea Haven, she'd come to care for him, in a way she hadn't cared for any man since before David died. She wasn't foolish enough to think he felt the same, but when he looked at her with such desire, she could almost dare to hope...

But once this was all over, once he was exonerated and came to realize exactly who she was, how would he look at her then?

The muscles in his back flexed as he set down the mug to reach for the razor and tested its edge on his thumb. Finding it sharp, he lifted the blade to his face, then hesitated as he tried to find the best angle against his cheek.

That brought her out of her reverie. "When was the last time you shaved yourself?"

"Years," he mumbled, trying not to move his jaw. "Most likely when I was still in the army." He gritted his teeth and took a tentative swipe—

"Stop!" With a sigh of exasperation, she held out her hand. "Let me do that before you cut off an ear."

He arched a brow, his manly pride clearly offended. "I'm quite capable of shaving myself."

She shot him a dubious look and gestured at the remnants of the wounds she'd stitched up on his shoulder and thigh. "Haven't you shed enough blood recently?" Snatching the razor away from him, she pointed at a wooden chair by the window. "Sit."

Conceding that she was right, he sat and leaned back, tilting his face into the air the way he surely did for his valet. She applied more lather to his jaw.

He eyed her nervously. "Do you know what you're doing?"

"Well, last month I scraped all the hair off a pig's head we'd planned on making into soup." She raised the blade. "In my experience, there's not much difference between a dead pig and an earl."

He grabbed her wrist and stilled her hand, the blade an inch from his throat.

Slowly, his gaze lifted to meet hers. His face remained carefully stoical, but amusement shined in his eyes. "Try not to cut me into bacon, will you? I think my arse might already be cooked."

A soft laugh spilled from her.

He smiled, a lazy and relaxed grin that warmed low in her belly. Then he let go of her wrist, eased back in the chair, and closed his eyes. It was a posture of complete trust.

"How did you learn to do this?" he mumbled, careful not to move as she carefully scraped the blade across his cheek, swiping away both lather and beard in slow, short strokes.

"My father taught me." She smiled at the memory, which now seemed like a lifetime ago. "I would shave him in the mornings before he dressed or for any special event."

His brow wrinkled with a small frown. "Didn't he have a valet?"

She paused in her strokes of the razor, debating how much she should tell him. More than endangering her true identity, what she revealed would be a blow to her pride. "He had to dismiss his man when we ran out of money."

He cracked open one eye to look up at her. "How?"

"How does anyone go bankrupt? Too much property to maintain, bad business investments, falling wool prices, drought…" She shrugged a shoulder as if losing the fortune of six generations was an everyday occurrence. Yet she was surprised that talking about this to Ross came so easily and, for once, without the bitterness or anguish the memories of that time had always roused before. "We sold whatever we could, let the bank foreclose on whatever we couldn't, and scaled back our lives, which meant that most of the servants were let go. After all, there's no good justification for keeping a valet if you cannot pay your rent."

"How old were you?"

"Fourteen." She brushed her fingertips across his cheek, to feel his skin in the wake of the blade and gauge the quality of the shave. Warm, soft, so very smooth…"Anyway, it was only for two years. Once I married, Papa came to live with us, and he was assigned a footman to serve as his valet."

He stiffened, not enough to be visible, but she felt it beneath her hands. "You were sixteen when you married?" He couldn't keep the surprise from his voice. "Good God, you were young."

"I was never young." Her voice trembled with the raw honesty of that.

He said nothing, and his silence proved more unsettling than his gentle questioning.

Avoiding his gaze, she focused her attention on the shave. "I had to marry well in order for us to survive, and I couldn't wait until I was eighteen. I had no dowry of any kind, but I was a gentleman's daughter and well-schooled." She wiped her fingertip at a patch of lather clinging to his upper lip and frowned softly. "And I was pretty."

"Beautiful."

She shivered heatedly. That he could give that compliment in such a matter-of-fact way, as if it were an irrefutable fact—the sun rose in the east, rains came in April…she was beautiful. She gave a dismissive laugh. "But you don't remember me!"

"How is that even possible?" he asked carefully between small strokes of the razor, although she wasn't certain if he took care because he didn't want to move and be cut or because he was prying so unapologetically into her personal life when she held a razor at his throat. "I was a rogue of the worst sort back then. I made certain to claim the attentions of every beautiful woman I met. How did you slip through my fingers?"

"Because my husband stole me away." With the pad of her left thumb, she pulled at his chin to smooth out the soft indention of his cleft, then carefully stroked the razor against his skin. "It was during my first ball and so early in the season, in fact, that it snowed that evening. My first waltz, too." She smiled faintly at the memory. "You had requested it, but he was just arrogant and audacious enough to steal it from you. Not that you cared overly much. Rumors at the time claimed that you were quite happily involved with Lady Middleton."

"Half of the men in Mayfair were involved with Lady Middleton, but *I* was not one of them," he muttered, then arched his brow indignantly before closing his eyes. "So he stole my waltz." A trace of pique laced through his voice as he added, "And you."

"He did." She wiped the blade on the towel and tipped up his chin to shave his neck. "And with such charm that I couldn't be angry at him for it."

Ross gave a scoffing half-grunt.

"By the end of the dance, I knew that he was going to marry me. I never danced with another man after that. We were wed in June. And you—" She playfully tapped the tip of his nose, earning a scowl from him. "You were on the continent by then, fighting old Boney, seducing Spanish women, and not giving a single thought to some miss whose waltz with you was stolen away."

A moment of silence fell between them, with only the scratch of the beard beneath the razor breaking the stillness.

He asked softly, "Did you love him?"

His unexpected question jolted through her. Hiding her unease, she traced her fingers down his throat to smear more of the lather across the stubble there and dodged, "I was very fond of him, and we had a good marriage. He was a generous and kind man who treated Papa and me well. He gave me everything I wanted." Her voice softened when she added, "Eventually, even the child I wanted. But by then it was too late."

When he opened his eyes to look up at her, she could read the truth in their blue depths—he knew she'd never loved David. Thankfully, instead of pressing her about it, he asked, "He didn't know about Ethan?"

"I didn't know," she whispered, following along with her fingers over his soft skin in the wake of the razor. She prayed he couldn't feel the trembling in her fingertips at revealing these secrets to him. "Not until after the funeral, when the estate was being settled. That was when I knew I had to flee London, that I had to do everything in my power to protect my baby." *Then and now.*

"The courts would have waited to see if you delivered an heir before granting the inheritance to another," he reminded her gently. "You didn't have to flee."

She stilled, her fingers in mid-caress against his neck. Not daring to raise her gaze to meet his, afraid of the accusation she might see there—or worse, pity—she trained her eyes on her fingers and welcomed each beat of his steady pulse beneath her fingertips. Alive and strong…so intoxicating as it echoed up her arm and down into her breasts, reminding her unwittingly of the life she'd forged from the ashes.

"You are assuming that I would have lived until my confinement if I hadn't," she answered, so softly that barely any sound passed her lips. Then, with a burst of inner strength, she lifted her gaze to meet his. "But I did flee. And we survived."

Falling silent then, she returned to her task, carefully shaving away the last of the beard, even as her hands trembled from her memories of that horrible time. She didn't regret the lengths she was forced to go to in order to hide her child's existence from Vincent, but she would never be proud of them.

When the last of the lather was scraped away, she set down the razor and then gently wiped the remaining bits of soap from his neck with the towel.

"There." She trailed her thumb along the edge of his jaw and back to his ear to gauge the closeness of the shave. "Nicely done." She crooked a smile. "And no earls were harmed in the process."

He quirked a half-grin at her quip and rubbed his hand over his face. "How do I look?"

As she tilted her head back and forth, pretending to study him, she couldn't prevent the catch of her breath at how handsome he was, how piercing his blue eyes as they gazed up at her. With the beard gone, he looked so much as he had ten years ago that she ached with a deep longing for the past. Her fingertips itched to touch him, to stroke over the smooth planes of his face and feel his warmth and strength. He would let her, she knew. If she reached out and touched him, if she dared to caress him—

She would be lost.

"You'll do." She forced a teasing smile and drew her traitorous hands into fists, turning away before she could be tempted further. "Don't forget to pay your barber on the way out. We put nothing on tick here, so—"

His arm went around her waist. She gave a soft cry of surprise as he tugged her to him, bringing her down onto his lap.

"Your turn." His eyes gleamed mischievously as he daubed a drop of lather onto her chin. "Hand me the razor."

Her mouth fell open. He grinned at her shocked expression and playfully placed a dollop of lather onto the tip of her nose.

She laughed, so hard that her shoulders shook with it. Oh, how good it felt to laugh! His arms tightened around her as the deep sound of his own laughs rumbled inside her.

For a moment, she forgot that she was perched across his thighs, forgot that she was still wearing her old-fashioned night rail that billowed around her like a ship's sail. She forgot everything except how wonderful it felt to be with him like this and buried her face against his neck.

"How do I not remember you?" he murmured incredulously as he nuzzled her temple, his laughter fading. "How is that possible?"

Her heart skipped, once, before it leapt into a wild tattoo that pounded so hard against her ribs that she feared he could feel it. Slowly, she shifted back, their faces nearly even.

"It was fate's doing," she answered a bit flippantly, yet more breathlessly than she intended. "I wasn't meant for you."

His eyes turned predatory as he reached up to tuck a curl behind her ear. The gesture should have been one of comfort. Instead, it was pure seduction, one that twisted an unbearable ache low in her belly.

"Not then, no," he acknowledged in what was little more than a husky purr. "But are you meant for me now?"

The heat of him tickled down to the tips of her bare toes. Electric. Thrilling. *Dangerous.*

How easy it would be to surrender, to simply turn toward him and whisper *yes*…

He would give her pleasure, a man with that body and those eyes, one capable of making her laugh with abandon. One with the reputation of a rake and the soul of a patriot. One who thought she was beautiful even with a scar marring her cheek. For a few hours in his arms, his body moving over hers, moving inside hers…*bliss.*

Until he slipped from her bed.

Then it would end. How could it not, when it could only ever be physical between them? He would give his body but not his heart, not to a woman who didn't trust him enough to share her identity. Not to a woman whom he would never love once he learned who she was and the havoc she could wreck upon his life. And in the throes of passion, if he called out her name, the name that was nothing but a lie, how would she bear it?

"No." She blinked hard to clear the sudden stinging from her eyes. "I'm not."

When she slipped from his lap, she froze. Her stomach lurched into her throat.

A man stood in the doorway at the top of the stairs, leaning a hip against the frame, casually watching them. At his side, his hand gripped a pistol.

"Well then." The man crooked a brow, his gaze sliding between the two of them. "Apparently, I've been going to the wrong barber."

CHAPTER 16

*R*oss stepped protectively in front of Grace, who had paled as white as her night rail.

"Don't be frightened." He squeezed her arm to reassure her. "This is my brother Christopher."

"That does not make this any better," she bit out in a hissing whisper in his ear, her fear turning to simmering anger. She folded her arms over her breasts as she tried to hide behind him. "I'm in my *night rail!*"

Ross bit his cheek to keep from laughing. The brave woman who had tied him up and then coerced him into helping her had been stopped in her tracks by modesty. But he couldn't hold back the possessiveness that warmed his chest at noting that she hadn't cared about wearing the night rail in front of him.

"It's all right," Ross returned over his shoulder. He somehow managed to keep a straight face as he lied, "He's going to be a vicar."

A groan of mortification rose from her. "*Not* any better!"

He couldn't help but laugh, and received a slap on the back from Grace.

He turned to face her, taking her shoulders and carefully

keeping as much of her hidden from Kit's view as possible. Odd, that he didn't like the idea of his brother looking at her in her nightgown any more than she did. "Go change while I talk to Kit. I'll introduce you when you're dressed, all right?"

She gave a grudging nod, then leaned around him to shoot a murderous glare at his brother.

"Vicar," Kit reminded her apologetically, holding up his hands in a gesture of innocence.

"*Carlisle*," she flung back.

With a toss of her head, she stalked into the adjoining bedroom. The door slammed shut.

"So," Kit drawled, amusement coloring his voice, "you've gotten yourself an asset."

"I've gotten myself a hellcat," Ross corrected with a grimace.

"And here I was, worried about you as a fugitive on the run, alone." Kit grinned admiringly. "Not so alone after all."

Ross leveled a quelling look at him. The very last person he wanted to discuss with his brother was Grace. That unwillingness was born of unrealized possession and utter confusion. And a hell of a lot of frustration. So he drawled instead, "Picking locks again, I see."

Kit slipped the pistol into its holster beneath his jacket. "Practicing for the gaol cell they're going to toss you into."

"Thank God."

He grinned as he hugged Christopher. Too many times in the past fortnight he'd been certain he'd never see his brother again. Now the rush of relief nearly overwhelmed him.

He slapped Kit's shoulders as he stepped back. "Evelyn got the message to you without any problems, then?"

"You have no idea," Kit muttered with a pained expression.

Ross laughed. "Thank heavens for bored shipping heiresses!"

He was more grateful than he could ever express to Evelyn Winslow for delivering the message, and to Kit for believing her. For the first time since he jumped into the Channel, he had hope.

"Ellsworth sent me here, but…" Perplexed, Kit glanced around the old groom's quarters. "What is this place?"

"A property he lets out to an artist for use as a studio." That was as much of an explanation as Ross was willing to give. He was one of a handful of people who knew the secret life that the Marquess of Ellsworth was leading, and he planned on keeping it that way. Even from his brother. "And the only safe place for us to stay in London."

Kit arched a curious brow. "When did *you* become an *us*?" He sat on the chair, settling in for a long story. "Start from the beginning, and don't spare the details."

With an aggravated sigh, Ross leaned against the wall and told his brother everything that had happened during the past few weeks, from the moment he found the list of names and could finally make all the connections between Wentworth and the French. Kit knew about the original letter, knew about Sir Henry's murder and why Ross was relentless in hunting down the traitors. But he didn't know anything about the past month, how Ross stole the list of names from the embassy, how he found the other documents that all pointed to Wentworth's guilt. So he detailed his every move, until he reached the point where he'd forced his way into Grace's cottage. Then details became heavily censored.

Kit listened intently, without interrupting. Thank God. Because he had every right to say *I told you so.*

As an agent working secretly for the Home Office, his brother had been invaluable in providing advice and connections during the past year. But Kit had thought him reckless from the beginning for going after Wentworth alone and had warned him that there would be no one to help him if something went wrong. That had launched the fiercest argument of their lives, with Kit publicly threatening to become a vicar in retaliation. *So my older brother won't be the only one who martyrs himself,* he declared right in the middle of Lord Hawthorne's ball the night before Ross left to return to Paris. He'd departed without a goodbye from his brother, not knowing when—or if—he'd ever see Kit again.

But now, Christopher was here, coming to his assistance when he needed him. Ross had never felt more gratitude for his brother in his life.

"And the woman?" Kit prompted as Ross reached for his shirt to dress.

He yanked it on over his head and tucked it into his breeches. "Her name is Grace Alden." Or at least, that was the name she used. It rankled him to know that she still didn't trust him enough to share her true identity. "I came across her in Sea Haven, and she agreed to help me travel to London."

"You're in London now. So why is she still with you?"

A damnably fine question. "Because in exchange for helping me, I agreed to help her secure her son's inheritance." Not a lie. But also not the reason she was still with him. Kit was right. He should have sent her packing back to Sea Haven by now, promising to help her *after* he was exonerated. Whenever that was. *If* that ever was.

No. The reason she was still here was that he simply didn't want to part from her.

"What does that entail, exactly?" Kit pressed, the suspicious agent in him rising to the surface.

"Hire a solicitor, make a few inquiries, serve as a character witness…" He shrugged a shoulder and fastened up the half dozen shirt buttons at his neck. "I told her that I couldn't make any promises on how successful I'd be."

Especially if he went to the gallows. Which was still a very real possibility.

"There are lines that agents should never cross with their assets." As Kit kicked his boots up onto the washstand and leaned back in the chair, he eyed Ross with a close scrutiny belied by his casual posture.

"Then it's a good thing that I'm not an agent and she's not an asset." He shrugged into his plain brown waistcoat and grumbled, "And no lines have been crossed."

Although not for lack of trying.

That thought only tightened the coil of frustration inside him until he thought it might just snap. No other woman had ever gotten to him the way Grace had. And not only physically, although he certainly wanted that pleasure. No, the woman had proven herself to be so much more than just a beautiful companion. Brave, brilliant, fierce, determined—

For once, he found himself respecting a woman for more than her physical attributes. It was damnably disconcerting.

"Does she know what you've been up to?" Kit asked quietly.

"Yes." He grabbed the hem of his waistcoat and yanked it into place.

"Yet she didn't turn you over for the reward."

"No." He pulled at each shirtsleeve in turn. "She's loyal."

When Kit said nothing, Ross glanced up at him, and his brother wordlessly leveled an accusing stare.

"No lines have been crossed," Ross repeated firmly.

"*Yet.*"

His mouth twisting in aggravation, he smacked a hand at Kit's boots, to make him drop his feet to the floor. More out of irritation that his brother could practically read the thoughts swirling through his mind than so he could use the mirror over the washstand to tie his neckcloth.

"Does she look familiar to you?" Ross asked as casually as possible, keeping his gaze on his reflection and his face inscrutable.

"No, and I'd remember that scar," Kit commented, completely unaware of the anger that off-handed comment shot through Ross.

She was stunning, damn it. Even with that scar. No, stunning *because* of it. He couldn't think of a better symbol of the contradiction she embodied than that scar—a life of struggle branding the beautiful woman beneath.

"Should I recognize her?"

Ross finished the knot and turned away from the mirror. "I suppose not." He couldn't fault Kit for not remembering her when he couldn't do the same. "Besides, Grace isn't your worry." No, she was a problem all his own. A deliciously enticing, incredibly frustrating problem. "The worry is what we do next. All I have is a handful of stolen documents, and they're not enough." He raked his fingers through his hair, his frustration mounting. "I need indisputable proof that puts Wentworth in Le Havre with the French."

"You're thinking of his personal diary," Kit said knowingly.

"Yes." A man like Wentworth would certainly keep a journal—in fact, he'd keep two. One that he could hand to the authorities in case he was ever questioned, in which he lied about his daily activities and recorded nothing but a fabricated, unblemished existence. And the real one that acted as his account book, in which he detailed all his illegal transactions, including bribery, murder, and treason. "It's his life. He won't have it far from his reach." It would be here in London, and in his private residence. He wouldn't risk keeping it at his office in St James's Palace. "The question is, how do we get it?"

Kit stood and turned to look out the window, pulling back the gauzy lace curtain to peer thoughtfully down at the alley below. A quiet gesture, one that could have been confused for contemplation, except that Ross knew that Kit was one of the best agents the Home Office possessed. That glance outside was one of survival, to make certain he hadn't been followed.

"We can search his house, but you'll have to wait to do it," Kit warned.

Hell no. Waiting was the last thing he could do. Not only was his own safety placed at greater risk each day he failed to act, but so was the safety of every man on that list. "I'll do it tonight."

"No, you won't." Kit let the curtain drop into place and turned away from the window. "The ambassador's masquerade ball is tonight, and he won't cancel it, not even in the face of the turmoil you've unleashed inside the Court. If anything, he'll make certain to host it because he won't want to appear to be anything less than fully devoted to the crown." He shook his head at the futility of what Ross was proposing. "All of Mayfair will be there. You'll be walking into a lion's den."

"All of Mayfair," Ross repeated thoughtfully. At the devilish plan forming inside his head, he smiled slowly. "All of them in masks." *Perfect.*

"Oh no." Kit's face turned grim. "That was *not* a suggestion."

"A crush of masked guests? Seems like the perfect cover to me." It was also the easiest way to gain entrance to the house. No one would give a second thought to a masked man entering along with the rest of the guests, his face safely hidden.

"Until you reach the front door," Kit reminded him pointedly. "Something tells me that neither of us made the guest list."

"Ellsworth most certainly did." As the most respected peer in England, Dominick Mercer received invitations to nearly every society event held during the season. But as one of England's most eligible bachelors, he rarely attended in order to avoid marriage-minded mamas and sisters eager to attach him to their families. Most likely he wouldn't be planning on attending tonight, and Ross could take his invitation. "We're of a size. Behind a mask, I'll resemble him enough that no one will suspect I'm not Ellsworth. Once inside the house, I'll sneak up to search Wentworth's study and bedroom."

"That floor will be guarded." Kit folded his arms over his chest, eerily reminding Ross of their late father whenever he disapproved of whatever antic his sons had done. "How do you plan to sneak past them?"

He frowned. "I'll need a distraction."

"You'll need me," Grace answered as she entered, putting the last of her hairpins into place.

Ross swept an appreciative glance over her, taking in the way she looked in the morning sunlight in a simple muslin dress, her toffee-colored hair now upswept to reveal a stretch of elegant neck.

He needed her, all right. More than she realized.

Her eyes shined with determination. "I'll create a distraction for you."

"Absolutely not." He'd already placed her into more danger than he should have. The last thing he would do was dangle her beneath Wentworth's nose like a shiny bauble. "I told you, no more play acting. I won't let you take unnecessary risks for me."

"What better idea do you have?" She looked at Kit and shook her head. "*You* can't do it. Ellsworth will be expected to arrive with a female guest." Her assessing gaze swept over him from hat to boots. "And I don't think you'd look attractive draped in ribbons and lace."

Kit winked at her. "You'd be surprised."

She laughed softly.

Ross clenched his jaw. *Nothing* amused him about what the two of them were proposing. If anything happened to her—

"I won't let you do this." He fought back the urge to shake sense into her. "This isn't like pulling the wool over the eyes of some country constable or a group of soldiers. These men are trained guards." And killers. "They'll see right through your act."

"What act? I just need to be female. I think I qualify, don't you?"

"Nicely," Kit murmured, raking a glance over her that set Ross's blood boiling.

He glared murderously at his brother, which only seemed to amuse Kit more. "We'll find another way."

"There is *no* other way." A mix of aggravation and resolve thickened her voice. "Something tells me that the marquess rarely attends such events without a female companion. If you show up without one, pretending to be Ellsworth, you'll draw too much attention." She held his gaze in hers and repeated softly, "You need me, Ross."

The harsh taste of capitulation rose on his tongue. *Damnation.* She'd cornered him. Again.

"Fine," he bit out, having no choice but to agree. "But you'll do exactly as I say."

She gaped at him, as if offended. "Don't I always?"

Good Lord, did she actually believe that? If so, he was in far worse trouble than he'd thought.

"So you take Ellsworth's invitation," Kit agreed, calling their attentions back to the plan for the evening. "That will let you through the front door."

Ross nodded. "Wentworth's personal assistant will most likely be overseeing the guards, so he's the one we have to distract."

"Just point him out to me in the crowd." A determined smile lit her face, but Ross would have sworn he heard uncertainty in her voice.

As he looked at her, with bravery visible in the firm hold of her shoulders, his chest tightened. He knew then that he'd protect her at all costs, whether she liked it or not. Including with his life.

"Once you have his attention, I'll sneak into Wentworth's private rooms and search for the diary. Alone, while you remain downstairs." He fixed a look on her that brooked no argument. "Then at midnight, we'll leave the party under the cover of all the noise and revelries of the unmasking."

"I-I have to be gone before then. I can't remove my mask, can't show my face—" She turned her head just slightly to the side, to hide her scar, but she couldn't hide the way she paled at the idea of the unmasking. "No one can see me there."

"Then perhaps you should stay here." He would give his right arm if she'd do just that.

"No. I'm going with you." Then her shoulders sagged almost

imperceptibly. But Ross noticed. Sweet Lucifer, he noticed *every-thing* about her. "But I'm not taking off my mask."

"Grace, if the unmasking will be a problem—"

"Then don't take off your mask," Kit interjected, anticipating Ross's objection but answering the complete opposite way. "You'll be leaving right at midnight anyway. No one will notice a single reveler still behind her mask as she heads out the door."

A flash of jealousy speared Ross at the look of gratitude Grace sent his brother.

"Once you have the diary, you'll come back here. In the morning, we'll take all the evidence you've gathered straight to St James's Palace." Kit's gaze softened somberly. "Hopefully, they'll believe you."

Ross sent up a silent prayer. But he'd never been fortune's favorite son.

"We'll need evening clothes," Grace reminded them. "And full-face masks."

Kit nodded. "I'll fetch them and return—"

"No," Ross cut in. "There's too much risk that you'll be followed. Ellsworth has to bring them."

Kit didn't argue that point, knowing he was right. "Fine for you. We're the same size. You can borrow a set of my evening clothes. But for her"—his eyes slid to Grace—"Ellsworth won't know which of his paramours to request a gown from that would fit her."

"I'll fetch my other dress." She hurried into her bedroom, calling out over her shoulder, "You can use it to match my measurements!"

When she was safely out of earshot, Kit murmured to Ross, "I like that one. She's got courage." He grinned. "I like her a lot."

Ross's gaze followed after her in a mix of admiration and concern for her. *So do I.*

CHAPTER 17

"There." Ross finished pouring the last bucket of hot water into the small tin bathtub behind the screen in the corner of Grace's bedroom. "All ready for your bath, my lady."

"Hmm." She bent over to dangle her fingers into the water to test its temperature and gave him that taunting smile he'd come to know so well. And liked a great deal. "Well done."

He set down the pail and watched as she considered half a dozen small bottles of oils sitting on a stand beside the tub. "Don't be so surprised."

"I'm not." Selecting a purple bottle, she removed the stopper and wafted it beneath her nose, then drizzled several drops into the water. Her eyes gleamed mischievously in the soft glow of the lamp burning on the wall sconce. "But if you grow bored of being an earl, you've got a second career ahead of you as a footman."

"I can only imagine the kind of reference you'd write for me," he drawled sardonically at her teasing.

She laughed, the lilting sound nearly as warm and sweet as the jasmine-scented steam rising from the tub. His chest clenched in visceral response. Being with her like this as she prepared for the evening felt relaxed and familiar. It felt...*right*.

He hadn't had that feeling in his life for far too long.

She paused, glancing around the small space behind the large Japanese-painted screen. "Why are there his and her bedrooms up here?" A small furrow creased her brow. "Shaving accoutrements in your room, a bathing area in mine…What kind of artist needs a space like this in his studio?"

"One with a scandalous reputation." Not technically a lie, although describing the artist's reputation as *scandalous* was the understatement of the year. "Vincenzo's famous for paintings that can be rather shocking. Including nudes. Most likely his models change up here."

She arched a brow. "Or perhaps this is where Ellsworth meets his mistresses."

Cheeky chit. "That, too."

"Where do you meet your mistresses, Spalding?" she challenged with a glint in her eyes. "Do you keep his and her bedrooms above a carriage house, as well?"

Not a chance in the world he'd answer *that.* "Who can afford mistresses? I'm only a footman in training."

She laughed again. When the delicious sound faded, she said sincerely, "Thank you for helping to heat and haul the water." She smiled in gratitude as her hand reached up to unbutton the front of her bodice. "A hot bath is going to be heavenly."

"You're welcome." Instead of leaving, he propped a hip against the wall, as if settling in to shamelessly watch her bathe.

Her hand stilled on the third button. "Don't you have your own clothes to ready?"

"My clothes are boring." He trailed a deliberate gaze over her. He did it only to goad her into another match of verbal sparring, taking a perverse pleasure in the chess-like matches of conversation they regularly fell into. But he also genuinely appreciated the view. "Yours are much more interesting."

She swept her gaze pointedly over him and crooked a brow in chastisement that he wore very little, having stripped down to his breeches to help haul up the water. "Yours seem to be nonexistent."

He winked at her. "We footmen in training don't make enough to afford proper attire."

Her eyes narrowed in rebuke, which only made him grin. "You'll never finish dressing for the masquerade at this rate."

He shrugged a dismissing shoulder. "I'm your selfless servant, here to help you however you need." He gestured toward the room. "Light your lamps, fetch your water..." He opportunistically drawled, "Wash your back."

Her lips pressed into a tight line. "I'm quite fine on my own, thank you."

"Pity," he sighed, yet made no move to leave.

Reaching the end of her patience, she snapped, "You cannot stay and watch me bathe!"

"Why not?" He glanced over his shoulder at the bed and the gold satin ball grown laid out for her. Ellsworth had gotten it from one of his paramours and sent it over, along with all the accessories necessary for her to be tonight's shiniest jewel. "After all, I'll have to help you dress when you're finished."

"Only with the final hooks that I cannot reach on my own."

"Pity. Ah, but there *is* a corset to be tied."

"No, there's not. That dress's bodice is based on the old-fashioned Italian dresses. It's reinforced and doesn't need a corset to hold me in place." Her cheeks pinked alluringly at that explanation. When he didn't reply to that, she eyed him suspiciously. "Aren't you going to say that's a pity, too?"

"To you wearing one less layer of clothing?" he asked in a seductive purr, raking his gaze over her. "Heavens no."

Her faint blush turned positively scarlet. Her reaction had him pondering all the other delicious things he could do to her to deepen that blush, to turn her soft breath into pants, and to part her lips beneath his so that he could take possession of that enticing mouth. He'd only been teasing her, but now—

Pity indeed.

"Stop that," she admonished, although her protest could just as easily have been a soft plea to continue, for all the lack of force behind it. "You're incorrigible."

"Can't help it." He took another languid look over her, from head to toe. This one, he noted with selfish pleasure, made her tremble. "You'd blame a man for wanting to watch a beautiful woman bathe?"

"Something tells me that you want to do far more than watch," she grumbled warily.

He feigned wounding. "Am I so easy to read?"

"Like a library." When he began to protest, she continued, "With every book spread open wide." She cut him off before he could interrupt, "Beneath magnifying glasses."

He threw back his head and laughed. Sweet Lucifer, how much he enjoyed sparring with her! More than with any other woman he'd ever known. Spirited, sassy, so very quick—a man could cut himself on that sharp mind of hers. A beautiful body to arouse the senses, a wit to challenge the intellect, and all of it wrapped in a woman whose mystery only served to draw him more strongly.

With a grimace of irritation, she shooed him away. "Go on! Go!" She took his shoulders, turned him around, and pushed him away. "Out from behind the screen!"

Calling out as he walked away, he repeated her words from Sea Haven, "You don't have anything I haven't seen before."

A high-pitched growl of frustration broke across the room. Seconds later, a wet flannel smacked him in the middle of his back.

"Unlike all those other women you've known," she called out, safely hidden from view behind the screen as she undressed—and for the moment safe from his retaliation—"*I* prefer to bathe in peace."

"*All* those other women?" He bent over to snatch up the wet facecloth and set it aside on the dresser. He enjoyed raising her ire more than he should, but he couldn't help himself. She was beautiful simply passing from moment to moment, possessing more presence than most of the women in Mayfair. But when she was angry, she was downright glorious.

A part of him wanted nothing more than to enrage her, just to see how magnificently she'd glow.

"I cannot even begin to imagine how many there must have been in your life," she taunted.

The sound of softly splashing water arrested him in mid-step. His gut tightened reflexively at the image that played through his mind of Grace slipping seductively into the warm bath. Naked.

"Thousands and thousands," he quipped. *Not a single one of them like you.* The raw honesty of that thought startled him.

When she laughed, he smiled wickedly to himself and turned around to look at the screen. The temptation to walk back to her was nearly irresistible.

"More like half the women in England," she corrected amid more soft splashes and the exotic scent of jasmine wafting its way across the room to him, "if rumors are to be believed."

"Rumors can't be trusted," he threw back wryly. "It was far more than that."

"Well, you *are* a rake, after all."

And who are you? Besides the woman who was driving him to distraction?

He rubbed at the tension knotting at his nape and trailed his gaze around the room, hunting for any clues to her identity that she might have accidentally left in view...*Nothing.* After all this time with her, he was still no closer to learning her identity, and the more time they spent together, the more she drove him mad. The most alluring yet mysterious woman he'd ever met, and the most damnably frustrating.

Tonight, they would walk into the lion's den. He needed to be able to trust her, to place his life in her hands. How did he do that, when he didn't even know who the hell she was?

His gaze fell onto the bed. He shook his head at the juxtaposition of the threadbare travel bag she'd carried with her halfway across England sitting next to a satin gown that cost more than Alice Walters would make in ten years at her apothecary shop. She was a daughter to one gentleman, a wife to another…yet also a mother who willingly became a fisherman's widow to protect her child. How did he reconcile the two very different parts of her life?

Who the blazes *was* she?

Throwing a glance over his shoulder at the screen, he crossed to the bed. "If you need any help washing your back, just ask," he called out, continuing with their taunting flirtation because she expected it. "I'm very good at washing women's backs." Only a fleeting guilt pricked at him as he searched her clothes. "And other places."

"With your reputation, I would have thought you'd prefer your women dirty."

He smiled at that barb—and at the frumpy night rail as he set it aside. He paused to consider her belongings, all spread out before him. There was nothing there to give any clues to who she was. Not even a monogrammed hairbrush or hand mirror. "Is that how you prefer your men? Disheveled, sweaty…" He grimaced painfully at his own uncontrolled behavior around her. "Shamelessly eager and panting for you."

From behind the screen, there was a silent pause. His arrow had stuck home.

What he wouldn't have given for a glimpse of her at that moment, sitting there naked and stunned that he dared say something so blatantly sexual to her, her sensuous lips parted and her eyes glazed with arousal. Would her nipples be puckered into hard, little points, ready and aching to be suckled? Would her bare thighs be warm and slick with soap? Would he taste the jasmine clinging to her skin, the tangy taste of it on his tongue when he licked down her body, until he had to duck his head into the water to reach—

"I prefer them to be gentlemen," she countered, once she'd found her voice.

Defying the softly splashing water's siren song, he took a moment to gather himself. "Then that leaves me out."

She gave a loud, haughty sniff and sarcastically drawled, "Pity."

He grimaced. He deserved that jab, yet he also found it alluring. Only Grace could make him want her more by attempting to drive him away.

He reached for her bag and searched it, checking every inch. "Perhaps you haven't been around enough sullied men," he mumbled, frowning into the bag.

"Perhaps you haven't been around enough unsoiled women."

"Dear God, why would I want that?" At that moment, there was only one woman who concerned him, and it was all he could do to shut out the images of her naked body bathing in the warm, soapy water and focus on the task at hand. "After all, half the women in Europe are simply holding their breaths as they wait for me to wash their backs."

He barely registered the splash of water behind him or her reply to that as he ran his fingertips over the inside of the bag. Then he felt it—a tear. Only a small rip in the lining, but its straight line was a purposeful cut, not the kind gotten through wear or accident. He carefully reached beneath the lining, and his fingertips brushed over something small and hard. He pulled out the hidden object and held it up.

A gold ring, decorated with rubies and diamonds. It shimmered brightly even in the dim lamplight, leaving no doubt that it was real.

He held it up toward the lamp and read the faint inscription on the inside of the tiny band...*To S, Love always D.*

Was it a leftover memento from her previous life? Had to be.

She was beautiful, but living under the pretense of being a fisherman's widow wouldn't have brought her anywhere near the kind of man who could afford to give her a bauble like this. Neither was she the kind of woman who sold her intimacies. Had to be from her gentleman husband then, who had to be *D. S.*...her initial?

Fresh frustration spiked inside him. If a few letters were the only clues he had, he would never be able to piece together her identity.

Love always. His chest constricted at that, but he refused to consider why. It couldn't be jealousy. Not of a dead man.

No, it was betrayal. She'd misled him by implying that she hadn't loved her husband. But *this*—keeping a ring like this was an act of love.

"You make it very difficult to trust you, Spalding," a soft voice said from behind him.

He froze. Caught. *Christ.* Rapidly trying to think of any viable excuse for what he'd done, he turned to face her—

And lost his breath.

She stood in front of the screen, wearing only a large towel wrapped around her, with her toffee hair falling loose around her bare shoulders and down her back. Her skin was pink from the hot water, with jasmine-scented droplets still clinging to her bare arms and legs. She reminded him of that Botticelli painting of Venus being born from the sea, with all of nature begging to be allowed to worship at her feet.

But it was her gaze that arrested him. She looked at him not in anger, but with acute disappointment.

He'd rather have had her rage. It would have been less biting.

"When you didn't answer, I thought you'd left to dress." She lowered her gaze to the bed and the clothes he'd gone through, and her disappointment deepened. "If you wanted to search my things, you could have simply asked. I would have let you."

Damnation. He gritted his teeth. She would *not* make him feel guilty about being cautious. Not with everything he was up against. His survival depended on tonight's search going perfectly, and he wouldn't let it be jeopardized because a former society miss refused to divulge her name.

"I did ask," he countered. "But you refused to tell me who you are."

"I told you that I would tell you later."

"You said when we reached London. We're in London now." He pinned a narrowed gaze on her. "Who are you?"

She paused, as if she might surrender her name after all. But then she shook her head, as obstinate as ever in keeping her secrets. "You wanted me to trust you, and this is how you repay me. By showing no trust in me." She held out her hand. "Give me my ring, please."

Her refusal to answer even now stoked his anger, and he stalked toward her, forcing her to retreat. The hand that had been outstretched now clutched at the towel to keep her covered from his eyes. Oddly, that only aggravated him more.

"I'm supposed to trust a woman with my life when she refuses to tell me her name?" he shot back, backing her up against the wall. He held up the ring in front of her and demanded, "Who's D?"

"My late husband." She snatched the ring away and drew her hand around it in a tight fist, as if afraid he might try to take it back by force.

"That's not what I meant."

She countered defiantly, "I know."

With a frustrated growl, his patience snapping, he leaned in and trapped her between the wall and his body.

Her eyes blazed, which only drew him closer, until her softness pressed along the front of his hard body. She shuddered at the contact with a soft little gasp that parted her lips in sensuous invitation. One he couldn't help staring at, and longing to accept.

"You hid that ring from me. What other secrets are you keeping?"

"More than you can count," she shot back, but the aching breathlessness of her voice undercut whatever indignation she'd been aiming for.

His lips curled into a wicked smile he couldn't prevent. He knew why she was trembling and panting. *That* wasn't anger.

He leaned closer, so close that her lips tickled against his as he murmured, "I think there are some secrets you want to share."

The heated flare of her eyes proved she knew he didn't mean her name.

"In fact, I think you're aching for it." He admitted in a rasping half-growl, "God knows I'm aching for you."

His arousal pulsed fiercely in his gut, flamed by the way she stared at his mouth. The front of her body moved against his with each panting breath she took, rubbing the towel against his chest and unwittingly sparking a delicious friction that stirred his cock.

He trailed a single fingertip down her bare arm, from her shoulder to her wrist, when what he wanted to do was grab her into his arms. Yet that slight touch was enough to blossom a trail of goose bumps in its wake and prove to him how much she wanted his hands on her. "Why deny yourself the pleasures you want so badly?"

"I can't," she protested, her hands grasping tightly at the towel.

"Oh, I very much think you can."

Unable to resist, he lowered his mouth to kiss her bare shoulder. When she sighed softly, making no move to stop him, he brushed his mouth over that delectably smooth patch of skin where her shoulder curved into her neck.

"You want me inside you, making you writhe in pleasure until you shatter from it." He smiled sinfully against her throat, reveling in the sensation of her pulse racing furiously against his lips in arousal. "You're craving it, so much that you're trembling." He placed a soft kiss against the tender flesh behind her ear, and she shuddered with longing. "Say yes and let me give you that pleasure."

"I can't...endanger Ethan." Her whisper came between soft pants, her breasts rising and falling rapidly beneath the towel.

"This has nothing to do with him." He dared to caress his hand over her bare shoulder in a featherlight touch. Then lower, to stroke his fingers teasingly across the top of her chest, where he could feel her racing heartbeat. "This is only about you and me, and letting ourselves have what we both want." His lowered his head to trace an open-mouth kiss along her jaw. "And I want you, so very much."

"But we—we don't trust each other."

"I *do* trust you. I trust you with my life." He nuzzled his mouth against her cheek, her jagged scar rough beneath his lips. He kissed it reverently. "So trust me enough to make yourself vulnerable to me, in every way."

His lips found hers. When her mouth softened with a sigh, he slipped inside to take sweeping licks into the delicious depths of her kiss, to tauntingly joust with her tongue and arouse her to give over to the hot ache he knew burned inside her. To the undeniable attraction that had crackled like electricity between them since the night of the storm.

"Say yes." He took her bottom lip between his and gently sucked. "Say yes and let me give you every pleasure you deserve."

"Ross." His name was a tortured whimper of capitulation as a hot shudder of permission swept through her.

She slowly opened the towel.

CHAPTER 18

*G*race caught her breath as the rush of cool evening air swept over her naked body, followed immediately by the heat of his predacious gaze. It raked over her with agonizing deliberateness, taking her in, from her breasts with her nipples puckered hard and aching with arousal, across the flat of her belly to the curls between her thighs, and down her bare legs. Dear God, he was like a wolf, contemplating which parts of her to devour first.

"So beautiful," he rasped out as he swept his hand down her front, teasingly stroking over her breasts before resting on her lower belly, his fingertips mere inches from the throbbing that sprang up at her core. He lowered his mouth to hers and murmured against her lips. "And finally mine."

His hand lowered possessively between her legs. When she gasped at the intimate touch, he drank in the soft sound. Then he smiled against her mouth when his fingers caressed her and the gasp became a throaty moan.

Grace closed her eyes and clung to him, the world around her falling away until all she knew was the delicious teasing of his fingers. For once, she didn't let herself consider the risk she was taking by letting herself be vulnerable like this, or if wanting this touch made her wanton. If stepping her legs apart so he could stroke more deeply and moaning when his mouth slid down her body to kiss at her breasts made her just another one of those merry widows who threw themselves at him. If the pleading whimper that fell from her lips when he pulled her nipple deep into his mouth and suckled hard acknowledged exactly how much she longed to be ravished by him.

None of that mattered as she arched herself against him. The need to be in his arms, to wrap herself around him until his strong body was both surrounding and surrounded by hers, had nothing to do with any of that. Just as it had nothing to do with the past ten years of loneliness and fear.

This desire was only for Ross and for the way he awakened the woman sleeping inside her. It was only his touch she craved, only his strong arms she wanted around her. His mouth caressing its way down her body, the same mouth that challenged her to such verbal sparring that her blood heated from it. His heroism and inner strength, his goodness. *All* of him aroused her and made her yearn for the pleasures she knew he could give her, every brilliant, dedicated, daring inch of him.

When he sank to his knees, she opened her eyes to find him staring up at her. His blue eyes gleamed like the devil's own, not leaving hers even when he placed a tender kiss against her soft belly. Not even when he nuzzled his mouth and chin against her feminine curls, as if daring her to stop him.

But she didn't—oh, how could she? She wanted this with every ounce of her being. When a knowing smile curved at his lips as his hands stroked up the backs of her legs and squeezed her bare bottom, Grace bit her lip to choke back a moan.

"You smell like jasmine." He nuzzled her again, this time slipping his mouth shamelessly lower until his warm lips tickled against her wet folds. "Everywhere."

His words spun through her, winding more tightly the throbbing need coiling inside her. She clutched at his broad shoulders to keep her knees from buckling beneath her.

Still, his gaze didn't leave hers, and a sinful glint shined in his eyes. "I wonder," he murmured against her, placing a kiss to her inner thigh, just below her aching center. "Do you taste like jasmine, too?"

She tensed with pulsating longing. "If you—"

He licked her. The sensation of his tongue stroking along the seam of her sex tore a shuddering gasp from her. Her fingernails dug into his hard shoulders as she fought to regain her breath.

When he did it again, this time stroking deeper into her folds and flicking across the aching nub hidden within, her hips bucked. "Ross!"

A pleased groan rose from the back of his throat. The soft sound rumbled into her, and her sex tightened reflexively, eagerly yearning for more. He obliged, this time swirling the tip of his tongue down into the hollow at her throbbing core. The rush of pleasure was so intense that she moaned, shamelessly not bothering to even attempt to silence herself.

He nudged her thighs farther apart with his shoulder until she stood wide-legged, all of her open to his seeking mouth that continued to kiss, lick, and nibble in turns, sometimes taking great greedy mouthfuls, other times only a tiny suck. Heavens, how good it felt! He had a hot ache pulsating inside her, her fingers and toes tingling, and her hair standing on end. Never had she experienced an intimacy as powerful as this. *Never.* And only, she knew, because it was Ross who was bringing her this pleasure.

"Do you have any idea how hard it was to sleep with you in the same room all those nights, wanting my mouth on you like this?" he murmured against her. Each hot word tickled over her wet folds and intensified the tightening tension. "Fantasizing about how good you'd taste beneath my lips, how soft you'd feel beneath my hands? You drove me mad."

"You deserved...to be tortured," she panted out.

She felt the tickling rumble of his laughter against the lips of her sex, which only increased the heated ache for him there. "Almost begged you to tie me up again."

She tossed back her head to laugh and was rewarded with a plunge of his tongue deep inside her, then another and another as he thrust into her, mimicking with his mouth the sexual act she was certain he wanted to perform with his body. She trembled as that tempting thought settled wantonly over her and flamed her fire to an all-consuming blaze.

His gaze lifted to hers, as if making certain she was watching his mouth working against her as he gave her the most intense sexual pleasure of her life. That same connection to him that she'd felt since the night of the storm engulfed her, only now so much stronger, so much more powerful. All of her shook wildly, and she grasped at his shoulders, desperate to keep his mouth on her as he drove her toward bliss.

He murmured soft words of encouragement against her as he circled her throbbing clitoris with his thumb, teasing but not fully touching. Such a wicked tease! To hold back from her what he knew she needed—

She needed *him.* She thrust her hips against him, begging in incoherent mewlings and whimpers for release.

He closed his lips around the aching point and sucked.

An exquisite pleasure shot through her, straight out to the tips of her fingers and toes. She bucked violently, and he grabbed onto her hips to hold her still, so he could suck again, harder and longer than before—

"Ross...*Dear God.*" She arched herself into him, her hands clenching around his head, her fingers wrapping in his silky hair. "Ross!"

A hoarse cry tore from her as she broke against his mouth. The ruby ring fell out of her hand and dropped unwanted to the floor with a soft ping. She shuddered as a wave of pleasure crashed over her with such force that it knocked the air from her lungs.

She crumpled against the wall, her upper body sagging as his large hands around her hips kept her pinned there on her feet, his mouth still against her. She quivered helplessly against his lips in a series of soft tremors as the intensity of the pleasure ebbed, leaving bliss behind.

She reached a hand down to stroke his cheek as he continued to kiss her tenderly, the soothing softness of his lips helping her come down from the heights he'd shot her to. Hot tears stung at her lashes and blurred his handsome face, and she choked back words of affection poised on her tongue. She'd given her body, but she wasn't yet ready to open her heart. There was still too much at risk.

When she'd finally caught her breath, he placed one last reverent kiss against her inner thigh and rose to his feet. He gathered her into his arms and buried his face in her hair.

"I'll bring you that pleasure again, if you let me." He shifted his hips until he pressed the hard length of his erection against her soft belly. There was no mistaking how much he wanted her. "This time, I'll be inside you when I do."

She clung to him, wanting exactly that. Now that he'd awoken the yearning woman inside her, she was far from satiated. If he could devastate her with only his mouth, she shivered to think of what his hard body could do.

"Grace," he whispered, his hands stroking over her as she pressed against him. "My beautiful Grace."

Grace.

Instantly, her blood turned cold. The fires he'd set only moments before were doused, and remorse replaced her desire.

"No." She tried to pull away, but his arms tightened around her. "I can't! I can't—I won't—no!"

He froze, as startled as if she'd struck him. Then he cupped her cheek against his palm and lifted her chin until he could search her face. Confusion flickered briefly in his eyes.

Then they darkened as his face grew hard. "Why not?"

She shook her head and pushed against his chest, but he refused to release her. "Ross, please—"

"You want me as much as I want you." He strummed his thumb over her bottom lip, and she closed her eyes against the sweet torture of that touch. "I felt your desire for me." He leaned in, brushing his mouth along her cheek to her ear. "For God's sake, I *tasted* it."

She choked back a sob. He had no idea how his whispers affected her, how the mix of arousal and anguish warred within her.

When she could no longer stop a tear from sliding down her cheek, she pulled away, turned her back to him, and reached down for the towel. Her hands shook as she wrapped it around herself.

He took her shoulders from behind, his mouth lowering close to her ear, so close that his warm breath tickled across her cheek. "You want this, too."

"More than you know." She ached to let him make love to her —but it wouldn't be with *her*. It would be with the woman she was pretending to be.

She couldn't have borne it.

The harsh edge to his voice cut like a blade of ice—"You still don't trust me."

"I *do* trust you." She trusted him with her life. But she couldn't yet trust him with her son's future. Until she did, she couldn't give herself—her *true* self—to him.

His hands dropped away. "Apparently, not enough."

CHAPTER 19

*R*oss glanced out the window of the carriage as Piccadilly passed by in the darkness. "Almost there."

Grace gave a tight nod. Whether because she was becoming more nervous the closer they drew to the ambassador's townhouse or because she was still upset over their earlier argument, he couldn't have said. Not that it mattered. He knew the rules between them now. He wouldn't attempt to touch her again.

He grimaced into the darkness. If tonight didn't go as planned, he wouldn't have the chance to.

"If we're caught," she said softly, "Ellsworth will be arrested for helping us."

Us. His damnable heart skipped, even though he knew it was nothing more than a slip of her tongue. He'd like to believe that she thought they were still in this together, but he knew better.

"In for a penny, in for a pound," he muttered. The Ellsworth town coach that they traveled in was unmistakable, with its gold coat of arms emblazed on the doors, but they'd had no choice. Ross *was* Ellsworth to everyone in attendance tonight, and they couldn't very well arrive in a hired hackney or on foot. "Don't worry about Mercer. He knows what he's doing."

Ellsworth was already in their mess up to his noose-clad neck if they were caught, but Ross had made certain that he couldn't be implicated. Amid the commotion and confusion that would surely happen, there would be enough wiggle room for the marquess to claim that he had attended the masquerade himself, that it was him and not Ross who had handed over his invitation, with his paramour wearing a similar gold brocade gown to the one draped over Grace.

What a magnificent gown it was, too. He didn't have to look at her to see it—the vision of her in it had already imprinted itself upon his mind.

When she'd stepped from her room and grudgingly asked for his help in fastening the last of the tiny hooks on the bodice, he'd been so struck by the sight of her that he'd been speechless. He let her believe his silence was lingering pique over their earlier encounter. No. It was because of the way the brocade shimmered like gold foil over her hips, how the sculpted bodice pushed up her breasts against the low-cut neckline and displayed their top swells. The gold color accentuated the highlights in her toffee-colored hair, piled in a riot of barely controlled curls on top her head. Midway through fastening her up, when she commented that the dress was so tight that she'd not had room beneath for a chemise, he nearly said to hell with the masquerade and scooped her into his arms to ravish her. Her true identity be damned.

Frustration flared hotly. For Christ's sake, he could still taste the tangy-sweet cream of her on his tongue, still feel her hot passion and pulsating pleasure when she broke. Having experienced that, he couldn't regret claiming that taste of her. Or wanting to feast on her until he was fully satiated, until the unbearable craving for her was satisfied.

But she refused to let herself share in that pleasure.

He bit back an aggravated laugh. How ironic that the most beautiful creature he'd ever known, one of the most inherently passionate and enthralling, had erected a wall of ice between them. And how fitting that his mystery woman now wore a mask that hid her completely from the world, except for her sensuous mouth, making her even more delectably enigmatic.

Fate was surely laughing at him.

When the carriage stopped in front of the townhouse, he sucked in a mouthful of air and checked his own mask. Time to focus.

Ross stepped to the ground, then turned back to offer his hand to Grace. She hesitated.

"I'll tell the coachman to take you back if you've changed your mind." He hoped she would ask for exactly that. He didn't want her here. Despite all that had happened between them—and all that hadn't—he still wanted to protect her. "You don't have to do this."

She squared her shoulders. "Yes, I do."

Then she took his hand and descended gracefully to the footpath.

As he led her toward the front door, he leaned over to bring his mouth close to her ear, his hand on her elbow pulling back to slow their approach. "If you're going to do this," he said, resigning himself to her involvement, "then you've got to do it for all you're worth, understand? Play the part as if you were born to it."

Water could have frozen on the smile she sent him. "I *was* born to it."

That reminder of her hidden identity pricked at him. But there was no time for an argument now. "Tonight, you are Francesca Bianchi, Contessa di Capodimonte, an old friend of Ellsworth's whose family holds lands near Florence. She's in London for the season, ostensibly to become reacquainted with European society after the death of her husband last year."

"And *un*-ostensibly?"

"Let's just say that the real contessa is most likely spending her evening becoming reacquainted with Ellsworth." His lips curled into a knowing half-smile. "*Well* reacquainted."

"Which is why he has no problem staying out of sight tonight while you pretend to be him."

"Dominick Mercer is one of the most-respected peers in the Lords, with an impeccable reputation above reproach. He is staid, conservative, and always restrained when he is in public. In private, he's none of those things."

"I see."

Ross was certain she did. She was no stranger to living beneath a well-crafted façade.

"Then we have a small problem." She gave a slight nod to the guests gathered just outside the massive front door as he led her inside the townhouse. "I cannot speak Italian."

"Then you're in luck, because you don't have to." He helped her remove her fox stole and handed it to the waiting footman, then froze for a beat at how lovely she looked, her bare shoulders as smooth and silky soft as the gold gown that shimmered exotically beneath the chandeliers. He couldn't help but let his eyes travel appreciatively over her, and murmured honestly, "Your beauty speaks for you."

Not breaking his gaze from hers, he took her hand and placed a lingering kiss in her palm. When she shivered, he felt that tremor travel up her arm, all the way to his lips.

She peered at him from behind the mask with dark desire, her lips parting delicately. Not even her satin gloves and his cotton ones could mute the fierce tattoo of her pulse when he caressed his fingertips over her wrist.

That she could want him so much that just his nearness made her tremble should have stroked his arrogant male pride. Instead, it irritated the hell out of him. How could she deny herself what they both yearned to have?

He forced his attention back to the task before them, placed her hand on his arm, and led her into the entrance hall. He handed his invitation to the Master of Ceremonies, who did not call out the guests' names in order to heighten the drama of the midnight unmasking.

"We're in this together now," he whispered to her as the man bowed to him and handed back the invitation. Instead of tucking it inside his jacket, Ross continued to hold it in his hand while he led her forward. "If one of us gets caught, so does the other."

"Then let's not get caught."

"I don't intend to."

Good God. How had his life come to this? Six months ago he never would have imagined that he'd now be wanted for treason and the murder of his mentor, that the country he loved would consider him a traitor. That he would be sneaking into a party under mask in order to prove his patriotism with a woman who refused to let him bed her.

Tonight, one way or another, the charge of treason would be decided.

His eyes slid sideways to Grace. Not so the other problem that plagued him.

"My apologies for our earlier argument," he offered sincerely as he lowered his mouth close to her ear, although he wouldn't have been overheard in the noisy crush around them if he'd shouted. "I'm certain you have good reasons for hiding your identity." *Whatever the hell they were.* Although, to be honest, what frustrated him wasn't that she was keeping her identity from him, but that she was keeping *all* of herself from him. Including her vulnerability and trust.

"I do." Her eyes glistened behind her mask.

"And I apologize for going through your things this evening." He gave her hand a repentant squeeze as it rested on his arm. "It was wrong of me."

She accepted that with a piqued sniff. "Yes, it was."

He couldn't help but chuckle. Her ice might have been melting beneath his contrition, but her claws were as sharp as ever.

"I understand why you would want to keep that ring." Yet it

still grated like hell. "A reminder of how much you and your husband loved each other."

She stiffened. The tightening of her fingers on his arm stopped him. He looked down at her, but the mask prevented him from reading any emotions beyond what he could see in her eyes and lips.

"I didn't keep it because of that." The chocolate depths of her eyes grew dim. "I have it because it's the last of the jewels I was able to take with me when I fled London. I'll have to sell it in order to afford a solicitor to press for Ethan's inheritance." Then her voice grew impossibly softer, but every word pierced him. "It has nothing to do with love."

A peculiar relief seeped through him. What kind of marriage she'd had shouldn't have been any of his concern. Yet it mattered. A great deal.

"You won't have to sell it," he promised, leading her forward. "I'll take care of everything."

He didn't dare glance her way to try to read the expression in her eyes, because he was afraid of what she'd be able to read in his.

As they moved into the two-story high stair hall, the townhouse unfolded around them, with the massive marble staircase marking the center of the building and a circuit of reception rooms on the ground and first floors encircling it. The house was built expressly for parties like this, with each room connecting so that guests could see and be seen walking through the house in two great circles. First on the ground floor, with its dining rooms and withdrawing rooms, then up the stairs to move through the long gallery, the music room, and the card room, before circling back down the stairs to join the dancing in the grand salon. The house could easily accommodate several hundred people, and it seemed that just that many—or more—were crowded into its rooms tonight. Most likely because the guests wanted to be titillated by stories of the Earl of Spalding's treason.

Ironically, Ross was glad for it. More people made hiding

among the crush easier, where he would be nothing but another masked man.

He innocently dropped the invitation to the floor. It was immediately lost beneath the trample of feet and so unable to place any blame on Ellsworth if Ross were caught.

He led her toward a spot near the wall from where he could assess the entire room, including the wide marble stairs that wound their way to the first floor. The crowd pushed in around them, the noise of conversation and laughter nearly drowning out the quartet of musicians playing from the first floor balcony.

"I don't want you taking any unnecessary risks tonight." He snatched two flutes of champagne from a passing footman and handed her one. "Understand?"

Ignoring that, she took a sip of champagne and glanced around at the crowd. "So what's next, now that we're through the door?"

He carefully kept his eyes moving around the room, turning his body halfway toward her. "Do you see those three men standing on the first floor landing, guarding the second flight of stairs? The ones without masks." None of the servants were wearing masks tonight, to distinguish them from the guests, including Wentworth's assistant and guards. "Do you see the one dressed in all black?"

She took her time in letting her eyes sweep around the room and on past the man he described. "Yes."

"He's Sir Anthony Patton, Wentworth's secretary, and the man in charge of making the party go smoothly. Including making certain no guests stray where they shouldn't, especially up to the private rooms on the second floor."

"Exactly where you're headed."

He nodded and took a swallow of champagne. "To his study. A man like Wentworth wouldn't hide anything of value in his bedchamber. Too many women coming and going who might stumble across it and decide that he pays his blackmailers better than his courtesans. It will be in his study." *Somewhere*. He trailed his gloved fingers along her arm, the gesture familiar and just innocuous enough that he could get away with it as Ellsworth. "I need you to distract Patton so I can sneak upstairs." With his fingers at her wrist, he gave her a hard look from behind his mask. "Then you are to leave the party immediately."

She froze with the glass halfway to her mouth. "We're supposed to depart together at midnight."

"Change of plans. I'm not leaving until I have that diary." He tossed back the rest of the champagne. "I want you to leave without me, and I'll meet you back at the carriage house."

"That's not what we agreed to. Your brother's expecting us back at the—"

"Christopher is waiting outside, to help us in case something goes wrong." When her lips parted in surprise, he explained with a faint grimace, "I know my little brother. Kit would never let me go into a fight without him. He'll be here to help if you need him."

Saying nothing to that, she took a delicate sip of champagne, her eyes thoughtful. If he could have seen beneath the mask, he knew she'd be frowning with worry.

"But you won't need him," he assured her. "Because as soon as I'm up those stairs, I want you to leave. Have the footman at the door send for Ellsworth's coach, and return to Chelsea. Understand?"

"No. I won't leave you here."

"You have to. I can't search for the journal if I'm worried about you."

She turned her face away, but not before he could see the emotion in her eyes. "I don't like this."

"It's the only way." He would *not* put her life in any more danger. In an attempt to ease the grim seriousness hanging over them, he added, "Besides, it's nothing new for us. We seem to be making a habit of being separated at masquerades."

Her slender shoulders sank, the small movement setting her

gown to shimmering like gold foil beneath the chandeliers. "I didn't like it then, and I don't like it now."

Lowering his lips to her ear, he placed his hand at the small of her back. Something Ellsworth would never have done in public, not even at a masquerade. But he didn't care. He *had* to touch her. "Tell me. If you could do it all over, would you still let my waltz be stolen?"

She paused for a moment, one heartbeat in which the two of them were frozen in place while the rest of the world went on around them. Partygoers talked and moved past, and beyond the salon door only a few feet away the whirling rows of couples reached the end of their dance. The musicians played the final resounding notes. Applause sounded, so did laughter. Isolated bits of conversation hung in the air, made overly warm by the crush of bodies and the beeswax candles that lit up the rooms and turned the crowd into a sparkling sea of glittering jewels and shimmering silks. All hidden behind the safety of masks.

But Ross saw and heard none of it. His attention was riveted on Grace as he waited for her answer.

"Yes." Her eyes glistened. "Because that night brought me David, and David gave me Ethan. I would never change a single event in the chain that brought him to me."

His throat tightened. "Of course not."

"But if not for Ethan," she whispered her confession, resting her hand on his arm, "I would have danced with you all night, if you'd have let me."

A knot coiled in his gut, a roiling mix of pleasure, arousal, and loss. *I wasn't meant for you...*He prayed that she was meant for him now.

From the salon, the orchestra sent up the first flourishes of a waltz, and a palpable excitement pulsed through the party.

Not letting his eyes stray from hers, Ross bowed and held out his hand. "Then this waltz is mine."

"After ten years." Disbelief colored her voice. She was just as struck as he that fate had brought them back to this moment.

He smiled. "Better late than never."

Her eyes shining, she slipped her hand into his and allowed him to lead her toward the ball.

As they neared the salon, a movement on the stairs caught his attention. The two guards with Patton stepped away. One man made his way down to the ground floor and the other up the next flight of stairs, which were recessed back from the formal staircase with its wrought iron railing and marble steps that curved up to the first floor's reception rooms like something from a palace. The second set of steps went straight up an enclosed stairwell that marked the boundary between public and private. The same route that Ross had to use to access the study.

He stopped her and with a glance drew her attention to Patton, who now stood alone. "Looks like we still won't have that waltz." He grimaced. "It's time. Are you ready?"

With a nod, Grace's presence changed as she slipped easily into the role of contessa. She flashed him a bewitching smile, then dribbled the rest of her champagne over her bodice. "Just watch me."

Trailing her fingertips down his arm, she slipped away.

WITH THE HEAT OF ROSS'S GAZE WARMING HER BACK, GRACE weaved her way through the crowd toward the stairs.

She didn't dare glance over her shoulder to look at him, but she could feel him, once again sensing that inexplicable connection to him. He trailed slowly after her, always several feet behind, as if he were just another man in the crush who happened to be moving in the same direction. But all pretense of being Ellsworth had now vanished, leaving only his true self—resolute and focused. *Dangerous.* Those same qualities she'd glimpsed in him from the beginning, once again heightened, just as they'd been the night of the storm when he'd come crashing back into her life. But the desperation of that night had been replaced by determination.

She wouldn't let him down.

Her smile not fading, despite the frantic pounding of her pulse, she reached the stairs. She paused with feigned uncertainty as she took a glance around her, then another up the stairs at the floor above, as if she didn't know where she was going. Then she glided up the stairs, her head held high. Every inch of her now proclaimed her as the regal Incomparable she'd once been so many years ago, but she now knew that so much more lurked unseen beneath her surface. She had the wits for deception, and the courage to carry it off.

When she reached the top of the stairs, she gave Patton a smile and slowly passed by on the landing, as if she was just another one of the guests who had moved upstairs to the circuit of reception rooms there. Then she stopped. With a touch of embarrassment, she turned and walked back toward the second set of stairs, her hips sashaying as she began to climb them.

"My lady." A deep voice and a hand to her elbow stopped her mid-step.

With a painful rush of fear and triumph, she glanced over her shoulder—

Patton.

Remaining right where she was on the second step, she slowly turned to face him, giving him a cool and assessing look. He could have been considered handsome, she supposed, with black hair and brown eyes, patrician angles to the planes of his face, and full lips now curved up into arrogant smile at having caught her. She also supposed that his broad shoulders on an otherwise lean and muscular frame would have been appealing to some women.

But compared to Ross, he was greatly lacking.

"Can I help you?" The same conceit that colored his smile laced through his voice.

More than you realize. "Unless the retiring rooms in England are much different from the ones in Italia," she commented in a thick Italian accent, standing her ground on the stairs, "I do not suppose that you could be of much help."

His mouth twitched at that, as if he didn't know for certain whether she was flirting with him or making fun. "The ladies retiring rooms are downstairs."

A tingling at the backs of her knees alerted her to Ross's presence as he walked up the marble stairs and onto the first floor landing, treating her as any other woman in the crowd. Which meant that he ignored her, except for a slight glance of bored interest as he approached, presumably on his way to the men's smoking and game rooms.

She descended to the landing to give him clear access to the next flight of stairs and brushed her hand at the drops of champagne on her bodice, drawing Patton's gaze to her bosom. "I have had an accident and need to attend to my dress." She reached out to brush her other hand against Patton's jacket sleeve to keep his attention. But she needn't have worried, because her hand at her neckline kept the man's eyes glued to her. "Do you see what I've done? Such a mess all over my front, no?"

Ross's step hitched. His back straightened for a beat before he sauntered on past her.

But Grace noticed his fleeting jealousy, and her heart soared.

"Would you be a gentleman and show me to the retiring room?" She linked her arm through Patton's in invitation to be escorted away, and away from Ross to give him an opportunity to sneak up the stairs.

From the corner of her eye, she saw Ross stiffen when she touched Patton. His jaw tightened, and beneath the mask, she was certain his expression was murderous.

Patton let her lead him a few feet away toward the stairs, then stopped. He turned her toward the balustrade overlooking the stair hall below and pointed. "Down there, my lady."

"Where?" She turned him sideways as she leaned over the balustrade, feigning ignorance.

He gestured toward the main doors leading into the grand salon. "The small door there."

She leaned out further. Her hand fiercely gripped his as if afraid she might fall, yet really to keep his attention on her and away from Ross. "I do not see...where?"

"To the left of the salon. The footmen below will be able to direct you." He leaned in uncomfortably close over her shoulder, and she suspected from the way his head tilted downward and his eyes latched onto the top swells of her breasts that he was hoping to see all the way to her navel. "While I would be very pleased to escort you downstairs, my lady, I cannot leave my post. But do come back later. I would be most amenable to taking a stroll around the party with you."

He shifted back to take her hand and lift it to his lips to kiss it, the same way Ross had done earlier. But it was all she could do not to snatch her hand away with a shudder.

Yet she forced a smile and purred, "Perhaps I will see you later then." *When hell froze over.*

As she slowly descended the stairs, she turned back to glance over her shoulder. A look that Patton pompously thought was for him.

Ross was gone.

CHAPTER 20

*R*oss sauntered as quickly as he dared up the second flight of stairs and out of sight of Patton and the rest of the ambassador's guards. He would have laughed to himself at the performance Grace had just put on if watching her with Patton hadn't infuriated him so. When this night was over, they were going to have a long talk about what kind of distractions were proper. And how she was never again to draw a man's attention to her breasts.

"Unless it's mine," he growled.

He headed down the hall to search for the study. He opened the first door—a bedroom. He moved on to the next.

"You there!" A man called out from the other end of the hall, where he'd just stepped out from the backstairs. "This floor is off limits. You need to return to the party."

But Ross ignored him and opened another door.

"I said you need to leave. *Now.*"

Ross muttered a curse. "I'm looking for a bottle of cognac." He flashed a friendly smile and flung open another door. His heart skipped. Wentworth's study. "And none of that watered down grape juice they're passing off downstairs as brandy."

"Stop where you are!" The man was enormous, all muscle and gritty brawn, and he drew his hands into fists as he started toward Ross.

Ross's smile faded. "No need for violence. I'm only searching for a good drink."

But the man kept coming, charging at him like a bull.

"All right, all right! I'll go." He turned around and started back down the hall toward the stairs, but he could hear the man's approaching steps as they grew nearer. Every inch of him alert, he waited until the guard was just behind—

He snatched up a silver candlestick holder from the narrow table beside him, pivoted, and swung.

The hard blow hit the man on the side of his head and sent him spinning. He staggered back against the wall. Then his eyes rolled up in his head, and he sank to the floor, unconscious.

Ross bent down to grab him by his arms. "I was wrong," he muttered through gritted teeth of exertion as he pulled the large man inside the nearest room. "Apparently, there was a need for violence after all."

After tying him up with a length of cord from the drapes, with knots not nearly as good as Grace's, Ross left him there and returned to the study, taking the candlestick with him and lighting it on the hallway wall sconce. With a glance over his shoulder, he slipped inside, closing and locking the door after himself.

He set the candle on the desk and began to search the room. Each drawer in the desk, then the side tables...but finding nothing. There were too many books on the shelves to go through them all, and no point since Wentworth most likely owned them only for show. So he returned to the desk and searched it again, this time removing every drawer completely and inspecting each from all sides before returning it.

He replaced the last drawer and bit back a harsh curse,

running a hand through his hair as he stepped back to survey the desk. Frustration boiled inside him. He *had* to find that diary, or every struggle during the past year would come to nothing.

Worse. He'd entangled Grace into his mess, and there was no way to protect her if he was discovered. He hadn't lied to her. If he was caught tonight, so was she. That was the *very* last way she should be repaid for helping him since he crawled ashore in Sea Haven. For God's sake, she'd sewn up his wounds even after he'd taken her captive and before she'd arrived at the notion of having his help in gaining her son's rightful inheritance. When she'd had the opportunity to turn him over, she'd not taken it. Even tonight she didn't need to risk herself in order to help him, yet she was doing just that. He'd been wrong to ever assume that her involvement was only mercenary when her own safety was the last thing she'd been worried about.

Being an ambassador had once been all that he'd wanted from his life. But now—

He wanted Grace.

The thought startled him, but the truth of it was undeniable. He wanted her. *All* of her. Her courage and determination, brilliance and sharp wit, competence and confidence—she was all that every other woman wasn't. When this fight was over, when he was exonerated and the traitors stopped, he would finally claim his waltz with her. And more.

But now he had to focus. Giving up on the desk, he scanned the room. That diary had to be in here somewhere. *Had* to be! Wentworth would keep it near him at all times. But where?

His eyes landed on a narrow side table pushed against the wall between the two tall windows. There were no drawers in it, and the underside of it was clean because he'd already checked it. Yet the wood grain on its front...*warped*. Significantly. He crossed to the piece and ran his hand over the front panel. Smooth, but with a telltale dip where the grain changed direction, indicating the

joining of two separate pieces in an attempt to hide it. No furni-
ture maker of any quality would make a piece with a flaw like this.
And Wentworth certainly wouldn't have paid good money for it.
Unless...

He pressed his fingers along the edge where the tabletop met
the base, feeling for any kind of mechanism—

His fingertip snagged on a piece of wood just barely
protruding from the flushed edge. A smile crooked his lips. He
pressed it, and a secret compartment sprung open.

His pulse pounded as he reached inside and pulled out a
sheath of papers. He scanned them. Not the diary he sought, but a
list of names and bits of information about each man. With a jolt,
he realized what he held in his hands—the list of men working
with Wentworth to trade secrets to the French, along with information that Wentworth could use to blackmail them. Or take
them down with him if any of them ever decided to confess.

He folded the papers and tucked them inside his breast pocket,
then closed the secret compartment and muttered a low curse.
These papers were helpful, but he needed the diary. Without it, his
only evidence for placing Wentworth in Le Havre was a single
signature. Not nearly enough to prove the ambassador's guilt and
his innocence.

Finding no more hidden spaces in the table, he turned back to
the room to begin a new search, and his gaze landed on a
matching table sitting between two bookshelves on the other side
of the room. He offered up a silent prayer that it also held a
matching secret compartment, and matching evidence of treason.

As he started forward, a shout went up from the hallway.

The guard had been found. More noise, more shouts, now
followed by the sounds of running feet and doors rapidly opening
and closing—

Christ. He was caught.

With a longing glance at the table, he ran to the window and
threw up the sash, just as the men reached the study. The door

handle rattled, then fists pounded against the locked door as Ross slipped outside onto the narrow brick ledge supporting the window casement, two stories above the side garden. He eased down the sash and pressed himself flat against the house at the side of the window, out of sight. The toes of his Hessians jutted out over the edge into thin air.

"Wonderful," he muttered sarcastically as he scanned the building's flat façade.

There was no ledge connecting the windows that he could inch his way down and use to escape through another room. And of no use even if there had been. Wentworth's men would be searching every room on this floor and standing guard at both ends of the hall, preventing escape down either set of stairs. No, there was no way back into the house, and no way back into the party to fetch Grace. She was on her own now.

So was he, with no means of escape. He couldn't help a dark laugh at the picture he'd create when dawn came and he was discovered, a masked man standing on a window ledge two stories above London. He couldn't think of anything worse, unless fate decided to punish him further by making it rain.

Rain. A desperate idea struck, and he slid his gaze to the side, holding his breath and praying...

He let out a heaving sigh of relief at the downspout that ran along the side of the house, from the roof all the way to the cistern in the cellar. Carefully, he inched his way to the edge of the casement ledge. His hand shook as he reached out to grab the downspout to climb to the ground. Suicide, most likely. But he had no choice. If he stayed here, death was certain.

He glanced at the ground in the darkness, thirty feet below him, and muttered, "Better to die in a flowerbed than by the hangman's noose."

But that sentiment gave little comfort as he swung over onto the downspout. The metal groaned beneath his weight, and he froze. *Please, God, let the fastenings hold!* After several deep breaths, with his hands gripped around the metal pipe and his feet pressed against it like a vise, he slowly lowered himself, yard by terrifying yard. The metal groaned and squealed as he climbed down as carefully yet as quickly as he could.

Above him in the study, he heard the door break open. The jamb splintered with a loud shattering as the lock popped and the door was flung open. Shouts and running boots filtered through the window into the night.

Christ. He moved quickly now, half-sliding down the downspout to move as far away into the darkness below as possible before the men discovered his escape route. But the metal length groaned beneath his weight and jerked sideways.

The last bracket tore loose from the brick. The pipe bowed out from the wall with a loud *pop.*

Ross jumped. He fell the last six feet into the side garden, his boots hitting the ground and throwing him forward. He tucked his shoulder and rolled, stopping just inches from a large blackthorn bush whose thorns were so big that he could see the thumb-sized spears shining in the moonlight.

He climbed to his feet, brushing the dirt and grass off his shoulders.

A surprised cry sounded behind him. He spun around. Among the shadows beside the house, a woman leaned back against the brick with her skirts bunched up around her waist. In front of her, staring at Ross with the same shocked expression, stood a man with one hand down her bodice and the other between her legs, his breeches down around his knees.

For a moment, none of them moved, all three simply staring in surprise. Then Ross cleared his throat and called out, "Lovely evening, isn't it?"

He nodded a polite goodnight and sauntered away toward the street at the front of the house, leaving the startled couple staring after him.

GRACE NERVOUSLY TAPPED HER FINGERS AGAINST THE CHAMPAGNE flute and once more glanced toward the marble stairs. A half hour had passed, and there was still no sign of Ross. She waited in the stair hall and pretended to enjoy her glass of champagne while her heart ticked off the seconds growing closer to midnight.

Ross had told her to leave, but still she'd stayed as the clock grew closer to the unmasking. Leaving him behind was unbearable. So was the thought that he might have been caught, that even now he was being led away by the authorities. That she might never see him again.

Her hand trembled as she raised the flute to her lips. A drink was the last thing she wanted, with the champagne tasting like vinegar on her tongue. But as she tilted back her head to sip, her eyes darted to the gold clock hanging on the wall, once more surreptitiously checking the time—

Five minutes to midnight. Panic squeezed her chest. *Oh God, where was Ross?*

But she didn't dare linger any longer. If her mask came off and someone recognized her, it would mean more than the end for Ross's burglary—it could very well mean the end for her and Ethan. Even now, so close to obtaining the information that would exonerate Ross, she couldn't put her son in jeopardy. With no other choice, she turned to leave the party.

A hand clasped her elbow from behind, stopping her.

Relief poured from her in a long sigh, and her shoulders eased down. *Thank God.* Ross had been delivered safely back to her. And just in the nick of time.

With a bright smile, she turned. "I thought you'd—"

Patton. The glass slipped from her fingers.

He caught it before it could fall and smash on the floor. Handing it off to one of the passing footmen who were busily bringing in dozens of trays of champagne for the midnight toast, he smiled at her in amusement. *Amused*...when what pounded through her was sheer terror.

"It's midnight," he told her, wrapping her arm around his and leading her not toward the front door and escape but toward the blue drawing room and further into the house. "My watch is done, and now I can enjoy the party for the rest of the evening." His eyes darted toward her breasts, and she forced back a shudder and threw a desperate glance toward the stairs. Dear God, *where* was Ross? He added in a murmur, "And enjoy the guests."

She remembered to use a fake Italian accent as she gestured back toward the door. "But I was leav—"

"Lingering right below where I've been standing all evening." Arrogance seeped from him at the idea that she'd been waiting for him. What would the egotistical fop say if he knew she was waiting there for a far better man? "Sending all those half-veiled glances up the stairs in my direction."

"I would never be so desperate." The only desperation she felt was to flee.

He chuckled, not releasing her arm even when she tried to pull it away.

Instead of leading her into the drawing room, he pulled her aside into an arched hall running alongside the room. When she turned to face him in indignation, he stepped forward, forcing her backward with his body as he closed the distance between them and maneuvering her behind a marble column and thick growth of potted bamboo. Cleverly hidden from view of the party.

"I would be very happy to entertain you now, my lady," he drawled, tracing his fingertip along the edge of her low neckline.

"Contessa," she corrected haughtily, smacking his hand away. She trembled, unable to do anything to defend herself except for being as icy and insulting as possible in an attempt to drive him away. Because any cry for help would reveal her presence. And Ross's.

"Contessa, of course," he repeated with a smile that was

anything but apologetic. He lifted her hand to his lips and mumbled, purposefully low and fast, thinking she wouldn't understand, "Doesn't matter what a woman calls herself once you're buried inside her pussy."

The unintended anguish of his comment sliced into her, and she forced out, "Pardon?"

"I said," he murmured as he removed her glove and brought her hand to his lips, to suck at her fingers, "that tonight I would very much enjoy a private party."

Unable any longer to force back a shudder, she yanked her hand away. "I have grown bored of your party."

When she tried to step around him, he blocked her way. He audaciously trailed a finger from her throat down between her breasts.

"I'll give you exactly what you need to keep the boredom at bay, Contessa." He leaned forward and whispered hotly in her ear as his hand continued to draw a line down her body and across her belly toward the space between her legs, "*Una bella scopata.*"

That Italian she knew, thanks to the sailors in Sea Haven. "You arrogant—"

Noise erupted around them. Shouts and cheers echoed through the house as the clocks' bells tolled midnight. The orchestra sent up rounds of fanfare, and fireworks sizzled and boomed over the square fronting the house.

"Midnight," he explained loudly over the racket. "Time for your unmasking, contessa." He lifted his hand toward her head. "Then the real party can begin."

"No!"

He grabbed the ribbon tie at the back of her head and stripped the mask away before she could stop him.

He gaped at her, wide-eyed. Startled by her scar, he stepped back. "What the hell—"

In that moment of confusion, she shoved at him with all her might and sent him staggering backward. Then she ran.

She pushed through the crowd pressing into the stair hall. In her hurry, her shoulder hit one of the footmen and sent a tray of champagne glasses crashing onto the floor. Everyone turned to look, and panic consumed her. Covering her cheek with her hand, she shoved her way through the crowd, into the entrance hall, and out the front door. Fireworks rained in booming showers over the square, lighting the night in flashes of red and blue. Her chest burned as she gasped for air, yet she ran on, stumbling along the footpath in her desperation to flee.

"Grace!"

She halted and snapped her head up, straining to hear anything else but the roar of blood rushing through her ears.

A man hurried toward her from the dozens of people gathered in front of the square, from the hundreds more now emptying from the house to watch the fireworks—

"Christopher!"

His face was set hard beneath the dark shadows as he approached, made eerily demonic by the flashes of red and blue. But this devil was her savior.

He grabbed her arm and hurried her toward the line of carriages waiting in front of the house. "This way."

She craned her neck to search for Ross. "Where's your brother?"

He yanked open the carriage door and placed her inside.

"Christopher, where is Ross?" she demanded, her voice rising with fear.

"I don't know. I've been guarding the front entrance all night and haven't seen him come out of the house yet." He shut the door and shouted up to the driver. "Chelsea," he ordered. "And protect her with your life."

Ellsworth's driver nodded and flipped the ribbons, sending the team forward. The carriage rolled away from the house, quickly picking up speed as it moved through the dark streets of Mayfair and carried her away into the night.

"Please God," she prayed as she squeezed her eyes shut and rested her head back against the squabs. If Ross wasn't with Christopher— She shook her head, unwilling to contemplate the worst. "Please let him be all right...because he's a good man. Because he's a hero..."

Because I love him.

CHAPTER 21

Dear God, where was Ross?

Grace wrung her hands as she paced the length of the dark studio, unable to sit still. She'd been back for over half an hour, delivered safely to the door by the coachman, just as Christopher had ordered. For all she knew, Kit was still out there lurking in the darkness, keeping watch over her, while Ross was God only knew where. Possibly captured and being taken away to Newgate at this very moment. Or worse. If he'd been found by Wentworth's men—

No.

She wouldn't let herself consider that! He was fine. He was safe. He was making his way back to her even now through the moonlit streets. He *had* to be, because the alternative was unbearable.

She reached the end of the narrow studio and turned back, pacing like one of those animals in the Tower Menagerie that was cruelly trapped in a cage. By a trick of light, her gold dress shined silver in the slant of moonlight that fell through the oversized fanlight above the double doors, and her skirts swished softly with each step and turn. Otherwise, the building was as dark and silent as a tomb.

Not a tomb.

She pressed a trembling hand to her forehead. *Where was Ross?*

"Grace."

She spun around and strangled back a cry of relief.

Ross leaned against the closed wicket, having entered without her seeing him in her distracted worry. Dark shadows hid his face, but she recognized him from nothing more than his silhouette... the breadth of his shoulders, his chest that narrowed to his waist, his long and muscular legs. Just as she knew him from that inexplicable bond that had connected them since the night he arrived at her cottage. Perhaps even before that. There must have been a reason that fate kept bringing them together at the most important moments of their lives, why she felt as if a silk ribbon tied them together. A ribbon that wound around her even now, drawing her to him with a magical pull she couldn't resist.

The air between them crackled with electricity, so much so that the tiny hairs at her nape stood on end. Every inch of her tightened in nervous anticipation, and she'd never felt more alive in her life.

"I was worried about you," she confessed in a throaty whisper. She blinked hard to clear away the stinging tears that distorted the shadows until his silhouette was little more than a watery blur, like a ghost in the darkness. "When midnight came and I couldn't find you—" She choked, too overcome to put voice to her fears.

As if in answer, he slowly reached inside his jacket and held up a sheath of papers. "The men working with Wentworth. We've got their names now."

She forced herself to breathe against the riot of her churning emotions, but each inhalation seared her lungs. "The diary?"

"No."

That single word pierced her like a bullet, and she winced at the fierce disappointment that slammed into her. The man she loved had returned safely to her, but without what he needed to save himself. Yet every bit of strength she had was focused on simply remaining standing, instead of falling to the floor in sobbing gratitude for this reprieve, no matter how fleeting.

Silently, he returned the papers to his breast pocket. Despite the shadows hiding his face, she could feel the heat of his predacious gaze that only grew more intense, more electric, with every pounding heartbeat.

"Say yes," he rasped out hoarsely. The soft order drifted through the moonlight and shadows between them, wrapping around her, engulfing her...capturing her. No movement, no other sound. Only the fierce tattoo of her yearning heart and the quiet urging of his deep voice. "Say yes, and let me come to you."

Since Sea Haven and the night of the storm, she'd denied herself the pleasure of him because she'd wanted to protect Ethan, because she'd doubted him and the vow he'd made to help her. But tonight, when he'd had the opportunity to leave her, he'd returned. Just as he'd promised.

All the wariness and fear of making herself vulnerable rose to the surface, all the uncertainty and hesitation—all of it extinguished by the irresistible need to be in his arms. The man she knew she could trust with her life, and her son's.

"Yes," she breathed, so softly that the whisper was barely audible.

But he heard and stalked toward her, his dark gaze never leaving hers in the shadows. When he reached her, he cupped her face between his hands and seized her mouth beneath his.

Heat and need flared instantly between them. With a throaty moan, she wrapped her arms around his neck to bring herself against him. The warmth of him reached her through her dress, so did the hardness of his body pressing against the softness of her breasts and thighs as she molded herself against him, to be as close to him as possible.

"Grace," he implored in a throaty murmur.

Knowing what he wanted, she parted her lips beneath his, and his tongue plunged inside. No exploring or teasing licks this time —only hard and desperate thrusts that captured her mouth completely in a singularly focused kiss that left no mistaking the way he planned on possessing all of her tonight. One filled with such desire and longing that she shuddered beneath the intensity of it.

When he shoved his hands into her hair, pulling the pins loose and scattering them across the floor, she gasped at the rough caress. But he drank in the sound, cupping the back of her head to hold her still as he continued to ravish her mouth.

She trembled. This wasn't kissing—this was *need*. Raw, hungry…desperate. Beneath the onslaught of his kiss, she moaned with increasing desire.

She tore her mouth away to pant for air, but he gave her no quarter, his hands sliding down her back to cup her bottom through the gold brocade dress as his mouth found her neck. Her pulse spiked beneath his lips. He groaned a satisfied growl as the tip of his tongue flicked rapidly against her throat, as if he could lick up her heartbeat and devour her desire.

Squeezing her bottom, he pulled her against him. An electric yearning pulsed between her legs at the sensation of his hardening arousal jutting into her belly. Tonight he would be hers. For once there would be no loneliness, no emptiness, no doubt or fear —there would be only Ross, wanting her as a woman, making her feel beautiful despite the scar that marred her. There would be the absolute certainty of knowing that giving herself to him was right and good.

He trailed his lips over her chin to once more capture her mouth. So *very* good.

"You have no idea how much I want you," she murmured against his mouth.

His hand swept up her body to grab her neckline and yank it down, revealing a single breast to his eyes. With a wicked grin, he strummed his thumb over the already hard nipple, making it draw up even tighter in the moonlight. "I have a pretty good suspicion."

Then he darted his head down to capture her breast in his mouth, sucking so hard and deep that his cheeks hollowed with every fierce pull. She inhaled a shuddering breath when he gave her nipple a sharp nip, followed by a soothing stroke of his tongue that turned her gasp into a whimper.

Her fingers twisted in his hair, and she arched into him, bringing him even harder against her, thrusting her breast even deeper into his mouth. He drew back his head, releasing her breast from his lips with a soft *pop*. The circle where his hot mouth had been glistened wet in the moonlight. When he blew against her nipple, the rush of cool air against hot flesh was jarring and flared an unbearable throbbing between her legs.

"Ross!" She tossed back her head at the exquisite torture. Oh, that mouth! She knew the pleasures it could bring, and she wanted him to lick and suck everywhere, as much as she craved having her own mouth on him.

Her hands tore at his clothes, fisting his lapels and trying to rip the jacket right off his broad shoulders. She nearly groaned. He'd spent most of the day walking around in practically nothing but those tightly fitted breeches that flaunted his hard thighs and the large bulge of his manhood nestled between, driving her mad with the temptation he presented and the wicked fantasies she'd let spin through her mind. But now that she wanted to give herself to him, to feel bare skin against bare skin with no more barriers between them, too many layers kept him from her.

A cry of frustration poured from her. "Clothes," she panted out. "I can't—get them off—I can't—"

He grabbed her shoulders and bent her forward over the

worktable. His hand yanked at the back of her dress, and the brocade gave way with a loud rip. With her back bare to him, he shoved his hands beneath the gaping bodice and reached around her to clasp both breasts in his hands.

"Better?" he drawled hotly in her ear as he kneaded her breasts. His fingers teased at her aching nipples, twisting them, pinching and pulling, with an expertise that sent her head swimming. The roughness of his caresses made the ache between her thighs grow more intense, more demanding for release.

"I meant *your* clothes," she protested, closing her eyes against the sweet torment as she lay bent over the table, with Ross's large body leaning rapaciously over hers from behind.

He licked between her bare shoulder blades, sending a hot shiver curling down her spine. "But removing yours is so much more fun."

A delicious rush of feminine power surged out to the tips of her fingers and toes. "Then remove them," she ordered, her voice trembling with anticipation.

With a growl, he grabbed her dress and ripped the fabric, tearing down her back and over her buttocks as they jutted into the air. Another hard tug, and the skirt and petticoat ripped in two all the way down through the hem, leaving her backside bare to the moonlight and to the heat of his gaze.

The front of her dress fell away from her shoulders, to land in the crook of her elbows as she leaned on her forearms. She was naked now except for her stockings, all of her laid out bare and vulnerable across the table. Like a feast for him to devour.

"Sweet Lucifer," he murmured, reverently trailing his hand down her spine, from her nape to that point where it disappeared between her buttocks. Then he caressed his hands over her bottom and down the backs of her legs, to tease at the lace hem where her stockings clung to her thighs.

But she wanted his hands higher, *needed* to have him stoking the throbbing ache at her core until the pleasure burst through her.

In wanton invitation, she stepped her legs apart. "Please."

A low groan sounded from the back of his throat, and he swept his hand up between her thighs to cup her sex.

She quivered against his palm and fought back a shout of joy when he began to stroke his hand against her. Long, smooth caresses, each one growing harder and deeper, until he slid a finger inside her.

Her breath strangled, all of her tensing at the new intimacy. Then she relaxed with a deep moan and welcomed him into her warmth. A second finger joined the first, stretching her deliciously wider.

"Do you like that?" he asked, the low rasp of his voice mixing with the wicked teasing of his fingers to melt all the muscles in her belly.

"Yes! Dear God, yes..." Her heart pounded so hard that she knew he could feel it against his hand that still kneaded her breast, knew that he could feel the ache of desire throbbing against his fingertips. Each teasing retreat brought a swirl of his fingers, each returning plunge a delicious brush against the sensitive bead buried in her folds.

"You're so warm and soft," he murmured incredulously against her bare back. "So unbelievably tight."

His words stirred the flames burning at her core. Only Ross could create such sensations of yearning, along with a ravenous need to be satiated.

"So slippery smooth." He bit her shoulder, his teeth sinking into her flesh. She jumped beneath him at the jolt of pleasure-pain, and her sex clenched hard around his fingers. She felt his wicked smile spread against her back. "And ready."

"Take me." She glanced over her shoulder at him and pleaded softly, "Now."

In the moonlight, she watched him unbutton his trousers. His hand reached inside and pulled himself free from the layers of clothes he still wore while she was so brazenly draped naked across the table before him. Her gaze was riveted on his erection...magnificently masculine, long and hard, with a thick girth that made her tremble. The tip glistened in the moonlight with proof of his desire for her.

He paused to let her look, a smile quirking at his lips at her shamelessness. Then he stepped forward and guided himself between her thighs, sliding back and forth against her folds from behind until her dew slicked his length. Each forward slide tickled his tip against the aching bead at her core in a fleeting tease that had her writhing against the table in silent pleading for him to give her what she needed. Her body and soul had been waiting for over a decade to quench this thirst, and that it would be with Ross...perfection.

"Please," she begged, shaking. The unbearable ache threatened to consume her if he didn't put out the very fire he flamed. "Ross, please—now!"

With a single step, he pushed his hips forward and thrust into her. She cried out at being filled so completely, at being stretched open wide to take all of him in, and her body tensed beneath his. Ten years' abstinence made the moment feel almost like losing her maidenhead again. But this time, she knew what pleasures came next, and there was no fear of making herself vulnerable to him, of showing him with her body the affections she now held for him in her heart.

The fleeting pain vanished quickly, and in its place came the most wonderful sensation she'd ever known. Ross moved inside her so tenderly that tears formed at her lashes. Her body welcomed his deep and controlled strokes as his hips rocked against her bottom, as his hands soothingly caressed large circles over her bare back. That inexplicable connection they shared bonded them together now, the invisible ribbon that joined them spooling more tightly with each plunge of his manhood into her tight warmth.

"Better," she panted out. "Oh so much better!"

He laughed. The low sound rumbled from his chest and along his erection as it stroked into her.

His hand slipped around to her front, between her legs to that place where their bodies joined. He delved down to find the engorged bead at her core and rubbed it as he continued to thrust inside her.

She gasped as the intensity of his touch overwhelmed her. With a yearning cry of capitulation, she grabbed the edge of the table to hold herself down against the unstoppable release—

She shattered, her hips bucking her bottom against him as the climax overtook her. Wave after gasping wave gripped her and then released with a shudder. Never...*never* had she felt such uninhibited joy as she did at that moment, with his arms around her and his manhood still inside her, now impossibly harder than before.

The lips of her sex tightened around him as her body attempted to milk his release from him. But he held himself still in hard-won restraint, gritting his teeth as he let her fall into her own bliss without him.

When she could find her voice, she whispered, "You didn't..."

"Because we're not finished," he ground out through gritted teeth.

Slipping from her warmth with a tortured groan, he turned her to face him, the gold dress falling to the floor at his feet. He set her on the table's edge and wrapped her legs around his waist, hooking her ankles together at the small of his back. Then he moved forward between her spread thighs, teasing just the engorged tip of his steely hard length into the sensitized folds. She whimpered, greedily wanting him again.

In one swift, smooth movement, he lifted her from the table and thrust hard, stepping forward to impale her against the wall.

HOLDING HER PINNED IN PLACE, ROSS THRUST INTO HER, HARD AND fast. All the hot desire and pent-up frustration he'd suffered during their time together surged to the surface, heightened by tonight's events. The only cure was to take himself as deep inside her as possible.

She clung helplessly to him, her face buried against his neck as new arousal coursed through her. He heard it in the moans that poured from her and felt it in the tightening of her sex encircling him, even as she grew so drenched that the wet noises of their joined bodies declared audibly the shared pleasure they were finding in each other. *Dear God,* what pleasure she gave him! It was all he could do to hold himself back when he'd taken her over the table. But she'd waited a long time for this, and he wanted it to last as long as possible.

Yet she quickly broke again in his arms, and her body shuddered violently as she clung to him. Her thighs gripped hard against his hips as she quivered helplessly around him.

Not withdrawing from her, he lowered himself to the floor, bringing her down onto her back beneath him. He grabbed her wrists and pinned her arms over her head.

She writhed with a low moan, begging for more.

"Insatiable," he admonished as he ground his hips down into hers, bringing him inside her to the hilt.

"I am." She hooked her left leg over his arm, opening herself wide beneath him. With an appreciative groan, he sank impossibly deeper, eliciting a shudder of pleasure from her. "For you."

A growl of masculine pride and possession tore from him. He wanted to claim all of her—body, heart, and soul—and mark her as his. She would never be stolen from him again, and he would never suffer another masquerade at which this amazing woman ended up with another man. She was his. Tonight, tomorrow...*always.*

This time when she came beneath him with a cry, he followed after, thrusting deep and holding himself there. His cock jerked in exquisite release, and he poured himself into her. She quivered around him as her body drank him in, and in response, his thighs and buttocks clenched as he strained to empty every drop. Until he'd given her every last bit of himself.

He collapsed on top of her, his body throbbing from exertion and blissfully tingling with utter happiness.

He placed a tender kiss to her flushed lips, then lowered his head to her bare shoulder, resting his forehead there as he struggled to calm himself. Good God, how she undid him! He'd never known a woman like her, one who could make him feel strong and masculine with only a glance. One who frustrated him beyond measure yet drove him to bliss when she finally granted release.

One who made him want to give her the world, and himself right along with it.

He gathered her into his arms and turned onto his back to nestle her into the hollow between his shoulder and his chest. With her eyes still closed and her face tantalizingly flushed, he'd never seen a more beautiful woman.

He placed a delicate kiss to her lips.

In reply, she placed her hand to his chest—

No, to his heart. Her fingers curled into the waistcoat he still wore, so desperate had he been to have her that he hadn't removed any of his clothes. He grinned. He understood that feeling of possession, because he felt the same about her.

"You are an amazing woman, Grace Alden," he murmured. "I've never...*never*."

He laughed with astonishment that he couldn't put to words the wonderful way she made him feel and nuzzled his cheek against hers. But he'd have the rest of his life to describe to her how happy she made him, how much he admired her, and if his blossoming joy was any indication, how much he cared about her.

She whispered against his shoulder, "Susan."

He froze, his heart skipping with a hard jolt that shook him to his core. He slowly rolled over on top of her, raising himself onto his elbow as he stared down at her, searching for answers.

She fixed her eyes to his chest, unwilling to meet his gaze as she confessed so softly that he could barely hear her, "My name is Susan Montague." A silver tear slid down her cheek in the moonlight. "Viscountess Lockwood."

CHAPTER 22

*R*oss climbed the stairs into the bedroom and silently held out a glass of brandy.

"Thank you," Grace whispered as she accepted it. Yet there wasn't enough liquor in the world to help her through this. Nothing could stop the shaking that had gripped her since she'd revealed her secret, or relieve the numbness that filled her after he'd gazed at her with such shock.

Or hide the bewildered suspicion that now registered on his face.

Only a few minutes ago, they had been wrapped around each other, desperate to touch and explore every part of the other until their passion was spent. Now he remained apart from her, and as she stood there, covered neck to ankle to wrist by her night rail, she felt more exposed and vulnerable than when he'd ripped her dress away.

He'd removed his jacket and cravat while she'd been changing. Now, with his shirtsleeves rolled up, revealing muscular forearms, he looked like the perfect picture of a gentleman at leisure as he sat back on the windowsill and watched her, his long legs kicked out in front of him. But his relaxed appearance belied the simmering tension seeping from him.

"Start at the beginning," he ordered quietly. "And tell me everything."

She took a deep swallow of brandy and welcomed the burn down her throat. "You were there at the beginning." She whispered in little more than a breath, "At Lady Hawthorne's masquerade."

His eyes flickered as the memory of that night finally returned to him. "The waltz that was stolen…It was Lockwood."

She nodded, suppressing a shiver as the memories flooded painfully back. "That was when I met David. We were married not that long after." She trailed her fingertip around the rim of the glass, watching it because she couldn't bear looking at him. "For two years, we had a pleasant marriage. He was kind and generous, always thoughtful…a good husband in every way."

"He loved you." The matter-of-fact shrug of his shoulder wasn't enough to hide the trace of jealousy in his voice.

"He did. But I didn't love him, not in the same way. Oh, I cared about him, certainly, but it wasn't love. I think he knew that and was hoping that I would come to love him in time." She didn't dare to speak louder than a whisper, not when the connection between them now felt so tenuous that she could destroy it with nothing more than one harsh word. "But we only had two years together."

Trying to gather herself enough to continue, she lifted the glass to her lips. She closed her eyes as the brandy warmed her throat, to shut out as much of the pain of that time as possible. Yet from the ashes rose life, because that horrible time also gave her Ethan. How could she wish for anything to be different?

"You said before that he died of fever," he prompted.

"Yes. We were in London and had just arrived for the season. Because we'd lost our land agent the month prior, David had worn himself out putting the estate in order for our absence. He was exhausted from working and traveling, and the fever came on so fast…" She pressed the back of her hand against her lips to keep down any errant sob that might escape at the memory of her sick husband and whispered through her fingers, "I sent for Doctor Laraby. At first, David seemed to recover, only to suddenly become worse. But I couldn't be at his side because I'd fallen ill myself—headaches, sickness in my stomach, dizziness…"

"Because you were with child."

Nodding, she felt the close study of his gaze on her, although she didn't dare look up from her glass. "I'd missed my courses the previous month, but that wasn't unusual. I was only eighteen, and since I'd missed my courses before but hadn't gotten with child, I thought that month was simply the same as before, that my sickness was the same that had gripped David. So did Doctor Laraby. He advised me to stay in bed in my room, and that's where I was when David died." The memory of that horrible afternoon rushed back so fiercely that she flinched. "I should have been at his side. I should have been there to comfort him. I should have—" A knot of self-recrimination in her throat choked her. "But at least he wasn't alone. His brother Vincent was with him when he passed."

"I'm sorry," he murmured.

She forced her gaze to his, to acknowledge his sympathy and show her gratitude for it. "The following fortnight was a blur. I stayed away from everyone because I couldn't bear to see their pity. It was easier to grieve in peace, and I was still feeling ill. We had the funeral, and as the heir, Vincent assumed the viscountcy."

"The heir presumptive," he corrected. "You were of child-bearing years, which should have given everyone pause. I cannot imagine anyone believing your husband wouldn't have made love to you, repeatedly and often." He murmured, "I damned well would have."

An embarrassed blush rose in her cheeks. It was difficult enough to share this with anyone after all these years, but discussing her marriage bed with the man she'd just given herself to with such wild abandon nearly overwhelmed her. "No one would have assumed that. I certainly didn't. After all, we'd been married for two years, and I hadn't become *enceinte* during that time. David wanted children, and I desperately wanted to give him a family. But after two years, even we had come to believe that I was barren."

"Surely the Committee on Privileges would have waited to see for themselves."

"I was too distraught and ill to speak with them. Vincent said he would take care of everything, so I let him, still believing that I couldn't possibly be with child." *Still believing his lies that he would protect me.* Oh, she'd been such a fool! "When he notified them of David's death, he told them that I was barren, and they believed him. I had no reason to think otherwise."

"When did you find out?"

"Two weeks after David died, when I missed my second month of courses." The bittersweet anguish of that day flooded over her, that day that had been both the happiest and most terrible of her life. "I began to suspect why they hadn't come, why I'd been so ill…When they didn't come the third time, I knew for certain."

"Why didn't you go to the Committee then?"

She slowly raised her eyes to his. "Because Vincent had already threatened my life."

His jaw tightened. But who was he angry with—Vincent for threatening her, or her for keeping all this awful truth from him for so long?

She swirled the brandy, took another long swallow, slowly lowered the glass, raised it to take another sip—doing *anything* to directly avoid his eyes. She couldn't have endured the anger she might see there. Or the cold accusation.

"It was shortly after the funeral and before I knew for certain about the baby," she whispered breathlessly. "We were at the London house. Vincent had already moved in. To help comfort me, he'd said. The family solicitors were there, to discuss the settlement of the estate. I let Vincent meet with them and went to my room to be alone. At the time, I thought he was being so kind to keep me from being burdened with all that. But when the men left, Vincent came upstairs." She squeezed her eyes shut against his face as it materialized before her, as if no time had passed at all. "I'd never seen him so angry, so *enraged*. Far beyond shouting and cursing. And his eyes—Dear God, Ross! Such hatred..."

"What happened to anger him?"

"The will wasn't at all what he'd thought. David had changed it without telling him. Or me. I had no idea—" She shook her head as an anguished pain pierced her. "Vincent inherited all the property entailed with the title, but most of the estate wasn't in that property but in bank investments. It came from their mother, whose family were wealthy factory owners in Manchester. David left everything that wasn't entailed to me. It was a fortune." A sad smile touched ironically at her lips. What a wonderful, kindhearted man. But his love had been her doom. And his son's. "Vincent demanded that I turn it all over to him. He said it belonged to the rightful heir and not to some trollop who'd bewitched his brother into marrying her."

Ross tensed. His hands gripped the window casement beneath him so hard that his knuckles turned white even in the dim lamplight.

"When I refused—" The words strangled in her throat, but she swallowed hard and forced out, "He shoved me toward the fireplace. I landed on my side on the fender, and my head—" Her hand shook so violently now that she had to set down the glass for fear that she would splash the remaining brandy onto the floor. "I missed the flames, but the iron cut my cheek."

She reached up slowly to trace her fingertip over the scar slicing from the corner of her mouth to her temple. Even after a decade, drawing attention to it like this was agony. The sweep of her finger pained her as much as if the wound were still raw.

"*Jesus*." Ross rasped out, stunned, "He tried to burn you."

"Yes," she whispered, knowing the severity of the accusation she was making, one of attempted murder. "Such an unremarkable way to die that no one would have given my death a second thought...the new widow so aggrieved by her husband's untimely death that she hadn't been minding her skirts around the fire, who died by trying to run away from the very flames that were burning her alive. Nothing more than a tragic accident. Thank God the maid heard my fall and came running into the room." She placed her hand over her scarred cheek, unable to tamp down her humiliation over being so helpless that day. "I knew then that he would kill me if I didn't do as he asked."

His expression was inscrutable despite the tensing of his body that was so fierce as to be visible. "So you signed over your inheritance."

"No." She lifted her chin in foolish pride at that obstinate act. "I never signed any papers, but how could I stop him from taking everything anyway? He was a viscount, after all, and my only male relative. All I could do was make certain that I was never alone with him, that my maid or one of the servants was always with me." She picked up the glass and drank the last of the brandy, then winced at the burn. "Already I was trying to figure out how to escape him, where to go, who I could call on for help. Yet I stayed because I was young and afraid, because I had no place else to go...until I discovered that I was with child."

Wrapping her arms around her middle for protection against the past, she stepped forward until she stood beside him at the window. She gazed out blankly through the dirty glass at the moonlit alley and the service gardens of Chelsea that lined it. Appearing so still and silent...a mirage that belied an entire world sleeping and at peace.

"I kept it secret from everyone. If my baby were a girl, she would have been no threat. But a son would have taken everything away from Vincent, including the title. He would never have risked that." She lifted her hand to the window, to feel the cold of the night—to feel *anything* except the omnipresent fear that still haunted her. "If he were willing to harm me to steal my inheritance, how far would he go to eliminate any chance of losing the title?"

Ross stepped up behind her but didn't reach for her. She felt the absence of that touch as coldly as the glass beneath her fingertips. "So you fled."

She gave a jerky nod. "I packed a bag, took what little money and jewels I'd secreted away in my room, and left that night. It was dangerous, but so was remaining in Mayfair. I found an inn where I hired a post-chaise. I didn't think to give a false name or hide my appearance—I was too concerned about simply fleeing, about protecting my baby." She forced a grim smile. "Which turned out to be the very best thing I could have done." Then her smile faded, replaced by grief so deep that she pressed her hand against her chest to keep breathing, to keep telling her tale. "Because when I finally stopped running ten days later, so tired that I couldn't go on, there was a fire at the inn. A terrible fire."

"Were you hurt?"

The thick concern in his voice nearly undid her, because it gave her hope that he might understand and accept the horrible things she'd done to survive.

She shook her head. "I was one of the lucky ones. But several people were killed, their bodies taken to the parish church and placed in the crypt to await burial. Somehow I knew that this was my chance for life, for me and my baby." She had to pause to gather herself before she could continue. "So I went to the church. I lied to the vicar and told him that I needed to search for my friend who was separated from me in the fire. He let me into the crypt, where I chose one of the women. A young woman my size, burned beyond recognition." She swallowed. Hard. "I told the vicar that the body belonged to her, to the woman I'd met while traveling…Susan Montague."

Ross said nothing, but in his dim reflection in the window

glass, she saw his hand lift to rake his fingers through his hair. That telltale sign of frustration she'd become so familiar with during their time together.

"I knew my word wouldn't be enough. Not to fake the death of a viscountess. So when the vicar wasn't looking, I put my wedding ring onto her finger so that Vincent would identify her body as mine. I knew he wouldn't look too closely. After all, he wanted me dead. It was the answer to his prayers."

She turned around to face him then, and the grim set of his face nearly undid her. Even in the dark shadows of the room, lit only by a slant of moonlight, she could see visible signs of his unease in the stiff tension in his shoulders, in the lift of his chin as he stared silently at her. Less than a foot separated them, but he felt a world away.

"That fire changed everything, you see," she whispered, desperate to make him understand. "Susan Montague died that night, and Grace Alden rose from the ashes. I took my new identity and bought a coach ticket for as far away as I could travel."

"To Sea Haven," he murmured.

"Not at first. I didn't trust that Vincent hadn't discovered what I'd done, and why. That he wasn't still coming after me. So I kept moving, never staying in one place for more than a few weeks. By the time I arrived in Sea Haven, I was nearly ready for my confinement and out of options. I had planned to make my way to the coast and then somehow find a ship that would take me away from England. But Ethan had other plans for us." She smiled wistfully and placed her hand over her lower belly. She could almost feel the babe that she'd once carried there. "Alice Walters saved our lives. She helped deliver him, then took us in when we had no place else to go."

"So you stayed and pretended to be a fisherman's widow."

"I had to protect my baby." Her chest tightened with that same dread that had hovered over her like a specter for the past decade, until it had become a part of her. Only during this time with Ross had it not haunted her, had she been able to shake off the oppressive fear. But his disbelieving expression made her hope sink. "I know what you're thinking—you, who's never backed down from a fight in his life, who is even now running toward danger rather than away from it." Anger at the weak woman she'd been filled her chest. "You think I was a coward to run and hide like that instead of fighting."

"I don't think that." Yet he made no move to touch her or take her into his arms to give her reassurance.

"*I* do." She blinked hard against the stinging tears as that old feeling of helplessness resurfaced. "I was a different woman then." *From a different lifetime.* She feared he might never understand the choices she'd made. "But I refuse to hide any longer."

Losing his battle to keep his distance, his arms went around her and pulled her against him. He buried his face in her hair. "You were eighteen, for God's sake, with no money and no relatives to take you in. What else could you have done?"

She choked down a sob as she slipped her arms around him and rested her cheek against his hard chest.

"But you were safe in Sea Haven," he murmured against her temple. "You two could have lived out your days there completely unnoticed. Why return to London now?"

"Vincent's second wife is expecting," she whispered. "His first wife was barren, so I thought I had time to claim Ethan's inheritance. But Cora died, Vincent remarried..."

And she'd run out of time.

The Committee on Privileges would never remove a sitting lord with a legitimate heir in favor of an heir whose legitimacy was suspect. If her son was to have the life that he deserved—the life that David would have wanted for him—then she had to act now.

From the way Ross tensed in her arms, he realized that, too.

He shifted away from her just far enough to cup her scarred cheek against his palm. "It's going to be an uphill battle, you realize that." His fingers soothingly stroked her cheek. "They most likely won't even agree to hear your petition."

"I know." She placed her hand on his chest and felt his heartbeat through his shirt, strong and steady. "But I have to try. Ethan deserves the life that his father wanted for him." Then she paused before admitting, "I can't do this without you, and I don't mean the influence of the Spalding title. I mean *you*, Ross."

His face softened at her words, even as he warned, "You'll be exposing Ethan."

"I'll keep him safe." Just as she always had.

"You'll also be exposing yourself." He gravely traced his fingertip over her scar to make his point. "Are you ready for that?"

"As long as you're with me."

His hand stilled for a moment against her cheek. Only a moment's hesitation, but she felt it.

Her stomach plummeted with a flash of worry. "Have you changed your mind, now that you know the full truth?"

She'd understand if he had, but dear God, what would she do without him? Not to have his support, not to have his strength to lean upon during the fight to come or his determination and resilience to see her through to the end—*unbearable*.

Not answering, he asked quietly instead, "Why did you give yourself to me tonight?"

The question pierced her.

"You said before that it would put Ethan at risk." He searched her face in the shadows. "What changed?"

"When you took so long to return tonight, when I didn't know if you were safe or captured—" *Dead or alive.* She pushed the horrible thought from her mind. "I realized then how much you matter to me."

Needing to touch him, she curled her fingers into the hard muscle of his chest. If only she could lay claim to his heart so easily.

"That's why I made love to you tonight. It was selfish and

risky." For the first time in a decade she'd put her own needs before her son's, and the enormity of that made her tremble. "But I couldn't deny myself the opportunity to finally be that close to you. To take what might be our only chance to have that."

Ross tensed in surprise. Yet he said nothing as he continued to study her, those blue eyes shining black in the shadows. Each passing beat of silence came as a tortuous thump inside her aching chest, increasing her nervousness until it blossomed into hot embarrassment.

She turned her head away to hide her humiliation. Oh, what a fool she was!

"I'm sorry," she whispered, blinking furiously to keep back the tears. "I shouldn't have said that."

In answer, he took her chin in his hand and lifted her face as his lips came down tenderly onto hers. The gentleness of his kiss stole her breath away.

"Yes, you should have, and I'm damn glad you did." Taking her hand, he moved back a few feet to sit on the bed. "Because it means you finally trust me." With a soft tug, he drew her forward between his knees. "As much as I trust you."

"I do." She placed her hands on his broad shoulders in order to ground herself as her mind spun, making her light-headed. All of her tingled with the faint stirrings of happiness that were coming to her slowly after so many years of loneliness and distrust.

"But we're a long way from safe." Although his words were meant as a warning, his deep voice curled an intensifying heat low in her belly. "Even if I'm exonerated, the scandal will linger. Any influence I had in Parliament is gone now." His eyes grew bleak. "I might prove more of a hindrance than a help."

How wrong he was! Just having him with her, giving her his strength and steadfastness, would help her more than he would ever know. A smile tugged at her lips, and her hand slipped down his chest to the buttons of his waistcoat as she kissed him.

"I've come to appreciate the value of your hindrances," she murmured against his lips.

From the way his frown deepened, she knew he wasn't reassured.

He tilted back his head to gaze up at her as his arms encircled her and gently pulled her closer. The sobriety in his eyes rippled uneasiness through her, and reflexively, her fingers tightened their hold on him.

"What do I call you now?" he puzzled softly, his deep voice contemplative as he searched her features. "You're not really Grace, but to me, you're also not Susan."

She shook her head as she unbuttoned his waistcoat and slipped it from his shoulders. "It doesn't signify."

"It does if—"

With a kiss, she silenced him. "It doesn't signify. I'm the same woman." Prompting him to raise his arms, she lifted his shirt over his head and off, tossing it away to the floor. She needed to be close to him, to make love to him again. This time, completely as herself. "No matter what you call me."

He arched a brow. "Truly?"

"Absolutely." Her hands roamed over the muscular planes of his chest, sifting through the dusting of hair and down over the hard ridges of his abdomen. Sweet heavens, he was magnificent. Every inch of him simply begged to be explored. Would she ever grow tired of looking at him? Of touching him or tasting him? With a wanton smile, she leaned down to place a kiss to the center of his chest, and the tip of her tongue darted out to lick—

"I've always liked the name Martha."

She froze for a beat. Then she stood up straight and smacked him on the shoulder with her palm. "Ross Carlisle, don't think for one moment that a *third* name—"

With a rumbling laugh, he grabbed her around the waist and pulled her down across his lap. His eyes sparkled with wicked amusement right before his mouth covered hers, kissing her so intensely that he drew a moan from her lips. When he looked at her like that, he didn't see her scar—he saw the woman beneath. One who was strong and confident, unmarred by her past. She thrilled with it.

"It's my turn to make a confession," he murmured against her shoulder as he nudged back the neck of her night rail and danced kisses across her collarbone. "About something I've wanted to do for a long time."

She exhaled a shivering sigh when he licked down into the valley between her breasts, as far as the night rail's neckline would allow yet still several agonizing inches from her taut nipples that ached to be between his lips. "What?"

"This." His hands slipped beneath the hem of her night rail and began to explore her body. "There's something about you in this frumpy old nightgown that drives me mad."

"Silver-tongued devil," she panted out teasingly as his low laugh rumbled into her.

With his caresses hidden from her eyes beneath the tent-like yards of cotton, his seeking hands gave her touches that left her yearning for more. Tender and gentle yet persistent, he stroked up the outsides of her bare legs, along the side of her torso, and up to lightly trace over the side swells of her breasts, before deliberately moving back down her body. The undeniable sensation gripped her that he was laying claim to every part of her that he touched.

"You're special," he whispered as he continued to caress her. "So very special to me, unlike any other woman I've ever known."

His soft words cascaded over her, spinning her in a whirlwind of emotion until she felt as if she were soaring, as if the only thing keeping her from flying away to heaven were Ross's arms around her.

"I'm going to make love to you again," he murmured against her lips.

Make love. He'd never used those words before, and something low in her belly told her that it wasn't because he wanted to avoid being coarse. She'd never met a man so careful with his choice of words, one who meant exactly what he said.

Despite the sudden knot of nervousness in her belly, she breathed out...*Yes.*

No sound came from her lips, but his eyes softened, registering his understanding.

In that moment's silence, she felt the undeniable connection between them again, returning stronger than before. She knew now that she had been wrong. It wasn't at all like a ribbon stretching between them. So much more powerful than that! Their souls had intertwined, and what she felt for him now inhabited a secret place in her heart that had never been full before he entered her life.

The shadowy depths of his eyes held her captive, as if he'd cast a spell over her. They never left hers, not when he reached down to take the hem of her night rail to lift it up and off. Not when she trembled at being naked and perched across his thighs. Not even when he shifted beneath her to remove his breeches, leaving him just as bare as she was, his skin warm and soft over steely hard muscles beneath. She couldn't look away—didn't *want* to look away. What she wanted was to drown in those dark depths, to find a way to crawl beneath his skin and become a part of him. The way he'd become a part of her.

She turned to straddle him and slowly reached down between them to take his manhood into her hand. He grew hard and thick against her palm as she stroked his length, teasing her fingertips lightly over his tip and drawing a bead of his essence from the tiny slit.

He squeezed his eyes shut to enjoy her caresses, sliding lower in the chair and tilting up his hips. She whispered his name and traced her thumb slowly over his bottom lip even as her other thumb swirled over the head of his erection, until he twitched in her hand.

He was wrong. He wasn't going to make love to her. *She* was going to make love to *him*, with every ounce of her being.

Holding him still, his tip tickling at her wet folds, she slid forward to sheath his length within her tight warmth. No pain this time, only the delicious comfort of having his hardness filling her. Never did she feel more feminine or more beautiful than when Ross was inside her.

With a soft sigh, she slowly began to rock herself against his hips. There was none of the fierce passion of before, none of the wild need to satiate their physical cravings. This time was slow and tender, so deeply affectionate that tears gathered at her lashes. This...oh, *this* was simply making love. In every way.

"Grace," he purred as his mouth slid down her neck and smiled against her wildly beating pulse. "My Grace."

With a trembling sigh, she wrapped herself around him and closed her eyes. Happiness coursed through her veins.

No—what she felt was far more than mere happiness. It was a feeling of being accepted just as she was, scars and past mistakes included. He knew the truth now about all her secrets, yet he still wanted her. Her love for him deepened every time he whispered the name of the woman she'd become. Grace...*his* Grace.

With a groan of pleasure, he buried his face in her hair and murmured, so softly that at first she couldn't understand what he was saying, until she heard—

"I will keep you safe." Then, in an aching vow for the future they might never have, "Always."

Her heart skittered, too full of love and joy to beat on as it always had. At that moment, with their bodies entwined and his promise lingering on the dark shadows surrounding them, she realized the truth about the woman she'd become. She was no longer the frightened young girl who had no choice but to flee in order to survive. Now she was strong and formidable, willing to lay claim to what she wanted for her future. And what she wanted...

"Ross," she whispered as the pleasure engulfed her in a soft shiver. It fanned out from her and into him as he followed after, breath by breath, heartbeat into heartbeat, until it was impossible to tell where she ended and he began.

Her heart—and her life—had changed once more. They would never be the same again.

CHAPTER 23

*R*oss came up behind Grace as she sat in front of the dressing table and put the last pins into her hair. In the morning sunlight, she was breathtaking.

He placed a lingering kiss to her nape and murmured hotly against her skin, "Good morning."

"A *very* good morning," she corrected as she snaked her arm up around his neck.

With a smile at her reflection in the mirror, one that looked just as wicked as it felt, he deliberately raked his eyes over her. Her luscious body gave every indication that she was a woman who had been fully satiated in those busy hours since midnight. Lord knew he'd certainly done his damnedest to make her just that.

She ran her fingers through his hair. The suggestive caress sparked all the way down the length of his cock and tingled at his tip.

"If you keep that up," he warned wolfishly, wanting nothing more at that moment than to strip off her dress and feast on her, "I'll have you on your back again before you can blink."

Her wicked smile matched his own. "That would be bad...why, exactly?"

He groaned at the temptation, yet he somehow found the resolve to unwrap her arm and place a chaste kiss to her fingertips before he set her hand away. "Because Kit's due to arrive at any moment, and I'd rather my brother never learn what you hide beneath that night rail of yours."

She bit her lip to keep back her amusement as he leaned against the dressing table, facing her. "A bit territorial, are you?"

Folding his arms over his chest, he arched an indignant brow, as if offended. "Absolutely."

She laughed, the lilting sound musical on the sunlight that streamed in through the window.

Warmth swelled inside him. At that moment, his world was perfect. Nothing existed outside the walls of this room. There was no espionage ring to expose, no threat of treason—there was only Grace and the way she smiled at him, as if he were the most wonderful man in the world.

"Does your brother really want to become a vicar?" She reached up to affectionately run her fingers over his waistcoat buttons. She couldn't keep from touching him, even so casually, and he certainly wasn't going to make her stop.

"Does rain fall up?" he countered with a shake of his head. "It's unnatural, as unnatural as Christopher Carlisle in a vicarage."

A puzzled frown pulled lightly at her brow. "Then why does he claim so?"

"Petty revenge." He grimaced. "When Kit learned what I was doing in Paris with Wentworth, he announced that he planned to become a vicar so that I wouldn't be the only martyr in the family."

Her hand stilled against his abdomen, and her bright smile faded. "Are you?" Her soft voice thickened with concern. "Martyring yourself?"

"There was a time when I would have said yes. Not so long

ago, I was willing to do anything to prove Wentworth's guilt, including sacrificing myself."

Her fingers curled into the brocade, as if she were afraid she might lose him right then. "What changed your mind?"

He stared into her eyes. A man could drown in those chocolate depths and never regret his demise. "You."

She froze for a beat. Then she drew her hand away.

He caught it up before she could pull back and wrapped his fingers around hers. He lifted a brow at her sudden unease. "You went there first, with your talk last night about lost chances."

"That wasn't the same thing," she countered with forced indignation, "and you know it."

"Then what was it?" He refused to let go of her hand. He wanted her to say it, *needed* to hear it—that she held an affection for him beyond physical pleasure, beyond worry about his safety and whatever help he could give Ethan.

When she tugged to free herself, his fingers tightened their hold, until she wisely gave up with an aggravated sigh. "You wanted to know why I gave myself to you." She lowered her voice to a whisper although they were alone. "And I answered you."

She was dodging the question, but this conversation was too important. So he pressed, "You said I mattered to you."

"You do."

He held his breath and pressed, "How much?"

Her eyes flared in surprise that he would dare to ask that. But the last few weeks of having his life constantly at risk made him appreciate the here and now, because he knew first-hand that tomorrow wasn't guaranteed.

"Ross, what you're implying…" She shook her head in exasperation. "You're hinting about a future when we have no idea what fate will bring for us."

"It's uncertain, granted."

"It's *bleak*," she corrected soberly.

"But not hopeless." Far from it. For the first time since he fled

Paris he was optimistic that all would work out in his favor, and he wanted Grace by his side when it did. "I didn't get the diary last night, but I now know where it is. Wentworth is keeping it in a hidden drawer in a side table in his study. With Kit's help, I'll be able to retrieve it."

"No." Her face paled, but her fingers tightened around his. As if she were afraid he might leave her right then to go after it. "Wentworth will be waiting for you. I don't want you to risk your life."

Her concern warmed his chest. With a tug on her hand, he gently pulled her to her feet and into his arms, then caressed his knuckles across her cheek. "Risking my life is the only way to save it now." When her eyes darkened with worry, he forced a teasing lightness into his voice to break the tension. "Unless you fancy a life on the run with me."

"A life of nights crammed into tiny inn rooms sandwiched beneath stairs and days riding on hard carriage seats? I don't think so." The smile she gave him wavered, but her false bravado kept it in place, to keep the teasing at the forefront of their conversation and the seriousness pushed below the surface. "But you could come to Sea Haven with me and Ethan and pretend to be my long-lost fisherman husband returned from the sea. No one would notice an earl among the dockworkers."

He couldn't find the strength to return her smile. She wanted a future with him as much as he did. She was simply too worried to let herself consider it, and it killed him to be unable to give her the reassurance she needed.

"That is," she continued, "if you think you could stand the life of a quiet seaside village over the excitement you had in the Court of St James's."

He'd had more than enough excitement for one lifetime, thanks to the Court of St James's. "I think I could." Then he threw all caution to the wind—"But I'd rather be in London with you by my side as my countess."

She tensed in his arms.

She'd accused him of hinting about a future together, but this was no hint—despite the teasing behind it, it was a firm offer. The first that he'd dared to voice. The idea shocked him nearly as much as her, but he couldn't imagine *not* having her with him now. No matter what fate threw their way.

She trembled, her lips parting silently with worry and the fear that seemed to always linger in her. He understood it now, but he refused to let her fall prey to it any longer.

He cupped her face between his hands and gazed deeply into her eyes, making certain there would be no misunderstanding on what he intended for them. "Once my name is cleared, I promise you that—"

A loud smashing of glass and splintering of wood shattered the quiet morning, followed by the shouts and running strides of men rushing into the studio below.

Christ. They'd been found.

Grace's eyes widened in terror. "Ross—"

"Hide!" He grabbed her by the shoulders as the men came closer. "Go into the other room. I'll keep them busy here."

She shook her head adamantly, grabbing for his arm. "I won't leave you!"

At that moment he knew—she loved him.

And he loved her too much to let her be harmed because of him.

He pushed her toward the door. "As soon as it's safe, go to St James's Street, to any of the clubs there. Ask for Kit. He'll take care of you."

"But I don't want—"

His mouth swooped down to capture hers. She gasped beneath his desperation, but his kiss silenced her, making it clear that he'd brook no arguments about this. He said he would protect her, and that's exactly what he was doing.

"Go, *now.*"

He pushed her into the room and closed the door after her, then turned to face the men who were storming upstairs.

When the first soldier reached the top of the stairs, Ross swung, his fist catching the man in the chin and snapping his head aside as he stumbled back.

Three more men came after, and he let fly punch after punch, ducking when the men fought back. He couldn't win against them, not when he was so outnumbered, but he fought as hard as he could to distract them from finding Grace.

A fist landed on his jaw, and he staggered back. Another struck in his stomach. He doubled over in pain. A slam to the middle of his back knocked him to his knees. But the kick to his already wounded ribs did him in, and he sank to the floor, this time unable to find the strength to stand back up.

"Ross Carlisle, you're under arrest." The same officer he'd first punched when the soldiers rushed up the stairs jabbed his knee into the middle of his back to keep him pressed against the floor, then yanked his arms behind his back. Iron manacles clamped tightly around his wrists. "For treason."

Ross remained still as the men grabbed his arms and jerked him to his feet. A trickle of blood seeped from the cut at the corner of his mouth, and his side hurt like hell, the pain so fierce that each ragged breath came with an agonizing shudder. But he smiled grimly, pleased with himself, when he saw the damage he'd done to the three men.

"And this one?" another soldier demanded from behind him.

His stomach plummeting, Ross turned—

Grace stood in the doorway. Behind her, one of the soldiers gripped her arms so hard to keep her from escaping that she winced. His teeth clenched in fury. If that man hurt her, he would kill the bastard.

"Arrest her," the captain ordered. "Same charge."

"She had nothing to do with this!" Ross protested quickly,

desperate to save her. "She's only a woman I tricked into helping me. Nothing more."

"Ross," she whispered. For once, stunned by the confusion and surprise of the arrest, she was unable to hide behind pretense, and the shock and hurt showed on her face.

Good. He needed to make the soldiers see that raw emotion and pain on her face, to convince them that she wasn't part of his crimes.

"She's no one," he told the men. Then he spat out the blood from his cut lip, but he couldn't purge the awful taste from his mouth that he'd put her into danger.

The hurt that flashed across her face nearly undid him. But he held her gaze fixed beneath his, praying she comprehended what he was doing, why he had to hurt her so brutally. Because he would do anything to protect her.

"Go," the captain ordered, shoving Ross toward the stairs. Then he called out over his shoulder, "Arrest her."

Ross glanced back as the men dragged him down the stairs and out to the waiting wagon in the alley. The last glimpse he had of her was of the soldier placing irons on her wrists.

CHAPTER 24

*H*er head falling back in exhaustion, Grace looked up from the cold floor where she sat shivering in the damp darkness as the sound of metal scraping on metal echoed off the stone walls of her prison cell.

Two large men opened the door. Their faces were hidden in the dark shadows, the blackness of the prison so deep that not even the flickering glow cast by the lamp one of them carried managed to light their features.

The men exchanged quiet words, then the man with the lamp hung it on a rusty iron hook jutting out from the stone wall and walked away. The other man remained.

"What do you want?" she called out, letting the anger overcome her fear. "I've already answered enough questions to prove that I don't know anything." Then, just for spite, she raised her chin and added, "And I wouldn't tell you even if I did!"

"I would expect no less from a formidable woman like you."

Christopher.

She jumped to her feet and hurried forward with a choked sob. She had no idea how long she'd been there, how many hours she'd suffered in the cold and filth—how badly beaten Ross had been when the soldiers took him away. "Where's your brother?"

"You've been released," he told her, avoiding her question. "All the charges against you have been repealed. I'm taking you out of here." His expression hardened as he took her chin in his fingers and turned her head to examine her. "And straight to a doctor to make certain you're all right."

She pushed his hand away. She didn't care about herself. "Where's Ross?"

He hesitated, glancing over his shoulder to gauge who might be near enough to overhear, then answered, his voice low, "Still in prison, awaiting trial in Parliament."

"But surely they realize that he's innocent." How had she ever doubted that? England should have been celebrating him as the hero he was. "He's certain to have been questioned by now, shown them the papers, and explained what Wentworth did."

When Kit said nothing, she knew...The Court thought him just as guilty of treason as when they'd first leveled the charges against him. Her eyes stung with hot tears of fear and frustration. Nothing had changed. They'd traveled hundreds of miles and risked their lives, and he was still regarded as a traitor, when in truth he was the furthest thing from it.

Unable to hide the concern that hardened his face, he answered grimly, "He will receive a fair trial, and it will all come out then."

She gave a bitter laugh. A fair trial in which he'd be found guilty, if only to save the crown's pride. King George never admitted that he was wrong, even when he so very clearly was. "We have to help him. What can we do?"

"We will help." He shrugged out of his greatcoat and slipped it onto her small frame. "But first, I have to take you out of here." He buttoned the coat and turned up the collar against her neck. "Ross's orders."

He took her elbow and led her from the cell.

"You've seen him?" She clutched at his arm, refusing to take another step until he told her. "How is he?"

"He'll be fine."

"You lie as badly as your brother," she bit out in worry and frustration, but she allowed him to lead her on. She needed to escape this hellish place so that she could think clearly. She, more than anyone, knew the details of what Ross had done and why, and it fell to her to find a way to help him.

As Kit guided her down the prison's underground aisles, he kept his eyes straight ahead and scanned through the darkness around them. His other hand stayed beneath his jacket, resting on what she knew was a pistol. As if he expected someone to jump out of the shadows at any moment.

"How is he? At least tell me that much." She sucked in a mouthful of dank prison air to steady herself, and immediately regretted it when the stench of the place filled her lungs and made her cough. "I saw how they beat him when they arrested him, and I need to know...Please."

His dark gaze flicked sideways at her, but he said nothing. When they reached the end of the aisle, where a set of stone stairs led up to the surface, he stopped and glanced into the darkness of a narrow corridor cutting perpendicular to the main aisle, as if contemplating...

He tightened his grip on her arm and tugged her into the dark corridor. "This way."

He pulled her quickly along beside him, catching her when her feet tripped over the uneven stones. As the darkness engulfed them, lit only by a single dim lamp hanging high on a post halfway down the corridor, the air grew colder, even more musty and dank. The pungent scent of human excrement suffocated her, and she could barely make out any of the shapes around her in the black shadows.

"There'll be hell to pay for this," he muttered. "Don't say I didn't warn you."

Fresh fear tightened a knot in her throat. "What do you mean? Where are we—"

"Here."

He stopped her in front of a small cell at the far end of the corridor, in what had to be the oldest part of the centuries-old prison. Rough-hewn limestone two feet thick formed short walls that shut out all traces of light and fresh air from the outside world. Thick iron bars rose from floor to ceiling, locking forgotten prisoners inside with the darkness. In the silence, she heard the steady drip of water trickling down the damp walls and puddling on the floor. Along the edge of the corridor, a rat scurried away into the darkness, and she bit back a startled scream.

He looked grimly down at her, even as he tapped the barrel of his pistol against the iron bars. The metallic sound jarred down her spine with each ping. He called out softly, "Ross, you have a visitor."

"Ross?" *Impossible.* He couldn't be here, not in this hell. He was a peer, for God's sake!

But one glance at Christopher's bleak face told her the truth.

A dark form moved forward from the blackness at the rear of the cell. The shadows were too thick for her to see him, but she *knew.* Because she felt it swell up inside her, felt it reach out through the darkness toward him—that same connection that had linked them together since the moment he forced his way into her cottage. Perhaps long before that, always with her but sleeping, waiting for him to come to her again after all those years. And it shattered her.

"Grace." Her name was a tortured whisper.

A sob fell from her lips. She was unable to speak as the pain overwhelmed her.

She pressed herself up against the bars and reached a hand into the darkness, desperate to touch him and prove that he was alive and unhurt. His hand slipped into hers, and she swallowed back a cry, refusing to let him know how terrified she was. She had to stay strong for him. He didn't deserve her tears, even though her desolation burned so viciously in her chest that she could barely breathe.

He reached between the bars to cup her face against his palm and stroked his thumb over her cheek to comfort her. But instead of providing warmth and strength, his touch pierced her. It was agony to be so close yet unable to wrap her arms around him, unable to protect him as she'd done since the night of the storm.

Hell. They'd been thrust into hell.

"You shouldn't be here. Kit shouldn't have brought you here."

"I had to see you," she choked out in a whisper. If she spoke any louder, she would break down into tears. Squeezing her eyes shut, she shook her head. "Those soldiers—the way they hit you—"

The warm softness of his lips touched hers between the bars. "I'm all right." His shoulders sagged with palpable anguish. "But what I said about you at the carriage house, I never meant any of it. You mean the world to me, Grace."

"I know." She reached up to stroke his cheek, her trembling fingers startled to find a prickle of beard. Just as he'd been when he first arrived at her cottage, as if she'd never shaved him. As if they'd never shared those wonderful moments together. "You were protecting me."

"Always." His arms slipped through the bars to encircle her and pull her as close to him as possible. His body was warm and strong, even in this dank hell, but the bars were a hard and cold reminder between them of their situation.

"Now it's my turn to protect you." Fierce resolve stiffened her spine. That same horrible feeling of helplessness that had driven her to flee all those years ago returned, but now it made her determined to stand and fight. "I'll free you from here, I promise."

His arms tightened around her, as if he were afraid of being dragged away from her at that very moment. "You can't.

"I'll explain everything to the authorities. They have to listen, and they'll understand. I'll make them."

He placed a somber kiss to her temple. "There's no way to prove my innocence."

"But the papers—"

"Are worthless." His hands continued to stroke across her back, as if he was afraid that she would vanish into the shadows if he stopped touching her. "Without Wentworth's private journal to prove that he was in Le Havre, they're nothing but speculation. Circumstantial at best."

"But we *have* to try to—"

He kissed her, silencing her. On that kiss, she tasted resignation, and grief shuddered violently through her. Dear God, she was losing him! Already she felt him melting away in her arms, like a ghost vanishing in the fog.

"Your fight is over," he whispered against her lips, lingering in the kiss as long as possible. "Let it go, love."

"I will *not* give up." Her fear changed into anger, and she let it come, seeking solace in the burning that kept her heart from shattering completely into a thousand shards of glass. "We're going to make them listen to you and prove that you're not a traitor. I'll go to the newspapers and make them publish those papers. The king and prime minister will have to listen to you then. There will be public outcry—"

"I'll accuse you of lying and deny every bit of it." That quiet comment sliced into like a blade of ice. "Because if you do that, they'll arrest you as my accomplice, and I will not allow you to put yourself in danger for me."

"Ross," she whispered, stunned. He was giving up on proving his innocence, in order to protect her.

"To endure what's to come, I have to know that you'll be safe," he whispered, his mouth close to her ear. "Let me have that solace."

She wanted to scream! She wanted to rage against every peer sitting in the Lords, against Wentworth—even the king himself.

Ross had risked everything for his country, only for them to turn their backs on him. And now he was asking her to do the same.

But she wasn't ready to surrender just yet.

"You want to protect me? Then give me the future you want for us." She choked as she repeated his words, "With me by your side." She shut her eyes against the anguish that squeezed at her chest like a fist. "I want that, too, Ross. I was afraid to admit that earlier. I've been alone and afraid for so long...but I want a chance at happiness, with you."

He held her as close as he could. But already he felt a world away, slipping through her fingers even as she clutched him so desperately to her.

The grief that swept over her was unbearable, and so much worse than when she lost David, because Ross was still here in her arms, warm and alive, so strong...the only man she'd ever loved. She simply couldn't fathom it, that they could do this to him, that they could rob him of his life. It was a nightmare. A horrible, surreal nightmare, one from which they could never wake up.

As she stood encircled in his arms, her cheek resting on his chest, she fought to imprint upon her mind every detail of him. The soft but strong heartbeat against her cheek, the way his arms held around her so tightly, the hard planes of his chest, the strength of his arms...She forced herself to memorize how soft his silky hair was beneath her fingertips, how tender his lips as he kissed her temple, the deep timbre of his voice that wrapped itself around her like a warm blanket...even that masculine scent of him, of port and cigars, leather and bergamot. She deeply breathed him in. She had to, during this short time they had together, this last time—

A single tear slipped down her cheek.

"You were right. I should never have spoken of the future." He buried his mouth in her hair near her ear and murmured in what was barely louder than a whisper, with emotion rasping his voice raw, "I couldn't help myself. The possibility of having a life with you was simply too wonderful to ignore." He inhaled sharply. "But that future is gone now. You have to live for Ethan, to give him the life he deserves. And you have to forget about me."

Never. He might as well ask her to stop breathing. "I won't—"

"You must." His arms tightened around her, even as his words sought to push her away. "Kit will take care of you. He'll make certain that you and Ethan are cared for, that you come to no harm."

The finality of that struck her so violently that she shuddered. The ribbon of connection that she'd felt pulling them together was fraying around her, snapping away one thread at a time. When it finally tore in two, leaving her once more without him...*oh God*, what would she do? How would she survive?

She buried her face against his chest through the cold iron bars that pressed against her cheeks and forced herself to nod, unable to speak without breaking down completely, because he wanted her acquiescence. Because she would do anything he asked of her. Because she would do anything to make these last days bearable for him, no matter how much it destroyed her. Because she loved him.

As if reading her fear, he caressed his knuckles across her cheek. "Don't worry about me, love." He placed a kiss to her temple to reassure her. "They won't send me to the gallows. I still have friends in Parliament I can count on to argue for trans-portation."

Exile. That's what he meant. *Not* innocence. He would be forever branded a traitor and banished to Australia, St. Helena, or some other godforsaken place where they sent criminals and trai-tors, never able to return. He would live...without her.

She could never follow after him. Her life was here. Her son needed her here. Ross knew that, too, which was why he didn't ask it of her. The only solace he could give her now was that he would still be alive, but she was too consumed by grief to accept the consolation he intended, because the thought of being apart from him devastated her. The darkness seeped into her soul, killing what last spark of hope she still possessed.

"Fate double-crossed us again," he murmured, releasing his hold on her. He caressed her cheek in the darkness. "Apparently, you're still not meant for me." His voice lowered to little more than a whisper, one laced with hopelessness. "But I so very much wanted you to be."

Pain splintered her insides. When he released her and stepped back from the bars, she reached for him, for one last kiss—

When her hand touched only cold air, her heart died.

"Christopher, take her away. Now." Grief roughened his voice into a harsh rasp. "And never bring her back here again."

But she didn't move, *couldn't bear* to move, to end these precious last moments she might ever have with him. Her arm remained outstretched toward him in the darkness, her hand through the bars grasping only cold air. "Ross…."

No answer came from the dark cell.

Kit took her arm and gently pulled her away.

He led her up from the bowels of the prison and out into the damp night that hung oppressively over the city. The loud clank of the metal door slamming shut after them reverberated through the street, the finality of the sound so harsh that she cried out as if a knife had been plunged into her chest. Only Kit's arm around her kept her from falling to the ground.

Kit signaled for a hackney waiting on the street, then put her inside the old coach and ordered the driver to take them to Mayfair. He sat on the bench across from her in the darkness, with the only light coming from the dim lantern dangling off the front corner of the carriage. The silence and darkness were oppressive, so deep that every clopping hoof against the cobblestones reverberated as loud as gunfire in her ears.

She pressed her fist against her chest to physically keep back the tears. She'd been torn in two, with half of her still back in the prison with Ross. But *all* of her had died in his arms.

"What happens now?" she forced out.

Kit turned toward the window, although she knew he could see very little of the passing city beneath the moonless night and thick fog that slowed the carriage traffic to a near standstill. His face was inscrutable in the jostling shadows cast by the swaying lamp.

"Parliament will convene for the trial tomorrow in the House of Lords. They're already sitting in session, so there'll be no delay in the proceedings. If history is any precedent, they'll vote their decision within a fortnight."

Two weeks. Then Ross would be gone from her forever.

"As for you, you'll spend the night at Spalding House. In the morning, I'll arrange for a driver and coach to return you to Sea Haven."

"*No.*"

The ferocity behind that single word forced his gaze back to her.

"Ross stands before the Lords tomorrow." She folded her useless hands in her lap. "I want to be there. I won't let him face this alone."

"Ross wants you safely home with your son." His firm tone told her that he'd brook no argument about that. "That's where you're going."

Her fists tightened. How dare he attempt to take away this last bit of time with Ross! "I'll leave when I know that Ross is safe, when the trial is over."

"You'll leave tomorrow."

"No, I want to be here in case—"

"For God's sake!" he snapped out furiously. "He doesn't want you to watch him hang!"

Her body flashed numb, followed by a blinding pain. But her foolish heart kept pounding, each jarring beat like a hammer to her breastbone, not knowing that she was already dead inside.

Hang…*No*. "He said they would transport him," she whispered, her stunned lips barely able to form the words.

"He lied." Christopher's eyes blazed with fury and anguish. "He's going to the gallows. The crown will make an example of him, and Wentworth will call in every favor he's owed to make certain it happens."

Her eyes burned, blurring his shadowy figure in the darkness. As silence fell between them, broken only by the rumble of the carriage wheels, her shock gave way to the brutal pain of helplessness. That same horrible helplessness that had nearly ended her ten years ago—this time, it was certain to break her. Even now she struggled for each excruciating breath.

"Ross is too proud to let you watch him beg for his life, and he sure as hell doesn't want you there when they take that life from him. He wants you back in Sea Haven, tucked safely into that cottage of yours with your son." He flicked the latch on the window and shoved it open, to let in the cold air of the damp night, as if he, too, were suffocating. "And I will *not* deny my brother his final wish."

"Neither would I." But he was so very wrong! Ross's wish wasn't to send her away. It was to thwart fate and find a way to finally be together. There was nothing under heaven that would keep her from making that wish come true.

Already a desperate plan was forming in her head. "Have you been to the studio?" *Had he found the papers?*

He shook his head. "As soon as Ellsworth notified me of what happened, I went straight to Newgate." He didn't look at her, his attention focused somewhere beyond the carriage in the night. "Ross wanted you freed. So I made it happen."

Then the papers were most likely still in the studio, still tucked beneath the floorboards where Ross had hidden them. Still waiting for her.

What she was contemplating was dangerous, utterly mad…and quite possibly his only hope. "What will happen tomorrow?"

He stiffened, clearly not wanting to discuss this. Or even look at her. He blamed her for Ross's capture, and she didn't fault him. If she hadn't been with Ross, he could have hidden someplace else where the soldiers would never have found him. He wouldn't have gone to the studio at all after the masquerade, choosing instead to move and change locations. But he'd returned because of her, and aching guilt sickened her that the night which had been so blissful for her might be his downfall.

"The Lord High Steward will call for the trial to commence," he answered simply, unwilling to offer up any additional information, "and Ross will be given the chance to plead his innocence."

But he wouldn't. That wonderful, honorable man would keep his silence to protect her. Which meant that she had to act now to protect him. "The trial will be closed to the public?"

"Yes. Only peers and solicitors will be allowed inside." His gaze flicked to her, then back to the passing streets outside. "Which is another reason why you can't be there."

Her belly tied into a tight knot at what she was contemplating. "But Wentworth will be?"

"He'll make certain of it."

She twisted her fingers into her skirt to fight back her rising anxiousness, hoping that in the darkness he wouldn't notice her desperation. "Not his assistants?"

"Not inside the chamber, no." He muttered into the shadows, "But you can damn well bet those vultures will be waiting somewhere nearby."

So not inside the ambassador's townhouse. *Exactly* what she needed to know to carry out her plan.

As the carriage traveled out of the City, with Fleet Street giving way to the Strand beneath their wheels, the traffic became heavier, until they were stopped completely near Covent Garden by the snarl of carriage traffic and pedestrians blocking their way. The theatres had let out. Despite the drizzling rain that blackened

London, it seemed that the entire city was out for the evening and clogging the fog-filled streets.

Quashing all signs of nervousness, she suggested as casually as possible, "Can we walk a ways? I don't think I can keep sitting here like this." *Without screaming.* "With all these people, we'll be safe from footpads."

He considered silently for a moment, then gave a curt nod. Pounding his fist against the roof to signal to the driver that they were getting out, he opened the door and swung to the ground. He reached back to help her down.

"Thank you." Then she pulled her hand away and stepped back several paces toward the footpath at the edge of the wide road.

When Christopher turned his back to pay the driver, Grace ran.

In a matter of seconds she was lost in the crowd and the dark of foggy night, hurrying as fast as she dared without calling attention to herself. She wove her way through the crush of people meandering along the street, past several carriages, and down a side street. Not daring to look back to see if Christopher was chasing after her, she darted into a dark alley that ran behind the theatre.

Only then, safely covered by shadows and surrounded by the noisy city night, did she stop. She leaned against the stone wall and gasped deeply to fill her lungs. She waited, straining to listen for any sounds that he might be pursuing her. But only the noise of distant carriages and horses reached her, along with stray laughter from one of the open windows in the building across the alley. The midnight bell tolled loudly from a church tower, a woman yelled—but there was no trace of Christopher.

She squeezed her eyes closed, allowing herself only this one moment of pain and fear. This one moment when she would let herself remember the feel of Ross's fingers caressing her cheek, the sound of his laughter, the exquisite joy of his hard body moving inside hers as he made love to her. There would be time later when she could have the luxury of more than just this quiet moment to reflect and remember.

But now, she had to act.

Pushing herself away from the wall, she hurried on through the night toward the Thames and the Chelsea Embankment. Always, she kept her head down, her face turned away even in the shadows, in case she was being followed.

An hour later, she reached the alley that ran behind Ellsworth's carriage house. She pressed herself against the wall, staying tucked away in the dark shadows. She cocked her head and listened…Nothing. Only the sound of drizzling rain dripping off the rooftops and striking the cobblestones. But the alley wouldn't be empty for long. Christopher would undoubtedly think to look for her here, and when he did, she had to be long gone.

She carefully approached the studio and reached to open the battered door that the soldiers had nearly ripped off its hinges when they'd forced their way inside. But someone had padlocked it during the day, and the lock wouldn't give. A cry of pained frustration tore from her as she yanked at it.

She slammed her fist against the door and stepped back. She looked up at the building, at the windows in the first floor bedrooms. All of them were shuttered, as they had been since the night she and Ross arrived here, to keep away the curiosity of prying neighbors. All the windows—

Except one. The window in her bedroom.

The window in the long side of the building whose shutters had been pushed open to allow in the sunlight where she'd sat to pin up her hair that last morning they were together. The soldiers wouldn't have bothered to shut it when they left, and Ellsworth had said that the building would be empty for the sennight, that neither the workers nor any artists would be here.

She hurried around the corner of the building and gave a quiet gasp of relief when she saw the unshuttered window, only for the gasp to turn into a cry of distress that it was a full story above her.

Even the rickety scaffolding that Ellsworth's workers had constructed in order to paint to the top of the eaves didn't reach that high and left a three-foot gap between her reach and the window. Dear God...to come all this way, only to be stopped by a distance of three feet.

No. She wouldn't let this stop her. She *refused* to stop now.

She glanced around the small service area between the studio and the main terrace house fronting Cheyne Walk. Her eyes desperately searched for anything she could—

An old barrel. It lay on its side on the ground behind a white-washed necessary, the weather having shrunk the boards in the side staves and head until gaps showed between. The metal loops were rusted and bent. She'd have to be a fool to trust that rotted thing beneath her weight.

"Then I'm a fool," she whispered.

With a soft groan of exertion, she picked up the barrel and heaved it up onto the scaffolding's boards, about five feet above the ground. It landed with a rattle of noise that made her flinch. But no sound or movement came from the surrounding houses, no lights flared—no one knew she was there. Or cared.

Summoning all her courage, she slowly climbed up the scaffolding, one tentative step at a time. Her hands and knees shook as she inched slowly upward and never let herself look down. Then she very carefully positioned the barrel and eased her weight onto it, standing slowly to her full height.

When she reached the window, she lifted a shaking hand toward the sill, to raise the sash—

Locked. Oh God, it wouldn't move!

"No," she whispered, her eyes stinging with helpless frustration. "No!"

She had to find a way inside. She *had* to!

With no other choice, she reached beneath the greatcoat and grasped her skirt. She gave a hard yank, and the fabric ripped. Pulling again and again, she tugged until the material tore away.

Then she made a fist with her left hand and wrapped the fabric around it until it was encased in cotton layers.

Closing her eyes and saying a quick prayer, she punched her hand through the window. It shattered, and she froze as the sound of breaking glass rained through the alley. She stayed perfectly still, waiting to be caught. But the night remained just as still as before, just as silent beneath the foggy black midnight.

Careful not to cut her arm, she reached through the broken pane of glass to carefully feel for the latch—

Her fingers touched metal, and a long sigh of relief poured from her as it gave way with a soft click. She pushed open the window and brushed away the remaining pieces of glass that had landed on the sill.

Then she jumped.

The barrel fell away beneath her, clattering to the hard ground. She lay across the window casement on her belly, just far enough inside not to fall back out. There was only one way forward now, so she kicked her feet against the side of the building and leveraged herself through the window.

When she landed on her feet in the room, she paused. She was unable to ignore the fierce stab of emotion in her chest at being back here, where she and Ross had revealed so much to each other. Where she'd made herself vulnerable enough to share all her secrets with him, to make love to him and open her heart the way she never had with any other man.

Her throat tightened—where she'd seen him beaten and dragged away as he was arrested.

"No time for that," she scolded, blinking hard and forcing herself forward. Later, she promised herself. There would be time later to think of Ross and all she was risking. Now she had to stay focused and numb to the pain.

Her belongings were still scattered about the bedroom, including the gold gown that Ross had torn off her in his desire to make love to her. Her hairbrush at the dressing table where he'd told her that he wanted a future with her, her little travel bag resting on the bed next to the night rail…all of it exactly where she'd left it, as if simply waiting for her to return and continue with her life right where she'd left off. But because of Ross, her life would never be the same again.

She changed quickly into a fresh dress but kept Kit's coat to protect her from the weather, snatched up the few coins leftover from their trip across England, and paused as she reached for her ruby ring.

Love always. Her life with David was so long ago that it now felt like a dream. He was her past.

Ross was her future.

She made her way downstairs in the darkness, where she knelt on the floor and felt at the boards beneath the central beam. One gave beneath her hands, and a soft cry of relief fell from her. She held her breath as she reached inside the small hollow—

Her fingers brushed against the papers, still beneath the floor where Ross had hidden them. *Thank God.* Her hand shook as she retrieved them, knowing those pages held the difference between life and death. Not only for Ross but also for every man whose name was on that list. For those men alone, knowing what Ross was sacrificing to keep them alive, she could never give up.

Not bothering to replace the board, she tucked the papers inside the coat's breast pocket and moved to the door. A flick of the lock on the big carriage doors, a hard shove and groan of wood upon stone—the doors parted just enough for her to slip outside into the alley. Without a glance backward, she hurried away into the night.

When she'd gone far enough away from the carriage house that Christopher wouldn't be able to find her, she stopped. Quiet stillness hovered around her. Now she could rest and plan out her next steps.

Beneath the doorway of an abandoned building, she sat down to take refuge against the cold drizzle and wait out the dawn.

CHAPTER 25

"*S*o you know what to do, correct?" Grace held up the few coins she had left and leveled her best motherly stare at the three boys standing with her at the edge of the square across from Wentworth's townhouse. Then she hesitated, frowning as she looked them up and down. "Perhaps you won't be able to do this after all." She lowered her hand, to make a show of putting the coins away. "I'll have to find other boys to help me. Boys who can run faster."

"We're fast, ma'am." The oldest of the three boys assured her, his shock of bright red hair nearly as arresting as the map of freckles covering his ruddy cheeks. He wasn't more than twelve.

"An' plenty big 'nough," the second—and smallest—piped up.

The third one knew to keep silent.

"Perhaps…" She drew out the word, letting her doubt register in her voice.

"We can do it, ma'am. Ain't nothin' but a little play o' tag wi' th' guvnor," the oldest boy assured her. He held out his hand for prepayment of services, his expression suddenly all business.

She nodded as she placed a coin onto the grimy palm of each boy. "And another coin for each of you when you complete your task." She pointedly jingled the pouch so they could hear that she had coin left. "Fail, and you'll get nothing more. Understand?"

All three boys nodded with stubborn boyish pride, and she fought back a pleased smile. Raising Ethan had taught her that getting what she wanted from young boys required a combination of reverse persuasion, bribery, and old-fashioned threats.

"I'll be waiting over there with your payment." She pointed toward the corner of a narrow alley that cut through the stretch of terraced houses and gave access to the service yards behind. "Go!"

With excited grins, the boys ran away, laughing as they charged up to the front door of the grand townhouse. Grace watched as the two smaller boys stood to either side of the doorway and crouched down, hidden just out of view from the sidelights. The oldest grabbed the brass knocker and began to beat it furiously, as if he were attempting to wake the dead.

The butler opened the door and scowled when he saw the boy. Even from this distance, Grace could see the venom with which the paunchy servant began to berate the lad, moving to yank the door closed as quickly as he'd opened it.

But the boy lowered his shoulder and plowed into the door, shoving both it and the startled butler out of the way as the two smaller urchins jumped to their feet and ran inside the house, setting a merry chase. Shouts went up throughout the townhouse as the butler raced after them. But they were too fast for him to keep up.

Stifling a smile, Grace calmly strolled down the street to the alley, as if she were just another household servant, coming and going for work. She waited out of sight around the corner.

Less than ten minutes later, the three boys came running up to her. They laughed so hard that they nearly doubled over from their glee and giggles. After their sprint through the house, the three weren't even winded, although she was certain they'd worn out the servants who'd chased them. In the distance, she heard a fierce shout from the butler and a slam of the front door. She had to bite her bottom lip to keep from laughing.

If what she was about to do wasn't so dangerous, its endgame the only thing that would save Ross's life, she would have taken a moment to enjoy it. But too much depended upon every step she made now, and there wasn't a minute to spare.

"You did as I asked?" she pressed.

All three boys nodded.

"Aye, ma'am." The oldest held out his hand for the promised coin. "The first door i'' th' side garden."

Her belly tightened. It was her turn now.

Doing her best to press down the nervousness that rose so intensely that her hand trembled, she paid out the promised coins. The boys clutched their booty tightly in their fists as they ran away, down the narrow path toward the rabbit warren of back alleys and side streets that filled this part of Piccadilly like a maze. In a matter of seconds they were gone.

She inhaled deeply for courage and set off.

Unhurriedly, she strolled her way down the alley to the back of the terrace houses, looking for all the world as if she belonged right there. Anyone who saw her wouldn't think to question her presence, not in a dress that four days of travel and sleeping in a doorway last night had dirtied to the point that she could have passed for any common lower-class laborer simply going about her morning business.

But the alley was mostly empty, except for a groom who was too busy flirting with a scullery maid taking out a bucket of slopes to notice her. Yet even then she kept her face lowered, her scar turned away.

When she reached the end of the terrace, where Wentworth's townhouse mansion capped the row, she slowed her gate just enough to take a casual glance into its service yard, to make certain no one was there when she unlatched the garden gate and let herself inside.

Now—she hitched up her skirts and ran, to duck out of sight behind the outbuildings.

She crouched low and circled the perimeter of the service yard to arrive at the wooden gate that separated the yard from the formal side garden beyond. The same garden whose three sets of French doors had been thrown open wide for the partygoers the night of the masquerade. Their grandeur was impossible to miss that night, and she prayed that they would be her way back into the house this morning.

She slipped through the gate and closed it silently behind her.

Behind the cover of flowered bushes and thick arbors, she finally let herself pause, to catch her breath and steady her nervous shaking.

She thought of Ross and pushed on toward the house. Careful to keep out of view of the windows, she reached the set of doors that she'd instructed the boys to unlock in their chase through the house. She whispered a prayer and reached for the handle—

It turned. The door swung open. She slipped inside the grand drawing room, then silently closed the door behind herself.

The house seemed so much bigger without the crush of hundreds of guests. And terrifyingly silent, which only made each faint footstep she took register in her ears like the sound of cannon fire. But she tried to take courage in that silence. It meant that Wentworth and his cronies were in Westminster, just as Christopher had predicted, gleefully relishing Ross's downfall, while she was here to stop it.

She carefully moved through the house. As she did, she sent up a silent thank you to fate that she'd been at the party and so knew the layout of all the rooms and where little alcoves and corners were located where she could hide if someone happened upon her. But so far, there was no need to hide, the house remaining silent and still around her.

When she reached the stair hall, that enormous room that stretched two stories tall and could have engulfed her entire cottage between its walls, she hesitated. She would be exposed here, with no way to hide as she ascended the stairs. But the only other choice—unless she wanted to scale the downspout, and who would be mad enough to do a thing like that?—was the backstairs. Not a choice at all, given that the servants would be coming and going in their duties. She'd be seen the moment she took her first step.

No. It was up the grand staircase or nothing.

Hitching up her skirt, she raced up the stairs. Dear God, how had she not noticed the night of the masquerade how tall these stairs were? It took an eternity to reach the top and duck into the second set of stairs that led up to the ambassador's private rooms above, and to the study, where the journal waited for her.

Although she'd not been into this part of the house during the party, the study was easy to find, because its door hung half off its hinges, the frame around it broken into shards. Good God, what had happened here with Ross that night?

Her hands shaking, she slipped inside and closed the door behind her as fully as she could, shutting herself into the lion's den. Every heartbeat made her wince with pain and terror, yet she forced herself to stop and take a moment to quiet herself, to look around the room and gather her bearings. No good would come of being panicked in her search. Calm, controlled...*Just breathe!*

But the bell of a nearby church tolling the noon hour startled her. The morning was gone, and Ross would be facing the Lords even now. She had to hurry.

Her gaze swept around the room and landed on the side table that Ross had described. She ran her fingers over it, testing every surface and joint, every hidden place where a latch might—

Her fingertips found it, and she gave a soft cry of relief. She pressed it, and a front panel gave way, opening a hidden compartment. Her hand dove inside.

Only to come up empty.

She bit back a frustrated cry and sank down onto her heels. No! To come this far, through so much—

But the journal was here in this study. It *had* to be! And she wasn't leaving until she found it.

She pulled herself up to her feet and turned back to face the room, determined to search through every inch of the place if she had to. Then she saw the matching side table on the opposite wall and smiled.

Shaking so fiercely that she could barely control her hands, she went to it and once more searched for the hidden compartment. Once more finding the latch. The panel fell open, and she reached trembling fingers inside—

They brushed against something hard and flat. She pulled it out, blinking against the stinging in her eyes as she stared down at what she held in her hands.

Wentworth's private journal. Her hands shook as she opened it and flipped through the pages to make certain it was the proof she needed. *Breathe.* Each entry was meticulously dated and entered in an elegant but masculine hand, listing names and bits of information, places, favors granted, favors given. Her chest burned with each mouthful of air she forced herself to take. *Just breathe!*

The journal. It was more precious than its weight in gold, and she could scarcely believe that she'd found it. Ross's salvation. And hers.

"Put it down," a deep voice ordered.

With a startled cry, she spun around. A man stood in the doorway—

"Patton." Panic spiked in her chest. *Dear God*, what was he doing here? Why wasn't he in Westminster with the ambassador?

"Put it down," he repeated as he stalked toward her.

She lifted her chin. "I'd rather die."

An evil smile tugged at his thin lips. "All right."

He lunged.

She darted aside, with her hand clamped around the little

book like a vise. He turned and charged back toward her. She snatched up a brass blotter from the desk and heaved it at him as hard as she could.

The throw missed, but he ducked his head. In that moment, she turned to run. Her hand reached for the door—

An arm clasped around her waist and tackled her to the floor. She slammed hard against the rug, the journal flying free from her grip and across the room. Large hands grabbed her shoulders and twisted her arms as he rolled her over and pinned her down. His heavy body straddled hers.

"Well, well, Contessa," he leered as he leaned over her. "You've returned. Looks like we'll have that private party after all."

The sadistic look of violence on his face pulled a cry of terror from her lips. She struggled beneath him to free herself, but he was too strong, too heavy. Helplessness crashed over her in a terrifying flood.

"That's it, pet," he purred as he pinned her arms over her head and reached down to grab up her skirt. "Fight your hardest. It's always more fun when the lady struggles."

Bile rose in her throat, and a fierce hatred instantly flashed over her, pushing out all traces of fear and leaving only blinding fury in its place. She yanked her arms as hard as she could, and her right wrist slipped free of his grasp. Desperately, she flung her hand out around her, reaching for anything she could grasp. Cold metal touched her fingertips—

The brass blotter! Her hand tightened around it, and with a groan of exertion, she swung. It struck him on the temple and knocked him off-balance, dazing him just long enough for her to swing again. Another strike against his head, and he fell over onto the floor beside her, moaning with pain as he reached a hand to the trickle of blood at his cut brow.

She scrambled to her feet and backed away. The journal lay on the floor behind him, just out of her reach.

"You bitch!" He climbed unsteadily to his feet. Stalking toward her, he circled her around the room.

Never taking her eyes off him, she backed slowly away, matching him step for step, and waited for the shift of his body that signaled another lunge for her. How many times had she replayed in her mind the memory of Vincent doing just that, until she knew exactly when a man's posture changed, when his shoulders stiffened and his thighs tensed, ready to spring? More than enough times to have imprinted that hard-learned lesson forever on her mind.

From the corner of her eye she saw the fireplace behind her. A flash of dark memory—the hard shove, the fall, the sickening give of her cheek as it ripped open on the iron…barely inches from the flames, so close that her hair singed and her fingertips burned on the iron fender when she pushed herself away…The pool of blood on the floor, her face mercifully numb in her shock…And Vincent's eyes blazing at her, black murder in their depths. He'd reached for her a second time, to grasp her dress and toss her into the flames. But her maid screamed from the doorway at the sight, of what she mistakenly believed was Vincent hauling her back from the fire, to save her—

Her terror rose as the memories flooded back, until Patton's face blurred with Vincent's, until there was no difference between the two men who wanted to harm her.

She'd died that day, as surely as if Vincent had managed to cast her into the flames after all. But from the ashes rose another woman, one so much stronger and more powerful than he would ever know.

A murderous look blazed in Patton's eyes as he reached up to touch the trickle of blood at his brow. "You'll pay for this."

She took another step back, angling her body toward the marble fireplace surround, reached her hand back to feel for the set of iron tools—

He pounced.

Her hand closed over the poker. With a fierce cry, she swung with all her strength. The metal rod hit the side of his head with a dull thud. He froze, momentarily stunned, and then collapsed onto the floor at her feet, unconscious.

"No, I won't," she muttered, wiping the back of her hand across her mouth .

She hit him a second time. For good measure. Then she tossed the iron rod aside, grabbed up the journal, and ran.

But the servants had been startled by the noise of the fight. Sounds of bewildered calls and running footsteps filled the house. When she reached the bottom of the stairs, she looked behind to see the butler and two large footmen running toward her, anger distorting their faces.

She ran on without hesitating into the entrance hall toward the front door and escape.

But they were close on her heels, their pounding strides gaining on her. She grabbed at the lamp on the table as she raced past and flung it behind her, shattering glass across the floor in an oily mess. The men hesitated before following across the puddle of slippery oil, for only a few precious seconds, but that was all she needed to open the door.

Her feet hit the footpath at a dead run. Not glancing back, she darted down the street and away from the house, turning randomly down street after street, alley after alley, and paying no attention to the strange looks the pedestrians and carriage drivers gave her. Behind her the two footmen gave chase. She ran on, propelled by panic and her fear for Ross's life, going deeper and deeper into the maze of back alleys and narrow streets, until she had no idea in which direction she was heading, how far she'd run, or if the men were still chasing her.

When she could run no longer, her chest heaving and her side twisting into an agonizing knot, she stumbled to a stop and sank to the cobblestones beneath her. Resting on her knees, she wrapped her arms around her belly and gulped in large mouthfuls of air. Her stomach roiled from exertion and from the terror she finally let come over her, unable to tamp it down any longer now that she clasped the journal so tightly in her hands that her fingertips turned white.

She staggered to her feet and limped painfully down the street until she reached a wide avenue. It took the last of her strength to raise her arm to signal for a hackney.

A black carriage stopped at the side of the street, and she bit back a cry of relief.

"Westminster—Parliament," she rasped out, her throat raw. "As fast as you can!"

With a knowing look at her disheveled and filthy appearance, the coachman held out his hand for payment up front. Panic seized her as she frantically searched her pockets. Dear God, she had no more coins! She'd given the last of them to the boys.

With no choice, she pulled the ruby ring from her finger and placed it into his palm.

"As fast as you can," she repeated in a whisper, blinking hard to keep back her tears. Then she climbed inside, squeezed her eyes shut, and prayed.

CHAPTER 26

*R*oss gritted his teeth as he gazed out over the chamber, not knowing whether to shout in anger or laugh in bitter amusement. The House of Lords had erupted into chaos and confusion already, after only two hours of a trial that was expected to last at least a fortnight before the verdict was pronounced. Just long enough to have every embarrassing bit of his life—and then some—flayed open for public scrutiny.

Good Lord, he'd rather be hanged now than suffer a moment longer of this.

The Lord High Steward pounded the end of his white staff against the floor, but none of the men paid him any mind. They were too busy squabbling and arguing amongst themselves, with the solicitors and barristers doing the same right there before the bar. The Duke of Wembley nearly came to blows with Lord Houghton, their fisticuffs broken up only by the quick action of the chamber guards, one of whom lost his hat in the scuffle.

"Point of order!"

The trial had turned into a debacle. Because not one of the so-called quality wanted to miss what was certain to be the trial of the century, peers filled the chamber to overflowing. Including some who rarely attended the sessions, some who had been far into their cups only a few hours earlier, and all of them loudly opinionated on whether Ross had actually committed treason, petty treason, or simply espionage. As if any of it made a difference to how tightly the noose would fit around his neck.

Then, there was Wentworth.

Ross slid a murderous gaze sideways to where the ambassador sat, surrounded by his cronies. A smirk on the man's face showed how much he was enjoying bearing witness to Ross's downfall.

"Point of order!"

This time, the loud shout from the floor caught enough attention that voices fell quiet just long enough for Lord Batten to be heard as he waved his hat in the air to be recognized to speak. But as with everything else that had happened so far, proper procedure fell by the wayside as men began to jeer at him, behaving more like the MPs in the Commons than distinguished peers of the realm.

"Point of order!" Batten tried again. This time, he ignored the jeers and continued on, shouting them down, "This is the first trial of a peer for treason in nearly one hundred years." He turned in a circle so that his voice would carry above the din to the far corners of the room. "The proper procedure is in question."

More jeers and boos went up, until the entire room had joined in.

Ross inhaled a deep breath for patience and kept his expression inscrutable, not allowing the humiliation of this debacle to register on his face. For his entire adult life, he'd worked tirelessly to serve England, to be a statesman with decorum and dignity. Only for his reputation to be sullied by this.

"Spalding is an earl," Batten continued, drawing boisterous laughs at that embarrassingly obvious statement. His face reddened, yet he pressed on, "It is not our place to try him for treason."

That statement shocked the room. Even the lawyers were

taken aback as indignant shouts went round of *Trial of peers by peers!*

"It is our right—nay, our very responsibility—to ensure an attainder first!" He pounded his fist on a table when astonished gasps went up at that declaration. "His crimes have betrayed England, and he does not deserve any of the privileges afforded him as a peer. He has forfeited the respect and dignity of the title, and so he should be stripped of all rank and privilege, to be tried like a common criminal!"

His jaw tightened at that. So much for a fair trial.

"The king must attaint!"

More angry thumps of Batten's fist were lost beneath the noise of confusion and chaos that erupted so loudly that they could have been the crowd at the Ealing races instead of England's so-called finest. Wentworth's knowing smirk only deepened at the unfolding fiasco.

Batten pointed an accusatory finger at Ross as he sat on the platform that served as the trial's dock, placed on display like a stuffed peacock for all to gawk at.

Ross's eyes met Christopher's as his brother crowded into the rear of the chamber with the guards, even then allowed only just inside the door. Kit solemnly returned his gaze.

Guilt gnawed at his gut. His brother didn't deserve to have the family name dragged through the mud like this, to lose their fortune, or have his future ripped away the way it would be once the trial was over and Ross was hanged. Kit would be expelled from the Home Office and marked forever as the brother of a traitor, having no peace for the rest of his life.

What Ross regretted most about this—the *only* thing he regretted—was what his conviction would do to the people he cared about. To Christopher, for destroying four hundred years of family legacy connected to the Spalding title, to Mary Jacobs for never bringing to justice the man who murdered her husband,

and to Grace, for not giving her and her son the future they deserved.

"Attainder is meaningless!" Lord Daubney shouted at Batten from his seat at the side of the chamber. "A peer cannot claim privilege in cases of treason, you pompous blowhard of a—"

Laughter and shouts drowned out the end of that tirade. The pounding of the High Lord Steward's staff went unheard, so did pleas by the lawyers to allow them to continue to present their evidence.

"The Spalding title must first be attainted," Batten insisted, his cheeks now turning scarlet. "It is a matter of *moral* principle!"

A final insult, and it galled him. It wasn't enough for them to destroy his family's reputation beneath a charge of treason. No. They wanted to humiliate him first.

Amid the clamor and confusion, Ross stood and stepped forward. He shouted out, "I claim only those rights due to me as a servant and citizen of England!" He glared at Batten, so ferociously that the man's ruddy face paled to white. "Unless you prefer to play at being king, to strip even those God-given rights away from me."

Hoots and howls filled the room as Batten sank down onto his seat.

"But if you feel the need to rob me of my birthright before you have even heard the evidence against me," Ross continued, shouting out the challenge, "then so be it! Attainder changes not one of the facts, nor does it nullify the sacrifices I have made in service to my country." Then he drawled distastefully, taking direct aim at most of the peers surrounding him, "While lesser men have sacrificed nothing."

Duly chastised, the room fell quiet, the jeers and laughter fading to murmurs and whispers. The Lord High Steward gestured with his white staff for the barristers to continue.

Ross straightened his shoulders. *Finally.*

A commotion went up from the rear of the room as the

chamber door was pushed open wide. Shouts from the guards, jostling and confusion—a flash of toffee-colored hair—

Grace.

Unable to believe his eyes as she pushed her way into the chamber, his heart stopped. Then jarred back to life with a painful thud when he saw the papers she clasped in her hands. *Christ!* The damned woman had disobeyed him, and now, she was putting her own life on the dock next to his. Worse—if she'd brought with her the list of names, she'd sealed both their fates.

Shoving aside the surprised men blocking her way, she stumbled forward, breaking through the hold of the guards and the hands that reached to stop her. An uproar erupted inside the chamber as she rushed toward him, with Kit barely breaking stride as he followed after to keep her safe.

"I have them!" She thrust the papers toward him. Then she turned to shout out to the entire room. "I have documents that prove the Earl of Spalding innocent of treason!"

"They're not enough," he rasped out, shaking his head. "Without the journal—"

"I have it!" She held up a small book and smiled at the stunned shock that pulsed over him. She repeated his words to him from the night of the masquerade, "Better late than never."

Impossible. It simply couldn't be…Yet he took it from her and flipped through it, scanning the pages for proof that it belonged to Wentworth. That it held the evidence he needed for his own exoneration and for the ambassador's guilt.

"That's it, isn't it?" she asked intensely, her eyes glistening as if she couldn't believe it herself.

"Yes." He leapt the low railing and jumped to the floor, then grabbed her into his arms and shouted with joy as he twirled her around in a circle. "Yes!"

Beaming at her, he set her down with a quick kiss, then strode into the middle of the chamber. He held up the papers and journal as he called out to the room. He paused to let them all take a good long look. Exoneration was proving sweeter than he ever imagined.

"My noble lords!" he shouted above the bewildered cacophony as all the peers shot to their feet. "I beg your attention!"

The noise quieted just enough for him to be heard.

"I am innocent!" He shook the pages in the air over his head. "And here is the proof."

A fresh round of shouts went up, this time followed by calls for more guards. The uniformed men grabbed Ross by the arms and began to drag him from the chamber.

"Silence!" The word reverberated through the chamber as Sebastian Carlisle, Duke of Trent, shouted down the crowd of peers. "Stop this madness!"

"Come to order!" the Duke of Chatham demanded.

Beside Chatham, Edward Westover, Duke of Strathmore, rose slowly to his feet and immediately drew the attention of the chamber, which quieted into muffled whispers beneath his ire.

"Release that woman," Strathmore ordered the soldiers who had shoved Kit away and were struggling to drag Grace from the chamber, hanging on to her as she fought to remain. Every inch of the duke resonated with the commanding authority of the decorated army officer he'd once been and with the imperial presence of the powerful peer he'd become. *"Now."*

The soldiers froze, as if debating whether to carry out their duty as guards or follow the duke's orders. Thinking better of it, they let her go.

The guards holding Ross loosened their hold. He tore himself away from their grip and rushed back to the center of the room. He faced the guards now, not turning his back on them, because if they changed their minds and dragged him from the chamber, he was as good as dead.

"The Earl of Spalding has always been a well-respected peer of the realm," Trent called out in the growing calm that was settling over the chamber, now that the shock of Grace's arrival had worn off. The presence of guards had sobered all of them. "As such, he deserves to be heard."

With gratitude toward his cousin lightening his chest, Ross seized the opportunity. "I am not a traitor! I have dedicated my life to my country and to my king, first as an officer in His Majesty's army and then in service to the Court of St James's. I have served here and on the continent for over a decade, even during those dark days against Napoleon. My brother fought valiantly against the Americans and the French, and my father, the late earl, always sat in service to this House. *Always*." A few nods of agreement acknowledged his family's dedication to their country. He placed his hand over his heart as he turned in a slow circle to face all the peers sitting in judgment of him. "I'll admit—in my younger days, I was a bit of a handful." He allowed himself a half grin of arrogance. "I am a Carlisle, after all."

Uneasy laughter went up at that.

Encouraged, he continued, "But *never* have I been disloyal or unwilling to serve England and her king to the best of my talents and resolve. And you, my most noble friends, are well aware of that. In your hearts, you know it."

The soft rise of murmured whispers acknowledged the truth of that. He held up the papers again, like a battle flag.

"I know what you've heard, those accusations and baseless rumors that have permeated London, claiming that I committed treason and murder." His eyes moved deliberately from peer to peer now, daring each of them to make eye contact with him and challenging them to believe him. "I was unable to be here to defend myself against them because I was still making my way back to English soil from France. But these pages show my innocence. They prove without doubt who is responsible for the real acts of treason that have occurred." Now going on the attack, he swung his gaze to Wentworth. As the man's face turned white, a sweet vindication cascaded through Ross. The swirling emotions of grief and overwhelming relief stung at his eyes. "And for the murder of Sir Henry Jacobs."

At that announcement, the chamber filled with new shouts and arguments, including among the solicitors and barristers. The Lord High Steward gave up trying to enforce order and slammed down his white shaft on the table, ordering that the session be dismissed and the chamber emptied. In the confusion, the guards stood uncertainly at the sides of the room, not knowing what to do.

The Marquess of Ellsworth picked up the Lord High Steward's staff and snapped it in two, symbolically ending the trial.

"Take him out!" the Lord High Steward ordered the guards to remove Ross from the dock. Then he gestured at the entire room. "Clear out the chamber! We'll sort through this in peace and quiet. Clear them out!"

The guards came forward through the confusion and took Ross's arms. He caught a last glimpse of Grace as they pulled him from the chamber, her eyes meeting his through the crowd. The joy that filled him was immeasurable.

Not moving, Grace watched until Ross stepped from the chamber, and the crowd closed in around her. Curious stares came from the men, who whispered to each other about her, all of them frowning and scowling in turns. Despite the Lord High Steward's orders to clear the chamber, even more men pushed in though the wide-open doors, to find out what had happened and why the trial had been stopped. MPs from the Commons, more guards, secretaries, assistants—the room had become a crush, with even more stares and whispers, now joined by pointing and loud calls that brought her to the attention of the room.

She rubbed her clammy palms against her skirt as the metallic taste of uneasiness grew on her tongue. She needed to leave, to find space and air, to hide from the unwanted attention. Slowly, barely able to shuffle forward through the press of bodies, she started toward the doors.

A flash of blond hair caught her attention, the line of a familiar jaw, narrowed eyes—

Vincent.

A shoulder slammed into her from behind. The force of the blow shoved her forward, and she stumbled, nearly falling. The gentleman grabbed her arm to catch her and muttered his apologies for not seeing her, then released her and pushed his way forward.

Panic roiled in her stomach. Her gaze darted back—

He'd turned away in the crowd as he made his way toward the door, his back turned to her and his face hidden. *Turn around so I can see you, so I can be certain…*An icy fear slithered up her spine. If Vincent had seen her, if he knew she was there—*Oh God.*

"Grace!"

Christopher shoved his way through the crowd to her side, but when he reached for her, she pushed him back. She couldn't look away, not until she knew. *Turn around, damn you!*

Sensing her distress, he took her arm, not letting her dismiss him a second time. He demanded with concern, "What's the matter?"

"I thought—" The knot of fear in her throat choked her. She started again, breathlessly, "I thought I saw someone I used to know…"

"Who?" He craned his neck to see where she was staring.

"Lockwood." The single word was nearly lost beneath the cacophony around them.

"*Who?*"

The man turned. Finally she had a clear view of his face—

Not Vincent.

Relief poured from her. She clutched at Kit's arm to steady herself as she saw the blonde gentleman laugh at something the other men with him had said, a wide smile beaming from a face that had to be ten years younger than her brother-in-law would have been now. A man who wasn't nearly as tall, not nearly as wide or solid as Vincent.

Her shoulders dropped as she let out a harsh exhalation, expelling the fear that had attacked her. She corrected, "A ghost."

Kit frowned in confusion, unable to fathom what she'd meant by that or who she'd been looking at. But deciding that there was no threat after all, the tension drained out of him as he grinned down at her. "A ghost would never be foolish enough to haunt such a formidable woman."

She smiled, half at the flattery of his compliment, half with relief. A ghost, that was all. Just like the other ghosts she'd seen of Vincent along the road from Sea Haven. How foolish she was to think she'd seen him! They'd both changed over the years, certainly—would she even recognize him now if she saw him, or him her? Would he even consider that she could be here, when he thought she'd died a decade ago? She nearly laughed at herself that she'd let her past conjure up specters when her future with Ross now spread out so gloriously in front of her.

When Kit led her forward through the crowd, she craned her neck around for one more glimpse of the door that the guards had led Ross through. It led into the depths of Parliament, surely only accessed by MPs. But the longing to prove that he was finally safe was too much to quash. "Can I see Ross?"

"Not until tonight, I'm afraid." He grimaced, not looking down at her, his attention on the crowd around them. "We're likely to be questioned for hours."

She tensed. "We?"

"They'll want to speak to me, too, to find out what we knew and when. I'll take you to Spalding House, then come straight back here." He frowned down at her in stern warning. "*Don't* run away this time." He grumbled, "I don't fancy another chase through the streets of London after you."

Placing a reassuring hand to his upper arm, she laughed. The worry and fear eased away completely as they stepped through the chamber door and into the far less crowded outer hall. Closing her eyes, she drew in a deep breath and relished in it.

"You're an amazing woman, Grace Alden." He lowered his mouth to her temple but didn't slow his strides to escort her away as quickly as possible, to get her safely tucked into Spalding House and himself back to saving Ross. "What you did…"

"Was exactly what Ross would have done to save me."

"That's the God's truth." He smiled knowingly. "He loves you, you know."

All of her tensed for a fleeting moment as sheer happiness poured over her. Then she nodded against his shoulder with a soft tremble as they passed through the door and outside into the sunlight. She whispered, "I know."

The nightmare was finally over.

CHAPTER 27

"That's everything." Ross finished relating the events of the past few months to the Home Secretary. The same details and events he'd shared earlier with the Secretary at War, the Prime Minister, the Lord Chancellor, and the Master of Ceremonies for the Court of St James's. The same details he was certain he'd have to relate again to King George tomorrow. But now, he wanted to end this and go home to Spalding House, where Grace was waiting for him. "Any more questions?"

The expression on the secretary's face remained solemn as the man sat across from him at a table in a reception room in the Palace of Westminster, where officials had been questioning him since they escorted him from the Lords. Beyond the tall windows, the dying reds and purples of the fading sunset fell mutedly across London, and an attendant had already come into the room an hour ago to light the lamps and stoke the fire.

The secretary shook his head. "I think you've told us everything we need to know."

Thank God. Only then did Ross allow himself to ease back in his chair. Only then did he let himself completely believe that he would be exonerated.

The secretary rose to his feet, prompting Ross tiredly to his. Then the man extended his hand and said simply, "Welcome home, Spalding."

"Thank you." Gratitude warmed inside his chest. He didn't want to be lauded as a hero. He simply wanted to move on with his life. As a man who had dedicated his own life to England, the secretary would undoubtedly understand. Being welcomed home was better than any kind of honor the Court and crown could bestow.

The Home Secretary left the room, and Ross reached to pour a glass of whiskey from the tray that had been brought in hours ago and thus far remained untouched. He removed the crystal stopper and splashed the caramel-colored liquor into one of the glasses, then wordlessly held it out.

As if on cue, Christopher strode into the room. Not breaking stride, he snagged the drink on his way past the table toward two leather chairs positioned in front of the fire.

Ross filled the second glass, took a large swallow, then topped off his drink. When he slumped into the chair across from Kit, the rush of relief at putting an end to this long day swept over him with a shudder.

After that performance in the Lords, he wasn't surprised at what they'd both been put through this afternoon. While he'd been subjected to meeting after meeting, repeatedly explaining in excruciating detail the connections he'd made between the pages he'd brought from Paris and the treason that the ambassador had committed, Kit had been interrogated by the Home Office Secretary and the Lord Chancellor. By the time this last meeting ended, Ross was certain both brothers had detailed every step they'd taken for the past ten years of their lives.

The only way he'd been able to tolerate the questioning was knowing that Grace was safely tucked away at Spalding House, where Watkins and Mrs. Mabry had strict orders to tend to whatever she needed. He had no doubt that eventually the authorities would ask to speak with her, just to confirm her innocence, but Ross would be right there at her side when she was. He owed her his life.

More. He wanted to dedicate the rest of that life to her.

Kit heaved out a tired sigh. Good Lord, his brother looked as haggard as he felt. Thoroughly exhausted, Ross wanted nothing more at that moment than to drink himself to the bottom of his glass. Repeatedly. Then fall into bed and not wake up for three days. Judging from Kit's slumping shoulders, his brother wanted the same.

Yet Kit frowned darkly into his glass. "When?"

Ross's throat tightened, knowing what he meant. When did he plan to visit Sir Henry's widow, to inform her that he'd caught the man's murderer. "Tomorrow."

Then the ordeal would be over. *Finally.*

Kit studied the golden liquid as he held it up against the fire-light. "You're England's newest hero."

Ross grunted out a scoffing laugh.

"You'll be made an ambassador yourself now."

He stared tiredly into the fire, ignoring the quick squeeze of longing in his chest. He'd once wanted nothing more than exactly that. "Perhaps not."

"Assuredly."

But his career wasn't the only one which had suffered acute scrutiny today. "And you?"

Kit shrugged. "Only a man helping his brother."

So he would continue as a Home Office agent. The publicity hadn't revealed what he'd truly been doing these past few years, when he'd pretended to be nothing more than the shiftless brother of an earl. *Good.* Christopher needed his work the way men needed air to breathe.

Ross took a sip. "At least now you can stop pretending that you want to be a vicar."

"Never."

His brow inched up.

"Women love it." A crooked grin twisted at Kit's lips, and despite his fatigue, his eyes sparkled. "Who am I to stand in the way of their spiritual enlightenment?"

Good Lord. But Ross was too tired to roll his eyes.

"Congratulations," Kit said quietly.

Ross nodded, his jaw tightening against a grimace of remorse. It was damnably hard to feel victorious when a good man had died and another he had long admired proved himself a traitor.

"But don't ever risk your life like that again," Kit added somberly. "I couldn't bear it if something happened to you."

For a moment, the two brothers held each other's gaze in silent connection. Then Ross let a teasing smile tug at his mouth. "Don't want to be earl, hmm?"

"God no!" Kit gave an exaggerated shudder of horror.

As Ross chuckled, Kit slumped down into the chair and kicked his legs out in front of him. It had been a long and draining day. Tomorrow would prove equally grueling for both of them, but for now, they had a few hours of reprieve.

And important matters yet to discuss.

Ross shoved himself out of his chair to refill their glasses. As he topped off both drinks, he tossed out casually, "Grace is quite a woman, isn't she?"

"Very much so."

"Brilliant, kindhearted, loyal to a fault…a wonderful mother." Keeping his eyes on Kit to gauge his brother's reaction, he lowered himself into his chair and said quietly, "I want her to be the next Countess of Spalding."

Kit's gaze darted to his in surprise, for a moment attempting to discern if Ross was serious. Then, despite his fatigue, he grinned and repeated, this time with delight, "Congratulations."

But Ross couldn't let himself give over to happiness. Not yet. "I want your blessing."

"Of course you have it."

He shook his head. "It isn't that simple. My marriage to Grace will affect the Spalding title and you. I need you to know what you're letting yourself in for."

Kit didn't move, but Ross sensed a hardening in him. An invisible alertness that made him one of the Home Office's best operatives.

Leaning forward in his chair, his elbows on his knees and his hands folded around the glass he held between them, Ross never moved his gaze from Kit, even as he explained quietly, "Grace isn't who she seems."

"Tell me something I don't know," his brother muttered with a smile.

"When her husband died, she was robbed of her inheritance. She feared for her life and that of her unborn child, so she went into hiding. Eventually, she faked her own death and has lived under a false identity for the past ten years."

Kit's smile faded. "I was kidding."

"I'm not." He took a large swallow of whiskey, welcoming the burn. He'd determined to marry Grace. Nothing would dissuade him. But he also wanted his brother's blessing, despite the potential upheaval to both their lives. "When the Earl of Spalding weds a dead society widow, returned from the grave and demanding restitution, scandal will rain down upon us like fire and brimstone."

"Then let it rain," Kit murmured, his gaze steely with determination. "When have we ever cared what society thinks of us?"

"And King George? We're both serve at the pleasure of the king, don't forget. The kind of scrutiny we'll receive from society will make it damnably hard to do your job, and I'll lose my post out right. My diplomatic career will be over."

He wasn't prepared for the stab into his chest that uttering it aloud brought. Kit had been right earlier, when he said that Ross would have been offered an ambassadorship. Perhaps even the newly vacated post in France, now that its former occupant sat behind bars in Newgate, awaiting trial and certain execution. It would be the apex of Ross's diplomatic career, one befitting the duty and loyalty he'd shown to his country, and exactly what he'd wanted since he joined the Court of St. James's. No, since long before that, when he donned his first uniform and realized what it meant to serve England.

Now, though, he wanted Grace. More than he wanted an ambassadorship. More than he'd ever wanted anything else in his life.

"Despite all that, I am marrying her." The resolve in those quiet words sounded with the force of cannon fire. "I don't know that I deserve your blessing, Christopher, knowing the hardship that's going to befall you. But I'd very much like to have it."

Kit said nothing for a moment, studying him over the rim of his glass. "You love her."

Not a question, he noted. Yet he admitted quietly to the new truth that would guide his future, that he knew in his gut with a certainty unlike anything else he'd ever experienced before, "More than life itself."

"And she loves you."

An electric jolt sparked inside him. "How do you know that?"

"For God's sake, I'm not blind. That woman loves you." Then he murmured against the glass as he took a sip, "Damned if I know why."

Ross smiled hopefully. "So I have your blessing, then?"

His eyes softened on Ross. "You have my blessing." Then he slumped further down into the chair and grinned. "As the vicar in the family, I'll even preside over the wedding."

"Not a chance," he countered. Yet his chest warmed with love for his brother and with thoughts of his future with Grace. "Come back to Spalding House with me. We'll have a quiet dinner and put this day behind us."

"Something tells me that a quiet dinner with me isn't how you want to spend your evening." His grin faded into a tired sigh.

"Besides, I promised to pay someone a visit as soon as everything was settled."

Ross drawled with a smile, knowing his brother well, "And what's *her* name?"

"Evelyn Winslow."

That made him sit up straight, nearly spilling his whiskey. "*Pardon?*"

"I promised her that I'd let her know how everything turned out." He shook his head and muttered, "Damned chit thinks she's the Baroness d'Oettlinger."

Ross grinned. Evelyn Winslow was certainly one of kind. And speaking of formidable women..."Thank you for getting Grace released from Newgate." Then he added, "And for caring for her when I couldn't."

A short sentence of understated gratitude, but there was nothing simple behind its implications. Last night, he'd wanted Grace away from Newgate in order to save her life and keep her from seeing the end of his. He'd had no idea that she'd risk her own neck to come to his rescue. Thank God she did.

"You're welcome." Kit solemnly met his gaze and held it, a flood of understanding passing between them in that moment. "Although from what I've seen, she's plenty capable of taking care of herself." He gave a chagrinned grimace. "Chased her for three hours last night and couldn't catch her."

Ross smiled to himself. "It took me ten years before *I* finally caught her."

Now he had no intention of ever letting her go.

Kit frowned into his drink as he swirled it slowly in his glass. "There's one thing I don't understand, though. Why would Grace need your help in regaining her inheritance? Why not just petition to reopen the will in court?"

"Because it involves a peerage. Her late husband was David Montague, Viscount Lockwood. She doesn't have the money or the power needed to pursue restitution on her own."

"Lockwood?"

He grimaced into his whiskey. The last person he wanted to think about then was her dead husband. "She's worried that her brother-in-law might try to harm the boy if he knew about Ethan's existence. I told her that she had Parliamentary precedent on her side, but she—"

"Christ!" Kit shot out of the chair. "Grace thought she saw him today. If Lockwood was there—" His face paled with a stricken expression. "He knows she's alive."

Ross's heart stopped.

CHAPTER 28

*G*race stepped out of the cooling bathwater and sighed softly. For the first time in a decade, she was at ease, and her hope for the future burned bright.

So did her love for Ross. She couldn't wait until tonight, when she could hold him in her arms and tell him exactly how much he meant to her. And that she loved him.

Humming happily to herself, she emerged from behind the screen in the bedroom where they'd spent the past few nights— where Ross had so breathtakingly made love to her. Around her, the converted carriage house was quiet and peaceful, made even more so by the soft glow of the lamp on the writing desk, where she'd started another letter to Ethan. To let him know that she was safe and that everything was going to be just fine.

Perhaps it was cowardly of her to flee Spalding House and come here, but the chaos that had descended upon the townhouse had been too much to bear. It seemed as if everyone in London had rushed to Ross's front door upon hearing the news of what happened that day in the Lords. A few of the crush sincerely wanted to wish Ross their congratulations, but the overwhelming majority simply wanted to gawk. Of course, they refused to return the next day and insisted that Watkins allow them to wait for Ross to arrive, which meant dozens of people in the house. Which meant noise and commotion.

She wasn't ready yet to face society's suffocations, so she'd escaped for the peace and quiet of the carriage house, leaving instructions with Watkins to send Ross here when he arrived home. She had a feeling that tonight might be the last peaceful one they'd have together for a very long time to come, and she wanted to savor every moment of it.

Of course, she'd also left Spalding House because she couldn't bear the stares of the servants. Including Watkins and Mrs. Mabry. Oh, they were certainly all very nice and attentive to her—although she suspected that Kit's private conversation with the butler and housekeeper might have been the reason—and the stares they gave her were more curious than gawking.

Yet they still stared. After ten years in Sea Haven, where no one paid her any mind, to have that kind of concentrated attention made her extremely uneasy. So did their obvious curiosity about why she, someone dressed no better than the woman who sold fish in the market, should be given such special treatment.

"But I'm a viscountess," she whispered to herself, so softly that the words barely registered to her own ears. That was her marriage right, and nothing could take that away from her. Not Vincent, not David's death, not ten years of hiding. Yet speaking it aloud, even now that she was on the verge of regaining that old life, still felt foreign. And dangerous.

She pulled on the satin dressing gown she'd found in the armoire, most likely left there by one of Ellsworth's mistresses. Her lips twisted into a knowing smile. Italian paramours, indeed! One day, she and the Marquess of Ellsworth would have a good long laugh over the ambassador's masquerade and her role as the contessa.

"I am a viscountess," she repeated to herself, this time slightly louder and with more confidence, as she reached for a bite of food from the little basket Mrs. Mabry had insisted she take with her. She popped the strawberry into her mouth and stifled a laugh, her hand going to her lips.

What would Ross think if he could see her like this, so carefree and happy? Her laugh faded into a blissful sigh.

He cared about her, even after he'd discovered her real identity, even after he'd learned the truth of her past. One month ago, she never would have imagined such a thing could ever have happened, yet the gleam in his eyes in the Lords had proved its veracity. In that moment, she knew exactly what she wanted, then and for the rest of her life. She wanted to be his wife and countess, make a loving home for him, and carry his children in her womb.

The look in his eyes had told her that he wanted the same.

"I am good enough to be loved by the Earl of Spalding," she affirmed, finally casting away all the demons of doubt that had plagued her. Then with a happy laugh of abandon, she exclaimed confidently, "I am Viscountess Lockwood!"

"You are dead," a voice countered from behind her.

She froze in terror. Malevolent fingers of darkness slithered up her spine and ripped the air from her lungs.

Vincent.

She squeezed her eyes shut and willed herself to wake up from the nightmare, but that only intensified the fear clenching her chest and constricting her throat as she felt him stalk closer, like a specter expelled from hell.

Slowly, she turned to face him.

"Hello, Susan."

His face blurred beneath the hot tears gathering in her eyes until she couldn't recognize him, but the icy hatred that radiated from him was undeniable. So was the malice lacing through his voice. It took every ounce of her strength to simply keep breathing, to keep her gaze locked with his black eyes.

"It's been a long time." A chilling smile spread across his face. "But then, one of us was dead."

She slowly tightened her hands into fists at her sides. She wouldn't let him cow her into begging for mercy or terrify her until she screamed, with no one to hear her cries. *Never.* She'd become someone far different from the timid young lady he'd known before. What filled her now was fury, and sheer resolve to never again be his victim.

"You left this behind." He pulled something out of his pocket and tossed it toward her. It landed on the floor with a pinging clatter and rolled to a stop at her feet.

She looked down and swallowed back a shocked gasp. Her wedding ring.

"How careless of you to leave behind such a token of your undying love for my brother." He mockingly shook his head. "Oh, that's right. You never loved him." A pitiless smile curved at his lips. "But then, neither did I."

Something about the way he said that coiled a cold warning inside her belly. A voice screamed inside her head to steel herself—

"Which made it so much easier when I killed him."

The stab of pain of that was brutal, but she forced herself to not react, biting the inside of her cheek so hard that she tasted blood. What he wanted from her was shock and fear, and she refused to give him either.

"He had the money and the title, and I had nothing." A hard glint sparked in his black eyes. "And no way to possess it unless he died. Fortunately, he was already ill, so it wasn't difficult to speed him along." Clucking his tongue, he turned his attention to the room around them, examining the perfume bottles and jeweled brushes sitting on the dressing table. "So trusting to drink that potion I placed at his lips, believing it was medicine."

As he talked, he slowly circled the room, picking up various objects and examining them before setting them away disdainfully. As if women's things repulsed him.

"I hate poison. Such a coward's way. So weak...so *Shake-*

spearian." He gave a dramatic sneer at that. "Would have been much more satisfying to smother him with his own pillow. But his lips would have turned blue, you see, and with the doctors watching him so closely, they would have suspected foul play. But no one suspected poison in his medicine. Not even David."

Despite the fury that seared her insides at his heartless confession, she followed his every move, watching and waiting for him to attack.

"Of course, my first wife Cora was much more suspicious, so I had to be more persuasive." He shrugged and reached for a pot of rouge on the dresser. "But the effect was the same after I forced it down her throat."

She gasped aloud this time, unable to stop herself.

His eyes gleamed brightly at her reaction. Exactly what he'd hoped. *Damn him!*

"Don't seem so surprised. As viscount, I needed an heir, and Cora failed to produce one." He smiled to himself in private amusement as he stopped circling the room, standing much closer than before. "But the new wife is bred. An heir is on his way, I'm certain."

Grace recognized in his eyes the hatred he held for her, because she hated him in kind, with every ounce of her soul. Once upon a time, that raw hatred would have immobilized her with helplessness. But no more.

He paused at the writing desk, and terror gripped her as he picked up the first page of her unfinished letter to Ethan. Dark amusement curled his lips as he scanned over it.

"When you disappeared so suddenly all those years ago, I'd suspected that you might be with child. I had to question your maid quite thoroughly before she admitted that you'd missed your courses. But then you died, burned to death in that fire." He chuckled, and the evil sound turned her blood to ice. "The doctor I hired to examine your remains assured me that you weren't carrying a child, that it must have been the illness and David's death that had prevented your courses." Disgust darkened his face. "Women are such weak things."

His eyes glowed like brimstone in the lamplight, hoping she'd rise to the bait and react. But she knew better, even though terror gripped her chest like a fist. Instead, she watched him, noting every breath he took, each tensing of every muscle, and waited.

"With David and you both dead, I focused on building my legacy, on making the Lockwood title powerful and strong. There's only one thing now that can destroy all I've worked so hard to achieve." He set the letter down and turned to face her. "Your son."

Panic struck her like lightning, forcing the air from her lungs. All of her began to shake.

"Where's the boy, Susan?"

"Go to hell!" she cried out. "I won't let you hurt him."

"I don't plan on hurting him, you stupid bitch." A look of pure evil gripped his face. "I plan on killing him."

He lunged for her.

Grace darted to the side. He raced past, his hands grabbing only empty air. She ran into the other bedroom, but with a growl, he dove in front of her, cutting off her escape down the stairs.

With a fierce scream of fury and frustration, she swung her fist as hard as she could, clipping him on the chin and momentarily stunning him as he staggered back a step.

He grabbed for her, this time catching her arm and yanking her off-balance. She fell toward the dresser. Her hand skidded across the top, desperately searching for anything she could use as a weapon—

The razor! A cry broke over her lips as she closed her fingers around the ivory handle. She swung. The blade flashed through the lamplight and sliced through his arm, the sickening parting of flesh giving as little resistance as soft butter.

Vincent bellowed in pain and released her as his hand flew to his arm.

Grace staggered away, futilely trying to catch back the air in her lungs as she ran toward the stairs. She didn't look back as she raced down into the dark studio below, nor could she hear him over the drumbeat of blood coursing through her ears and the pounding of her footsteps. The wicket gate stood open to the moonlit alley beyond the door, its lock broken—

An arm looped around her waist from behind and flung her into the air.

She landed on her back on the worktable, the blow of her body against the wood so jarring that her teeth rattled. The jars of pigment fell from the table, smashing onto the stone floor with the percussion of cannon fire and shards of flying glass.

As she gasped frantically to catch back the air forced from her lungs, he leaned over her. His hands went to her neck.

"I should have done this to you all those years ago," he hissed, "when I found out how you'd cheated me out of what was mine. But I gave you the chance to turn everything over to me and live." His hands tightened around her throat. "I won't make that mistake again."

His hot breath flared across her cheek as she turned her head away. The last thing she would see in this world would *not* be this bastard's face!

She couldn't stop a tear from sliding down her cheek, or unbidden thoughts of Ethan. Oh God, her baby! Her little boy… agony ripped through her. To never see him again—

But he would live. That was her only consolation as Vincent tightened his hands around her throat. Ethan would live. Ross would care for him and protect him, send him to school, give him the life she was never able to.

He laughed and licked her cheek, the tip of his tongue tracing her scar. When she shuddered in revulsion, he taunted, "You always were such a pathetically weak little thing."

Something deep inside her snapped. Her eyes shot back to his as pure rage and fury consumed her. She ground out, "I'm *nothing* like the girl I was before!"

Summoning all her strength, she twisted beneath him and kneed him hard between the legs. He bit out a fierce curse and fell onto his side in a spasm of pain.

She struggled to shove him away, but he was too large, too heavy. With one hand grabbing at the edge of the table, she clawed viciously at his face and eyes with the other, to cause as much pain as possible so he would move away. But he only growled and grabbed her by the throat again, squeezing hard.

Choking as black circles blurred her vision, she tore open the drawer. She reached inside, searching frantically—

Her fingers touched cold steel. As the pain in her throat grew worse, his hands crushing at her windpipe, she pulled out the pistol, cocked back the hammer, and shoved the barrel against his ribs.

She closed her eyes and squeezed.

The gunshot reverberated through the studio. Vincent staggered back from the force of the blow, then immediately wheeled to his left as another gunshot rang out. For a beat, he stood there, swaying unsteadily on his feet, his face white and his mouth gaping like a fish. Then he crumpled to the floor.

Behind him in the open doorway stood Ross, a white tendril of smoke curling from the spent pistol in his hand.

All of her flashed numb and pained in rapid turns as she saw Christopher move quickly past Ross and hurry to kneel beside Vincent, his own pistol in his hand. Feeling Vincent's neck, he sat back on his heels and gave a single shake of his head.

Her gaze fixed on Vincent's body as Ross slowly stepped toward her. She didn't move. *Couldn't* move. Through a fog, she heard him softly repeating her name, felt his hand touch her arm and slide down toward the gun in her grasp. Her fingers released their hold, and the pistol clattered against the floor.

With a soft cry, she turned into his arms.

He held her tightly against him and whispered, "It's all right, Grace. You're safe."

She was only dimly aware of his words. The aching anguish slowly ebbed from her beneath the softness of his voice and the strength of his arms as he held her close.

"I'm here now." He placed a tender kiss to her temple. "You're safe, my love."

She rasped out, her throat burning, "And Vincent?"

Ross turned her in his arms, blocking her view with his body. "Lockwood's dead." His arms tightened their hold as she shuddered one last time. "He'll never be able to hurt you again."

She squeezed her eyes shut and buried her face in his chest.

"We stopped him. *You* stopped him." He cupped her face between his hands, and when she opened her eyes, the promise in his blue depths filled up her soul. "I will never let anyone hurt you again. Or Ethan." He touched his lips tenderly to hers. "With my last dying breath, I will keep you safe." Then he whispered the single word against her lips, one that held all the love and dedication he felt toward her, "Always."

Trembling, she wrapped her arms around his neck and hugged him tightly to her, never wanting to let go. Her heart gave its own promise as she repeated, "Always."

EPILOGUE

Kingscote Park, Hampshire
Six Months Later

*R*oss smiled at Grace as they paused together at the
marble balustrade framing the south terrace of his
country house, to share a rare moment alone today. Dear God, she
was stunning. Her hair shined in the afternoon sun of one of the
last warm fall days of the year, and her white dress, with its old-
fashioned beaded bodice layered over a brocade skirt, accentuated
her slender curves. In that gown, she was simply beautiful, inside
and out.

He took her hand and raised it to his lips. During the past few
months, she had become the center of his world and the most
important part of his life. Safe and loved. Exactly what she
deserved.

She laughed with happiness, the musical sound lilting on the
soft fall air. Even though she was now Susan again, he insisted on
calling her Grace. That was the woman she was when he'd fallen
in love with her. The same woman he would always hold in
his heart.

"I love you," he murmured, folding her hand in both of his.

"You'd better," she teased as she traced her fingertip over the gold band on his left hand. "It's too late for doubts now."

"Then it's a good thing I have none." Making Grace his wife and countess was a choice he'd never regret.

They'd both been through hell during the past six months. Turning a blind ear to the salacious gossip that poured through society about them had been much harder than either of them had imagined. So was making certain that Ethan's rightful claim to the viscountcy was upheld. Despite Vincent Montague's widow not protesting the claim and leaving England to return to her own family in America, where she delivered a healthy baby girl, the Committee on Privileges wasn't willing to grant Ethan the title. Just as Grace had feared, they dismissed her evidence of his birth, claiming that his legitimacy could not be proven. Even Ross's popularity as England's greatest hero since Wellington couldn't mitigate the most brutal aspects of the ordeal. Only a direct appeal to King George finally ended it, because not even the crown could refuse this request—the only one Ross made for all he'd been through to bring the ambassador's treason to light. And when the king learned that he could use Parliament's own precedents against them, he gleefully called the Prime Minister to account, setting everything to rights.

The boy had held up well under all the changes, Ross had to admit. Even now, as he watched him playing pall mall on the lawn with some of his tenants' children, he was proud of the way Ethan had given support to Grace during that trying time. Oh, he'd still be difficult for a while yet. What boy didn't push the boundaries of his world in his rush to become a man? But he'd begun to show more affection to her. To Ross, as well, although that was more likely because Ross had gone to Ethan to ask the boy for permission to marry Grace and because he had insisted that Ethan stand up with him as his best man, with Kit right beside him.

He'd also asked the Spalding solicitor to begin the necessary paperwork for Ross to legally adopt Ethan. The boy could never inherit the title or the Spalding entailments—those would be left for the children that he and Grace would have together—but Ethan would have the earldom's protection, with Kit as his uncle to ensure it, should anything happen to Ross.

The smile on her face faded, and he felt the absence of it like a blow to his gut. "But you can never be an ambassador now," she reminded him. "Do you regret that?"

"I don't need to be an ambassador. Being an earl is more than enough." He stepped forward to slip his arms around her waist. "As long as you're my countess."

He boldly kissed her, not caring who saw. For a moment, she let him, and he enjoyed the sweetness of her lips, the warmth and softness of her.

Then she lightly slapped her hand at his shoulder to scold him, turning her head away to break the kiss as her cheeks flushed pink. "You're being scandalous, kissing me like that!"

"Am I?" With a self-pleased grin, he glanced around them at the hundreds of guests who'd joined them for their wedding and the large tents erected across the lawn to hold the celebrations that would go long into the night, far after he'd absconded with her to their bedchamber and made love to her for the first time as her husband. "But I'm a Carlisle," he told her, taking another kiss. "So are you now. And we Carlisles have reputations to uphold, you know."

"Not anymore," she corrected, letting him take her hand and lead her down the terrace steps to the lawn. "I don't want any more scandals or sordid reputations, and no more gossip. I only want to spend a quiet life loving you." She reminded him over the opening flourishes as the orchestra struck up the first dance, "It took me more than a decade to find my way back to you. Now that we're together, I don't want to waste a moment more."

"I wouldn't have it any other way." He pulled her into position and twirled her into their waltz.

AUTHOR'S NOTE

I'm sure you noticed in the epilogue that Grace wears a white wedding gown. No, this was not historical inaccuracy on my part. The reason is a far more practical one.

As you probably know, white did not become the traditional color for wedding dresses until Queen Victoria wore white in 1840 and sparked a new wedding fashion. Before then, however, there was nothing stopping a bride from wearing white if she chose, and in fact, among the wealthy in the decades leading up to the Regency, white had been regarded as the preferred color. But women who were not wealthy (which means most women) often just wore their best dress to be married in, regardless of color, although yellow seemed to be very popular for a time. But if a special dress *was* wanted for the big day, a practical woman would often have planned ahead to make certain that the dress could also be worn beyond her wedding day. Therefore, most wedding dresses were not white. Why? Because women owned very few white dresses because they were incredibly difficult to keep clean. This meant that they couldn't be worn for most daily activities, and so usually only the wealthy could afford to be so impractical about their dress. (BTW, why do so many Regency-era heroes wear white breeches, cravats, and waistcoats? While I don't know for certain, I would venture to say because white clothes symbolize wealth: 1) they have the money to afford to throw them away when they get dirty and buy more to replace them, and 2) they are wealthy enough that they don't have to do any kind of work that would dirty them in the first place.)

So, if I could have picked any color wedding dress for Grace to wear, why did I pick white? For my own very practical reason: the cover model is wearing white. Yes, it's as simple as that.

DEAR READER

Greetings! I hoped you enjoyed reading **HOW THE EARL ENTICES**. There's just something dreamy about a man who's dedicated to both his country and to his true love, isn't there? I loved telling Grace and Ross's story. What you might not realize is that I wrote it in less than two months—mostly because I had to keep writing to find out what happened next! And isn't Evelyn Winslow wonderful? She was simply too much of a force of nature to keep silent, so I've given her a romance of her own (and a dashing marquess!) in my next book, **WHAT A LORD WANTS**, coming in early 2019. Her craving for adventure gets her into more trouble than she can handle...and right into the arms of scandalous Italian painter Domenico Vincenzo. When two worlds collide, is Evie prepared for learning the art of seduction?

Ross, as you know, is a Carlisle cousin to the Trent side of the family. Haven't met the Carlisle brothers yet? Then are you in for a treat! The three overly protective brothers from **HOW I MARRIED A MARQUESS** (a RITA Award finalist!) have gone from being the scourge of Mayfair to heroes of the *ton*. When they meet three very special women, they've met their matches—in more ways than one. A sneak glimpse into Book 1 in the series, *IF THE DUKE DEMANDS*, follows below. Enjoy!

If you want to stay in touch and keep up with my latest releases, best contests, exclusive content, and more (including all those pictures of the roses from my garden—I cannot help myself!), be sure to sign up for my **newsletter.** You can also follow me on **Bookbub,** where you'll receive news of all my releases, and on all of my **social media sites.**

♥ Happy reading!
Anna

EXCERPT FROM IF THE DUKE DEMANDS

Enjoy this special glimpse of *IF THE DUKE DEMANDS* by Anna Harrington, the award-winning Book #1 in the Capturing the Carlisles series:

Miranda Hodgkins has only ever wanted one thing: to marry Robert Carlisle. And she simply can't wait a moment longer. During a masquerade ball, Miranda boldly sneaks into his bedchamber with seduction on her mind. But when the masks come off, she's horrified to find herself face-to-face with Sebastian, Duke of Trent—Robert's formidable older brother. Sebastian offers her a deal to avoid scandal: he'll help her win his brother's heart if she'll find him the perfect wife. But their simple negotiation spirals out of control. For the longer Sebastian tries to make a match for Miranda, the more he wants to keep her all to himself.

Sebastian nuzzled his mouth against her ear.

Miranda gasped. That, oh, *that* was clearly not an accidental brush of whispering lips! He'd meant to caress her, and the warm longing it sent spiraling through her nearly undid her. Drawing a deep breath as she threw all caution and sense to the wind, she tilted her head to give him access to her neck, unable to deny the temptation of having his mouth on her.

With a pleased smile against her ear, he murmured, "What is it about my brother that draws you so?"

The tip of his tongue traced the outer curl of her ear. She shuddered at the delicious sensation, and his hand pressed tighter against her belly to keep her still in his arms.

The confusion inside her gave way to a tingling warmth that ached low in her belly. With one little lick, Sebastian had set her blood humming, making her body shiver and her thighs clench the way he had that night in his bedroom when she thought he was Robert. She knew who was kissing her this time, yet knowing he was the wrong Carlisle brother made no difference to the heat rising through her traitorous body. She should step away—this was *Sebastian*, for heaven's sake, and the most wrong man in the world for her, save for the king himself—but she simply couldn't make herself leave the circle of his strong arms.

"Robert is masculine," she breathed, her words barely audible above the aria swirling around them.

"Most men are," he answered, dancing kisses down the side of her neck.

When he placed his mouth against that patch of bare skin where her neck curved into her shoulder, a hot throbbing sprang up between her thighs. She bit her lip to keep back a soft whimper.

"He's handsome," she forced out, hoping he couldn't hear the nervous trembling that crept into her voice.

"Hmm." His hand on her hip drifted upward along the side of her body, lightly tracing across her ribs. She trembled achingly when his fingers grazed the side swell of her breast. "We're brothers. We look alike."

Oh, that was *definitely* jealousy! But her kiss-fogged brain couldn't sort through the confusion to discern why he'd be jealous of Robert. Especially when his hand caressed once more along the side of her breast.

"Not so much alike," she countered, although she'd always thought Sebastian would be more handsome if he wasn't always so serious and brooding. If he did more spontaneous and unexpected things...like licking a woman on her nape at an opera. *Oh my.* She shivered at the audacity of his mouth and at the heat it sent slithering down her spine.

"Very nearly identical," he murmured as his hand roamed up to trace his fingers along the neckline of her gown. Completely unexpected yet wantonly thrilling, the caress sent her heart somersaulting just inches from his fingertips.

"He's exciting...a risk-taker..." Her voice was a breathless hum despite knowing that in his rivalry with his brother he didn't want to touch her as much as he wanted to touch her before Robert did. At that moment, though, with his fingertips lightly brushing over the top swells of her breasts, she simply didn't care. At least not enough to make him stop. "He's thrilling."

When his fingertips traced slow circles against the inner curves of her breasts, she was powerless against the soft whimper that fell from her lips.

"Lots of men are thrilling." He smiled wickedly against her neck at the reaction his seeking fingers elicited from her. "I'm thrilling."

"*You?*" She gave a throaty laugh of surprise. "Sebastian, you're the most reserved, restrained man I—"

In one fluid motion, he turned her in his arms and pushed her back against the set wall, his mouth swooping down to swallow her words as he kissed her into silence. Her hands clenched into the hard muscles of his shoulders, and she stiffened beneath the startling onslaught of his lips, of his hips pushing into hers, all of him demanding possession of the kiss. And of her.

Click here to continue reading *IF THE DUKE DEMANDS*.

DISCOVER MORE BY ANNA HARRINGTON

Capturing the Carlisles
If The Duke Demands
When the Scoundrel Sins
As the Devil Dares
How the Earl Entices

Secret Life of Scoundrels
Dukes are Forever
Along Came a Rogue
How I Married a Marquess
Once a Scoundrel

Standalone Titles
Say Yes to the Scot
A Match Made in Heather
No Dukes Allowed

ABOUT THE AUTHOR

I fell in love with historical romances and all things Regency—and especially all those dashing Regency heroes—while living in England, where I spent most of my time studying the Romantic poets, reading Jane Austen, and getting lost all over the English countryside. I love the period's rich history and find that all those rules of etiquette and propriety can be worked to the heroine's advantage...if she's daring enough to seize her dreams.

I am an avid traveler and have enjoyed visiting schools and volunteering with children's organizations in Peru, Ecuador, Thailand, and Mexico, and I have amassed thousands of photos I unleash on unsuspecting friends who dare to ask about my travels.

I love to be outdoors! I've been hiking in Alaska, the Andes, and the Alps, and I love whitewater rafting (when I don't fall in!). I earned my pilot's license at Chicago Midway (To all the controllers in Chicago Center—I greatly apologize for every problem I caused for you and Southwest Airlines), and it is my dream to one-day fly in a hot-air balloon over Africa.

I adore all things chocolate, ice cream of any flavor, and Kona coffee by the gallon. A *Doctor Who* fanatic (everyone says my house *is* bigger on the inside), I am a terrible cook who hopes to one day use my oven for something other than shoe storage. When I'm not writing, I like to spend my time trying not to kill the innocent rose bushes in my garden.

https://www.annaharringtonbooks.com/

facebook.com/annaharrington.regencywriter

twitter.com/AHarrington2875